PENGUIN BOOKS

I LOVE DOLLARS

Zhu Wen is the author of a novel and several short story and poetry collections, and has been published in China's most prestigious literary magazines. He has also directed four films, including *Seafood*, which won the Grand Jury Prize at the 2001 Venice Film Festival. He lives in Beijing.

Julia Lovell has translated the novella *Lust, Caution* by Eileen Chang and is a lecturer in Chinese history at the University of London. She is the author of *The Great Wall: China Against the World 1000BC – AD2000* (2006). She lives in Cambridge, England.

I LOVE DOLLARS

AND OTHER STORIES OF CHINA

ZHU WEN

TRANSLATED FROM THE CHINESE BY JULIA LOVELL

PENGUIN BOOKS

PENGUIN BOOKS

Published by the Penguin Group
Penguin Books Ltd, 80 Strand, London WC2R ORL, England
Penguin Group (USA) Inc., 375 Hudson Street, New York, New York 10014, USA
Penguin Group (Canada), 90 Eglinton Avenue East, Suite 700, Toronto, Ontario, Canada M4P 2Y3
(a division of Pearson Penguin Canada Inc.)
Penguin Ireland, 25 St Stephen's Green, Dublin 2, Ireland (a division of Penguin Books Ltd)
Penguin Group (Australia), 250 Camberwell Road, Camberwell, Victoria 3124, Australia
(a division of Pearson Australia Group Pty Ltd)
Penguin Books India Pvt Ltd, 11 Community Centre, Panchsheel Park, New Delhi – 110 017, India
Penguin Group (NZ), 67 Apollo Drive, Rosedale, North Shore 0632, New Zealand
(a division of Pearson New Zealand Ltd)
Penguin Books (South Africa) (Pty) Ltd, 24 Sturdee Avenue, Rosebank, Johannesburg 2196, South Africa

Penguin Books Ltd, Registered Offices: 80 Strand, London WC2R ORL, England

www.penguin.com

First published in the United States of America by Columbia University Press 2007
First published in Great Britain in Penguin Books 2008
1

Printed in England by Clays Ltd, St Ives plc

ISBN: 978-0-141-03397-6

CONTENTS

TRANSLATOR'S PREFACE

IN 1989, the twenty-two-year-old Zhu Wen graduated in electrical engineering from a university in Nanjing (eastern China). For the next five years, he worked in a thermal power plant, during which time he began writing fiction. In 1994, he resigned from his state-allocated factory job to become a freelance author. That same year, he wrote and published *I Love Dollars*, a novella whose caustic vision of a spiritually bankrupt post–1989 China—about a father and son searching for kicks in a provincial Chinese city—caused an immediate sensation on the mainland literary scene. Whether feted or excoriated, *I Love Dollars* established Zhu Wen as a pivotal figure in Chinese literature of the 1990s and beyond.

Zhu Wen's development into a professional writer coincided with one of the most traumatic transitional phases experienced by Chinese authors in the post–Mao era: the shift from the intellectually elitist 1980s to the frenetic commercialism of the 1990s, via the bloody suppression of the 1989 pro-democracy protests. After years of Maoist repression, many of them spent in internal, rural exile, over three million intellectuals and writers returned to public life in 1979, and the ensuing ten years were dominated by a "high culture fever"—

high-flown cultural debates about China's rightful path to enlightenment and modernization, about the role of Western influences and the place of tradition in this process—that climaxed in the political turmoil of 1989. As often as not, the weighty sociocultural and linguistic questions raised by "serious" literature lay at the heart of these discussions: contemplating the national character and the cataclysms of Maoism, rediscovering local traditions, defining a modern Chinese literature and its relationship to its Western counterpart. Chinese writers today still look back nostalgically on the 1980s as a golden age when authors were celebrities or spokesmen for the nation, when poetry and fiction led the way in pushing back the boundaries of liberalization and freedom of expression, and when the whole country could seemingly unite around discussion of a new work of literature.

All of this ended abruptly in early June 1989, when the Politburo headed by Deng Xiaoping authorized People's Liberation Army troops to clear the demonstrators from Tiananmen Square, and to open fire on civilians who barred their way. The bloodshed of that summer was rapidly succeeded by a crackdown on the pro-democracy movement's intellectual leaders that brought to a peremptory close the climate of serious, intensely questioning discussion that had nurtured so much of the creative output of the preceding decade. Those writers who had publicly ventured out of the literary arena and into Tiananmen Square and the sphere of political debate found themselves, along with student protest leaders, facing harsh political censure: interrogation, imprisonment, or exile. The famous satirical novelist Wang Meng—responsible, in the second half of the 1980s, for promoting several liberal authors to influential positions on the literary scene—resigned as Minister of Culture, and the works of prominent writers were banned.

In the immediate aftermath of the June 4 repression, the intellectual heterodoxy of the high culture fever was ousted by a resurgence of political orthodoxy. After a decade during which writers and thinkers had struggled to break with the constrained, xenophobic worldview of Maoism, they found themselves once more confronted by the Communist government's attempt to refit thoroughly old-style socialist manacles on them, as party novelists denounced the "Western bourgeois liberalization" and "spiritual pollution" that had turned mainland culture into a "disaster area." As the questioning, liberal spirit of the 1980s was excoriated as ideologically degenerate, the establishment apostles of political correctness called for "cultural works that reflect socialism, give expression to communist ideals and the spirit of the socialist age . . . and that can fill people with enthusiasm and create unity among the masses."[1] Party stooges churned out invective against prominent literary liberals, while urging upon the literary rank and file the Communist canon on literary theory: *Deng Xiaoping on Art and Literature* and the *ur*-text of Chinese socialist realism, Mao's 1942 "Talks on Art and Literature at the Yan'an Forum."[2]

In January–February 1992, however, China's supreme leader, Deng Xiaoping, offered his subjects a way out of the threatened political and cultural ice age of the very early 1990s. Convinced that Communist China's stability depended on the spread of material prosperity, he called for an end to ideological hang-ups about the capitalist nature of economic liberalization, and for an unleashing of market forces and encouragement of foreign investment in the interests of achieving "faster, better, deeper" economic growth.[3] To the ever-pragmatic Deng, it was irrelevant whether the means were capitalist or socialist, provided that the end of preserving party rule was achieved: "It doesn't matter whether a cat is black or white," he had argued years before. "So long as it catches mice, it's a good cat."

Translated into the cultural sphere, Deng's exhortations to profit made commercial, popular success, rather than stultifying ideological diktat, the new bottom line for literary production. As the catchphrase of the 1990s became *wang qian kan* ("look toward the future," which, in Chinese, neatly punned the word for "future" on that for

---

1 Quoted in Geremie R. Barmé, *In the Red: On Contemporary Chinese Culture* (New York: Columbia University Press, 1997), 26.

2 For these and further details, see the account in ibid. 20–37.

3 Joe Studwell, *The China Dream: The Elusive Quest for the Greatest Untapped Market on Earth* (London: Profile Books, 2002), 56.

"money"), many writers abandoned the idealistic intellectual stance of social responsibility and reflection dominant in the 1980s and joined in the capitalist free-for-all. With the literary market flooded by entertainment products (love stories from Taiwan, kung fu novels from Hong Kong) and the government phasing out the iron rice bowl (the Communist promise of a salary for life to state-sponsored writers), some serious novelists abandoned literature almost totally and instead took the plunge into business. A number of those determined to live off their writing watched, and tried to learn from, the trails to commercial success blazed by two of their peers: Wang Shuo and Jia Pingwa. Having won national, popular acclaim in the late 1980s with a string of best-selling novels that specialized in lampooning intellectuals and their (sometimes pompous) sense of national historical mission, in the early 1990s Wang led the way in showing his fellow authors how to squeeze maximum profit out of their words, repackaging his own as songs, screenplays, and television shows. A year or two later, in 1993, Jia—a critically acclaimed nativist chronicler of northwest China in the 1980s—became one of the first and most notorious cases of a serious writer surrendering to lurid populism, with the publication of *The Ruined Capital* (*Feidu*), a best-selling, sexually explicit tale of a male writer's spermatic journey through the spiritual corruption of contemporary China for which, rumor had it, Jia was paid an advance of one million *yuan*.[4] Despite its explicit sexual content, the Chinese authorities failed to ban the novel until 1994, when the sensation was in any case dying down; Jia himself was not persecuted. The political message was clear: sex and sensation meant high sales figures, and high sales figures promoted state ideology, "to get rich is glorious." However writers chose to adapt to the economic realities of 1990s China, intellectual elitism was out and profit-seeking decidedly in.

Written a year or so after *The Abandoned Capital*, *I Love Dollars* is unmistakably a product of its time, its focus on the new materialistic, libido-driven realities of 1990s China the obvious offspring of the

4 Jia Pingwa, *Feidu* (Beijing: Beijing chubanshe, 1993).

bewildered post–1989 climate of numb disillusionment, cynicism, and commercialization. The title alone is an eloquent mission statement: a shockingly candid paean—five years after the Tiananmen crackdown blamed the turmoil of 1989 on the corrupting influence of the West—to the American dollar, taking to a logical extreme Deng Xiaoping's directive to embrace capitalism. Set within the context of a nominally still-Communist China, the title jarringly illuminates the intense ideological inconsistency that has lain at the heart of the People's Republic for the last dozen years.

By the close of the first two paragraphs, Zhu Wen's straight-talking narrator—a swaggering, sex-obsessed writer who shunts his women out the door once he's got what he wants from them—has given his readers the measure of the brave new world of the 1990s. A few pages on and our narrator is urging his father to try his luck with a waitress his sister's age and musing on how useful it would be if this same sister decided to become a prostitute. The remainder of the novella is spent cruising the city for women, and punctuated by the random, pettily bloody-minded encounters of an urban China in which an overwhelming preoccupation with money—how to get it, how to spend it—has eroded basic social and familial civilities: the pavement policewoman screaming for her 2 *yuan* ($0.25), the narrator attacking his father for failing to get his 30 *yuan* ($3.75)'s-worth out of his cinema escort. Arrogant, cynical, greedy, incapable of valuing women for anything other than their willingness (or otherwise) to offer him sex, Zhu Wen's "I" is a man of his time: in his own words, "a cheap person, in an age that burned to sell cheap, my natural habitat the clearance warehouse, pushed carelessly to one end of a shelf, happy to write for anyone who tossed me a couple of coins." When the father, speaking like a relic of the 1980s, reproaches him for failing to offer "something positive" in his fiction, "something to look up to, ideals, aspirations, democracy, freedom," his novelist son has a 1990s answer ready: "Dad, I'm telling you, all that stuff, it's all there in sex."

The only two relationships that contain a flicker of conventional social warmth—the narrator's alleged love for his father and brother—are debased by the novella's merciless debunking of one of China's oldest social conventions: the bonds of Confucian filial piety. A son's filial responsibilities, the narrator believes, are to "search out a few glimmers of fun for his hardworking father"—in other words, to find him as many women as possible—not "to offer a pious faceful of empty respect"; spare moments away from this worthy undertaking are filled with propositioning his brother's girlfriend. In *I Love Dollars*, the officially sanctioned greed of the 1990s has erased the traditional debt of respect owed by son to father, by brother to brother, and replaced it with an overwhelming desire for money and pleasure seeking.

Devastatingly frank in his descriptions of provincial city life, Zhu Wen tells 1990s China exactly as he finds it: seedy, selfish, amoral, corrupt. Although his narrator has thrown himself wholeheartedly into the early 1990s embrace of commercialism, although he is the archetype of the new, compromised, and compromising post–1989 model of Chinese author, and although, in a literal sense, his life choices chime harmoniously with official state policy, the world of *I Love Dollars* is no earthly paradise built by socialist orthodoxy. Nowhere in its account of the vacuousness of contemporary, market-economy China does the novella imply that the narrator's lifestyle is doing him much good, either physically or emotionally—despite the bravado with which he informs his father that "he's leading the life he was meant to lead, he's leading a life that has a future." Throughout, he not only fails to realize his limited personal goals—making and spending money to his own satisfaction, sleeping with younger women—but his attempts to do so leave him sick, tired, and blank. The novella's final tableau—of self-disgust at the nonachievements of the day just passed, in which official directives to spend and consume have been tirelessly followed—is no kind of advertisement for the potential for personal fulfillment offered by Deng Xiaoping's China.

The audacious plain speaking of *I Love Dollars*—its relaxed, colloquial narrative voice, its long, hard stare at the indignity and iniquity of a Chinese society in meltdown from communism to capitalism—instated Zhu Wen as a representative writer for his own and for succeeding literary generations. Almost uniquely among his peers, he has fully succeeded in facing up to one of the most significant challenges that confront Chinese writers today: making literary sense of the bizarre, ideologically confused amalgam that is contemporary China (cut-throat free market economy fronted by Communist platitudes).

As they began to receive increasing critical attention, Zhu Wen and other authors of his age group came to be labeled the "New Generation" (*Xinshengdai*), a loose classification that referred, at its vaguest application, to novelists born in the late 1960s and early 1970s who began publishing after 1989, but also, more usefully, implied certain shared literary characteristics: a strongly individualistic and, particularly in the case of its female representatives, intensely interior, private voice, often combined with a focus on the patterns, cadences, and banalities of everyday life. As much as anything, this generation defined itself by what it vehemently believed it was not, dismissing many of the themes and concerns—in particular, the idealism and social commitment—espoused by the writers of the 1980s. Li Feng, a friend of Zhu Wen from university days at Nanjing who also drifted into full-time writing in the early 1990s, recalls how, in the 1980s, he and his undergraduate friends used to think all contemporary literature "terrible. . . . If ever we were feeling bad about ourselves, we'd go to the library to read some recent fiction and feel much better."[5] The gap between new and old generations resulted not just from subject matter and style but also from outlook and lifestyle. With the collapse of the iron rice bowl, many of the New Generation—Zhu Wen included—were obliged to become "free writers" (*ziyou zuojia*), existing outside the old-style socialist literary system and forced to live by the market economy. Little wonder then, perhaps, that the New Generation's writing has often been a mirror of the new urban society that surrounds it, of the (at times hedonistic) individualism that has developed alongside the growth in economic opportunity.

In 1998, Zhu Wen published "Rupture," a manifesto-like survey polling the iconoclastic opinions of his New Generation on the Chinese literary scene, past and present. Its respondents dismissed canonical establishment authors, contemporary critics, literary magazines,

5   Li Feng, interview by translator, Beijing, April 6, 2000.

philosophy, and religion as utterly irrelevant. Questions such as "What assistance does the Writers' Union offer you?" garnered the response "public washroom." "Dressed-up piles of shit," someone else commented on state literary prizes.[6] Read today, "Rupture" resounds with the posturing swagger of a brat pack too myopically sure of its own defiant originality to contemplate its relationship to the past and to its immediate context; three years after it was published, Zhu Wen himself called his survey "a childish game that set out to achieve a certain, limited purpose."[7] Nonetheless, for anyone with even a cursory knowledge of the smug literary bureaucracies of the former Soviet Union or the People's Republic of China, "Rupture"'s demolition of the institutional totems to conformist mediocrity—the prizes, journals, and canonical authors—that prop up the Communist Writers' Union still packs an entertainingly irreverent punch.

In their diverse ways, the other four novellas and short story translated in this collection all develop, with increasing narrative sophistication, inventiveness, and variety, the themes and preoccupations Zhu Wen first laid bare in *I Love Dollars*. All feature his trademark narrative style: a loosely punctuated, first-person voice in which speech, both direct and indirect, runs on within sentences of descriptive prose, designed to capture the unceremonious, free-flowing rhythms of action and dialogue in contemporary China. They chronicle a society in which anything, it seems, can happen, where everything is decided by the vagaries of chance encounters and decisions, and where stable, regulated patterns of life and codes of behavior have long been swept away. Despite the individualistic, self-determining stance asserted by Zhu Wen's narrators, none seems to exercise any real power over his own destiny. The sequence of events that leads up to the violent denouement of *A Boat Crossing* is a chain of interlocking arbitrarinesses: the narrator's random decision to drift to Wan County, ten days

---

6 See Zhu Wen, comp., "Duanlie: yi fen wenjuan he wushiliu fen dajuan" (Rupture: one questionnaire and fifty-six responses), *Beijing wenxue* no. 10 (1998): 19–47.

7 Zhu Wen, interview by translator, Beijing, March 31, 2001.

after a vague premonition about Cape Steadfast; his collision with his three sinister cabinmates, and with Li Yan and her niece; his escape to Lin Yicheng's cabin in the second-class section; his snap decision to reveal his real name as the two of them part. The moment they step out into the maelstrom of Chinese society, Zhu Wen's protagonists lose all control over their lives. Even on an apparently straightforward mission to buy a pound of pork at a market, Zhu Wen's narrator in "Pounds, Ounces, Meat" is continually waylaid by the petty, small-change grievances of a furious girlfriend, a disgruntled old woman, a dishonest stall holder, and a cheated customer, pushing from his mind the original purpose of his expedition.

Zhu Wen's China is a country where the social contract—if it ever existed—is now in tatters; whose inhabitants, both materially and emotionally, are living on the edge; where every 0.1 *yuan* counts and charity is in short supply. Like China's population figures, Zhu Wen's fictional surroundings are always overcrowded, either packed urban streets or poky rooms, often shared; privacy is practically nonexistent. But this enforced exposure to others rarely brings out the kindness of strangers; a physical surplus of humanity does not generate an abundance of its emotional corollary. Only money—and plenty of it—buys any kind of solicitude or compassion. Although, thanks to the privatization of health care in Deng's China, all the inhabitants of Ward 4 in *A Hospital Night* are paying customers, only the ostentatiously rich manage to wrest any spontaneous tenderness out of the nurses; anyone else is treated with crushing brusqueness. In *A Boat Crossing*, the narrator is justifiably suspicious of Li Yan's obsequious overtures, motivated only by the desire to talk him into paying her 4,000 *yuan*.

At its darkest, in *A Boat Crossing*, Zhu Wen's bleak vision of a claustrophobically congested Chinese society translates into the narrator's Kafkaesque paranoia about being constantly observed and threatened by indifferent or ill-meaning strangers, into the vague, all-pervasive presentiment of animus that haunts the novella. (Kafka and Borges are two of Zhu Wen's acknowledged influences. Visiting Zhu

Wen in his apartment in 1995, an interviewer imagined the portrait of Kafka hung on one of the walls eavesdropping on their conversation.[8]) Often enough, the narrator is as guilty as his persecutors in contributing to the emotional indifference that surrounds him: in his deliberately stony response to the gloomy young man on the boat who tells him his father is probably dead; in his reluctance to engage with (the initially amiable) Lin Yicheng. The tensions generated by this absence of basic human sympathy find release in the climactic spasms of uncontrolled violence that punctuate the story lines: Lin Yicheng's near-homicidal fury at a minor deception in *A Boat Crossing*; the destructive frenzy that brings to a close weeks of intimidation by small-town mafiosi in *Wheels*.

If played entirely straight, Zhu Wen's dismal view of contemporary China—of its callous venality, its empty platitudes and opportunistic falseness, the overbearing obligations of reciprocity, the violent rage lurking just below the complaisant front of the downtrodden—might verge on the oppressively pessimistic. Instead, Zhu Wen manages to rescue his fiction, and his readers, from terminal despair through the easy, often playful informality of his narrative vernacular. It is the intriguing contrast between his lightness of tone and the gravity of his subject matter that succeeds in underscoring, without portentous overemphasis, the arbitrary, brutal absurdities of life in China today; that grabs readers' attention and holds their interest through a story. The surreally slapstick nature of the situational writing in *A Hospital Night*, for example, overlies a serious and sympathetic point about the harshness and indignities of life in contemporary China, unobtrusively affirmed by the narrator's final recovery of sympathy for the terminal patient in the middle bed. And with its eccentric cast of tragicomic drifters marooned on their sinking power plant—the mysterious factory director with his rumored homosexual predilections; Hao Qiang, the playboy; Xia Yuqing, the mahjong-playing, banqueting social climber; the melancholy Xiao Xie desperately, even

---

8 Lin Zhou, "Zai qidai zhi zhong qidai—Zhu Wen fangtan lu" (Expecting amid expectation—an interview with Zhu Wen), *Huacheng* no. 4 (1996): 107.

suicidally, casting around for a way to persuade the management to accept his resignation—*Ah, Xiao Xie* disarms with its light-handed, idiosyncratic account of mental and economic depression.

Despite Zhu Wen's eagerness to break social and sexual taboos of the China he observes around him, on one key question he holds back from open comment—politics. This is a near-omnipresent lacuna in contemporary mainland Chinese writing: the measures introduced straight after the Tiananmen repression to reestablish cultural orthodoxy notwithstanding, the ultimate consequence of 1989 and of the rise of popular market forces has not been more stringent political controls over literature, but in fact the further detachment of literature from politics. By 2000, overt political influences on Chinese literature were at their lowest ebb since the founding of the PRC in 1949. According to many critics and writers, Chinese writers can now write about anything they want without fear of severe reprisal, and even with the prospect of financial gain—*if* they don't write about politics, of course. For all their rebelliousness toward establishment literary values, the 1990s New Generation—Zhu Wen included—have largely fallen in with this tacit consensus. As one well-known mainland critic put it, "Zhu Wen is a rebel through and through, able to confront any contemporary taboo—except, of course, for politics, a subject which, it is universally understood, is at present to be passed over."[9]

But although Zhu Wen's criticism of the political status quo is never direct, it is ubiquitously implicit. In comparison with many of his peers—who are willing to reflect the commercialism raging around them without necessarily plumbing its shallowness—the darkness of Zhu Wen's fiction, at both its grimmest and its wryest moments, expresses an unremittingly negative vision of China today and, by logical extension, of the political architects of this society. (Socialist) systems and institutions constantly fail those they are meant to serve: the threadbare health care provided in *A Hospital Night*; the unfinishable, centrally (un)planned power plant in *Ah, Xiao Xie* that

9 Chen Xiaoming, *Wenxue chaoyue* (Literary excess) (Beijing: Zhongguo fazhan chubanshe, 1999), 199.

generates only melancholia and treats its employees like indentured serfs; the abusive, uncouth "People's Police" of *A Boat Crossing*. In *Wheels*, the narrator barely considers seeking protection from Nanjing's ineffectual police; the local mafiosi problem is viewed by the government as little more than an unfortunate but insurmountable social side effect of developing, at breakneck, intensely polluting speed, the industrial area adjoining the city. The lawless consequences are to be suffered by the hapless locals: if they have money, like Hao Qiang, they manage; the less financially secure take their chances.

★

In 2000, six years after *I Love Dollars* captured the seamy, cynical zeitgeist of urban China and established its author as one of the leading new novelistic talents of the 1990s, Zhu Wen made another career move emblematic of the bewildering fluidity of contemporary Chinese culture: abandoning fiction for filmmaking. His 2001 directorial debut, *Seafood*—the story of a friendship between a policeman and a prostitute in the Politburo's summer holiday resort town, Beidaihe—won three international prizes, most notably the Grand Jury Prize at the 58th Venice Film Festival; his most recent feature, *South of the Clouds*, was awarded the NETPAC Prize at the 2004 Berlin Festival. Yet while he has, for the time being, stopped writing fiction, and his books, thanks to the brief print runs dictated by a reading market governed increasingly by sensation, are now almost impossible to find in shops, his work remains a powerful and widely acknowledged influence on his own and subsequent generations of the Chinese avant-garde. He has not, he says, permanently renounced fiction, and plans to return to it when the time is right. On the strength of his output so far, it would seem he is a novelist from whom there is plenty more to hope.

—JULIA LOVELL

A NOTE ABOUT THE TRANSLATION

ZHU WEN is that rare creature among writers: a novelist who doesn't keep copies of his own books. My translations of some of his earlier work—*I Love Dollars* (*Wo ai meiyuan*, 1994) and *A Boat Crossing* (*San sheng xiu de tong chuan du*, 1995)—were therefore taken from manuscript versions of the novellas sent to me by the author. *A Hospital Night* (*Xingkui zhe xie nian you le yidian qian*, 1996) was translated from the version published in the fourth issue of 1996 of the journal *Huacheng*. For *Wheels* (*Ba qiong ren tongtong da hun*, 1998), *Ah, Xiao Xie* (*Xiao Xie a Xiao Xie*, 1999), and "Pounds, Ounces, Meat" ("Bang, angsi he rou," 1999), I used the versions printed in Zhu Wen's most recently published collection of fiction, *Renmin daodi xu bu xuyao sangna* (Xi'an: Shaanxi shifan daxue chubanshe, 2000).

—J. L.

GUIDE TO THE PRONUNCIATION OF
TRANSLITERATED CHINESE

According to the pinyin system, transliterated Chinese is pronounced as in English, except for the following:

VOWELS

a	(as the only letter following a consonant): *a* as in "ah"
ai	*I* (or *eye*)
ao	*ow* as in "how"
e	*uh*
ei	*ay* as in "say"
en	*on* as in "lemon"
eng	*ung* as in "sung"
I	(as the only letter following most consonants): *e* as in "me"
I	(when following c, ch, s, sh, zh, z): *er* as in "driver"
ia	*yah*
ian	*yen*
ie	*yeah*
iu	*yo* as in "yo-yo"
o	*o* as in "fork"

ong	*oong*
ou	*o* as in "no"
u	(when following most consonants): *oo* as in "food"
u	(when following j, q, x, y): *ü* as the German ü
ua	*wah*
uai	*why*
uan	*wu-an*
uang	*wu-ang*
ui	*way*
uo	*u-woah*
yan	*yen*
yi	*ee* as in "feed"

CONSONANTS

c	*ts* as in "its"
g	*g* as in "good"
q	*ch* as in "chat"
x	*sh* as in "she"
z	*ds* as in "folds"
zh	*j* as in "job"

I LOVE DOLLARS

AND OTHER STORIES OF CHINA

I LOVE DOLLARS

FATHER'S VISITS ALWAYS took me by surprise. But soon as I heard that heavy knock, I knew who it was, so I told Wang Qing to hurry up and get some clothes on. She tried to pull me back, get me to keep quiet, respond to the situation as I usually did. After they'd been knocking a while, callers tended to lose interest and go their own sweet way. I threw the dress draped over the cane chair at Wang Qing, gesturing at her to get a move on. There was no point in hanging around; I knew who was outside. To save my door from imminent destruction, I tried to strike up conversation with my unexpected visitor: When'd he get here, I asked, how're things at home, are you here on business, when're you heading back? Another round of violent banging: Let me in, he said, and I'll tell you. When she'd at last gotten herself more or less respectable, Wang Qing was about to straighten the bed—which was a mess—but I'd already opened the door. Father charged in and patrolled the room like a police dog, sniffing here and there, his gaze finally, inevitably falling on Wang Qing. She stood, rather uncomfortably, by the bed, her hair a bird's nest, face flushed red; not bad-looking, really, nothing for me to be ashamed of. Ignoring my greeting, Father took a step toward her: And you would be Miss . . . ? Father's accent was a mix of northern and southern, which Mother could understand only by ignoring what he was actually saying and concentrating instead on his facial expressions. What? said

Wang Qing. Maybe because her curiosity was slightly aroused, she was starting to give off this pungent, earthy scent—the smell of the local women—and I didn't want Father to think the woman his son had just been sleeping with was some random pickup, a divorced older woman. I'd lose his respect. What the hell do you care what she's called? I said to Father, signaling to Wang Qing to get lost. She picked up her small leather bag, smiled at my father, and left, asking me to call her. You won't understand, but I was terrified she'd smile: the moment she smiles, her eyes are all crow's feet. All this time, she kept her right hand tightly clenched into a ball, not relaxing it even slightly, for an instant; I think Father had noticed right away. She must have had inside it a bra or a pair of panties she hadn't had time to put back on. Father went over to open the window, and the door too, then sat down on the bed and pulled out a cigarette. It was only then that I noticed he was empty-handed, hadn't brought a single item of luggage with him. Just then, still half sunk in a postcoital daze, I couldn't quite be bothered to talk. I wasn't depressed: quite the contrary, I had this heady, unfamiliar sensation of floating slowly upward. Unable to sit still, Father got up again and took another restless turn around the room, ripping open any letter he laid eyes on, chattering away all the while, such a nice day, how many times have I told you, you ought to get more exercise, you ought to get out more, go where there's sun, sea, rivers, fresh air. Ah, but Dad, some things, unfortunately, you can still only do inside. One day, one day I dream of doing them outside, on sun-drenched grass, happy and uninhibited, just like an animal. You never gave me the courage I really need; you forgot, just like your father did with you.

After a discussion, the two of us decided first to go looking for my younger brother, then find somewhere to have lunch. Father communicated that he didn't mind what he ate, a bowl of noodles would be fine. I can't have you eating noodles, not when you're with me, I told him. My brother was still at college, in his fourth year, majoring in mathematical statistics. I hadn't seen him for ages either. We'd had an argument because he wanted to drop out and become a pop musician. In actual fact, I only went to read him the riot act under orders from Father; personally, I was right behind him doing what he wanted. Father knew I was the only one who had any influence on my brother, and the only one he could persuade to do his bidding; some years ago he'd worked out ways and means for talking around his elder son. In the end, my brother submitted and agreed to finish college before he did anything else, though he was disappointed by my treachery and expressed it by attacking everything I wrote. No one who lives a banal life will ever write anything decent, he lectured me back, a short-sighted person will never see past his nose into the bigger, wider world out there. But just because you've turned your back on the banal, little brother, doesn't mean you have the right to keep your entire family at your beck and call, following behind you, wiping your bottom. All my life I've done all I can for you, never complained, never grumbled, I've even been proud, really proud to do it. You're an adult now, you can do what you like, but I want you to swear that from now on, you'll clean up your own messes. My mother got migraines just thinking about what her two absent sons could be up to: for all she knew, they could be wandering the streets, begging for food. Now that—that would be too much for her.

"You planning to marry that woman I just met?" Father suddenly turned and asked me, perfectly seriously, in a public toilet by an intersection.

"Nah."

"She's not the reason you're still not married, is she?"

"No—no."

"Good." Father hurried outside without waiting to do his trousers up again properly, just like he always did.

When I went outside, I found it hard at first to adjust to the bright September sunlight. It was as if I'd passed, in one step, from dark night into a blazing white dawn. I hadn't, I should point out, been wasting this beautiful day in bed out of personal preference, but out of compulsion. If you wanted to sleep with Wang Qing, you had to do it during the day. She never had time at night—she might have already agreed to do it with someone else. Since this other someone, or someones, were unarguably more important than I was, she'd keep her best times for them. I had to give in: I had to keep my libido quiet, and this wasn't always easy. At college, I'd fed it pretty steadily, once or twice a week. My girlfriend, a perky student association official with a handful of keys at her disposal, had access to the small storeroom at the side of the students' club piled with sports equipment and other stuff. I still think back nostalgically to that time: if, as soon as we'd done it and each gone back to our respective dormitories, I got the craving back, I'd go drag my skinny little girlfriend out and make her open the room again. But after I left college, it all got much more uncertain; I never knew where or when it was coming from next. The main problem was time, or the lack of it: to make ends meet, I had to work seventy-hour weeks, doing night shifts in a factory. This didn't cure the sex problem in my head, as I'd hoped, but made it even worse. It was like a kind of madness: whenever I met a woman I'd set about getting her into bed immediately; if I didn't manage it pretty quickly, I'd just walk away, no hanging around, because my time was limited, I had to use it to achieve something concrete. It was a sickness that needed daily treatment to keep it under control. So I turned to a sort of intellectual laxative: writing, endless writing. Once I'd rushed through maybe a dozen pages, I'd finally start to calm down and think about more complex literary issues, such as where's this coming from, where's this going, psychological insights, *le mot juste*. So there I was: an incurable case, happy to give anyone who wanted to medicate me a go.

My brother, we soon learned, was no longer living in his student dorm but was renting an apartment with a few friends off campus. Shit, I'd had no idea. When we got to his dorm, the fourth morning period had just ended and the corridors echoed with the hungry clanging of food bowls. Maybe they were all venting their sexual repression. I grabbed hold of a tall, skinny boy, hoping to get my brother's new address out of him. But he said he didn't know. Father was rooting around in the dorm, as if he thought he'd be able to turn my brother out from under the monumental piles of crap on his bed and desk. Come on, there's nothing here, let's go. No, said Father, let's wait a bit, someone's bound to know where he lives. And as luck would have it, a boy wearing glasses turned up, told us he'd been there, and, throwing down his bowl, sketched us a map. We managed to find the place, a single-story hovel behind the municipal gym. But my brother wasn't there either. When I bent down to peer through the window, I could see an electric guitar, a bass, and a few hand drums. No beds, only a few mats laid out on the floor, with blankets scattered on top. Father crouched down to have a look after me. Is that what they sleep on? he turned back to ask me. I could hear a note of reproach in his voice. Yup, that's right, that's the kind of older brother I am, enjoying my own bed with my own nice warm woman to hop into it from time to time, while little brother roughs it. Looked like it was going to be just me and Father for lunch. While we dithered in the entrance to a small restaurant nearby, an over-made-up waitress bustled out and yanked us inside.

I studied Father carefully as he sat opposite me on an old train seat. Now he'd lost a lot of hair, his forehead gleamed baldly, like a pebble rubbed smooth along the passage of time. But though he was past fifty, he was still as vigorous as a young man. He had a scar on his forehead, a great discovery we'd made about him in recent years. For decades, we'd never even noticed it. Father said he'd been a real daredevil in the town he'd grown up in, that he could climb trees, scrambling from one branch to another, nimble as a monkey. But he'd never explained how he'd ended up with that scar. Ask him, I said to the waitress when she came over for our order, introducing myself as the office boy, Father as my boss. Father did actually bear more than a passing resemblance to some cocksure manager of a small-town business, and started to respond, smooth as you like, to the woman's ridiculous attempts at flirting. But he didn't let it go to his head, you could tell by the food he ordered. We ordered one bottle of beer, then, when we'd drunk that, we ordered another. Father's face brightened, ironing out some of its creases; even his luminous baldness started to look almost distinguished. The waitress was leaning on the counter like a prostitute, smiling at us in a way that was seriously affecting our appetites. Someone like Father, I reckoned, would be quite a catch for someone like her.

"She's smiling at you," I told him.

Father turned to look, drank a swig of beer, then turned to look again.

"Looks a bit young to me," Father said, "about the same age as your sister."

"Don't say that, what d'you want to say a thing like that for?"

"Why not? She must be about Xiao Qing's age, don't you think?"

"Sure, but you don't want to be making those kinds of comparisons."

"Why not?" Father really didn't seem to get it.

"Because, if you start thinking like that, you won't want to get it on with her."

We both started laughing, Father almost choking on his beer. Dad, if I wanted to sleep with an older woman, I'd just want to do it, I wouldn't start thinking how she was as old as Mom, or Grandma, because then I'd lose it completely, it'd be hopeless. So you want to sleep with a woman as young as your daughter? That's when they're in their prime—have you forgotten what their fresh, beautiful bodies are like? Like juicy summer grapes, in hundreds of varieties, at all kinds of prices. If we wait till winter when there aren't any grapes on sale, we have to go back to eating raisins. That's what life's like: one minute there are grapes, the next they're gone, or they've been banned from sale on the free market. Though there's always ways and means. You should give them a try, if you get the chance. Soon as we began laughing, the waitress who was the same age as my little sister grabbed her opportunity and casually sidled over, sitting down next to my father, her last few traces of false innocence obliterated by a faceful of white powder. Though her top was unbuttoned low, it wasn't doing her many favors, as somehow she'd failed to grow any breasts during puberty; maybe she just forgot and it was too late by the time she remembered. Women like this always made me sad; even now I could almost feel the tears itching the back of my throat.

"I know you're saying naughty things about me, I heard you both!"

No, no, Father quickly said, shifting his buttocks over toward the wall, because she was practically sitting on his lap. I picked up a glass from the next table and poured her a generous half glass of beer.

"My boss was singing your praises. Have a drink with him."

"Really?" Without needing any further persuasion, she lifted her glass and clinked Father's. The discomfort I could read in his eyes told me he hadn't yet succeeded in turning her into a woman he could have sex with, that he was probably still seeing her as a classmate his daughter had brought back home.

"Why'd we lie to you? My boss was just saying how pretty you are; he was about to ask you out dancing tonight."

"Really?" She looked at me, then at Father.

"Where're you from?" Father suddenly asked.

"Anhui."

"I know Anhui very well. Where in Anhui?"

"What's this all about? Chaohu."

"I've been to Chaohu, where in Chaohu?"

I had no idea what Father was up to, I felt this line of conversation was pointless, going nowhere. So I interrupted.

"How about it, are you free tonight? I'll pick you up, for my boss."

"What for?"

"What for? You really don't know, or are you just pretending? Pick you up to go out."

"Okay, let's go to Manhattan, or . . ."

"No, no, he doesn't want to go dancing tonight, he wants to do something else."

"What, then?"

"My boss is on the early morning plane tomorrow, so he just wants you to keep him company tonight."

"Get out of here, now I've got it, you want me to do bad stuff."

"What d'you mean, bad? It'll be great."

"Going out's fine, but I never do bad stuff."

"I don't believe it. Not ever?"

"Never. Really. People ask me out every night, but I've never done bad stuff with them."

"Amazing. A-ma-zing." I turned to Father. "Hey, boss, I want to marry this woman. If you'll let me."

"Risky," said Father. "What if she still won't do bad stuff with you after you're married? Then you're in trouble."

"Listen to you both!" She was now starting to look distinctly aggrieved.

"Well, are you up for it or not?"

"No. But I'll introduce you to my friends. I've got lots of friends, all very pretty, they'll do it."

"They're not like you, not playing the game?"

"Hey, so not doing bad stuff means not playing the game? You're really something, you know that?"

"What, think we're being unfair? Then just try it, just once."

"It's no good you trying to hassle me, there's no way I'm doing anything bad."

"You're bound to start doing it sooner or later, so how about we look you up again a year from now?"

Though Father was clearly getting less lunch down him than he usually did, he looked to be enjoying himself. That woman back there, he said to me, totally serious, as we left, the one with no breasts, she really wasn't a prostitute. How can you be so sure? I said. She was a bit like Xiao Qing, he said. She was still a child. So what if she's like Xiao Qing? Don't you think your daughter could turn herself into a pretty passable prostitute? Oldest profession in the world—older than any of our traditions. If my beautiful little sister stepped outside the school gates and onto the streets, as long as she enjoyed her work, I wouldn't mind at all. In fact, it has a good ring to it: my sister the prostitute. I could introduce all my friends, get their spare cash together, give them a good time, and make her rich at the same time. And if she stayed a good, loyal sister, she'd get her colleagues to go and see her brother in their spare time, at a whopping discount, or if they're really decent, for free. Fantastic. Father and I started arguing about whether prostitution was women's natural vocation. In fact, we held identical opinions on the subject, it was just that he felt there were some things we needed to debate. Father gradually lowered his voice as we neared my brother's place again. He still wasn't back. Does your brother have a girlfriend? Father suddenly asked me, as he bent down to peer through the window. I said I didn't know, or at least I'd never seen one. There had to be something wrong with my brother, I thought, to get to his age and prefer guitars to women. Father leaned over the windowsill, writing a note, then slipped it through a crack under the door. He'd asked my brother to come over to my place when he got back.

★

In the end, Father agreed to let me arrange his activities for that afternoon and evening. He had to get back early the next morning: he'd been at a meeting in a nearby city and thought he'd come and see us while he was in the area. He was always deciding to show up at the last minute like this, and sometimes if he didn't catch either son, he'd take a couple of turns around the main street of the city, buy a pair of socks, then go home. Thinking about it, I realized Father was a man with quite a libido, just that he was born a bit before his time. In his day, libido wasn't called libido, it was called idealism. Early every morning, Father used to go to the sports field or run six miles along the highway, but he'd dropped that habit by now, I suspected, because there was no need for it. So I knew his few remaining ounces of congealed gasoline had to be used sparingly, that he couldn't go full throttle all the time. Energy: it's a problem for the planet, it's a problem for us, both now and in the future. I left a note on my door as well, telling my brother we'd gone out, and if he came by he should wait in the room for us. He had a key. Shouldn't we stay in, Father said, not keep him waiting? No need, I said. I've got the feeling he's not going to come by this afternoon. He might come if it was just me, but he won't if he knows you're here. So we shouldn't waste a long, beautiful afternoon inside for no good reason. Father said he wanted to wash his face before we went out again, he seemed a bit tired, but I didn't even have a Thermos of hot water in the room. How about, I said, I take you to a hairdresser's at the bottom of the building? I'll treat you to a facewash, and get a woman from Wenzhou who works there to dye your hair. Naturally, I took out with me all the money I had stuffed under the mat. It was everything I'd saved; I wanted to spend it all, didn't want a single cent left at the end of the day—I could think of nothing more satisfying. Sadly, I didn't have that much money to squander in the first place; maybe I've just been unlucky so far in my life. But one day I'm sure I'm going to make it big, great handfuls of bills will hit me in the face whenever I open my door; there'll be nowhere to hide. Dollars—they have this intoxicating, exotic generosity of spirit. The way a dollar bill can generate endless *renminbi* out of thin air, it's like magic; down they float into your outstretched hands, your eyes raised heavenward, gratefully receiving this riot, this shower of fortune. Just give me a chance and I'd show the world exactly what kind of a carefree, rustless spending machine I could be. Then, after throwing it all away, just as my friends have predicted, I'd live out my later years in lonely poverty. This kind of finale suited me down to the ground: even if I still had a thing for younger women, I wouldn't have enough gas to get me going again, so it wouldn't matter whether I had money or not.

Father stood in front of the hairdresser's mirror, scrutinizing his reflection. He looked satisfied, more than satisfied, with his new image, even though his new head of black hair looked far more like a wig than anything remotely natural. My father had been pretty good-looking in his youth, handy at basketball too; and he'd known it. He was a mid-court player, and in later life, he'd always be at his best there. At college, Father, the star of the men's team, coached the women's team, often escorting his dozen-odd pert trainees to brother colleges for games. He'd showed me his yellowing black-and-white photos, hoping to impress me. Instead he made me wild with jealousy. From that time on, I'd always be pestering Father for the truth about which of them he'd screwed. If he'd said he'd screwed all of them, now that would have been something, but he gave a very uninspiring reply: None of them, actually, that kind of thing didn't happen back then. Now he turned around and tapped me on the shoulder: Let's go, he said. Looking like he wished he had his basketball team with him now. Hold on, I said, I haven't paid yet. I gave the short woman who reeked of hair spray a hundred-*yuan* note and asked for change. Every time I did this, my ears rejoiced to hear the tinkle of metal on metal, like the delicate strike of a tuning fork, as one bill precipitated a succession of smaller coins. Of course, I could've told her to keep the change, just to do me a favor and take my father behind the door curtain, give him his money's worth. But she had nothing going for her aside from her youth: she was so pug-ugly I was afraid my father wouldn't be able to get it up. And I wouldn't have been in the least surprised if she had some unpleasant variety of STD. So I thought better of it, thought I'd be betraying the years of friendship between Father and me. I must admit, though, I've screwed women even uglier than her, and nothing wrong with it, I'm not ashamed. But when I pictured my father or one of my good friends messing around with her, it felt like an outrage. I love my father.

As we walked along the city's busiest street, I noticed a lot of passersby doing double takes at Father: not at his face, but at his hair. He walked at tremendous speed, cutting through the crowd, often leaving me lagging behind. I liked watching him take off, both hands stuck in his pockets like a young man going places, and with places to go. Sometimes, from where I was, I could see nothing but a head of black hair bobbing up and down, like a pennant carried along in the river of pedestrians. This was the beauty of a wash-in dye job, paid for—don't forget—by yours fucking truly. Just thinking about it brought a lump of emotion to my throat. In time, we'd all get to disappear off into the crowds in front of our descendants: my son trailing behind me, my grandson behind my son, and so on it would go. We formed a continuous, generational line, spreading, as we procreated, out into a fishing net, like the kind I used to see around the town I grew up in on the southeast coast, with women of every age and era shuttling back and forth through its folds like multicolored tropical fish. Some we pulled in, others we didn't, expressing neither jubilation nor regret either way; simply getting on. As I might already have mentioned, I was unfortunate enough to have the sex sickness; they say it's hereditary, but you can also catch it through contact. In any case, whenever I suffered a severe attack, my mouth and tongue would go dry and I'd start gibbering. On this count, I envied my father more than I could say: he must have had the sickness too, but he always kept a grip on himself; it was never chronic with him, the symptoms never any more intrusive than those of a common cold. I think I've got that about right. And that, precisely, was the main reason I had it so badly. Quickening my step, I caught up to Father in a few strides. Speed you're walking at, I said, looks like you already know where you're going. No, said Father, didn't we agree you'd decide?

"If you haven't decided where you're going, why're you walking so fast?"

"I'm just enjoying myself, wandering. So you tell me: where're we going?"

I didn't know either. I dragged Father over to a drinks stall at the side of the road and bought two paper cups of Coke. Father's face glowed in the sunlight, a healthful radiance gleaming out of every pore. He was sweating a little, his hair gluing together in clumps, no longer quite so salon-perfect. I was terrified a small, thin trickle of black dye would run down his forehead—promise me, please God, don't let that happen. Didn't Mother ask you to buy anything for her? I asked him. No, Father said, your mother doesn't even know I'm with you. You mean to say, we're both free as each other? Of course, we're just two men together. So what should we do? Well, we should go and do the things men do together, of course. But it's still only afternoon, the sun's still too high in the sky. Come on, what difference does that make? These days all you need is a couple of coins and it's night when you want it. Squatting on a step by the sidewalk, Father and I both raised our cups of Coke, glancing regularly across at each other, maintaining a silent dialogue. I ought to understand what my father needs, I thought. A son shouldn't shirk his filial duties. If, some distant day in the future, I should ever find myself at a loose end and free of the self-importance that comes with age, and run off to visit my son, I'd want him to figure out what was required, to be able to search out a few glimmers of fun for his hardworking father. I wouldn't want to end up with some idiot who only knew how to offer a pious faceful of empty respect. Listen to me, son, wherever you are right now, this thing they call respect is too intangible for me. We've all got things we could learn from money, from the beautiful dollar, from the strong yen, from the even-tempered, good-humored Swiss franc, from their straight-up, honest-to-goodness, absolute value.

★

I'd never have thought that a simple paper cup would cause me so much trouble. As he walked along, Father was ranting about the situation in the Gulf. War, or talk about war, has always been a way of letting off libidinal steam. While he was gesticulating with his left hand, I didn't notice his right drop the crumpled cup into the doorway of a clothes shop. He didn't normally do things like that, I swear; it was all because of the Gulf War. Or maybe it was because of me, Father always forgot his manners whenever he was with me. Screeching something in a local dialect, a middle-aged woman wearing a red armband scrambled up behind us and grabbed Father's arm. Soon as he'd worked out what was going on, his face went tomato red. Stuttering a stream of apologies, he ran back, picked up the paper cup, and threw it into a grass-green bin. But this was too little, too late, in the professional view of our middle-aged persecutor, who issued an on-the-spot fine; just a couple of *yuan*, nothing crippling. Father stood there, paralyzed, the three of us facing off. Several passersby ran into us, as if we were a submerged reef, invisible to the naked eye under a sea of concrete, until, after multiple collisions, our unmoving presence finally began to be noted. I've always hated this kind of thing, never bothered to argue it out: even if I'd only had two *yuan* left in the whole world, I'd have given them to her without a flicker of hesitation, just to save myself the aggravation. But as the blush faded from Father's cheeks and his calm returned, he reached out and pressed down on the hand I was about to dig out the money with. Now you listen here—and full battle was joined between the two of them, while we steadily acquired an audience hungry for entertainment. I felt desperately uncomfortable: I hate being a public spectacle like that, it's a major weakness of mine, and soon my right hand started twitching back toward that money. Maintaining his rhetorical flow without a break, without even glancing across, Father reached out and pressed back down on my hand, in precisely the right spot. Less than delighted at how the afternoon was progressing, I tried to shake him off, to get at that damn two *yuan*, but, imperceptibly to any onlooker, Father increased the pressure. Sensing his resolution, I let it lie. As a son, a filial son, the only thing I could do at a moment like this was stand shoulder to shoulder with Father, no matter how many people had gathered to gawk at us. I didn't speak out, not a word on Father's behalf—even now, just thinking about it, I feel disappointed in myself. Bent on taking those two *yuan* home with her, the woman started screaming like she had a grievance against the whole street. Unfazed, Father began to explain his actions with sophistry of increasing ingenuity: he'd been planning on taking that paper cup home to use again, such a lovely paper cup it was, why would he willingly throw it away? To his eternal chagrin, however, he'd dropped it, this cup that felt as precious to him as his wallet. Wasn't this enough bad luck for one person for one day—did he have to pay a fine too? Broke your heart, it did. If you were going to take it home with you, she retorted, then why did you just throw it in the bin? Father smiled: It had been on the ground, he said, it was covered in dirt, it was, in other words, no longer the paper cup I'd wanted to take home, no longer the paper cup I'd once known and loved, so I threw it away.

When we finally managed to drag ourselves away, my mood was ruined. But Father seemed rather pleased with himself: he'd kept that 2 *yuan* tucked up, nice and safe, in our pockets, still cosily soaking up our body heat. At the present exchange rate, 2 *yuan* were 0.25 dollars, or 25 cents. I slouched alongside Father, hoping to be left behind. Father failed to notice my nonpresence until he'd covered another 50 yards. He then stood where he was, waiting for me to catch up.

"You think I embarrassed you, don't you?"

"Think it's that easy to embarrass me? I just stood there, saying nothing—don't you think I embarrassed you?"

"Nope."

"No? Don't you think I let you down?"

"Nope."

"No?"

Father and I laughed. We started moving again, but still in silence. Near the overpass, a few women dressed in Miao minority costume walked up to us, peddling trinkets. Everyone knew they were phonys, but their outfits were so bright and unusual against the drab urban landscape, they were instantly forgiven. Father stood and stared at them, oblivious to the silver necklaces and bracelets they were hawking. Unable to help myself, I pulled out some money and bought a silver necklace. I didn't care how cheap they were, I knew they were fakes, only two *yuan*, but they were very pretty, prettier even than the real thing. Father wound the necklace around his hand and looked it over: Nice, he said, really quite nice. Buy another one, will you? I knew he wanted to take it back home as a present for my little sister, two *yuan* to keep her quiet—cheap at the price. She was still in high school, though she wasn't doing that well, because she was as glintingly pretty as the necklace I'd just bought her.

"Look, two *yuan* for something as pretty as this!"

"What's that supposed to mean?"

"Nothing, but if we'd paid that two *yuan* fine . . ."

"Aren't your eardrums worth spending two *yuan* on?"

"Let's not argue about relative values. If we'd surrendered those two *yuan*, I'd feel we'd shown a lack of respect, see? Two *yuan* ought to get the respect due to two *yuan*."

Eventually, we made our way to Southern Cinema City. As chance would have it, some prize-winning love flick was about to start, so there were crowds of people hanging around the foyer, waiting to have their tickets checked for the 3:30 show. Though there were still plenty of seats left, satisfactory escorts were much scarcer. It was never normally like this: normally, all you needed was about 40 *yuan* and a couple of box tickets, and you were set. Soon as the film began, once all the lights in the theater were down, you could sit in your own corner doing your own thing, half an eye on the screen. Of course, there were limits to how far you could get, but then you could talk the whole thing through like mature adults on your comfortably padded seats and, once the film was over, find someplace else to resume. Five minutes after the film began, I eventually managed to collar a couple of girls. They weren't exactly ideal in the looks department, pacing up and down the lobby together, their black miniskirts revealing legs as emaciated as forked branches in winter, too thin to betray even a single knot of covering flesh. But neither was I about to forget what, in the normal run of things, should be situated at the point of their intersection. At any rate, beggars couldn't be choosers, and time was short. I reserved two boxes, one for me, one for Father. Who seemed a little disorientated by this way of going about things, but in whose age, experience, and ability to adapt to novelty I had total confidence. The tickets cost 40 *yuan*, I muttered into Father's ear as we entered the cinema. By the present rate of exchange, that was $5. I just wanted to warn him that it was 40 *yuan*, that it ought, as he would say, to receive the respect due to 40 *yuan*.

★

This was the gist. The hero, Xiao Lin, is a struggling artist who can't sell any pictures. When he winds up too poor even to buy oil paints, let alone hire a model, he's forced to become a street portrait painter, just to make enough to eat. Business isn't that great because he doesn't paint likenesses and his customers can never recognize themselves, so they refuse to pay up. At this point, the heroine, Xiao Ai, turns up and sticks herself down on the square stool opposite Xiao Lin. She's soon joined by some fat guy, who makes Xiao Lin all anxious, sitting behind him and watching every brushstroke like a rabid dog. Of course, Xiao Lin paints like crap, and his portrait of the beautiful Xiao Ai comes out ugly as sin. The guy jumps up, throws the picture on the ground, and is about to punch the living daylights out of Xiao Lin when Xiao Ai walks over, picks it up, and says she likes it. Xiao Lin, to his amazement, then gets paid double his normal fee. And that's how Xiao Lin and Xiao Ai's love story begins. The details get more painful further on. Xiao Ai, it turns out, is a sing-song girl, a prostitute. Every week she comes to Xiao Lin's picture stall, asks him to paint her portrait, then pays him enough money to live on for a week and buy a few paints. When the money's gone, she comes back. In other words, every week Xiao Lin paints a portrait of Xiao Ai, every week he falls deeper in love with her. But Xiao Ai rejects Xiao Lin's advances, keeps her distance. Xiao Lin suffers, of course, but at least he can keep painting through the most difficult period of his career as an artist until, eventually, his paintings begin to sell; he becomes quite famous and decides to move away to make his name elsewhere. He tries to find Xiao Ai to tell her and, I reckon, to sleep with her, so that things can be left a bit more definite between the two of them. But what with the *yin* being crossed with the *yang,* et cetera, et cetera, she's nowhere to be found. So he sticks a note to Xiao Ai on his picture stall, saying that he loves her, that he wants her to come and find him, and leaving a contact address. After Xiao Lin leaves, he waits and waits for a letter from Xiao Ai, but none ever comes. Despite or rather because of his lovesickness, he becomes more and more famous as an artist. And, inevitably, the vulgar finale: a now-celebrated Xiao Lin returns to his former hometown, where he runs into Xiao Ai, now an aging, faded low-grade prostitute, scarred and ruined by her trade, and barely able to bring in any customers. The ever-faithful Xiao Lin takes her back to his hotel, and the two of them finally have sex. But Xiao Ai refuses to admit she's Xiao Ai and accuses Xiao Lin of inventing the whole story to trick his way out of paying. Whenever Xiao Lin tries to reply, Xiao Ai screams at him to pay up until, in front of a large, curious audience and more miserable than he's ever been before in his life, he's forced to throw a pile of money at her. This scene, please note, is filmed in slow motion, each beautiful dollar floating, pirouetting lazily through the air. After grabbing the money, quick as she can (she hasn't made that much in one night in years), the prostitute leaves the hotel, still spitting obscenities. And finally, of course, there's the scene where Xiao Ai rushes from one street corner to another, before finding a dark corner against which to lean and weep crystalline tears. A sorrowful Xiao Lin plods back home, now plagued by melancholy, which naturally helps make him an even more successful painter. And there we have it: the love story of how a great prostitute made an artist; screenplay by Zhu Wen. Stories like this are a dime a dozen, so go on, enjoy them, as many as you can stand.

I badly wanted to find out how Father was doing. But I couldn't see a thing: the theater was barely light enough to grope your way toward the toilet. The girl I was squeezed up against—I use this term advisedly, because she'd told me she was only seventeen—asked me for a can of Coke. I gave her a piece of chewing gum. Why d'you want to drink so much? The toilet's miles away. You're a stingy bastard, aren't you, she said back. Ah, I see, I said, it's not that you're thirsty, is it? You think just because you're letting me feel you up in here, you're entitled to make me spend another 4 fucking *yuan*, that's point five of a dollar, don't you forget. I'm right, aren't I? Well, don't you worry: in a minute, when the film's over, I'll give you another 4 *yuan* in cash, straight. She pulled my hand out from inside her skirt: God, you're a pain, you know, she said, you've got no . . . subtlety. Subtlety? What was that supposed to be? This got me thinking: I had to have a novice on my hands here, if she was still talking about this thing called subtlety. She was in the wrong trade: she ought to have been a writer or a poet. The subtlety of the film had her completely entranced: she sat there, mesmerized, dead as a block of wood, leaving my hand to go about its own subtle business on her. When eventually I got bored, I left my seat and tried to figure out where Father was. No joy, even after an extensive tour around the theater: occasionally, in among the dim, tight huddle of smooching couples, you might catch the gleam of a long, slender leg, but you couldn't make out any of the faces. Faces no longer mattered, in this kind of light. There was nothing to do but make my way back to my own box, bitterly regretting not having memorized Father's seat number, because I was very interested to see how he performed at this kind of game. Sitting back down, I leaned over and half-reached out again, before I noticed, in amazement, the girl still staring, spellbound, at the screen, her own crystalline tears hanging at the corners of her eyes. After a brief hesitation, I pulled back my hand. What was I thinking of, you might well ask, and I did feel disappointed in myself, truly, that I should be ruled more by a prostitute's tears than by any other bodily fluid. It ruined everything for me from then on, I couldn't help myself, so I frittered away the time that remained. How old's the girl who was with you? I asked her, when we got to a slightly happier bit in the story. Same as me, she replied. Shouldn't you both still be in school? Oh yes, she told me, very earnestly, they were both in their second year of high school. Now this was a funny coincidence. My little sister also happened to be in her second year of high school. Did both your parents die when you were very small? I went on to ask, out of idle curiosity. They're as dead as you fucking are, she spat back. So are you in this line of work to buy new clothes? My quick-fire questioning style was obviously starting to piss her off: What d'you mean, line of work, she scowled at me. You know what I mean, the one you're in now. No, you tell me, what line do you think we're in? You really need me to spell it out? You're the whores, we're the customers. Am I right or am I right? A long silence, then her last word on the subject: God, you're a pain, you know that? After another little while, she said she needed the toilet. You find it on your own, I said. Off she went, slinging her little bag over her shoulder, her face sunk into a deep scowl. She didn't come back.

I sat in the empty box on my own, watching the film through to the end. As I followed the rest of the audience out afterward, though I was in my usual postcinema daze, I could still recognize that feeling you get when you've not seen something—sex—through to its logical conclusion. I didn't know whose chest Wang Qing would be buried in right now. I looked all around, hoping to spot Father and his own little whore, hoping he'd had better luck than me. Thinking about it, I'd probably only gotten about a quarter of my money's worth, i.e., I'd pissed away a whole 30 *yuan*—$3.75. I stood for an age on the steps leading up to the theater entrance; no sign of Father. After another five minutes, he finally reappeared, shouting to me from over by some market stalls opposite and waving a skewer of roast mutton. He needed to cross the overpass to rejoin me. Tipping my head back, I watched Father struggle up, glide over the torrents of traffic, then descend, two steps at a time. From the bounce in his step, he must have gotten value for money on at least some of my lost $3.75. My father was a practical man, never one to waste time down dead ends or worry about subtlety. He never let me down.

★

But this time he failed me. Long before Xiao Ai had even made her first appearance, he'd slipped out of the theater and begun an hour-long stroll around the streets, eating, in the process, five mutton ke-babs, a bowl of beef noodles, and a stick of candied haws. Not for the first time, he'd managed to channel his libido into an unnaturally healthy appetite for food. I was not impressed. And to top it off, before he'd spent ten minutes in her company he'd given his skinny escort that silver necklace. You didn't even touch her, why'd you give her a present? Father's response was confused: She was very young, he stuttered, she was only a child. What Father meant was, if a woman was still very young, not old enough to make her own living, she had the right to expect whatever she wanted, free, gratis and for noth-ing. Recognizing this for the rank falsehood it was, I decided not to let it go and launched a full frontal assault on Father's faulty logic. (Opportunities like this didn't grow on trees, I had to grab tight on to it.) First of all, I snatched the one surviving kebab out of Father's hand and wolfed it down. I then insisted he explain to me what respect he'd shown to the necklace and the two *yuan* it'd cost. Initially, he took no notice, smiling happily away as I ranted. But after a while, his face began to stiffen. Finally, he ground to a halt in the middle of a pedes-trian crossing. A black sedan car whistled past, grazing his elbow.

"Listen, if you could just calm down a bit, you'd realize that we don't need nearly as many women as we think we want. Only a few, a very few."

"I don't know about that. All I know is I'm different."

"No, no, think about it some more. You're not as unusual as you think, you've got it all blown out of proportion. Okay, you're younger than me, you're fitter, maybe you need more than me, but no way as many as you think. You just think it through."

"I'm not going to argue with you about this. In any case, I don't believe fitter, younger people need more sex than other people. Or, let me put it another way: libido's independent of the body. Even eunuchs crave sex. Sex isn't just about marriage or adultery or incest, it's much bigger, it's everywhere, all the time; sometimes it's psychological, sometimes physical. But it's everywhere. If you don't face up to this, you're not being honest. And I've no time for anyone who doesn't."

Father now began to get agitated, gesturing inarticulately at me, then shaking his head, until a traffic cop started yelling at us to move on. Once a bus had whipped past us, I guided Father safely across, my arm on his shoulder. We paused again, once we'd reached the curb, next to a stunned-looking decibel gauge that claimed to tell us precisely how noisy the city was. Eyes cast downward, clearly feeling betrayed by my refusal to trust him, Father suddenly looked his age, that of a man the wrong side of fifty. I hated to see him like that; I love my father. For years now, he'd unconditionally accepted me as I was—now this was worth remembering. He was my friend, and you don't pull your friends to pieces. I tapped him on the shoulder. Come on, forget it, let's go and find my brother, I suggested, see if he's back yet. But Father didn't move.

"I want you to say exactly what you mean. Are you saying I'm dishonest? If you ask me, sex has messed with your head. Not everyone wants to screw every woman he sees, is always thinking about sex, sex, and nothing but. Everyone's different. According to you, wanting to screw every woman you see is being honest, and anything else dishonest. Nothing's ever that simple."

"I just felt we'd been conned—we'd spent good money, but hadn't got anything back on it. Maybe this isn't about sex, maybe it's about business. No one wants to make a loss. As you yourself would say . . ."

"You've loved misquoting me practically ever since you learned to talk. Take that girl just now: while I was with her, the idea of sex didn't cross my mind once, not once—what's so abnormal about that? Are you saying you'd think me more genuine if I'd forced myself to feel something else, just to keep you from laughing at me?"

"Look, I don't know what I think. But you still haven't gotten to the heart of the matter. I wanted you to explain why you gave her that necklace. Was she Xiao Qing? Was she my sister?"

"There she was, sat up close to me, of her own free will, and that's exactly how I felt toward her at that moment, kind of warm. Not sexual warm, though. So I gave her the necklace. Okay, it was a cheap kind of feeling, but so was the necklace, wasn't it? What else do you want to know?"

I smiled at Father.

"All right, let's drop it. Whatever else, I saw for myself today that you have your limits. But I haven't completely given up on you yet."

"You laugh now, but just wait till you get to my age."

As we waited for bus 31 to take us to my brother's, Father grabbed hold of my arm. I'm telling you, he said, very seriously, you've got a problem. For me, remember, sex is a necessary part of life, but that's it—it's not the be-all. Those are just hollow words, I objected, anyone can come out with them. But they're not enough to live on. We know sex isn't a bad or a good thing; all we know is we need it. If we're not getting any otherwise and it's being sold on the market, why shouldn't we go and buy some? As long as we're paying for the genuine article, at a fair price, into the shopping cart it goes, just like everything else; no need to waste any more mental energy on it. It's like eating meat: open your mouth and swallow it down, just don't choke. And sure, you want to eat well, with as much dignity, in as much comfort as you can, to get variety in your diet. Nothing complicated about it, nothing worth engaging with emotionally or intellectually. Sex is the same: you eat, and you're done. Father had soon had enough of my analogy: All right then, he said, I'll put it in your terms this time. Sex is only the meat in your diet, it can't be your staple, your rice or flour. But why am I bothering? he went on. Time will teach you these things.

★

My brother still wasn't home, and his single-story apartment was still completely deserted, with Father's note still stuck on the door; no one, it seemed, had been home. But after Father had peered in through the window by the half-light of dusk, he concluded that someone had been back, because he reckoned a green blanket had been moved. Father was always able to spot details I never noticed, and if you hadn't noticed them to begin with, you had to believe him, as you had no way of knowing whether or not he was right. Because he was proving so elusive, the search for my brother started to take on a new, urgent importance, with Father insisting on going back to his college for another look before dinner. I advised him to forget it: even if we found him, there wouldn't be much joy to be had in the reunion, so why put ourselves through the agony? Wait till next time, when you have more time, and we'll try finding him again. So what should we do this evening? Father asked. I could sense a glimmer of concealed expectation in his question. Surely you know me better than that, Dad, you must know I'll entertain you the best I can, I know it hasn't been easy for you, supporting your family all these years. I'm the eldest, I can see that better than anyone. If only I'd had more time to prepare: I'm not running an escort service here, I don't have an address book bulging with eligible phone numbers. You see for yourself how things are: I'm not rich, I can only do the best I can in difficult circumstances. Then there's the problem of your own preferences, which are a little, well, eccentric, should I say, in this day and age. I'll be honest with you: I can't 100 percent guarantee you complete satisfaction tonight, we can only see how it goes—what d'you say? We both paused as the rush hour traffic surged past: all that sexual possibility skillfully shoehorned into stockings and dresses, riding the crest of the torrent. Suddenly, bewilderingly, I began to find them all dazzling, as they glided—their faces painted with arrogant self-assurance—past Father and me. What was so wrong with us that none of these women would stop—where were they all slipping off to? All this constant motion, all these darting, glinting shards of color pricked at my tired eyes. Father turned toward me: shit, he actually had tears in his eyes. As the grit was getting to both of us and there seemed little to be gained by standing on this sidewalk much longer, we set off in search of my brother.

I'd guessed my brother knew by now that Father was around, so I didn't hold out much hope of him letting us find him. Plenty of times I'd talked to my brother about this: Father, I'd told him, was like another brother to us, a friend, he only sticks his nose in because he means well, because he's older than you, you shouldn't take it the wrong way. Of course Father doesn't like your music: he'd never admit it, but he's basically tone-deaf. He doesn't like my writing either, he thinks my fiction's stylistically and morally retrograde, and my poetry undistinguished. But so what? Whenever I've needed help, Father's been there. That's what matters. You've got no reason to go around feeling so sorry for yourself all the time, thinking there's this great virtue in not compromising. Remember, by refusing to compromise, all you do is make Father dig his heels in and act like more of a vulgarian. We'd been strolling for what seemed like hours around the part of the campus where all the classrooms were. No sign of my brother. Not that this blind search strategy had any sense behind it, not in a college of at least 10,000 students. We lingered for several minutes in front of the crammed bulletin board. Today was the first time I'd been in a university since graduating; for Father, I suspected, it had been even longer. It felt different now: I started to feel nostalgic about a period of my life I'd found irredeemably tedious at the time. Both lost in our various memories, barely aware of what we were doing, of where we were going, Father and I began tagging along, like a couple of sleepwalking stalkers, behind a group of 4, maybe 5 female students, probably freshmen or sophomores. One of them, a girl with a ponytail, immediately spotted what we were up to and kept on turning back to glance at us. I noticed she suddenly came alive, started to perform, now she'd sensed she had an audience of two to entertain. Fuck, now I thought about it, college was a great place to be: if your pockets were full of dollars and you were someone like me, someone who wanted more than your fair share of women, college was a paradise, brimful of opportunities for self-fulfillment. Our new guides took us on an enormous, circuitous detour around the campus, emptying our heads of our original purpose in returning. At the entrance to the gymnasium, we were forced to a halt: only female students—some in aerobics clothes, others about to change, all of them radiant with youth—were allowed in and out. Their ostentatious glow of health filled us with feelings of inadequacy. Looks like we've tracked them back to their lair, Dad. I handed Father a cigarette and we stood, serious-faced, under a large tree, each silently working on strategies to bag the lot of them. A few minutes later, after a whistle blew and a middle-aged woman in sports clothes clapped her hands, the girls assembled, chirping and twittering, on the grass in front of the gym, splendid in their exercise plumage. Looking all the more splendid, of course, in the places their plumage didn't conceal. Lined up in a square formation, they stood with legs apart and arms spread, staring up at the sky and waiting for the music to start. In no hurry to make this happen, the coach—lucky, lucky coach—wove in and out of their ranks, adjusting postures here and there. Our old friend, the girl with the ponytail, came in for repeated correction. She looked terrific to me, but the coach thought her stance exaggerated, her arms and legs too far outstretched. This brief calm before the music was becoming oppressive. Please, I begged her silently, press the start button. Which she did, eventually, mobilizing the entire square with some synthesized crap in a quick 4/4. To be honest, none of them was any good; they were dancing to keep warm, not to look beautiful. Then again, aesthetics, I've often thought, can be highly overrated. I turned to look at Father, but found I had nothing to say. What was there to feel depressed, dispirited about? It's a great life if you don't weaken. Or at least not as bad as you think it is. I wanted to walk into the epicenter of that square of femininity, open out my arms to the heavens, and bring down on these wonderful girls a wonderful, thick snowstorm, every snowflake a $100 bill, helping them savor to the full the rich possibilities of youth. Father stamped out his cigarette butt and nudged me with his shoulder: Let's go look in your brother's dorm, he might be back by now. After we'd walked a distance away, we both—without a word to the other—took a final glance back behind us. Relax, the look in our eyes seemed to say, we'll let you be, for today.

As we climbed up to my brother's floor, the lights along his corridor happened to flicker on, sparking an exchange of loud, incoherent greetings. I could only hope they made sense to their speakers. We were both regretting our decision: we knew my brother wasn't going to be there. We were only there because we didn't know what else to do. But now we were there, we might as well go and have a look. My brother's interpersonal skills, it would seem, weren't up to much, as his roommates were clearly far from delighted by our return visit. This time, they dropped even their empty show of welcome. One by one, they found an excuse to slip out, until only Father and I were left sitting on my brother's empty bunk. I guess they'd all taken refuge in some other dormitory nearby, waiting for us to give up and leave, at which point they'd scurry back in and bolt the door after us for good measure. As it was probably past dinnertime, my brother's zombie classmates would all be headed for the private study rooms to spend an evening masticating on their idiot books. I'd never seen the point, when I'd been a student, of studying in the evenings, and I felt the same way now. My brother never studied in the evenings either, or went to many classes; I entirely approved. The no-study lifestyle isn't as easy as it looks, and few manage it as well as we did. But the difference between the two of us was I could work my way through *Theoretical Mechanics* in one night, then pass the end-of-term exam the next day without any difficulty; my brother wasn't so fortunate. Luckily he had other natural aptitudes I didn't. He was not only fantastically good-looking, he was also the best, the most skillful cheater I've ever known. The way he did it, it was an art form; I've never seen anything like it. It convinced me he could make it as a pop musician. Any father who could produce sons like us, a father, moreover, who was now the proud model of a wash-in dye job, you just had to respect. He was getting hungry, he told me. You've been hungry for years, Dad, you just didn't know it.

★

A girl appeared in the doorway, a fashionable little backpack across both shoulders, hair cropped short, short as a boy's. Before she'd allowed us a good look at her face, she headed straight for us and asked us both to move over. We bent forward to stand up, then watched, nonplussed, as she turned over the pile of random objects on my brother's bed. What are you looking for? Father asked her, cautiously. Nothing, she said, without even looking up, then started rummaging through the heaps of unwashed food boxes, yogurt bottles, and textbooks on top of his desk. As she seemed very preoccupied about something, we didn't ask her anything else. Once she'd finished rummaging, she headed for the door, apparently disappointed, without so much as a backward glance at us, without even giving us another chance to see what she looked like. Hang on, I said to her, are you looking for Zhu Wu? She paused. She knew he wasn't here, she said, she'd come to see whether he'd left her a note. So are you one of Zhu Wu's classmates? No, she said, I'm his friend. Are you looking for him too? Father nodded. She turned back around and sat down on the bed opposite us. This time I got a good look at her face: quite pretty, granted, but I could tell from the confident way she carried herself that she thought her face was a damn sight prettier than it actually was. She told us Zhu Wu had moved out two months ago. I said I knew. So why're you waiting here? We've been to Zhu Wu's new place, I told her, and he wasn't there, so we decided to try our luck here. And here you are: maybe you'll tell us where we can find him. All she knew, she told us, a smile on her face, was that recently he'd been buying new instruments for his group, so in the evenings he played guitar at a bar to make a bit of money, but she didn't know which bar. Which left me nothing much else to ask. But I noticed her staring at me, more and more curiously.

"Are you his older brother?"

I nodded, and introduced the slightly outsized individual with the glossy black coiffure sitting next to me as Zhu Wu's father. Stiffening slightly, she reddened and quickly gave Father a friendly nod, then turned back to me, suddenly looking like a girl again.

"Zhu Wu told me about you, he said you're a writer who's not made it yet. I've read some of your stuff—'Moonlight in 1990,' is that one of yours?"

"Did Zhu Wu show it you?"

"Yes. 'Have a look at this,' he said, 'if I don't make it as a musician, I'll take up writing. I must be better than my brother.'"

"That's what he said?"

"Yes. He also said you're a hopeless degenerate, that when he's famous he'll have to lend you some money to get a book published."

Father, I noticed, had started laughing. How could the bastard talk about me like that, and in front of a girl as well? By "degenerate," my brother was presumably referring to my sex life. Anyone with a sex life, he thought, had to be degenerate. As he didn't have one himself, he didn't allow anyone else to have one either, for any length of time. It was ridiculous. I had a kind of grudging respect, too, for his ability to lie next to a girl, talking all night, without doing anything else. I didn't know whether the girl in front of me now had had the privilege. Just as I was about to ask her name, she spoke first.

"Actually, though, I really liked your stuff. I really did. Actually."

Whenever something like this happened, I never bothered concealing my delight. So as soon as I'd got a slight grip on myself, I began telling her about what I'd written so far, where you could get hold of it, what I was writing at the moment, and what I was planning to write next. She listened very intently, continually echoing my main points back at me, with this expression of mystified awe on her face. Exactly as she was meant to. I pretended not to notice Father skulking, cold-shouldered, on the edges of our literary salon. Now if there'd been a basketball in the room, Father would have known what to do; he'd have grabbed it and played around with it until he'd gotten our attention back, until the girl had eyes and ears only for him. Things being as they were, a basketball being absent, Father could only cough meaningfully while I gave my address to the girl, whose name I now knew was Xiao Yan, and invited her to come and see me when she wasn't too busy. To do what? I asked myself. Whatever she'd let me, of course. Xiao Yan, a student in the music school at the Normal University, had lost the look of pinched impatience she'd had when she'd first come in. Her face now had a kind of glow to it, the straps of her bag slipped lazily off her shoulders. It was obvious she'd love to stay talking to me. But Father spoke up.

"Have you had dinner?"

"I had something on the way over. Haven't you eaten?" Xiao Yan asked.

No, Father said, we haven't, then pulled on my arm and suggested we go and find something. I asked Xiao Yan if she wanted to come with us. Girls like you never want to eat much, Father interjected as she hesitated over my offer, they're scared of putting on weight. We don't want to force you. What are you talking about, Dad, I said. Xiao Yan smiled—shit, she even had dimples. She didn't worry about her weight, she said, but she didn't feel like anything else tonight. As we left the room, Father turned back to Xiao Yan: If you see Zhu Wu, please tell him to come over to his brother's place.

Outside it was now completely dark. Though there still seemed to be people playing on the basketball court to our right, they were barely visible to us: running feet, the thump of the ball, a crash against the basket, another patter of sprinting. Obviously a miss. Father stood a while, listening, then turned and spoke softly to me.

"What the hell d'you think you're doing? Hmm?"

Nothing, I replied, leaning over toward Father. I kept my voice down, like him.

I know what you're up to. From the moment she walked in the door, you were trying to impress her. Father's tone made it very clear he wasn't about to be argued with.

"All right, and what's wrong with that?" I kept my voice quiet, because I'd noticed someone emerge from the mouth of the stairwell and start unlocking their bike. And it looked like Xiao Yan.

"Wrong?" Father lowered his voice even further. "Xiao Yan is probably your brother's girlfriend, and you're checking her out before you know for sure?"

Just as I was about to reply, Father put out a hand to stop me. Xiao Yan was gliding past us on her bike, humming some song. After we'd watched her pass under the circle of light cast by a lamppost some distance ahead, her back momentarily painted in fluorescent white, I cleared my throat and continued:

"Look, I'm trying to see if I can cut loose from my family loyalties. It's like a personal challenge. I'm not saying I'll manage it. And if I don't, I'll probably end up impotent in the attempt, my body'll keep me in check, so you won't need to worry about me on that count anymore anyway."

"Shit, you've got problems. You really have. Come on, let's go eat."

It would have been an exaggeration to call this dinner a particularly happy one. Father ordered a few glasses of *baijiu*, an unreasonably potent Chinese vodka, from which I inferred he'd decided to opt out of the magical mystery tour I was supposed to be taking him on later. We went to the Yulin, a restaurant near the college that catered exclusively to students. It was pretty cheap, but very crowded, and the food took such a long time to arrive I had a quick nap against the back of my chair in between the first and second courses. Though I was tired, more tired than I could ever remember being, as soon as I closed my eyes, I kept on getting the same feeling I'd had coming out of the movie theater, the feeling of not having seen something, the same thing as before, through to its logical conclusion. Wang Qing: all right, so she was no longer in her first flush, but she looked after herself, she liked herself, and she wasn't a lost cause yet, she was the sort of woman whose age is breaking through, layer by layer, from the inside out; in quite a few places she was all right still. Father knocked his chopsticks against the table: The food's here, he said.

★

What do I think of myself, of my writing? I understand myself, I think, I know what I'm doing, I can take responsibility for it. You shouldn't lose confidence in your son, he's leading the life he was meant to lead, he's leading a life that has a future. He wants to stay friends with you, forever, he doesn't want to be your enemy. He likes women, the more, the prettier, the better, but he won't be destroyed by them. His only weakness is his stubborn, naïve refusal to abandon faith in the possibility of one true, great love. Yes, he yearns for money; his blood jingles through his veins, mimicking the musical tinkle of gold; he's prepared to work, honestly, but he wants honest respect, and honest money, more and more of it, in return. Price is the only true gauge of honesty. 10,000 *yuan* per 1,000 words has to be better than 30: keep the dollars flying at him, and inspiration will never dry up; poverty is far more corrupting than money. I respect my forebears, but those long-suffering earlier generations of writers who weren't interested in money or in sleeping with more than a dozen women doomed themselves to mediocrity. The next generation was just as bad: though they got a taste of sweetness, of money and women, they were either too nervous or too pretentious to write anything decent about either. But the next generation, my generation, is different: greedy for everything, everywhere, smashing, grabbing, swearing. Because they write for money, for women, everyone thinks they're going places. But it's exhausting, this life of theirs; not all of them can stay the course, they get kidney problems, they get beyond medical help. Drink up, Dad, I've told you all there is to know about me.

Father had more to say for himself than usual: though we'd known each other for years, there were still hundreds of stories from his past he'd never told me. Fuck, I said, when he'd finished, you're obviously not such a good friend as I thought. I've always told you everything, but you've been keeping so much back. I felt my tongue go numb as I said this, and I knew I'd had a bit too much to drink. But I wanted to keep drinking, because I felt we were getting somewhere, between us. I loved getting my elders and betters down and dirty on the floor with me, shouldering them back home senseless with drink, a merry tune on my lips. But this was no easy thing to accomplish. Father, you see, was very cunning when it came to drinking. It was like a conjuring trick with him: you thought he'd drunk a lot, when he'd actually done nothing of the sort. It wasn't that he was afraid of getting drunk, it was just that he thought it was more fun this way. As I recall, Father only acted a bit more genuine when he was drinking with me. By now his eyes were half closed, his body loose and floppy, slipping down against the chair back, as if all the bones had been filleted out of it. Behind us stood a crowd of dissatisfied would-be customers, waiting for us to leave, waiting for our table. Apparently exhausted by the effort of this, a couple of them sat down, unceremoniously, on the edge of our table, cigarettes in their mouths, eyeballing our every movement. The closer they watched us, the more sedately I ate. For years now it's been impossible to make me uncomfortable, though not for want of people trying, but everyone always loses interest in the end. Happily, I have an economical talent—happy, happy me—for spreading misery with just a few words.

"There's something I'd like you to do for me. Will you promise?" Father asked me, a falter in his voice, avoiding my eye.

"Go ahead—anything at all." Staring straight at him, I raised my glass, clinked it against his, still resting on the table, then tipped back my head to empty the glass, feeling the alcohol lapping against the sides of my throat.

"Give—give up writing." He gestured weakly at me.

This time, my stomach beat me to a verbal response, as a mighty croak of vomit surged up past my larynx and onto the table. Though the men standing by moved away with impressive agility, I at least succeeded in splattering one sleeve. But I didn't stop to argue with them or apologize: though my mind was lucid, my body felt like all the strength had been sucked out of it. Father—who, just a moment ago, had looked like he was about to pass out—sprang back to life, as if he hadn't touched a drop all evening. He stood up, coolly sorted out the mess in front of him, then, supporting me forcefully around the shoulders, navigated me past the bellowing chaos of diners and out of the restaurant. Fuck, Dad, you won again. When we got outside, the wind hit me in the face, carrying on it the intermingled taste of every imaginable human desire, giving me brief pause; I must have been feeling weak. I shook loose of Father's arm, then set off down the street next to him. My head was pounding. Father's shadow seemed to me to have changed shape, seemed free-floating and unanchored, as if every few steps he sprang up, began strutting along the crowns of an avenue of parasol trees. I reached out to hail a taxi. After we'd gotten in, I gave the driver directions to my apartment: it was a little out of the way, and taxi drivers never knew how to get there. Father rolled the windows right down on both sides and told me to sleep if I wanted to, he'd make sure we got home. That's what he said.

The red taxi plowed down the busiest street of the city. Most stores hadn't yet shut for the night, encouraged, maybe even forced by the government to keep their doors open later and later. We're all businessmen now, and the world is turning into one enormous mall, it gets bigger every day. If this city of ours is going to make it into modernity, it needs nightlife, twinkling lights, glorious Technicolor, consumption, it needs you—yes, you—to abandon all sense of restraint and moderation, to drive these outmoded concepts further and further from your mind, to fit into a future in which both will have been abolished, in which doomsday looms ever closer—closer and closer. Still looking forward to the future, are you? Better to be Father than me, me than my son, my son than my grandson. Whenever I see a baby, my heart fills with pity. Why so late, unlucky child? The noise of the city outside the car windows now seemed very distant, receding into remoteness as the taxi tunneled steadily, like an insignificant little beetle, into the vacuous center of my mind, into the absolute, screaming blank inside my head. As I turned to gaze upon the thin strands of hair scattered over Father's forehead, my tears began to fall. I didn't know why. I knew full well my tears were cheap, as were my emotions. I was a cheap person, in an age that burned to sell cheap, my natural habitat the clearance warehouse, pushed carelessly to one end of a shelf, happy to write for anyone who tossed me a couple of coins. I was ready and waiting: I'd even put my soul on special, on 70, 80 percent discount. But don't forget: I want to be paid in dollars—fucking dollars.

★

I didn't know how long I'd slept, because the moment my head went down, divisions of time became elastic, one moment stretched interminably out, the next shrunk into near nothingness. I had only one feeling of any clarity, clear as a ship's light on a dark ocean: that same old feeling, the feeling of not having seen something through to its logical conclusion. I pulled off the blanket and sat up. Father was sitting by the bed, a pair of half-moon glasses perched on his nose, leaning in to catch the light from the table lamp, a sheaf of my handwritten manuscripts in his hands. I felt moved, unbearably moved: it felt enough, it felt like I'd won, won a prize that only my father could give. As to what he thought of what he was reading, I could easily imagine.

"Is sex the only thing that matters? Is there nothing else?" Father threw the pile of manuscripts to one side, shaking his head furiously.

"Let me ask you a question: how come you only pick up on the sex in what I write, and nothing else?"

"A writer ought to offer people something positive, something to look up to, ideals, aspirations, democracy, freedom, stuff like that."

"Dad, I'm telling you, all that stuff, it's all there in sex."

My mind still an aching void, I was nauseated by the taste of stomach acid washing around my mouth. Around the whole room. Beneath the circle of light cast by the table lamp, Father's face, his high, angled nose and the shadow it cast, the chair, bed, ashtray, and cigarette burning down on it suddenly all seemed sunk into meaninglessness. Whenever someone criticizes my writing as Father had just done, I get this feeling that I'm an adulterer, that everything I do in the world is false and empty, like adultery. Do you know what I mean? I get an adulterer's misgivings, anxieties, guilt, unease. But then I carry on exactly as before. Father picked a piece of paper up off the table and passed it to me. It was from my brother: he'd waited all afternoon for us, he'd written. That evening we could find him playing guitar at the Jingang Nightclub. I turned over to glance at the clock by my pillow: a little after nine. Not too late still—what were we waiting for? A chance to check out some real women had to be better than staying at home arguing about fictional sex.

We went back out to the street and waited for another taxi, but very few came around here: it was too out of the way, there was too little business. In the end, we stopped a cheap, roofless minicab. Gliding through the corruption of a cool, breezy city night, with only the stars overhead, proved excellent therapy. Our spirits—both Father's and mine—began to rise, to return to something resembling happiness. By the time we got to the Jingang Nightclub, we'd never felt better about ourselves, about life. And so we cheerfully paid the cover charge and went in, heads high, chests puffed out like fighting turkeys. I hardly ever patronized this kind of establishment, though I knew there was fun to be had in them. For a very simple reason: I didn't have the money. It was only when rich friends found themselves in the mood for celebration that people like me got to see what went on inside. But Father's visit today had made me very happy, and whenever I felt happy, I felt rich. Happiness has never been all that precious or elusive a commodity: money can always bring you what you don't already have. A curvaceous waitress led us over to a table by the wall. It was a good table, placing a row of attractive young women, all of them sweeping us with a predatory gaze, directly in our sight line. The dim, lawn-green lighting inside the club fell upon that glossy file of legs, dappling them exquisitely, like dollar bills.

"Can I get you anything, gentlemen?"

Did she really need to ask? Just stick them all on a tray and bring them over. Two Cokes, Father said.

"Anything else?"

Did she really need to ask? Just that, Father said. His face had a serious set to it, because he was thinking my brother could pop out at any moment, from anywhere. At least in front of my brother, he still liked to keep up the front of wise experience that was useful for garnering public respect. Near the dance floor, over to our right, we could see a deserted podium filled with electronic instruments. I kept expecting my brother to appear from out of some green room, hugging to him his guitar and his appealing aura of despondency. For years now, I'd been waiting for a musical breakthrough from him—I was his most committed, enthusiastic listener. But he'd hit a wall. Musical talent wasn't the problem. It was more a talent for living that he lacked; he needed to spend a couple of years having sex, then go back to his music. But he wouldn't listen, so he'd run aground. I turned back to my left, sipping my Coke, appreciating at my leisure the ranks of young women laid out before me. When I'd first come in, all I'd been able to make out was a blurred, multifarious mass of color, but no faces. Father turned right and stared at the stage, waiting for my brother to come on. Lulled by the dulcet tones of a saxophone solo, about ten anaesthetized couples were shuffling around the dance floor. A handful of attractive girls, I sadly noted, had already been claimed by male mediocrities; all I could do was look on. For me, a self-avowed admirer of reason and justice, life could be painful. Men like me—men who were both outstandingly gifted and unusually sensitive—were thin on the ground these days. Your tragedy, I mentally addressed these unfortunate women, is that your beauty—which, let's face it, will be gone before you know it—hasn't won the public respect it deserves, just like my talent hasn't won the acclaim it deserves. But don't lose heart: the rise and rise of money—the only truly objective mediator between buyers and sellers—is good news for us, it'll rescue us from the obscurity and neglect in which we unfairly languish. We all need to respect money: it corrupts us, it makes us arrogant, but it doesn't mean to; it abases only so that we're forced to strengthen ourselves; it erodes our self-restraint only to make us realize we never had any in the first place. From day one of life on earth, money has quietly, unwaveringly, ubiquitously striven to help us, to ease our impoverished condition. We should be fair to it. The intoxicating drone of the saxophone finally stopped and the lights abruptly flickered on over the dance floor, interrupting my thoughts.

Father, I noticed, deftly readjusted his posture, anticipating the imminent appearance of my brother and his skeleton band. But after a momentary quiet, prerecorded music erupted out at us and a line of fashionably dressed models emerged from backstage, as a smiling young woman on a microphone announced a fashion show. Because of our disappointment, we were in no mood to enjoy the spectacle that followed, even though shows like this are always worth watching: the models might be amateur, but they all give of their best. In their own way, they were all worth having. But for now, there was no more time to be wasted around here: we'd come to find my brother. I waved at the waitress standing by the wall.

"Can I get you anything else, gentlemen?"

I told her we didn't want anything. But could she tell us what time the live music began? It's finished, she told us, every evening from 8:30 till 9. Now it was 10:30. Well, are the musicians still here? She didn't know, she said. I told her we were looking for the guitarist, could she ask backstage for us? She said she would. A little while later, she came back out, still wearing that regulation smile: They left as soon as they finished playing, she told us. We could try coming back tomorrow, just remember it's 8:30 till 9. Let's go to your brother's place now, Father immediately said. We're bound to find him there. I voted against: Don't you have to leave early tomorrow? I countered. Forget it. But I did promise Father that tomorrow or the day after, I'd be sure to go and see Zhu Wu; he was a big boy now, he could look after himself. Father finally settled back down in his seat. I smiled at him, then motioned leftward with my chin. Even though we missed my brother, Dad, no reason for a wasted journey, now we're here. Father began to take in the over-made-up, overdressed line of young women seated by the wall. His eyes lit up, as if he were seeing them for the first time. I had to admire his guileless guile; I couldn't match it.

"What are they all doing sitting there?"

I didn't know whether Father really didn't know or was just pretending. They're waiting for customers, I informed him, they can chat with you or dance with you or go home with you and screw you. They're businesswomen, engaged in business, controlled, like we all are, by macroeconomic price regulations.

"What—all of them?" Father couldn't believe it. There were two basketball teams' worth of them, one team to play each way. I still couldn't tell whether Father was truly unsure: he'd been around, seen a lot, the old man. In any case, if his middle-aged innocence was just for show, it was a show I was happy to humor.

"They look good, like they know how to make themselves up," Father went on, as if to himself.

Of course, because they were based here, they'd charge more, and you had to have the money there and then or you'd get nowhere. But I was certain that screwing a woman for 1,000 *yuan* would be 20 times more exciting than screwing her for 50, it had to be. It was a fundamental truth, even if you thought it shouldn't be.

"But they all look so young," Father meditated wonderingly, his face sagging faintly, but perceptibly.

Dad, I said, you have to get over this psychological barrier, it's terrorizing you, it's surplus to requirements. For you, sleeping with girls as young as my sister is no different from me sleeping with women as old as Mother or Grandmother. It's just a challenge that we, as men, must rise to. There's no reason not to: we have a responsibility to ourselves, and to others. Try and be a bit more like me, forget your family, and just take a look around you.

★

I was first home, in the taxi I shared with a delicately pretty girl who looked like she should have been back in middle school. She was exactly my type. In the car, I put on this experienced, great lover act, holding her in my arms, having her cling to me like a little bird. Fuck, it was all too frighteningly convincing. We both entered into our roles, the one playing off the other. She said I could call her "Little Bell." I liked it, liked the idea she'd tinkle whenever I touched her. I also made use of the journey home to work out how I'd allocate the space in my one-room apartment. As soon as Little Bell got out of the car, she started complaining about the lack of streetlights, about how far we'd driven. Don't worry, I told her very earnestly, more earnestly than I can remember being in years, we're good people. Father's car pulled up soon after, his unmissable dye job emerging first into the night. I then watched him walk over to the other side of the car, and open the door—ever the perfect gentleman—for his girl, Li Hong. I couldn't believe my eyes, seeing my own father open the car door for a whore and help her out, his every action gleaming with a lustrous, classical polish. Dad, I know you're nervous, I can tell, but you make me so proud. You're amazing, you really are. Li Hong was clearly the oldest whore in the club, much older than her colleagues, chosen, naturally, to cater to Father's own libidinal limitations. Of course, she was no older than thirty. Only a part-time whore—her day job was working at a watch factory—she was obviously well pleased by her night's catch. Not that a smug whore is particularly pleasing to behold. The four of us split into two couples, one in front of the other, and set off in the direction of my apartment. I guessed it was now past midnight, as the streets were practically deserted. Leaving Li Hong a few paces back, Father caught up with us from behind and pulled me to one side, his face anxious.

"I've got a bad feeling about this."

"What?"

"Maybe Zhu Wu's in your apartment right now."

"So what, we'll get him to join us."

"Look, if Zhu Wu's there, we'll take this no further."

As we were speaking, I noted with some disquiet that Li Hong and Little Bell had also gone into a huddle. Shifting back around, I saw Li Hong cast hard stares in my direction as the two of them discussed something in low voices. Father's worries turned out to be unfounded: when we got to my building, I looked up and saw all the windows were pitch-black. Only one apartment on the first floor still had lights on, its interior echoing with intermittent coughs. But now the women refused to go up any farther with us, holding their ground at the mouth of the stairwell. Come on, I muttered, beckoning behind me in a low, impatient voice. But they wouldn't budge.

"Let's talk money first," said Li Hong.

"How about when we get inside? It's only on the third floor."

"No, we'll do it here." She'd made up her mind.

We had no choice but to agree. Though Father did ask them to have a bit of respect, to do it by the garage with me, not to fucking haggle over money in front of other people's windows. Father stayed where he was, alone, by the stairwell; I thought I could handle this myself. After a bit of preliminary business, Li Hong gave it to me straight.

"A thousand."

Now I knew, I knew that a thousand was a very small sum of money in the great scheme of things. But even now, and still to my eternal regret, I have to admit that to me it's not a small sum, it's what I'd get paid for an entire novella. $125 by the current exchange rate—look, not so frightening when you think of it like that. Put another way, half an hour of their labor was worth at least a month of mine. A bit unfair, perhaps? Or just another example of the unfair social division of labor: it happened all the time, no point in griping about it. I turned to Little Bell, who'd said nothing so far. I still held out some hope for her.

"How about you?"

My question seemed to surprise her: Of course it's the same, she said, they came out together. Little Bell, you've cut me to the quick, I felt this bond with you, I thought we were like family, how can you do this to me? Embarrassed by my reproach, she eventually lowered her price to 800 *yuan*—$100—but wouldn't budge any further. I could go and ask, they said, at Jingang, or at Longmenhun, everywhere, everyone costs the same, they couldn't break the rules. I asked them to wait a second, then went over to Father. How much money have you got on you? I asked him, in a low voice. Three, maybe four hundred, he said. Even including coins, I reckoned I only had about the same amount. Calmly, lucidly, I turned to gaze at the two slim, well-proportioned girls standing five paces and $100 away under the moonlight. Such a small thing: if there'd been dollar and not *yuan* signs on the bills sitting in my pocket, I'd have been all right. In Chinese, dollars are called *mei yuan*: beautiful, good *yuan*, better versions of our flawed, *renminbi* selves. But things being as they were, I had no choice but to make a painful decision, to forget about myself for tonight, to pool our money and give it all to my father. He was the honored guest: he'd come a long way to see me, he'd suffered for his trouble. But Father seemed amazed by what I had to say. What? They want how much? He became more obstinate in his refusal to pay up than the girls had been in naming their price. When push came to shove, it seemed, Father belonged to a generation that could completely negate their libido. I know what you're thinking, Dad, you're thinking 800 *yuan* ought to get the respect due to 800 *yuan*. But how well do you really understand 800 *yuan*? They're worth it, this is what they charge everyone, inside their heads they're just a mass of small change. I got a grip back on myself: I didn't want an argument with Father here and now, didn't want to wake other people up from their sweet dreams. I hated myself and my situation, doomed to run uselessly between two irreconcilable camps, like a sweaty, out-of-breath clown. Expressing no sympathy for my predicament, the girls accepted my 50 *yuan* taxi money without any embarrassment and began discussing how to get back to the main road and find a ride home. And so they left. I couldn't forgive them, even though I still had a kind of grudging respect for them. They lived according to one kind of principle; the problem was, I'd hoped against extravagant hope that they could have given the principle just a bit of heart. This extravagant hope—the hope for a bit of heart—was always getting me into trouble, refusing to lie down and die, popping out at inconvenient moments. It was this hope that had forged me out of the desolation that lay everywhere around me, that had so carelessly allowed me to become—some kind of—an artist.

Father climbed the stairs ahead of me with heavy steps; neither of us spoke. After opening the door and flicking on the fluorescent light, we both exclaimed in surprise. There he was: my brother, fast asleep on my bed, fully dressed—wispy beard, shoes, and all. Father, I noticed, had been aged by our ordeal at the bottom of the stairwell, his hair drooping lifelessly, his skin waxy, his forehead creased. Arms splayed, he sat down on the chair, the bleak white light of the fluorescent lamp bleaching his face, illuminating a fatigue I could hardly bear to contemplate. Heaven's will had spoken to us: my brother—we both of us still needed a dignified father worthy of our filial respect.

As my brother wasn't prepared to share the sofa bed with me, much less share with my father—and the ghosts of so many other passers-by—my wooden plank bed, he insisted on going home. In fact, he sat up and left as soon as the lamp had woken him. He barely said anything to Father: as he understood it, the aim of this meeting had been for Father to lay eyes on him. Now that that had been accomplished, he could leave. I went back downstairs with him, to the bottom of the building. My brother had come on his bike, so of course he'd bike back, but it was a long way. Why didn't you talk more to Father? I asked him. I know you don't see it now, but friends like him don't come along often. He was just tired, my brother replied, they'd talk more next time. I had nothing else to say, my mind still an aching void. Anything else I happened to come out with, I had no advance idea what it might be. But after my brother had said good-bye, pushed his bike out onto the main road, and swung his leg over it, ready for departure, I suddenly thought of something and called him back. The bike wheeled a very slow turn in the deserted main street and came to another halt in front of me.

"What is it?" my brother asked, in the tone of someone who wanted to be asleep soon.

Nothing, I told him. I just wanted to know whether it was Xiao Yan who'd brought him the message. He said it was. That's funny, I said, how come she managed to find you? Ask her yourself, my brother said, how should I know.

"Is she your girlfriend?"

"No. Maybe she thinks she is. Why'd you want to know?"

No reason. As I had a feeling Xiao Yan would come and visit me, I now had even more reason to get straight to the point with her. Ideal. While I was thinking about this, that old, familiar feeling, the feeling of not having seen something through to its logical conclusion, washed back over me. My brother swayed off, then finally disappeared over to one side of the street. I stood where I was, thinking of Father, feeling guilty. Personally, I'd never be short of women, but things weren't necessarily so straightforward for him. Father had put up with a lot today from me, without getting anything back. If a panther spends a day searching unsuccessfully for food, he's bound to feel guilty when he returns to face his den of cubs at night. Just as a healthy panther cub feels guilty when he encounters an old panther that, because of age, injury, sickness, or some other reason, can't hunt. So when a taxi that had just deposited its fare swooshed past me to my left, I automatically stuck out a hand to stop it.

Eyes drowsy, Wang Qing was wearing a white nightdress when she opened the door. The moment she saw me, she started screaming: Which half of my brain cells had I lost today, why'd I come looking for her at this time of night? And so on. She never had me over to her place, in the normal run of things. I knew where she lived, but this was the first time I'd been there. So that was another rule broken. But she started to soften when she saw how pathetic I was looking. She told me to come in, quickly, as if I were some underground party activist with an arrest warrant on his head. She even poked her head out the door to have a look around before quietly closing it. Looked like I was in luck, like I hadn't collided with one or more of Wang Qing's other beaux. I sat on the sofa, dully eyeing the soap-scented body that lay visibly beneath her thin nightdress. It was 10, maybe 15 degrees warmer than comfortable room temperature. Thrust inside my trouser pocket, my hand encountered a cold, hard object, and pulled out the necklace that had cost $0.25. Wang Qing's eyes lit up: Is that for me? she said. All right, I said, yes. She wrapped the necklace around her fingers; it was nothing special, I knew she knew what it was worth. She had sharp eyes for things like this, years of experience, I suppose. So what is it? Wang Qing asked. Nothing, I said, nothing serious. What the hell is it? she repeated. So I asked her (that's what I did, I'm being as frank as I can here) whether she would agree that, quite apart from the sex that was between us, there was also some friendship? Or, put another way, that we were friends, weren't we? I suppose so, Wang Qing replied, very cautiously. Well, I was just wondering if you could do me a favor. I then fixed my most imploring gaze on her and, as luck would have it, strengthened my hand by squeezing some tears out of eyes made raw by the day's tribulations. Nonplussed by this sudden show of solemnity, by this serious side I'd so far successfully kept concealed from her, she immediately agreed: she'd do whatever was in her power to help me. This was entirely in character: she was always boasting to me about how generous and resourceful she thought she was. So what I wanted to ask you, I said, was, would you sleep with my father? I love and respect him more than anyone else in the world, and I know you'd love him as much as I do. Wang Qing's face told me my words had gone down the wrong way. Though I could easily have ducked her slap, I chose not to, watching, eyes wide and alert, as her right hand drew a perfect arc in the air before crash-landing on my left cheek. As I took the blow, my mind became a lake of calm: I thought of Little Bell, of Li Hong, of other, much more attractive whores, all far more real than Wang Qing was, of all the unresolved problems and issues we would talk through together, frankly, amicably, listening to our teeth clink together like cold coins, if only first we could sit ourselves comfortably down on a carpet of dollars. All these things, and many more, so many things Wang Qing would never understand, because whatever the fuck was between the two of us had never been anything more than a hallucination.

Things soon returned to normal. Half an hour later, as I lay on Wang Qing's soft mat, drifting toward sleep in her single woman's bedroom, I was attacked by self-disgust. I suddenly felt that I hadn't done anything or been anywhere in the entire day just past. All I'd done, inside the vacuum that had been the last twenty-four hours, was take to its logical conclusion the most logical thing you can do with a thirty-four-year-old woman.

A HOSPITAL NIGHT

LI PING TOLD ME on the phone to show up at the Workers' Hospital at one o'clock that afternoon, that she'd be waiting for me at the main entrance. That got me worried: What's up? I asked. Tell you when I see you, she said. I'm too busy right now. Come on, I said, you've got to tell me what's up. Long story, she said. At least give me a clue, so I can prepare myself, I said, about the kind of thing it is. You know I can't stand shocks. It won't shock you, she snapped back, it's nothing to do with you, all right? All right? Keep your hair on, I said, I was just a bit worried, that's all, about you-know-what, okay? Look, she said, after a brief silence, you coming or not? One o'clock this afternoon, right? Right, this afternoon at one o'clock, she said, at the main entrance of the Workers' Hospital. Okay, I said, see you then. After hanging up, I dug out 30 cents, left it on the counter, and turned to leave. Which was when the wife of the bike repairman started going Hey! at me. Puzzled, I looked back at her thin, dark face. You still owe us for a phone call you made yesterday, she said with an embarrassed smile, don't you remember? I was miles away, had no idea what she was talking about. She pressed on with the particulars: You took out a 100-*yuan* note, we didn't have the right change, so I said to pay when you had change, right? I finally remembered and started rifling through my pockets. But I knew I had no money on me: after Li Ping'd paged me, I'd picked up a grand total of three 10-cent pieces off the table and rushed out of the building. Sorry, I said, I'll go home now and get it, back in a sec. Forget it, doesn't matter, pay whenever, or not at all, doesn't matter. This was from the bike repairman, as he squatted on the ground with his back to us, busy changing a tire for a girl with thick calves. His face was thin and dark, very like his wife's; when he smiled, he showed all his gums and screwed up his eyes deep into their sockets. The reason I took the liberty of thinking them man and wife, and not brother and sister, is because there was a little girl with a very dark, pinched face often playing by the bike repair stand, who liked weaving around and staring up at me, and who looked entirely normal physically and mentally. I'll get it right now, I told them. Even when I'd walked off some distance, they were still yelling, Forget it, forget it! What can you do with 30 cents these days? at me.

I insisted on repaying the 30 cents I owed them. The scale of their reaction made me feel like I was committing some terrible sin, like I wasn't really playing the game. But it's just a principle of mine, never a lender or borrower be and all that. It's one of Li Ping's principles too, or should I say, a shared principle. She doesn't usually page me when I'm working, so I thought something must be up. My instincts told me it might have something to do with her ex-husband. He'd struck it rich lately, much richer than when he'd been married to Li Ping, and had taken to driving over in his flash car, angling for a rapprochement. It was just an excuse, he wasn't really brooding over their break-up; the only thing a man got out of a wife, he'd been known to say, he screwed out of her in bed. He couldn't let Li Ping be, but not because he was short of women: a pretty high school girl had just dropped out, with her parents' permission, to keep his bed warm. The reason he came looking for Li Ping was simply to remind her of the wonderful fact of his existence. If she couldn't appreciate exactly how wonderful his millions made him, then at least she'd have to accept they gave him the moral right to terrorize her whenever he felt like a bit of fun. Li Ping didn't dare rub him the wrong way, always took great care to keep her voice all meek and mild when she spoke to him, because her ex-husband wasn't quite normal, psychologically; one careless word and he'd have a knife to your face. He'd been just about manageable when he didn't have any money, but now he'd made a pile he was totally out of control and was rapidly driving Li Ping to the end of her tether. One day she ran straight over to my place in tears. I was upset too, but what could I do? More importantly, what business did I have poking my nose in? So I suggested she turn to the police for help, but this just made her cry even harder: The police are no good to me, she sobbed. He hasn't done anything illegal, what can they charge him with? All he wants is to show you how much money he has, make you feel bad, what can the police do about that? I hate to see people crying, so I offered to get a knife and sort him out myself. That's no use either, said Li Ping, his bodyguards'll make chop suey of you. So what can I do, then? I said. As we were getting increasingly despondent, I tried a joke, not a very funny one: I've got an idea, I said, I'm a writer, my pen's the most developed part of my body, right, so how's about I flatten him with some devastating satire? No impact on Li Ping's worry lines—and my attempt at humor sounded like it was designed to comfort me more than her.

I showed up at the Workers' Hospital at 1 p.m., on the dot. Li Ping rushed out of the hospital like a human whirlwind, wiping the sweat from her face with a hanky as she ran. I went up to meet her. What's up? I asked. My father's under the knife right now, he's in the operating room, she said, he's got gallstones. What? I said. Meaning: what's this got to do with me? I want you to come with me to see him, she said. Hold on a sec, I said. Does your father know who I am? I've never met him, and I don't think I need to meet him, right? That's neither here nor there, said Li Ping. Anyway, he's under anaesthetic right now, the main thing is that my little sister, my big sister, and all their families know who you are. This was an even bigger surprise—I'd no idea Li Ping had any sisters, much less met them. I don't mean they know who you are, Li Ping said, of course they don't know who you are, what you look like, what you do, all they know is that you exist, in my life, right now. So what? I said. Calm down, said Li Ping, I'm not asking much. Look, this is how things are: my sisters are hardly ever around normally, but now something's up with my dad, everyone's gathered together, looking each other over. And there's my mother too. It doesn't matter what is or isn't between us two, if you don't show right now, they'll all be passing judgment on me, I'll feel I've lost face. I just don't know what to do, don't know what to say—by this point, Li Ping was on the point of tears—I don't want much, she said, all I want is a little performance from you, just show your face, won't kill you, will it? This is where I started to get nervous: Don't you think, I said, you should have talked something like this over with me first? And that was when Li Ping started to get angry. What am I doing now, then? You don't want to go in, I won't force you—just go home. I should get back in there, the operation'll be over about now.

So Li Ping and I made our way to Zone 4, our path there lined by the sick and by those who weren't sick for the moment but to whom sickness would sooner or later come. I was sick, Li Ping was sick, we all of us were sick. When we got to the second-floor mezzanine, Li Ping stopped a little way in front, pointed upward, and said, The operating room's on the third floor. Meaning, she was giving me due notice to put my stage face on, so I lifted my head, straightened my chest, and shoulder to shoulder, we climbed up to the third floor. By this point, my mind was a total blank. On the chairs outside the glass doors of the operating room sat a huge noisy group of people who suddenly fell silent, all sizing us up in their different ways; principally, of course, sizing me up. Since every seat was taken, we had no choice but to stand in the middle, as if in the dock. As I gazed at the notice that said NO SMOKING, I suddenly got an overpowering desire for a cigarette. At that very moment, a thick, throat-tickling trail of smoke wafted out to my right. I turned to look. An old woman wearing a cream brushed-cotton mandarin jacket was bent over a cigarette butt, sucking the life out of it. Must be Li Ping's mother, I thought. Is he out yet? Li Ping asked, probably hoping to lighten things up a bit. In a minute, a brattish-looking boy, about seven or eight years old, answered. Mustering all the calm I could, I took a look around at this group of strangers. I easily picked out points of family resemblance: like Li Ping's, their foreheads were all inscribed with indelible worry lines—clearly a family destined for ill fortune. What'd I ever done to them, to make them stare at me like that? If only I'd known six months ago that I'd suddenly be confronted with this unholy gang, I'd have faded myself right out of the picture with Li Ping. There was no need to be like this, I thought, we might only meet this once in our whole lives, why not try to make a positive impression? So I said to Li Ping in a low voice, how about some introductions? Maybe that'll break the ice. The idea seemed to amaze Li Ping, who stared doubtfully back at me for a while before shaking her head. So I just let it lie.

The glass doors of the operating room opened, and out came a rather overexuberant doctor with a mask hanging on his chest and a white tray in his hands. He went straight up to Li Ping and me: Look, out it's come, easy as pie, pea from a pod. The mob who'd been hogging the chairs immediately crowded around. The tray contained some blood-covered object that looked like a chicken gizzard. What's this? everyone was asking. The gallbladder, said the doctor. The little boy, who'd wormed his way in front of me, clutched at the side of the tray with both hands, trying to effect an introduction between his nose and the liberated organ. Are these the stones in granddad's tummy? No, said the doctor, the stones are inside. With a pair of medical scissors, he snipped the gallbladder open, producing the kind of dull sound wet fabric makes when you cut it. The massed spectators sighed in astonishment: the gallbladder was stuffed full of stones of different sizes. The doctor counted them over with his scissors: eight in total. Shit, I heard someone next to me say, no wonder Dad was in so much pain. A woman of about the same age and height as Li Ping took the doctor's scissors and gave the stones a few curious pokes. You couldn't see much of the stones' texture, as they were a bloody mess on the outside. She stopped fiddling: They're so light, she remarked. But worth a lot on the open market, said the doctor. I'll go and rinse them for you at the sink—did you bring a bag? Another woman, taller and younger than Li Ping, waved a hanky: Wrap them in this, she said. Okay, said the doctor, come with me. And off they went. Doctor! a shout rang out from behind me, followed by a cough, what about Old Li? It was Li Ping's mother, who'd been standing on the edge of the throng, unable to push her way in. Don't worry, the doctor turned to say as he walked away, he'll be out in a minute.

Dad's gallstones are shaped like pearls, a thin, middle-aged man wearing glasses commented. No, they're not, another man, this one fat, disagreed. The two of them started arguing. They're gross, a girl with pigtails interrupted. At this riveting moment in proceedings, two nurses came out of the operating room, pushing open the two spring-hinged glass doors and securing them with a bolt. A second later, a gurney emerged, on top of which lay a green-faced man with a full head of white hair, both his eyes screwed shut and an oxygen tube stuck in his nose. Must be Li Ping's father, I thought. There was some white foamy debris around his mouth and nose, and just then he looked worse than dead. A few nurses expertly directed the gurney onto the elevator. The group of us followed cautiously behind, but there was no way we'd all fit; what were we to do? No one knew. A nurse ordered the little boy, who'd squeezed into the front of the elevator, to get out, then told us, go straight up to the ward, you're not needed here. Group impetus then forced me up six flights of stairs. The patient had been laid out in a bed by the window in Ward 16, and wasn't going to give us any more trouble for the moment, as the anaesthetic hadn't worn off. Why're you all here? the nurse on duty shouted at us. What number bed? She insisted that only one family member could stay, that everyone else should leave immediately. The fat, middle-aged guy, who was probably married to Li Ping's big sister, started playing leader: Come on, he called to everyone, let's talk this through. Meaning: the duty question; Li Ping's father had to have someone by his side twenty-four hours a day. Mom, you take care of Dad's meals, he said, and we'll divide the shifts between our three families, okay, so you don't get too tired. I sensed, alarmingly, that Li Ping and I had just been turned into a family unit. The thin man, who was probably married to Li Ping's little sister, came straight out with it: My work unit's on a quality-control drive right now, I just can't spare the time, and I need to help my kid with his midterm exams. He dwelled particularly on the fact that their family had put up the cash for this operation, on the added bearing this had on the above-mentioned factors. Li Ping's face was not a pretty sight by this point, and she said nothing for some time. I noticed a lot of people were now furtively looking me over: Just look at that fine, sturdy young man, I knew the bastards were thinking, he could do *ten* night shifts without batting an eyelid. I glanced up at the nurses going up and down the corridor, hoping to find one or two good-looking ones. Meaning: if I was going to end up looking after this cranky old stranger, I had to find something—someone to make it worth my while. Then Li Ping spoke up, suggesting they find the money for a private nurse, as everyone was too busy. Her suggestion met with immediate and unanimous opposition: What about when Dad needs to pee? Find a male nurse, said Li Ping, they must exist, or hire a laborer. At this point, the old woman who'd said nothing so far, Li Ping's mother, could restrain herself no longer: Just leave, all of you! she started shouting, just piss off! I'll do it myself! Tightly clutched to her chest, in her right hand, was the small, hanky-wrapped bundle of gallstones, somehow giving her words an added moral force. Everyone grumbled all the louder about Li Ping and her stupid idea: How could they leave Dad with a stranger, at his age? Out of the question, no way. By the time Li Ping had fumbled a hanky out of her pocket, her tears had already started to fall. Now, though I'm pretty suspicious of women's tears, I'm a total sucker for them too, and immediately reached a hand out to her shoulder. But she shook it off. Li Ping wiped at her eyes: What d'you want me to do? she shouted, I'm on my own! I've got my own problems! Don't look at him, she went on, pointing at me, he's nothing to me! Nothing at all! She then cried even harder. I stood where I was, my head empty of thoughts, quietly putting up with the curious stares that were coming at me from every imaginable angle. All I wanted was for someone to stand up and pronounce the sentence. Things, it seemed, were just starting to get interesting.

The next day, at 5:50 in the afternoon, I arrived punctually at Zone 4 of the Workers' Hospital. I had a book in my pocket that I hoped would get me through the long, dark night that stretched before me. This was pure phony, of course: the more bored I get, the less likely I am to read. The book was called *Resisting Death*, and for some years now I'd taken to picking it up whenever I was leaving the house or had nothing much else to do. Although I did like the book, and had actually read it quite carefully in the past, I hardly ever opened it these days, just brought it along to places, like a security blanket, or a prop. I waited a while at the elevator door, which showed no interest in opening. This gave an old guy sitting by the entrance wearing a red armband time to interrogate me. Visiting time's over. Hey, comrade, I'm talking to you, visiting time's over. He waved me over. Though it was the last thing in the world I wanted to do, still I went. I'm not here on a visit, I said, I'm here to look after someone during the night. When the old guy first started persecuting me, he'd seemed a bit unsure of himself, but now he'd had time to nail himself good and firm to the moral high ground, or that's how it seemed to me, at least. Number ward? Sixteen, I said. Name? He flipped through a register as the cross-examination progressed. I couldn't remember what Li Ping's father was called; or rather, it wasn't a question of not remembering—I'd never known. I don't know what he's called, I said, but he's the one in the bed by the window. The old guy shook his head: You don't even know what he's called, what're you doing spending the night with him? Look, why should I want to lie to you? I said. I don't know the patient, I'm a friend of the patient's daughter, that's all, and I want to go up there now, I've got to take over from someone who needs to get home. But the old guy started getting all literal on me: Forget it! I don't care if you're Lei bloody Feng.[*] Rules is rules, you're not going up! When I saw on the elevator's floor indicator the third floor light go out and the second floor light come on, I started to get a bit anxious. The harder I tried to placate him, the more resistance he put up. You young people have no respect for rules! he kept yelling at me. No respect! In the end I had no choice but to ignore him and head back to the elevator. But even as I got in, even as the doors slowly closed behind me, I didn't hear a squeak out of him. His job was at an end; he'd already made his fuss, done his bloody-minded bit.

Li Ping's little sister was waiting at the entrance to Ward 16 and started waving frantically as soon as she saw me. I accelerated over

---

[*] The legendary model Communist do-gooder, acclaimed by Chairman Mao for staying up all night washing his fellow soldiers' underpants.

to her, only to discover that she was Li Ping's big sister with makeup on; all three of them looked pretty similar from a distance, though I probably could have picked Li Ping out close up. In a good light. You're just in time, she told me. I was getting worried, Dad needs to pee. Quick as a flash, she shoved me into the ward, then shut the door from the outside. I felt like I'd suddenly been pushed onto a stage, paralyzed by the lights; the moment I adjusted to the brightness of my surroundings, I got stage fright. I stood in the doorway, the five, six pairs of eyes in the room all fixed on me. I didn't know which to look at first. A fat, clean-shaven man lay on the bed nearest the door, about sixty years old, pink-cheeked, looking as healthy as—healthier than me. In the middle bed lay a middle-aged man with yellowed eyes like a dried fish and a very long upper body exposed outside the quilt; he slowly waved his right hand, gave a friendly smile, and nodded at me in greeting. This was unexpected, so my gaze lingered on him briefly, preventing me from focusing smartly on the bed next to the window. This was an unforgivable mistake. By the time I'd finally shifted my attention to the third bed, the long-ignored Mr. Li had turned his head to contemplate the bleak autumnal scene outside his window. Should I walk over to him? Or just turn around and leave? Someone behind me was tapping on the glass door; I looked around. Li Ping's big sister smiled, pointed downward, then made a rather anxious face. I couldn't figure out what she meant, so I looked at her again. She repeated this gesture at me, this time a bit faster. All I could do was smile at her, then turn back, open the door, and poke my head out. What? I said. What do you mean? First she yanked her face, that was suddenly a bit too near mine, back, then said, It's under the bed. What's under the bed? I asked. She frowned and lowered her voice: The pee bottle. Gotcha, I said. I turned around and bounded back to the near side of the bed. Li was still looking out the window, so I had to take a few more steps to move into his line of vision. I bent over and asked—in a very friendly tone of voice—Would you like to urinate? What with the whitish blobs in the corners of his eyes and one night's beard growth sprouting all over his face, he looked terrible.

An unidentified red streak was wrapped across the stubble at the right corner of his mouth. He nodded somberly at me.

I squatted down and groped under the bed: two washbowls, a ceramic chamber pot, and a plastic container that I thought had to be the pee bottle. I took it out and gave it a careful once-over, pretending to be very sure of myself, but feeling extremely anxious inside: what on earth was I supposed to do? Hand it over here! Li chose this moment to snap at me, his hand fumbling out from under the quilt, five fingers outstretched. Quick as I could, I handed over the bottle and began paying particular attention to whether the movements under the quilt progressed smoothly or not. Staring up at the ceiling, Li tried a few times to prop himself up, but soon after lay back down again with a grimace of pain. Are you done? I asked. He repeated his efforts, without responding. Finally, the quilt went still again. His forehead covered in plump drops of sweat, he stared immovably at the ceiling, suggesting to me he was starting to savor the happiness of an emptied bladder. I rejoiced for him. After a sufficiently long interval had passed, I bent down to ask: Are you done? No reply, so I waited some more. After another interval, I bent down again: Done now? I asked. What d'you mean, done? he bellowed, to my amazement. I haven't even started—I can't reach! More than a little worried now, I pressed him further: What d'you mean? Which made him roar even louder, even more incoherently, and left me still clueless what I'd done wrong. Luckily, the middle-aged man in the middle bed chose to enlighten me. Speaking very slowly, and with a smile on his face, he told me that as Li'd just gone under the knife and the operation scar was still very painful, he couldn't bend at the waist, so he couldn't position the pee bottle properly: You want to get in there, help your dad tee it up, young man. Oh, I said, right, no problem. While I squatted down and prepared for the plunge, the yellow-eyed middle-aged man gave me another helpful pointer: Be gentle! Don't lift the quilt, he hates drafts! So I carefully lifted one corner of the quilt with my left hand, then quickly stuck my right hand in, like I was dipping it into a particularly undesirable kind of grab bag. As my right hand was having some trouble acclimatizing to its new humid working conditions, it paused for a brief period of adjustment on Li's fleshy left leg. Which Li then impatiently shook. This left me with no grounds for further hesitation, with nowhere to go but onward. When my hand first made contact with the open mouth of the pee bottle, I began to feel much calmer. Following the leg upward, I reasoned, in the normal run of things, I should arrive at the hoped-for destination. Out of politeness, I didn't ascertain its precise position with my hand, but pushed the bottle up and in, little by little, asking all the time, there yet? There yet? Li shook his head wildly, looking very displeased, not to say irritable. I had no choice but to keep pushing upward, until I could push no further. His face twisted into terrible contortions of pain: What're you playing at? he yelled. Every gaze in the room had by now swiveled over to me, squatted down, bright red in the face, eyeballs rolling. It was at this point I noticed there were two old women in the room also, one seated by the first bed, holding a soup bowl, the other seated by the wall opposite the second bed, both hands stuck in her pockets and a vacant, sorrowful expression on her face. What was I to do? I told myself to be patient and try again. Forget it! shouted an outraged Li. I don't need to go! Take the bottle out! Y'hear me? Take it out!

To which my reaction was, if you don't want to go, fine, I'm not going to force you. I pulled the pee bottle out in one clean movement, then straightened up. I gave him a good, calm stare as I stood there, holding the bottle, but Li turned away to face the door. Li Ping's sister pushed it open and came back in. All done? she asked, big smile plastered all over her face. I silently showed her the empty bottle. She turned to her father: What's going on? she asked in tones of deep concern. Li was keeping quiet too, as if he'd suffered some terrible wrong. He obviously felt his silence was tremendously powerful. Li Ping's sister turned back to me, her face tinged with displeasure. What on earth's happened? she asked me. Was this a reproach? What had I done wrong? Damned if I was going to tell her anything. It was again left to the man in the middle bed, the one who was taking careful note of everything going on, to intervene to break the stalemate. Hey, Old Li, he said, what're you mad about? So the kid's all fingers and thumbs—what's the point in getting mad? Come on, let it out, a bursting bladder's no fun. Let it out, let it out, everyone else in the room immediately echoed. Still breathless with rage, Li was determined to stay angry. One, two, three! the middle-aged man shouted, conducting the rest of the room with his right arm. At which everyone chorused, Let it out, let it out! Let it out, let it out! Li's face relaxed, slightly. Li Ping's sister moved in a bit closer to her father and bent down: Let it out, she coaxed. Your dinner'll be here in a minute, you'll enjoy it more if you let it out, won't you? Though Li remained silent, his change of expression showed he'd relented. Come on, Li Ping's sister said to me, in imperious tones. She then turned on her heel. With a slightly sick smile, I squatted down again by the bed. Thanks to my sense of revulsion, my movements were much steadier this time. With admirable efficiency, I grabbed hold of the sticky object that lay at the crux of the problem, as a combination of despondency and impatience made itself at home on Li's face, his eyes kept deliberately closed. My left hand then introduced the pee bottle into the netherworld of the quilt. But operating undercover remained a tricky business, and even pulling this way and that, I still couldn't quite gauge the position *juste*. The presence of a rapt audience following my every move added to my awkwardness, making me feel like I was an incompetent magician fumbling to pull a rabbit out. So, to avoid any further mistakes, and to shed some very necessary light on the job in hand, I simply lifted the quilt covering Li's lower body. With admirable calm and composure, I stuffed his thing, which was too dejected even to squeak, into the filthy mouth of the bottle, then covered him up again. At first, he glared at me, his eyes bulging like a goldfish, as if he was about to explode, but then—détente, as we all heard the poignant tinkle of water on plastic. Li Ping's sister turned around in triumph, her mood of celebration infecting the entire room. Maybe we ought to clap and cheer, I thought. When the noise had completely stopped, I bent down and asked (with utmost gallantry): Done? He continued to ignore me. After a series of tiny ripples just beneath the surface of the white quilt, his right, not his left, hand emerged from the depths clutching the pee bottle, signifying that he was determined to give the bottle to his daughter and not to me. Should I have felt disappointed? Rejected? The white plastic sides of the bottle revealed that it was over half-filled with yellow, sloshing urine. Although I could see Li's right hand shaking with the effort, Li Ping's immaculately made-up sister seemed initially reluctant to accept its gift. Take it! Li started shouting again. Just take it! Though she still looked less than ecstatic at the prospect, she quickly extended a beautifully manicured hand, then headed for the door, forehead wrinkled, body bent slightly forward. Seeing Li's forehead bathed in sweat, I thought I might ask him if he needed me to wipe it with the towel, but he was keeping his eyes haughtily shut, as if determined to ignore me entirely. I let it lie. A folding chair was propped up against the window. I opened it, placed it on the floor, then invited myself to sit down. The cloth of my right trouser pocket stretched uncomfortably. I got up, pulled out *Resisting Death*, chucked it on the windowsill, and sat down again.

Li Ping's sister came back in, holding the empty bottle, a new urgency to her movements: she really had to go, she said, she had to cook dinner for her son. Calling me over to one side, she drilled me on all kinds of minutiae I should take note of; I listened carefully. My immediate task was to go and fetch two bottles of hot water; any later and the water heater would be locked up. And there was no smoking on the ward. Don't worry, I said, I hadn't expected to smoke while I was here. She wasn't bothered about me smoking, she said, she was just worried her dad would smell it. Then he'd want to smoke, then he'd start coughing, and once he started coughing his scar would give him hell. Can't Jianguo give the kid his dinner? Li cried out in panic. Jianguo's on duty shift, Li Ping's sister said, he's not coming home tonight. For a moment, it looked like Li was going to say something else, but then he kept his mouth shut. I knew what he was worrying about: he was worried that once his daughter had gone, he'd be at my mercy. I'd have been worried if I'd been him. Li Ping's sister said her good-byes, sent a look of silent entreaty in my direction, then threw her bag over her shoulder and rushed off. After she'd disappeared out the door, Li coughed, resonantly. I knew then I had him on the run, that he was trying to put up a tough guy act in front of me. I gave him the friendliest smile I could manage; no reaction. I kept looking at him, trying to make him feel guilty, but it was no use. Young man, the middle-aged man with the jaundiced eyes in the middle bed warned me, you ought to go and fetch the water, or you'll miss it. He turned back to the middle-aged woman, the one who looked like a peasant: You go too, he spat out, and get my dinner while you're at it. Her face totally expressionless, the woman slowly levered herself up from her stool. I got up and took two water bottles out of the cupboard at the foot of the bed: I'm off to get water, I told Li, back in a bit. I thought he needed some personal space, to collect himself. After all, we'd be spending a whole night together, and he had to realize that we need-ed a certain level of trust between us to get through it.

★

Outside the ward, things were happening. Nurses, patients, and pa-tients' relatives were coming and going up and down the corridor, carrying food boxes, water bottles, pee bottles, and washbowls. The nurses' long white gowns—white flowers blooming among the ranks of the sick—masked their wearers as in an expanse of fog. Waxing thus poetical and carrying my bottles, I tagged along behind three young nurses, with no specific aim in mind, just thinking I'd like to go along with them wherever they were going. Could you tell me where the water heater is? I darted forward to ask when they got to an eleva-tor door. The three of them looked me up and down before finally the least attractive one, a girl with a face full of freckles, answered. Over there, she said, pointing behind me, back toward the toilets. So I turned and went back. As I arrived, the middle-aged peasant woman was emerging with her withered face and her water bottles. Got your water? I nodded at her. Ignoring my inquiry, she stepped around me as if circling an obstacle, head down, refusing to take a break from her misery, even for a moment. Glancing at the thermometer on the water heater, I discovered the water was only at 70 degrees. I put the bottles down on the ground, preparing for a wait. But before long, a tall woman in a long, dirty white gown and gum boots rattled the big iron lock on the door: You done? she asked. Time to lock up! The ward cleaner, I surmised, from her sweaty face and loud, rough voice. The water's not boiling, I said. You'd better come back tomorrow then! You want water now, then get it now! But it's not boiling, I repeated. If it's good enough for other people, it's good enough for you! Get a move on! Just a couple more minutes, I said, and it'll be boiling. She rattled the lock menacingly against the door: D'you want it or not? Because if you don't, get out! I didn't seem to have much choice in the matter. I poured out two bottles of 70-degree water and carried them back. The tall woman then locked the door to the water heater room with a clang.

What was her problem? I wondered. Was is just me or was she like this to everyone? Was she the same with men and women? Why didn't she look anything like a woman? She needed to get treatment for that. Still lost in thought, I took a wrong turn on the way back to the ward. Three old women sitting on a bed stared expressionlessly at me. Garbling a surprised sorry, I beat a hasty retreat, keeping my head down, and immediately collided with another old woman on her way in; another torrent of apologies. I felt utterly exhausted by the time I got back to Ward 16. And surprised to find Li Ping by Li's bedside, wiping the sweat from his forehead with a towel. I put down the water bottles and smiled at her. I don't think I'd ever seen her as I saw her then, sitting there, warm, affectionate, composed, almost maternal. Her father instantly went all petulant again, like a kid in the nursery playing king of the castle, spying on me out of the corner of his eye. Have a bit of fish soup, Li Ping whispered, the doctor said you could. He was having none of it: I said no! How come you're here? I asked her. I brought Dad his fish soup, she said, to save Mom a journey. Oh, I said. I wanted to ask her something else, but just then two nurses came in, pushing a cart covered in bottles and jars. They doled out medicine to every bed, and stuck a thermometer in every patient's mouth. There was a bit more to do around Li: he needed his blood pressure taken, as a routine check. Li Ping gestured at me to come outside the ward with her. Where you going? Li roared, his voice muffled by the thermometer in his mouth, his beady eyes never leaving us. Don't worry, I turned to say, putting an arm around Li Ping's waist, back in a minute. I have to admit, I did that deliberately, just to show that old bastard. What's up? I asked Li Ping when we got outside. Nothing else, is there? No, nothing, said Li Ping. She turned to look into the ward through the glass. You all right? she asked me, after a pause. 'Course I am, I said, and smiled at her, everything's fine. I can get time off work, she said. I can take tomorrow off; worst they'll do is dock my wages. What d'you mean? I asked. She hesitated: If you don't want to do this, she said, if you're having second thoughts, you can go home now, I'll stay. Leave things as they are, I said. I agreed, didn't I? I've got the time, I want to help you out. I haven't had second thoughts, you don't need to worry. Well, if you're sure, she said. I nodded at her. By now, Li Ping seemed much more relaxed: Hey, tell you something funny, she said, he came looking for me again last night. Who? I asked, even though I knew perfectly well who she meant. Who d'you think? she said. He parked right in front of me, then said if I got in the car and went back with him for the night, he'd give me so much money I wouldn't have to work the rest of my life. Li Ping was trying to keep her voice as casual as she could while she told me the story. Sounds good, I said. Why didn't you go? A cloud passed over her face. She went up to the glass to look in: Dad wants me, she said, then pushed open the door to the ward.

At the far end of the corridor, a middle-aged man with his arm in a sling was squatting by a spittoon having a smoke, tapping in his ash, then spitting, tapping then spitting, as if permanently striving for bigger, better expectorations. The fluorescent lights were rippling on along the corridors, dominolike. The man shrunk into the wall at the other end of the corridor looked up and stared blankly along the line of ward doors, his head turning nervously as it followed the sequence of illuminations. I slowly walked toward the mouth of the stairwell, up toward the smoker, decelerating as I approached to get a good look at him. What did I see? Nothing: there wasn't a single memorable thing about him. He stared expressionlessly back at me, forcing me to follow my course, and the dictates of inertia, to their end. When I reached the stairwell, I paused, then began my steady descent of the building. I maintained my speed, taking one mechanical step after another, until the stairs came to an abrupt halt in front of me. With a leaden thump of the heart, my sense of inertia gave way to waves of depression and desolation. The old janitor wearing the red armband had seen me, but when I looked up at him, he averted his eyes. If I left there and then, no one would have cared, not even Li Ping up there. All along, I'd had nothing but the most insignificant, dispensable role to play in this entire microdrama. I could walk out of this building back home, or I could turn around and go back up, but I couldn't for the life of me work out which choice was preferable. But, I said to myself, you should at the very least go and get your book. Clutching at the one consideration that could help me toward a decision, I turned and headed back up the building, back up to the now deserted mouth of the stairwell. The only sound I could hear was the hollow echo of my own footsteps. Though I tried first a heavier, then a lighter tread, still the hollowness remained.

After putting the empty bowl down on one side, Li Ping used a towel to wipe the wreckage of the soup from the corners of her father's mouth, as a mother might mop spilled breast milk. Now he was half sitting up, he was endlessly, inventively uncomfortable, one moment wanting her to raise the foot of the bed, the next to lower it. I was just in time to give her a hand. Li Ping smiled at me: I thought you'd gone, she whispered. Higher! Li roared, higher! I didn't know what to say to her. I still hadn't decided not to leave, but neither was I in a hurry to tell her anything; just then I had my hands full trying to steady the bed head. But wasn't this a kind of tacit compliance, I kept thinking to myself, hadn't I been about to leave? What had I been meaning to do? She pointed at the Thermos on the cupboard at the foot of the bed: There's still plenty of fish soup left, she said, d'you want some? Li turned his head suspiciously to eyeball the flask. No thanks, I said, save it for your dad, he'll want it later. Oh, I almost forgot, she said, after smoothing the hair off her forehead with her index finger, that's your dinner in the takeout carton. I had noodles before I came, I said, I don't need it. I'll leave it here, she said, so you can eat it if you get hungry during the night. You might as well take it back, I said, it'll get wasted otherwise. I'm not going back to my mom's tonight, she said. I'll leave it here, less trouble than carting it back and forth. What could I say to that? There, on the battered old cupboard at the foot of the bed, now sat the object that would decide my staying or going. Whether I ate it or not, as long as the carton was there, I felt as though I was bound to stay in this random ward with its random inhabitants. Although Li was lying down with his eyes apparently shut, he was maintaining a close watch on his daughter and on the man who was with her. I sat down on the folding chair and sized up my greasy plastic foe: how long, wide, deep, heavy it was. Keeping her voice low, Li Ping remembered to tell me that in a while her father would need another drip set up: The nurse should be around soon, but if she doesn't come, you should go and remind her. I mindlessly nodded my head. Well, I'll be off then, she murmured, even more softly. Li's eyes were instantly wide open: Where you going? Where you going? he barked, before succumbing to a violent coughing fit, his whole face contorting into a scarlet grimace of agony. Maybe he genuinely was in pain, but I didn't see any point in sympathizing; after all, he'd brought it upon himself. Li Ping wrinkled her forehead and swung her bag onto her shoulder: Must get going. That's how it always is with you! her father complained. Especially when there's trouble! So, what is it exactly you've got to go do? Calm down, she said. Calm down? he said. You want me to calm down? Just listen to yourself! And you want me to calm down! More anxious than ever to disappear into the night, Li Ping gave me a quick nod, then flounced off. Was she really gone? Li and I listened to her footsteps fade into the distance of the corridor and set off down the stairs; then nothing. We exchanged glances: Can you still hear anything, our eyes seemed to ask, anything at all? Everyone in the ward, I noticed, was looking at us. Sitting myself back down, I turned to look out the window, which by now was pitch-black. I wanted to show I was no longer listening for those footsteps, that they mattered nothing to me. But Li continued to lie there, concentrating, his expression growing more somber, more distracted by the second. She really does have to go, I told him, she's very busy at the moment. He snorted indeterminately. Why was he treating me like this? She's gone, I told him again, your daughter's gone. Still no response. I told myself to be patient, not to lose my temper, or at least not to lose my temper quite so quickly. Affecting nonchalance, I tried focusing on the white takeout carton on the bed cupboard. But it started to irritate me, more and more, till I could no longer stand the sight of it. I got up, picked it up, and walked out the door. Li stared after me, puzzled. Once the carton was in the trash, I started to feel a bit better. So now I could leave, right? Or could I? After pacing up and down the corridor a few times, I eventually paused in front of the door to the nurses' office. Inside, four nurses seemed to be having fun fighting over something, the right hand of one kept tightly clenched against her chest, while the other three had her pinned down on the table. I wanted to know what was in her hand, but couldn't see. I needed to knock but held back, hoping they'd carry on, hoping I'd see what she was hiding. A tall nurse with her hair in a long braid was the first to spot me. What're you looking at? she snapped, scowling at me. What's so interesting, huh? I flashed a polite, embarrassed smile at her. By now, the other three had all straightened up and were glaring belligerently. A patient needs a drip, I told them. Which ward? the tall nurse snapped again. Sixteen, I said.

★

Li finally spoke: Slow it down a bit, will you? I had no idea what he meant. He gestured impatiently with his left hand, the one that hadn't had a tube stuck into it, at the saline bottle in the iron frame by his bedside. I immediately went over to the water bottle, repeating cluelessly to myself, slow it down, slow it down a bit. The man on the middle bed, the one with the long upper body and yellow face, came to my rescue, yet again: Underneath, he said, underneath, there's a valve on the tube, you see it? Tighten it a bit and the water'll come out slower. Once I'd discovered the valve, I tightened it two turns. When I returned to my chair and sat down, I discovered my benefactor was still grinning at me and nodding his head, as if he had something else to say to me. I flashed a deeply grateful smile at him. Which he then took as his cue to offer further instruction: If the water comes out too fast, you get bloat, see? Blood vessels aren't very wide, so if the water comes all at once, and too much of it, it can't flow, it all gets bloated, see? I immediately nodded, terrified his explanation might go on any longer. It's too slow now! Li started yelling again. Speed it up! Obediently, I went over and unscrewed the valve a turn. That all right? I asked him. He scrutinized the drip in silence. I returned once more to the chair and sat down. The man with the long body was still smiling at me, so I had to smile back. He responded with more advice: It's no good if it's too slow either, the drip'll still be going tomorrow morning, you want it not too slow and not too fast, about the speed of a second hand. I decided the only way of escaping my interlocutor's inexhaustible solicitude was to focus very hard on getting the water drips in the transparent tube to move at second-hand speed, to convince him he could turn his attention elsewhere. The drops of liquid started to resonate louder and louder, until they were deafening me, until I had to open my mouth, as wide as it would go, just to ease the pressure on my eardrums. I glanced shiftily around me, to check whether this was my own personal hallucination. Every gaze in the room was on the drip. Li lay on the bed, his face contorted, his whole body twitching in pained, rhythmic response to each drop. The fat, pale man on the bed by the door attempted a laborious imitation of Li's spasms, but soon paused, exhausted by the effort. Though he eventually went back to it, after a few embarrassedly self-conscious glances about him. I stood up, walked over to the water bottle frame, and tweaked the valve a few more times. If I loosened it, Li would yelp it was too fast; if I tightened it, he growled with impatience. The fun we had, with that fascinating little valve.

Three or four men—office workers by the looks of them, smiles wrapped around their faces—pushed open the ward doors, bearing gifts of fruit, tins of food, and turtle extract. They'd come to see the patient in the first bed. They put down their things, exchanged a few nominal greetings, then took their leave. The patient in the middle bed immediately started simpering ingratiatingly at the strangers, and snapped at the unfortunate peasant woman, probably his wife, perched at the foot of the bed to get up and give her seat to the visitors. All this was quite unnecessary, as the person in the first bed completely ignored his generosity and, in fact, seemed very nervous about striking up any kind of relationship with him. The peasant woman with the miserable face was left stranded, bewilderedly on her feet while the stool stood pointlessly vacant. As all this played itself out, Li determinedly faced the other way, an expression of disdain on his face. Although Li Ping hadn't said anything to me, I had a fairly good idea her father had pretensions to being what we Chinese would term an "intellectual." It was also pretty obvious that the patient in the first bed and his visitors—the yapping middle-aged woman with small eyes, the daughter wearing glasses to hide the small eyes she'd inherited, and then those guys who'd just come in, with their mobile phones and perfectly coiffed hair—all wanted to demonstrate some absurd sense of superiority in here. When they talked, their voices were needlessly loud, their laughter unnecessarily uproarious. If there really is a God up there, an all-knowing and all-seeing one, he'd make sure to send the clean-shaven, pink-cheeked man to an early grave. And the shriveled man in the middle bed? Though time and life had already dealt him a bum hand, drying him out like a piece of salt cod, he too deserved an early death. Don't worry—I know I shouldn't say all this. I need to pee again, Li chose this very moment to inform me, with due solemnity. Am I saying, then, that Li deserved to live? No, no, he had to die too, ideally before he pissed, or at the very latest just after he'd pissed this time, but absolutely definitely before the next time after that; that way he'd make things a lot easier for everyone.

I know I shouldn't say all this either, and if there really is an all-knowing, all-seeing God out there, it's people who say things like this who ought to die, ought to die as soon as they've thought they shouldn't think them. I got up, lifted the quilt covering his lower body, bent down to extract the pee bottle from the underbelly of the bed, helped him get all fixed up, then covered him over again. I didn't look at Li once during this entire operation; I knew he'd be furious but couldn't care less—he'd just have to put up with my way of doing things. After I'd sat back down on my folding chair, I unintentionally glanced at him. Instead of the ire I'd expected, his face wore an expression of helpless, elderly tranquility. This made me a little uneasy. I'd made at least one mistake, I thought, I should've pulled out the bottle first, *then* lifted the quilt, not lift the quilt first, then pull out the bottle. For this tiny, irretrievable mistake, I would've been quite happy to condemn myself then and there: instant death, no mercy. Done? I asked him. Predictably, he refused to respond. Managing to intercept his roving gaze, I stared pointedly at him: Done? I repeated. This time, my question enraged him: What the hell are you doing? he yelled. What the hell d'you think you're doing? I'm not doing anything, I replied, I'm just asking you whether you're done or not. Mind your own business! he said back. No one asked you to stay, no one wants you here! All this shouting got me thinking clearly again. Keep it down, I said, I'm here by my own free will, and all I want to know is whether you're done. All I want is a straight answer, okay? Fully focused on gasping for breath, he ignored me. So I sat it out on my chair, smiling wryly at the back of his head. After a while, the man in the middle bed decided it was time to put an end to this watch-and-wait business: You ought to take the bottle out, he said, beaming away as usual, he must be done, awful uncomfortable if you don't, just be a bit gentler this time. His opinion delivered, he nodded encouragingly. There was something in what he said, I thought, so I leaned forward and extended a cautious right hand under the quilt. Just when my outstretched fingers were preparing to cross the twisted crook of Li's leg, his fleshy left thigh shot up, followed by a strangled yelp: Mind your own business! After a brief instant of numbness, my right arm began hurting so badly I almost whimpered. I left my arm undercover for a few moments longer, contemplating its next move, and the funny thing is, I could feel Li's leg trembling slightly: from fear, perhaps, or from excitement? I slowly withdrew, pretending I didn't care; now things had gone this far, my curiosity was up—why was he treating me like this? One other thing: if, for the time being, he was going to insist on keeping that pee bottle down there, if he was getting such a buzz out of holding on to it, there was nothing I could do. You just keep hold of it, then. Fine by me.

I opened *Resisting Death* and started to read, page after page, an entire chapter. I failed to take in a single word. But I had this vague sense I'd made a new discovery about the book. As I groped for the words to express this sense of discovery, only one thought barged its way into my head: Li still had that bottle in his groin. By this point, the drip had almost finished and had started spewing bubbles out of the nozzle of the bottle, so I took it upon myself to get up and call the nurse. By the time the nurse had shifted her skinny ass after me into the ward, he'd yanked the needle from his own hand and was keeping hold of it, pointed upward, in his left hand, eyeing me closely all the while, as if armed for combat. The nurse darted forward, seized the needle, grabbed his left hand, dabbed the back of it with a cottonball soaked in rubbing alcohol, then threw the hand to one side, as if discarding a piece of rubbish. Her lack of solicitude, I'm sure, left him feeling pretty lost and abandoned by life. But before she left the ward, she took herself over to the first bed to ask, in tones of warm concern, how its patient was doing, did he need anything. After he'd assured her everything was fine, she left. I glanced at my watch: about 9 p.m. All was quiet in the corridor. Night, I felt, was about to fall on the ward: both patients and caretakers should prepare for rest. The night watch for bed number 1 was a young man with a mobile phone who, after directing a few more totally unnecessary words into its mouthpiece, busied himself unfolding a camp bed by the door. The peasant woman sitting by the wall had to shift her stool over in my direction to give him room. Given the facts before me—he'd be spending the night on the camp bed, while I'd be spending the night on this chair—I quickly calculated that he, too, now deserved death. A painful one. Anyway, soon his bed was all ready, mattress, quilt, pillow all present and correct, but instead of lying down right away, he sat down on it, picked up his mobile phone, thought long and hard, then put it by his pillow. I get the picture, I wanted to say to him, I've seen just how very vital you are to the future of human civilization, so now you can lie down and quite happily die of your own importance. He seemed pretty uneasy, I must say, continuously looking over in my direction. He's not watching me, is he? I suddenly thought. Glancing around the room, I discovered to my surprise that except for Li, who was staring straight up at the ceiling, everyone else had their eyes directed at the two of us. Very odd. What were they waiting for?

Oh—the pee bottle, I finally remembered. Li was still nursing the pee bottle, preventing everyone else from getting to sleep—this was clearly quite wrong. So, a big idiot grin plastered over my face, I reopened negotiations: Would you permit me to remove the bottle? Just take it out, I then added in an undertone, show a bit of mercy. It's not just your problem anymore; if you want to nurse that pee bottle all night, fine, that's your business, but you're making everyone else feel like they've got a plastic bottle stuck in their groin. Not nice. Show a bit of public spirit, take it out. Go on, show some mercy, I urged, giving his shoulder a manly punch through the quilt; solid as a battlement it was. He turned, silently, to face me, his trembling, whitened lips framed by an inch of beard growth. Then: Forget it! Though the disappointment throughout the room was universal, out of politeness no one did or said anything directly, merely muttering quietly to themselves. Feeling it was time to take a stand and he was the only one to do it, the pink-cheeked man propped himself up with both arms: Look, Li, he said, very earnestly, everyone wants to go to sleep, so just show some respect and take it out, will you? The half-dead patient in the middle bed quickly reinforced the point: You heard what the gentleman said, Mr. Li, so why don't you just take it out? Li shrank back nervously before settling on his response: Ass! What he meant by this, I couldn't say, and I'm sure no one else could either. It now looked as if only collective action would win the day. One, two! I shouted, conducting with my right hand, at which everyone else in the room immediately chorused: Take it out! And again, One! two! Take it out! After five or six repeats, group feeling was riding high, but results were nonexistent; Li simply shrank even farther down into his bed. My only option, amid mounting anxiety, was to conduct a few more rounds: One! Two! Another five or six choruses. Li suddenly, unexpectedly, started crying: Screw the lot of you! I'm not taking it out! he repeated over and over. I shrugged helplessly at the rest of the room: Any ideas, anyone? After a quick glance around at each other, everyone else raised their right arms and shouted: Get it off him! And fast, the pink-cheeked man helpfully finished. So, in one clean movement, I lifted the quilt, drawing a tragic wail from a terrified Li, who tried to prop himself up but was forced to lie back down again by the pain ripping at his liver and kidneys; like an old turtle turned on its back, all he could do was twist his short, fat little limbs inward to shelter the pee bottle in his groin, as if he was protecting his last turtle egg. Would a turtle risk his life to protect an egg? I've no idea. With some difficulty, I inserted a hand into the crevice between his thrashing legs and grasped the warm handle of the bottle. But the damn thing wouldn't move, even after several violent tugs, and I was worried if I kept pulling on it, the handle might break. Fight with your mind, young man, the pink-cheeked one advised me, not with your body. So I decided upon a stealth attack. Deliberately letting go, I made as if I was giving up the fight, turning to hum a little lullaby out of the window. Then, faster than you could say "pee bottle," I spun around to whip it out. A volley of amazed cries rippled through the room. But all I got for my pains was a string of ghoulish chuckles from Li, shaking his head smugly from side to side, with the pee bottle still firmly lodged in his groin—he'd seen my ruse coming a mile off. Tell the truth, by now I was beginning to feel a little dispirited. The dried fish in the middle bed shook his head at me: Look here, he said, it's pointless fighting him with your brain, you're bound to lose. As the saying has it: his ginger's hotter than yours. Overcome mental weakness with physical strength, young man: fight with your body! With your body! The rest of the room voiced its agreement. All right, I said, rolling up my right sleeve with my left hand, tell me what to do. Best if you give the orders, boss, the dried fish said to the patient in the first bed, with an embarrassed smile, go ahead, please. Requiring no further persuasion, the pink-cheeked man cleared his throat: Are both sides fully prepared? he asked. I nodded, as, with utmost solemnity, did Li, his face bathed in sweat. Ready, steady—go! And so, after the starter's orders, my struggle to part Li's legs began: a truly titanic stalemate, accompanied by the epic creaks of the bed and the rhythmic cheers of our fellow inmates: Come on! Come on!

But it was my adversary, and not me, who drew strength from their shouts. Though he was panting for breath, his veins bulging, the hair on his head soaked with sweat, he was gaining on me every second. My throat was dry, my limbs jellylike: I knew I was near collapse. At which point the young man with the narrow eyes tiptoed over, mobile phone in hand, and, when Li wasn't looking, tickled his groin with his phone aerial. Li shuddered, then miraculously, wondrously relaxed his plierlike legs. As I finally whipped the bottle out, the crowd went wild, largely with relief. After scrutinizing the pee bottle, now severely misshapen, in my right hand, I covered Li up again with the quilt. To my enormous regret, only a tiny amount of yellow liquid was sloshing about in the bottom of the bottle. Having now lost interest in the whole matter, everyone in the room got into bed and lay down; someone asked for the lights out. Night, I sensed, had truly fallen on Ward 16.

★

To begin with, the peasant woman with a face full of misery sat, like me, by the wall. Soon, however, she took off her jacket and shoes, went over to the middle bed, and lay down, curled up at the feet of the patient lying in it. And then there was one: just me, still marooned on that rock-hard folding chair. The beams of fluorescent light bleached the white bedsheets and the patients underneath them with a deathly pallor, overwhelming every other color in the room. I could almost smell the whiteness; I was dizzy with it. Unable to sit still, I eventually stood up and quietly walked up and down in the small empty space available to me in the ward. Li's bedsheets were heaving violently: I knew he was still furious, but he'd calm down in the end, I thought. I'm thirsty, he suddenly yelled into nowhere, I want some water! I could have ignored him, but thinking back to what could be construed as my recent lack of respect for the old gentleman, I decided to go over. His lips were, in fact, cracked and he seemed to be gasping for breath. I poured a bit of hot water into his tea mug, then carried it over to the bed. Impatient for the mug, Li tried to sit up, though of course he couldn't. I lifted the mug a little higher, to save him the effort. I felt much more patient, much more relaxed than before, because although the other patients in the room were still under death sentence in my mind, for the time being they were busy dreaming their beautiful dreams, no longer monitoring my every move. Looking for a straw in the cupboard at the foot of the bed, I found only a soup spoon, so decided to use it to feed him mouthful by mouthful. I should have expected the unexpected, though: as I reached for the spoon, he spotted his opportunity and sprang a surprise attack on the mug, like a wounded orangutan. Though he didn't win his prize, he did succeed in spilling the water. His left claw now soaking wet, his eyes remained anxiously pinned on the progress of the mug in my hand. Now was that really necessary? I asked. The failure of his punitive raid—on top of the inevitable pain from his scar—now shamed Li into rage: Give me the water now! he wheezed, beard standing up like hedgehog spines. Hey, we're trying to sleep here, someone in the room grumbled. Think about it, I told him, with all the quiet forbearance I could muster, even if I gave you the mug, you couldn't drink from it, so just let me feed it to you, okay? He continued to grope around with his right hand, leaving me no choice but to play up. Like the master of cunning I was, I slowly lowered the mug to a height at which he could reach it, then moved it from side to side just to piss him off. He was a sly one all right, feinting with his left hand, then attacking with his right. But I read him like a book, and moved the cup away just in time. Li was left clutching at thin air. This whole performance was repeated three times, without him getting even a sniff of the cup, but still he wouldn't give up. Closing his eyes, he breathed raspily, as if his energy was at a low ebb. I wasn't fooled, though. And, predictably enough, he suddenly opened his eyes wide and propelled his upper body into the air with a great war cry, both hands flailing away pointlessly like eagle's talons, until his shoulders and torso thumped heavily back onto the bed. He whimpered in agony. And what'd he gotten out of it all? Only the lid of the mug, which I'd purposely dangled over his head; the mug itself and its watery contents were long gone, behind my back. He pursed his lips with the pain from his scar, as he turned the stainless steel lid over and over in his hands, sniffed at it, then threw it savagely onto the concrete. It clunked jarringly. The dried fish in the middle bed slowly raised his long, thin head, eyes barely able to open under the fluorescent lights: Was that an earthquake? he asked. I cautiously shook my head at him. He lay back down again.

Mr. Li, we need to have a talk, a proper talk. Why do you have to be like this? I put the mug on the windowsill, shifted the folding chair over to the foot of the bed, then sat down. But before I'd gotten myself settled, Li turned away, silencing me with his substantial bottom. Even though there were certain things I badly wanted to say to him, I kept them to myself, stunned by the sight of his buttocks, which seemed to be inflating before my very eyes. Wondering if I was truly hallucinating this time, I reached out to prod them—their warm elasticity was quite alluring in its own way—and concluded they were indeed getting bigger. I must find a needle, I muttered to myself. Soon as the words were out of my mouth, his buttocks immediately shrank back again, as if deflated, although, to my mind, they remained objectionably substantial. No, I said, I've got to go and get a needle to let the air out, I can't cope with something this big. They shrank again. Couldn't they get a bit smaller still? I asked. They shifted in the bed. Hold on, I said, I'm off to get a needle. I got up, scraping back the chair. Suddenly on the alert, he whipped around: Look, he asked, with a gratifying note of panic in his voice, are you going to be reasonable? Hmm? I was about to ask you the same thing, I said. Are *you* going to be reasonable, hmm? What d'you mean? he asked, looking anxious. Me, unreasonable? Eh? Shhh, I said, then bent over: If you were a reasonable being, you wouldn't have such a huge bottom, now would you? He had nothing to say to this, and as far as I could make out, had silently admitted to himself the profound truth of what I'd said. I can't help it, he said, more seriously, but still with insufficient contrition, what can I do? It's the bottom I was born with. Contemplating his face, I sank into deep thought. After a brief pause, he suddenly tossed his head, like a fat-bottomed duck might shake the water off its feathers, and resumed his glaring: Give me the water, now! Water? I said. Sure, I'll get it for you, no problem, but I still think we should work through our interpersonal problems first. Cut the crap, give me the water! He rubbed his parched upper lip over his cracked lower lip, making a rather intriguing noise, the kind of noise you get when you sandpaper wood. I turned to pick up the mug on the windowsill, but guessing the water inside would by now be cold, I bent down to throw it into the ceramic chamber pot, planning to replace it with hot. Rot in hell, he spat at me.

I stood at the side of the bed, holding the empty mug, feeling chilled all over. What did you just say? I asked him after a long pause. He now fell silent, his eyeballs darting about nervously, but I'd heard him, loud and clear. The curse—the first curse I'd ever taken the full weight of—reverberated through the bleached, formaldehyded air of the ward, draining the energy out of me, clouding my vision. Slowly dropping from my flaccid hand, the cup went briefly into free fall, sprawled over the concrete floor in a series of jarring metallic clunks, turned a semicircle, and ground to a halt by the chamber pot. I reached out a hand to support myself against the bed cupboard, to steady my overwhelming sense of dizziness. The other four people in the room raised semiconscious heads, their faces inscribed with expressions of untold suffering: Was that an earthquake? they wanted to know. I shook my head weakly at them. Unsettlingly, the heads refused to lie back down, forcing me to keep shaking my head, until all four of them reclined. But all this head-shaking only exacerbated my dizziness. I sat, both eyes screwed shut, my body rocking helplessly from side to side. Cut the zombie act! snarled Li. Give me the water now! His barking snapped me out of my stupor; suddenly no longer dizzy, I opened my eyes wide and smiled at him. What the hell are you smiling at? he said. Give me the water! His constant shouting was beginning, understandably, to vex me. One more word out of you, I said to him, and you'll get nothing at all, and then what'll you do? Yeah, don't give it to him, let him stew, someone in the room—a crisp, clear voice that seemed to be coming from offscreen—added. Li and I looked all around us, trying to figure out who'd spoken, but the four faces submerged in whiteness remained immobile, as if frozen in coma. You see, I said to him, no one wants you to have the water.

You've made your own bed, you might as well lie in it. Fine! he started spluttering. Fine! Red-faced with the effort, he tried to struggle clumsily up from the bed, to stretch down to the floor to pick up the mug, to punch me, to jump out of the window—he could have been trying to do any of these things; I had no idea. Whatever he was trying to do, it was futile. I stood up, walked over to the window, and gazed upon the night outside. I wanted a break from this bloody-minded old man and his ill-mannered old face. But still the view in the glass was dominated by his flailing limbs and torso: there he was, clenching his teeth, trying to clamber out of the darkness; all futile, of course, he belonged to that darkness, deserved to remain in that darkness. Why don't you just stay there, don't fight it? He was, I saw, finally calming down, wiping the sweat from his forehead with the pillowcase. He needed to start learning a bit of humility, I reckoned, a bit of self-awareness, a bit of gratitude. Why, I'd do anything to help a needy old man ready to show some gratitude. That was when I turned around.

He'd pulled the quilt off from his chest and was pointing solemnly at his heavily bandaged abdomen with his stubby index finger. Look! Look what you've done! I failed to spot anything of note. With a gigantic effort, Li raised his head and pointed again, then fell back down. I felt obliged to go in and take a more careful look. A blood stain was slowly spreading through the fibers, a blooming red flower, uncurling its petals, one by one. I was hypnotized by the way it opened out, staring as it transformed from a tiny rosebud into a camellia the size of a bowl. Seeing that this flower clearly still had some more opening out to do, I started to get a little anxious: maybe something had gone seriously wrong. A smug—and to my mind deeply vindictive—expression settled over Li's white death mask. Though it wasn't exactly what I wanted to do just then, I rushed out the door to get the nurse. The duty room was quiet as the grave, with just one nurse lying facedown on the table, asleep. I went straight over and rapped on the table. She suddenly lifted her head in fright. Then it was my turn to be frightened, by her sallow, sagging thirty-five-year-old face. I looked all around: where had all those young nurses gotten to? Surely they couldn't have aged this much by midnight? She was still staring straight at me, as if caught inside some terrible nightmare. What the hell d'you want? she asked. Nothing, I muttered, unable to suppress the bitter disappointment in my heart. She suddenly got up, still staring like the undead, grabbed my hand, dragged me to the doorway, kicked the door shut with a clang, then yanked me over to the wall left of the door. Throughout this entire maneuver, I was like a lump of wood, unable to respond with anything but paralyzing stupefaction. Moving in menacingly, she forced me into the corner and began running her hands roughly over my body. For a moment, I felt I had no means of counterattack, that I was faced with a terrifyingly unassailable adversary. But then, thinking it over again, I suddenly realized things didn't have to be like this: she hardly came up to my chest, probably weighed only half what I did—why the hell *shouldn't* I be able to fight back? So I grabbed her shoulder and shoved her backward, using only about 50 to 70 percent of my strength. This pushed her some way away, into the desk in the office, which scraped backward from the impact. Her hair all over the place, her face bright red, she rubbed at her bruised back. By this point, my head was clear as a bell: A patient in Ward 16, his operation scar's bleeding! I told her. Please come and look! No reaction. What're you waiting for, I said, it's bleeding! Badly! If you don't go and look, you'll be responsible for whatever happens. She smoothed the hair over her forehead: Okay, she said, I'll go and have a look, but first you've got to let me grope you a bit more.

I never know what to do in these situations.

Soon as the nurse and I appeared in the doorway of Ward 16, Li started acting strangely, opening both his arms out as if waiting for someone to embrace him. The nurse paused, not daring to go any nearer. What the—what the hell's he want? she whispered to me. I shoved her gently from behind: Go on, don't worry, what can he do to you? Nurse! Nurse! he cried out, almost in tears. Oh, nurse! What're you shouting for? she snapped. People are trying to sleep. He stretched a hand out, flailing for the nurse's hand, but she batted him away. Slightly subdued, he lowered his voice: Would you, he begged in tremulous, wheedling tones, give me a sip of your water? Just a sip, a tiny, weeny little sip! The nurse took a step backward and rested her shoulders against my chest, her right hand stretched out behind her, desperately trying to grab hold of something. Finally, she grabbed firm hold of the part of me that was easiest to grab hold of: That filthy old man! she complained. Concerned just then with other things, I made no reply. Her right hand gave a couple of insistent squeezes: How'd you wind up with a filthy old man like him? Gritting my teeth, I prised those fingers of hers off one by one, then pushed her forward. He's not my old man, I said. If my old man was anything like him, I'd have had him shot a long time ago. Quick, go and look at his scar. By now Li's discomfort was getting the better of him. Water! Water! he kept on shouting. What d'you mean water? said the nurse. Didn't you just say he was bleeding? Yes, I said, he's bleeding. I stepped forward and lifted the quilt covering his upper body. The nurse moved in close to have a look at the blackish-red bandages around his abdomen; he chortled with pleasure. Cut that out! the nurse immediately told him off. What d'you think you're playing at, comrade? Saying nothing, he lay on the bed, making bending and wriggling motions. The nurse's face reddened again. Look, I said to her, his scar's burst open, probably due to sudden violent movement. Violent movement? she turned to ask me, a lewd glint in her eyes. Is that right? she repeated the question to Li, who rather bashfully nodded his head. She stamped her foot: Serves you right! She then turned and left. I tried to reach out a hand to stop her, but she gave me such a vicious elbow in the groin I had no choice but to get the hell out of the way. Li was now frantic with worry, desperately trying to prop himself up, wailing as if it was his own funeral: Nurse, oh nurse! Forget the scar, I don't care about that, but you've got to give me some water, have mercy, water, water! It was only then that I suddenly realized: fuck, I'd almost fallen into his trap, the cunning bastard blackmailed me with his bleeding into getting the nurse, just to get a drink of water. I waved the nurse off—she'd reached the doorway by this point—You can go, I said, don't worry, if he wants water I'll look after him, not your problem, you go back and sleep.

The ward fell quiet again. I gave Li an approving nod. By now, he ought to understand exactly how things were, that there was to be no sympathy for old men who played with themselves. He was still rubbing his upper lip over his lower, the noise getting fainter but more jarring—one of his revenge techniques, perhaps? He pulled the quilt over his head, probably trying to block out the fluorescent lights, or trying to ferment new plots under cover of darkness. I felt like I was dealing with a corpse. I'm sorry, but I truly felt like I'd been landed with a corpse, lying there waiting for rigor mortis to set in. Just then, a tiny window opened on one side of the shroud, revealing one of his hands and a pair of sneaky eyes behind it. Shit, he was beckoning me. Over here, young man, over here. Now this was really testing my patience: Just say what you've got to say, what the hell's with all this cloak and dagger stuff? He was still beckoning away, forcing me to bend in closer. His breath was nauseating enough, but what he was about to say was worse. Bit closer, he said, I don't want them to hear, they're all bastards, the lot of them, let's not sink down to their level, come on, Uncle Li wants to talk something over with you. Fuck off, I said. Uncle my ass. He narrowed his eyes: Calm down, he went on. Now d'you want to stay with Li Ping? What business is it of yours if we stay together or not? I said. Don't be like that, young man, he said. I know your type, you're only with Li Ping for the sex, you don't want any commitment, do you? Put it bluntly, you're screwing with my daughter! Y'hear me? You're screwing with her! She's an unlucky one, that little girl of mine, her ex-husband was a pig, so she ought to know a pig when she sees one, and she's gone and ended up with you! She'll be too old after you're done screwing her around, you'll have screwed the fight out of her. And what'll she do then? You don't know what you're talking about, I interrupted him, feeling this was all in rather poor taste. He pulled back the quilt, fully exposing his head: Don't know what I'm talking about, you say? Then take Li Ping to the registry office tomorrow, go on, go! Where's your big talk now? Think I brought her up just to have her screwed senseless by you? What've you got to say to that? I didn't have anything to say to that. Reckoning he had the upper hand, he paused briefly, then suddenly changed tack: But I've got a plan to help you out, he went on, quite amicably. All you have to do is agree to one tiny little condition of mine and I won't ever bother you about this again, you can go and screw away to your heart's content. So what is it? I felt myself forced to ask. He signaled I should come closer: Just give your uncle a sip of water, he whispered. I contemplated him humorously for a while, chuckling away despite myself. Without even looking down, I kicked the mug all the way under the bed: Think you've got it all worked out, don't you? I said to him. Well, don't waste your time. You could call *me* uncle, and I still wouldn't give you any water. You want someone to help you, then take a good long hard look at yourself first. Soon as I'd said this, the young man sleeping on the camp bed by the door sat up with a start and pointed the mobile phone in his right hand at me: Now that's not fair! He bent over, looking for his shoes. Li and I looked blankly at each other: what the hell was he doing? Once his shoes were on, he shuffled over to Li's bedside. If he calls you uncle, the young man said to me, now pointing his phone at the invalid's stubbly beard and frowning, you really ought to give him some water, you ought to take pity on him. You didn't hear right, I said to him, he didn't say he'd call me uncle. I was about to explain further, when the interloper interrupted: Listen here, I'll be your witness, all you have to do is call him uncle, and he'll give you some water, okay? If he doesn't, I'll make sure you get some, what d'you say to that? Li tore with his teeth at a piece of loose white skin on his lower lip, a fire raging in his eyes. Slipping around to one side of me, the young man tapped me on the shoulder: Whaddya say? Look, we all have to get along somehow. Let bygones be bygones. I nodded, rather uncertainly. Look, he said, he's agreed, now it's over to you, Mr. Li, say it quick, it's getting late, you'll get your water once you've said it, then you can go to sleep. Li cleared his throat, then pronounced in clear, ringing tones: You little bastard! The young man and I looked at each other, and smiled. Shaking his head in disappointment, he made his way back to his bed. Before lying down again, he reached out to turn off the lights, muttering away to himself: It's your own funeral, Li, it's your own funeral.

Unable to acclimatize to the darkness in the room, I groped my way, off balance, back onto the chair behind me and slowly sat down. Amid various snores of diverse frequencies, it was Li's panting that I found most grating; he was, I sensed, still locked in some unfathomable but violent inner struggle. Then a cry in the dark: I need a piss! It was the patient in the first bed, I surmised, nothing to do with me. But for ages no one answered him, no one said a thing, even though the room's discordance of snoring did come to a miraculously abrupt halt. I began to think the patient in the first bed was talking in his sleep. But after a while, a repeat: I need a piss! He spoke calmly, almost lyrically, in the assured, measured tone you'd use to declare I Love You. The speaker sounded an altogether more mature, reasonable specimen than Li, so if everyone else kept ignoring him, I figured I'd be willing to go and help him out myself. Just at this moment, there came an answer: Look, couldn't you wait till the morning, I'm half-asleep. It was the young man, rolling over impatiently on his bed. Another silence, then another repeat, in exactly the same steady voice as before: I need a piss! Yet another silence. Then, a sigh from over by the door, followed closely by the musical tinkling of a relieved bladder. Done? Done. Sure? Done. Really? Done. Another sigh, then the young man could be heard lying back down on the bed. Vaguely, dimly aware of the general outlines of the room thanks to the light on in the corridor, I was still having difficulty adjusting mentally to the fact that I was going to have to sit here till daylight. I got up and stretched, then went over to a bit of empty shelving in one corner, to do a few exercises to shake out my back and legs, trying to recover the will to live. Would you mind not doing that? someone immediately piped up. You look like a ghost, swaying all over the place. As several other voices echoed their agreement, I had to submit and sat, disgruntled, back down on the folding chair. Maybe, I thought, I could take a walk outside the door—why should I molder away in this godforsaken darkness? So off I went. I need a piss! someone else said, just as I got up, in a strong provincial accent, the voice slightly tremulous, as if it realized, as it produced the words, just how outrageous its demand was. I identified it as belonging to the dried fish in the second bed. But the peasant woman asleep at his feet was snoring, louder than anyone else in the room, like a great stuck pig. Forgive me saying this, but truly, that's exactly what she sounded like; I can't think of a better comparison. Hearing the second bed creak, I guessed he'd given her a violent kick. Only momentarily stemmed, the torrent of snores immediately resumed. I need a piss! he shouted again, followed by an even heavier kick; still no reaction. Sounded like she was utterly exhausted, so I decided to go and do the honors myself.

Spotting me approach, he must have picked up on my charitable urge, and immediately sat up in a panic, as if overwhelmed by the scale of my generosity. I could see the valiant efforts his face was making to smile, glowing in the dark with a bluish efflorescence. If only he hadn't smiled at me like that, I'd have done almost anything for him. It also occurred to me that he seemed pretty flexible (for a dried fish, at least), perfectly able to resolve for himself the difficulty that was troubling him. Under the bed, he whispered. I bent down and produced the pee bottle. His scrawny grin was piercing through the darkness of the ward, sending shivers down my spine. Please, I had to beg him, would you mind not smiling, not like that, otherwise you're on your own here. His smile went into slow fade-out, taking some of the unearthly shimmer off his face but leaving it devoid of life, like a wax effigy; equally unnerving. I'm sorry, I quickly said to him, I'm not a fussy person, but that, that face is not working for me either. So the efflorescent smile gradually returned. I kept my head down, because I was going to get nowhere if I looked at his face. He shrugged his shoulders into a weird little contortion: There's no opening in my pants, he said, you'll have to undo the waist cord. Like a man with a gun in the small of his back, I bent forward and with some difficulty undid his pants cord, making strenuous efforts throughout to avoid brushing against his body, because I knew just one touch of that desiccated flesh would give me waking nightmares for years to come. After finally getting his pants undone, I helped him pull down his sticky underpants, releasing a fearsome smell into the pure, innocent air of the ward. I held my breath and handed him the pee bottle; my humanity, I felt, had already been pushed to its limits. But there was more to come. Go on, he said, leaning over to one side of the bed, it won't bite you. Finish the job off, would you? After a brief, appalled moment of hesitation, I gritted my teeth and stuck my hand in, driven on by some unknown, probably supernatural force. Suddenly, he regained power in his arms, placing both his hands over mine in his repellent groin area. It's okay, he said, I can manage, thanks, thanks very much. He plucked the bottle out of my hands and arranged matters for himself. After the deed was done I expected he'd hand the half-filled bottle of urine over to me like some great lost treasure of the ancients—but he didn't. I watched, astonished, as he rolled over, got off the bed, walked around me, one hand holding his trousers, one hand holding the bottle, tottered out of the door, placed the bottle on the ground, carefully closed the door, walked around me again, then jumped back into bed and lay down. Up until this point, I'd stood there, rooted to the spot: what the hell was the dried fish playing about at? Trying to make a fool of me? You go back to sleep, young man, he said, waving his hands at me airily. What the hell else could I do? I certainly wasn't going to help him do his pants up. I returned to my folding chair, seriously vexed. The more I thought about it, the angrier I got: my every step was dogged by urine, urine and human plumbing, on and on it went—where would it all end? The next person to call me into service in the name of urine, I promised myself, is a dead man.

I need a piss! This, but of course, was Li; no one else it could be. Were bladders telepathic? That was when I lost all pretense of self-control. Why d'you have to piss? I screamed, springing up from my chair. I thought you wanted a drink of water! How come you need a piss? Where's it coming from? You haven't had a drink in hours! Hours and hours! Why couldn't you piss earlier, or later, why's it have to be now? What d'you want me to do about it anyway? Just at that moment, the light in the room clicked on, the sudden bright glare forcing my eyes shut. I felt, again, as if I'd been pushed under stage lights, that there was nowhere to hide. But when I opened my eyes,

I discovered, to my surprise, that there was no audience, that everyone else in the room was peacefully asleep as before, or at least was pretending to be asleep, trying to stay out of whatever was brewing between me and Li. Who turned on the lights, though? Must have been the young man by the door, but just then I had other things to worry about. Lips and throat cracked, Li stared fearfully at me, clearly experiencing a spot of rather gratifying terror. I turned to the window to inspect my own face: It wasn't as bad as all that, I thought. I need a piss, he mumbled again. The way he was trembling made me realize maybe I'd gone too far, I shouldn't have gotten so angry with an old man. All you said was you wouldn't give me any water, he resumed after a pause, sounding aggrieved. You didn't say you wouldn't let me piss, did you? Okay, okay, I said, I'll come and help you. Feeling unnecessarily apologetic about the whole business, this time I was very gentle. But this put him even more on his guard: he tensed up, like a tiny frightened animal, whenever I drew near, trembling whenever I bumped against him. So it didn't take long for me to start hating him as much as before. He then began to wriggle around vigorously in the bed. Imagining he was trying to yank the misshapen pee bottle out, I bent over to give him a hand. Don't worry, he kept saying, shrinking nervously to the other side of the bed. I nodded approvingly at him, fully supportive of his struggle for personal independence. Eventually managing to get hold of the bottle, he pulled it out from under the quilt. But just as I turned an almost appreciative gaze on him, he sent an unexpected but intensely sneaky look in my direction. I reacted instantaneously: fooled, fooled again! Like a man crazed by thirst, he raised the pee bottle to his mouth. What the hell are you doing? I yelled, rushing forward to intercept. He put up quite a fight, both legs thumping wildly on the bed, but he never really had a chance. What the hell do you think you were doing? I asked him again, with my last few grains of patience. I want some water! he shouted back. That's not water, I said, that's urine! Let go! he said. I want to drink it! What could I say? It's your own funeral? With a flick of the wrist, I snatched the bottle away, to ensure all hope was lost, and put it outside the door, by the wall, next to the bottle from the middle bed. Now although, on one level, this latest perversion of his was deeply upsetting, on another there was a certain tragic dignity to it, at least compared to what had come before. Back inside the ward and shutting the door behind me, I spotted him silently mopping his tears with his pillowcase. As this was a sight that brought me no pleasure, I turned off the light, then slowly made my way back to my seat. But the darkness failed to have any calming effect: the more I thought things over, the less I knew what to do. Backward and forward I went, mulling over Li's plot: pissing to get a drink, that wasn't just cunning, it was gross. Couldn't he be just a bit less perverse? If he'd only come out with what he wanted, I wouldn't have said no, not in the normal run of things. But he didn't believe in being straightforward. Let him do things his way, I was going to keep well out. By the time I'd worked that out, I was starting to feel a bit tired myself, mainly from disgust; but I didn't want to sleep, I wanted to lie down and die. If only—Li still wouldn't let it, or me, lie: It's mine, he declared as insistently as he could manage, it's mine, you've no right to take it away. You still going on about that urine? Hate to disappoint you, Mr. Li, but once a thing's out of your system, it's finders keepers.

I moved the chair backward, to lean my poor confused head against the wall. The reek of urine in the room had seeped into my brain, squeezing out all the oxygen. The young man by the door, typically enough, was grinding his teeth. It's mine, mine, Li was still mumbling away. Absolutely typical: on top of everything else, he talked in his sleep. I was starting to feel that all this just had to be a dream. But suddenly I couldn't stand it anymore: I opened the middle window a chink and poked my nose out, feeling like a fish that had eaten too much and couldn't swim out of a crack, that would die before it lost enough weight to pass through, a fish bloated with urine. I hadn't expected to be quite so overwrought by this point. And yet I managed to sleep and even to dream—quite pleasantly. But when I realized it was just a dream and found myself waking up in the inescapable world of Ward 16, I felt pretty oppressed by life, as I'm sure you can imagine. For quite some time, I couldn't face even opening my eyes. But I did, of course, in the end. Could there be someone standing right next to me? Fucking hell: there was. Tall and thin, dressed in a white robe. Both hands stuck through that narrow crack in the window, looking out. I'd probably have taken it better if it'd turned out to be a ghost. I sat where I was, my nose almost grazing the person's clothes, too horrified to react in any way at all. After about a minute or so, I finally came to and sprang up. His hands stayed where they were, motionless. What the hell are you doing? He turned to face me: it was the dried fish from the middle bed. He smiled so ingratiatingly at me, I was forced to take a step backward. I knew there was a crack there, he muttered to himself as he tottered back to his bed, I felt it, and look, I was right. He slowly reclined again; but my desire for sleep had completely evaporated. As dawn approached, the room was still enveloped in darkness. Suddenly realizing not a sound was coming from Li's bed, I couldn't help feeling uneasy: if he were to die, his blood would be on my hands. So I wandered up close and stuck a hand under his nose to check his breathing: not bad, just a bit hot. The patient in the middle bed was waving to me again: Young man, over here a minute. My feelings toward this man, I probably should point out, were no longer as warm as they once had been, so I ignored him. But still he kept waving. What the hell d'you want? I asked in my most indifferent tone. I want—to say—a few words—to you, came the disjointed reply. You don't want another piss, do you? I asked. No, he said. All right then, I said, say what you've got to say, and say it now. No, he said, come over here, I don't want to wake everyone else up. I made my way around the side of Li's bed over to him: Go on then. But then, damn it, the dried fish wanted me to squat down. Fuck off and leave me alone, is what I wanted to say. But in the end, I kept my opinions to myself and squatted down obediently—again, I have no idea why. He very suddenly, very deftly took hold of my right hand and pressed it hard between the two of his. I felt myself go cold all over. There aren't many young people like you these days, he sighed. I was temporarily thrown by this: was he taking the piss, or what? I whipped my hand away, but he left his hanging open there. D'you know what, he said, I've three sons, the eldest's a dad, the youngest got married last year, but they're rotten, all of them, like leeches on my back, sucking me dry. When there's nothing but skin left, they'll all disappear. They hardly ever visit when I'm well, so when I'm ill, no chance, I should've drowned them all in the toilet when they were little. If I were you, I said to him, I wouldn't say things like that. If your sons heard you they'd drown *you* in the toilet, easy as blinking. As she shifted in her sleep, the peasant woman asleep at his feet raised the volume of her snoring one—more—agonizing notch. The dried fish gave her a vicious kick; no result. He repeated the exercise, several times, until the unfortunate woman rolled off the bed—*ba-doum*. But still not the hoped-for result: her snores just started up again from her new sleeping position. As spectator sport, I was finding this of limited entertainment value and was about to get up and leave when he started talking again: D'you know what? I was testing you before. An indulgent expression came over his face. I didn't understand: What d'you mean, testing me? I asked. Don't you remember? he said. When I was pissing. Sure, I'm in pain, like I've been knifed in the stomach, but I can still piss for myself, I don't need anyone's help. I can see that much, I said to him. But d'you know why I did it? He, unlike me, seemed to be finding all this deeply fascinating. He suddenly raised his voice: I wanted to find out whether you had any compassion, I wanted to find out whether there's any good left in the youth of today, and I'm happy to say, you passed the test. After telling me this, he made another grab for my hand. Well, that's all very nice, I said, getting up, but you, to me, are a mighty pain in the backside.

★

It was completely light outside. I glanced at my watch: 6:20 a.m. My heart danced and sang at the thought of this farcical night coming to an end. As I stretched, I discovered a book on the floor that, when I picked it up to have a look, turned out to be *Resisting Death*. I idly flicked through a few pages, but for some reason found it all very unfamiliar, unfamiliar and inane. I put it back on the windowsill. I could hear footsteps down the corridor, and washbowls scraping the sides of the water trough, but Ward 16 remained quiet as the grave.

I bent down and looked under the beds, toward the door. The peasant woman was still on the floor, her body rising and falling rhythmically. I watched her for a while, even envied her a little: how could anyone sleep so deeply? I got up, folded the chair, leaned it against the wall, then tiptoed over toward the door. I needed a piss, yes, a piss. It was as if I'd only just realized it. Funny: all night I'd been on urine maneuvers, without being aware of my own full bladder. Just as I was about to open the door, someone behind me burst noisily into tears. I turned to look: Li, of course. His crying rang out loud and clear as a newborn baby's—Ward 16's wake-up call. Rubbing the sleep from their eyes, everyone looked over at the bed by the window. I immediately rushed over and took him by the shoulders: Calm down, what's wrong? Uncle! Uncle! he howled at the ceiling, between sobs. This time, I thought we'd really lost him. I shook him by the shoulders, trying to quieten him. Don't shout, don't shout, I hushed, what on earth's wrong? He continued to shout, the same thing, till he was hoarse. Marvelous! Bloody brilliant! The stubborn old bastard's finally cracked! The young man, dressed only in his white underpants, bounced for joy on the camp bed by the door. What's happened? I asked him in total incomprehension. He ran over to me barefoot and clapped me on the shoulder. Oh—I finally remembered the pact he'd worked out for us last night: all Li had to do was call me uncle, then I'd have to give him his water. Stop shouting, I said to Li, I'll give you your water, all you needed to do was ask nicely and I would've gotten it for you. Stop shouting, any more shouting and I won't give it to you. He fell quiet, desperately tugging at his collar with both hands, as if it were a noose around his neck. The mug, if I remembered rightly, should still be minding its own business next to the chamber pot under the bed.

First of all, I fed him with the spoon, but as he looked about to swallow the spoon down too, in the end I just had him open his mouth and poured the water straight in. You can imagine his joy, I'm sure, as the water encountered his parched throat. Glug-glug-glug, he tinkled away, his Adam's apple rising and falling in swift, neat, graceful movements. He finished the mug in seconds. The final mouthful he didn't swallow right away but instead gargled it over and over, wanting—perfectly understandably, I thought—to enjoy to the full this last mouthful of nectar. I picked up the towel hanging at the foot of the bed, intending to wipe his mouth. It was then that I spotted his eyes shift with fiendish sneakiness, it was then that I knew he was up to no good, that I'd been had. Again! Fuck, again! But it was already too late. That last, fateful mouthful of water, laden with a whole nightful of Li's accumulated rage, sprayed all over my face. He started laughing hysterically, shit, I've never seen anyone laugh like that. But the good times couldn't keep rolling, thank God, and the scar on his stomach soon shut him up. And I could use the towel I happened to be holding to wipe my own face, so things weren't as bad as they could have been. His expectoration not only cleared my early morning head, it also improved my mood no end. I smiled beatifically at him as he gasped and heaved away: Thanks, I said, thanks a lot, saved me washing my face. By now it really was high time for the piss I'd been storing up all night. After a long, staggered silence, everyone else in the room finally remembered to clap. Was this applause for indomitable Mr. Li, or for magnanimous me? Or was it for neither, was it for the long, dark, and uniquely infuriating night of the soul that had just passed? I had no idea.

When I came back from the toilet, the young man was standing, fully dressed, in the doorway to Ward 16, unlocking his shoulders. He stopped me and insisted on offering me a cigarette. As he was smiling full-beam and, much more importantly, was without his mobile phone, it looked like I had no good reason to refuse. But I still didn't feel much like talking, so I said I wanted to go and check on Li. Everything's fine in there, he said, thrusting the cigarette into my hand, don't worry so much. What could I do? Light the cigarette. The two pee bottles were lined up by my foot, one misshapen, as I've said, a poor excuse for a pee bottle, the other far more dignified-looking. I really admire you, the young man said to me after a couple of speedy drags, that's how you gotta be with them, fight to the death, them or you. Though I had no idea what he was talking about, I didn't plan on asking either, because I really wasn't in the mood for conversation. But the young man didn't give a damn about whether you responded or not, the problem was he was the sort of person who made you feel bad about being a taciturn bastard. I mean, take my old man, he went on, warming to his topic, what's wrong with him? Not a damn thing, I'm telling you, but still he insists on going into the hospital, stays there two weeks at a time, throwing money at it, great handfuls of the stuff, like it's his personal bank, but what can we do? It's not just medical fees and food, there's the bribes too, it all costs money. If you don't have money, no one gives a shit. He's nice enough, my old man, no point in giving him a hard time, but it's like he's addicted to this place. I mean, I've heard of drug addicts, but hospital addicts? What can you do? He tilted his head to one side, gesturing strenuously, his tiny eyes fixed insistently on me. What could I say—did he want sympathy? Dragging on my cigarette, I studiously contemplated the pee bottle so exquisitely fashioned by Li. And then there's Zhang, the young man continued, the dried fish in the middle bed. A retired worker, from some village somewhere: stomach cancer. Got to the operation, the doctor had a look inside, saw it'd spread. Nothing to be done, just sewed him up again and sent him back home to die. I couldn't help shivering: The doctor really said that to him? I asked. No, he said, 'course he couldn't say it to his face, but it's pretty obvious what he thought. Every day the hospital tries to kick him out, but he refuses point-blank, says if he goes home there'll be no one to look after him, sons don't care. But even if they did care, what's the point if they don't have any money? When the doctor comes on his morning rounds, you'll see for yourself; and all the patients who're about to kick the bucket get treated like shit. Staring down at his toes, he sank back into silence. Suddenly, he shook his head and began to laugh. Tell you what, though, the way my old man messes with us, no way we'd've put up with it before now, out of the question, but we've had a bit more money these last few years. It's all about money. All about money, he repeated, nodding away like an idiot.

I threw my cigarette butt on the floor and stubbed it out with my foot, feeling justice had been done to it. I didn't want to listen to him jabber on anymore, not a single word. Before he could open his mouth again, I pushed open the doors to Ward 16 and walked in. Sitting up in bed, a piece of clothing draped around his shoulders, the dried fish slowly raised his right hand, flashed me a genial smile, and nodded me a greeting, just like yesterday, when we met for the first time. But this time it didn't surprise me, and I nodded back.

A BOAT CROSSING

1

I LEFT LIKE I was running away from something. Qi and Chen insisted on coming to the wharf to see me off, but neither really knew me; I wouldn't have said they were my friends. The person who'd entrusted me to them in the first place wasn't a friend either; none of them was. When it emerged that my steamer, the *Orient*, was going to be late, I urged them not to wait. I was perfectly polite, but my tone ought to have made them realize that I wanted to wait alone, that I was finding their presence upsetting. More upsetting than they could know. The wharf at Cape Steadfast—like Cape Steadfast itself—was very small, so small it consisted of only two, recently repainted jetties. Qi stood on the deck of one, my travel bag hugged to his chest, silently refusing to let go. Keeping his arms locked securely around the bag, every so often he'd shrug his right shoulder upward to rub the side of his jaw. Whenever my gaze came to rest, blankly, on his face, Qi would smile brightly back at me: Come again soon, he'd say. He'd said this several times before, but this time, before he'd even gotten the words out, I was seized by this sudden, powerful urge to escape, to go anywhere, to get away first and worry about where I was going later. Ten days earlier, I'd had a premonition, a serious one, that if I stayed on here, trouble would come knocking at my door. Ten long days it took me to act, to make my move—too long. You don't know this—no reason you should—but my premonitions are never wrong. Every time something bad has happened to me, it's not been for lack of a premonition or because my premonition was mistaken, but because I lost my nerve and didn't follow my instincts, or because, as I'd done this time, I took the premonition seriously but took too long to react. Chen was middle-aged, same as Qi, but for some reason people tended to tuck the diminutive in front of his name, to call him Young Chen; the only reason I ever called him that was everyone else did. By "everyone," I mean the few people I'd met during the two months I'd spent at Cape Steadfast. Chen was carrying a string bag for me, as he gawked around at the quayside. The bag, containing five pounds of the goose-egg oranges that grew so plentifully around here, was a present from a girl who worked in the broadcasting station at Cape Steadfast. The evening of the day before yesterday she'd offered me a choice: I could either take these oranges or agree to let her come and see me onto the boat. When I say "girl," it's just because that's how I liked to think of her. She was a married woman, I'd met her husband, too: a worker in the cement factory on the other side of the river, nickname Big Dick, one of the "everyone" I mentioned above. The wind was gusting strong and cold over the river: Qi's and Chen's faces were frozen blue, and I had long since forgotten what it was to have sensation in my own cheeks. So I got two oranges out of the bag and offered them to my companions, urging them, yet again, to go home. It was getting dark, and they both had wives and children, terrifying wives at that; I knew from personal experience there were always things they were supposed to be doing at home. They weren't needed here, not in the slightest. But all Qi and Chen did was peel and eat the oranges, ignoring my suggestion. They left me no choice but to go and stand on another side of the jetty, staring down at the murky river water. I resolved to take no further notice of them: if they thought me rude and ill-tempered, I didn't care. Because I was genuinely unhappy, and could feel a vague, unfathomable anxiety welling up inside.

The Yangtze was very low at this time of the year, exposing a large, sallow expanse of bank along Cape Steadfast's wharf. A number of wooden boats had run aground, transformed on dry land into crude, ghostly looking shelters. The riverside was crowded with girls from mountain villages come to look for work in the towns, filled with their excited chatter, their delight at the prospect of leaving home. They, too, were waiting for a boat, but in the opposite direction to me. They looked to be headed downriver, while I was going up; they were going off to work, while I didn't know what I was going to do. They had reason to be happy; I had none. In among this chirping mass of femininity, I noticed a middle-aged man sitting cross-legged and straight-backed on the bank, looking straight ahead, out over the surface of the river, an aged blue cotton padded jacket over his shoulders, a carrying pole and a securely trussed bedroll by his feet. His face was thin, wan, and completely expressionless: to me, he looked like a piece of flotsam washed up on land, like one of those useless wooden boats. Qi and Chen stood upwind of me, untroubled by my behavior, chatting in low, hushed tones. Qi still had my travel bag wrapped in a tight embrace. I could hear what they were saying perfectly clearly, I could even smell the sour gastric vapors wafting in and around Chen's mouth. They both worked in the local Communist Party Cadre School, two out of a staff of no more than ten, both very aware of their status as officials and, of course, as party members. As they said themselves, they'd opted for the path of the straight and narrow, they weren't risk-takers, not like me. But what path was I following? There's going to be a shake-up in the party school administration, have you heard? Chen was saying. Qi affirmed, cautiously. They then took turns suggesting likely end results, before dismissing each of them, one by one. The truth of the matter, I felt, lay locked within their silence. Chen was forever reminding me that rankings in party schools were very high, that the head of the Central Party School, for example, ranked one official grade higher than the principal of Qinghua University. I turned back around. Are boats often late here? I asked. They couldn't have been expecting my question, as they neglected to reply for some time, too involved in, too consumed by their own conversation. Then they looked not at me but at each other, as if first they had to decide whose job it was to answer. Who should respond? Sometimes they're late, Qi said, shrugging his right shoulder to rub his right jaw, but I wouldn't say "often." Usually then, I asked him, when they are late, how late are they? Sometimes half an hour, Qi said, sometimes two, hard to say. The main issue was the weather, Chen interrupted, if there was fog, there'd be delays. But the weather's fine today, isn't it? I don't know in that case, but if the boat doesn't come, it doesn't matter, you can stay on an extra day, go tomorrow instead. Everyone wants you to stay around a bit longer. That's what he said: Everyone wants you to stay around a bit longer.

I was the first to hear pounding footsteps, hurtling unmistakeably in my direction. Jerking my head up, I began scrutinizing the quay-side, but spotted nothing untoward. A stream of people were trick-ling steadily through the ticket check at the entrance to the wharf; no one who looked to have any connection with me. The footsteps drew nearer, their direction more assured. Spinning back around, I now saw three men charging toward me, over from the right-hand side of the jetty: one in front, head down, running hard, the other two following a little way behind. I tried to get a good clear look at their faces: none of them I'd seen before. But as they rushed at me, I almost got to thinking that these were the very three faces I'd been so afraid of encountering. I didn't know what to do; no idea. At this moment of indecision, the man in front collapsed at my feet, with the two men behind surging forward to catch up. Pinning the other man to the ground with their knees, they started searching his body for some-thing. Satisfied—by the discovery of an intensely crumpled cigarette pack—they hauled themselves back up. After drawing out two ciga-rettes, one each, they returned the pack to the man on the ground. Swearing, the latter got up, brushed the dust off himself, took a ciga-rette out of the pack, straightened it out, and headed off to join the other two. After the three of them had lit their cigarettes, they moved off leftward to another part of the jetty, pushing and jostling one an-other as they went. As I recovered my calm, I discovered, unnervingly, that I was being watched, by a nonplussed Qi and Chen. My heart skipped another beat. What was I giving them to stare at? Did I look unbalanced? After an uncertain pause, Qi walked over, still hugging the garishly colored travel bag to his chest for comfort. Listen, don't worry, he said, his chin jutting out as it always did when he talked. In any case, the boat to Wan County always has to stop and wait, it can't sail into the gorge till seven a.m., so whether you board early or late, you won't get in until seven tomorrow morning, you see? No point in worrying, what's your hurry? I shook my head at him. I'd never been to Wan County; I'd only just discovered it even existed, another forgettable town among hundreds along the Yangtze. I wanted to get to Wan County because I'd bought a boat ticket there.

How long're you planning to stay in Wan County? Chen asked me. Don't know yet, I said. I know a few people there, he went on, I met them the year before last on a course at the Provincial Party School. D'you want their details? You could look them up if you have time, they could show you around. That's what Chen said: You could look them up if you have time, they could show you around. No need, I immediately interjected, I've already got friends there. Where do they work? Chen's ears pricked up. In the local government, I said, off the top of my head, because I thought that way I couldn't be caught out; however big or small a place is, there has to be a local government. Chen's eyes sparkled with interest: Now is that right? What are your friends called? We all looked up as a steam whistle shrieked across the river. My patience was wearing thin: Why the hell d'you want to know? I asked. You don't know them. No, you don't understand, Chen said, smiling. Didn't you just say your friends work for the government? Now my friend works in the party school, and people in the party school, you see, are always friendly with people in government, that's how it always is. So I think my friend will know your friends, that's why I asked you what they were called. Your friend won't know mine, I told Chen, every word spat out through clenched teeth. Not necessarily, not necessarily, Chen still insisted, albeit with fading enthusiasm, as he drifted over to where Qi was standing. A moment later, Chen turned back, handed the string bag to me, pointed west, then pushed his glasses up his nose and strode away. I figured he was going home, angry, tired of seeing me onto the boat. I didn't try to stop him: I had no reason for and much less interest in keeping him with me. You should have gone a long time ago. This left only Qi and me standing together on the deck. My bag enveloped by his arms, he smiled brightly at me, then turned to squint down off toward the lower reaches of the river. He wasn't angry, he was sticking with me. Offending Qi was no easy task, but I was still willing to give it a try. I moved a couple of steps closer. I heard you got arrested once—what for? I asked, looking all interested. Antisocial behavior? Indecency? A blank—shocked—look flickered across Qi's face. For counterrevolution, he told me. That was years ago. Sure it wasn't for indecency? No, counterrevolution, then later on most of my ideas were proved correct. Like dividing farmland into private plots, everyone agrees with that now, don't they? I was suggesting it about twenty years ago, back when no one else was talking about it. I wanted nothing more to do with the conversation, now that Qi seemed to be enjoying it. I turned sharply and walked a distance off. Chen, to my amazement, now reappeared, looking down to adjust his fly as he approached. His head was crowned, I noticed, by a bald patch, a pale, hazily shaded spot on the dark sun of his scalp, blurred around the edges, dilating, enlarging as it drew closer to me. I glanced back at Qi, who looked entirely unsurprised by this latest turn of events. Chen had never thought to leave early—he was staying to the bitter end.

I spent an age looking for the toilet to which Chen had given me directions. I just wanted to find somewhere quiet, deserted, out of the way, somewhere I could relieve my problem. But there was nowhere, the entire length of the two jetties. From one angle or another, I was always visible to other people. I couldn't repeat my search a second time, because clusters of people waiting for the boat were starting to notice me, to concern themselves over my movements. In the end I had no choice but to go back where I'd come from. You were gone a long time, Chen said to me. Well, you're still young, aren't you. That gave me pause: I had no idea what he was trying to imply. I couldn't find it, I told him, eventually. My revelation was the cause of much hilarity to the two of them. How'd you miss something like that? they asked. You should have followed your nose. Accompanied this time by Chen, I set off once more to our right, in search, yet again, of the toilet. Before long, Chen pulled me up from behind and pointed out a nearby door. Here it is. There being no notice hung on the door to indicate its state of occupancy, I stepped forward to tug on the handle. The door wouldn't open, apparently locked from the inside. I would have to wait. My string bag in hand, Chen leaned on a nearby railing, as if settling down to wait with me. You go, I said to him, I can wait on my own. I don't mind, Chen said to me. That's what he said: I don't mind. That instant, I heard the sound of running water from inside the toilet; I knew whoever was in there would be finished soon. But minutes passed and still no one emerged. Twice I rapped lightly on the door, then stood back and continued to wait. But still, after another several minutes, no one came out. Chen started chuckling. Just as I was hesitating over whether to knock a couple more times, a man with a scanty, sallowed goatee wandered over, a cigarette in his mouth, a rolled-up newspaper clutched in his hand. After throwing me a suspicious look, he stepped forward to pull on the door to the toilet, which of course didn't open. He then gave the door two sharp kicks on its bottom right-hand corner, and yanked violently on it. Fucking hell. The door opened, announcing its vacant status to the outside world. More than anything in the world at that moment, I wanted to tell him that I was first, I had priority, but somehow I felt I lacked the moral right. So I just stood and stared, as he glided in. Forget it, just wait a bit longer, Chen said to me. Are you very desperate? Struggling and failing to recover a sense of personal control over the situation, I ignored Chen's question. A diabolical stench gusted out of the toilet, forcing me to retreat several paces. Chen stayed where he was. After that, I had to get moving again, straight over to the waiting area. The few benches there were crammed full of people, patrolled by a handful of peddlers selling what looked like some rocklike variety of cake. I stood on the edge of the waiting area, where the air was a little clearer. A woman in a black jacket got up from the middle of a bench and slowly pushed her way out of the crowd. Though I'd gotten a good clear look at her, she didn't seem to have seen me. Or maybe she'd spotted me when she was sitting down, and that was why she stood up. From the direction she was headed, I guessed she was about to walk over to me, or pass directly by on her way to the toilet. I spun around and started moving toward the other end of the deck as fast as I could, out of sight off to the right. What the hell're you doing? Chen asked when I passed him. Didn't you want the toilet? No, I told him as I walked off, not anymore. As I reached the right-hand edge of the deck, I seemed to hear the clatter of high heels far behind. I didn't know whether she'd seen me disappearing off into the distance.

★

The *Orient* was a full two hours late. Qi helped me haul the travel bag onto my shoulders, while Chen continued to hang on to the string bag, as if he'd forgotten it had originally belonged to me. People were beginning to have their tickets checked and board the boat; I offered Chen and Qi a cigarette each, to delay getting on, to stay on shore as long as possible, to avoid seeing people I didn't want to see. Thinking the time had now come, Chen said his first good-bye to me. He still owed me money, he said, he felt really bad. Chen, I should probably tell you, was one of the best of that bunch; at least he remembered that he owed me money. I didn't say forget it, don't worry. I didn't say that. Not because I still cherished hopes of him paying me back; I just didn't want to let him off the hook. Qi had also borrowed money off me, privately, but we'd already settled the debt in another way—privately. It being six o'clock in the evening, darkness had more or less fallen, and I contemplated the lights of Cape Steadfast twinkling and flickering amid the obscurity. Qi assumed I was regretting my decision: the night boat was the most boring way to travel, he said, because you didn't get to see anything. If the boat hadn't been late, I'd have gotten to look out along the river for two whole hours before nightfall, but now I wouldn't see a thing. It doesn't matter, I said to him, I hadn't expected to see anything. Let me tell you, Chen told me, very seriously, the scenery along this part of the river is really something, you're missing out. I didn't know if Chen was upset because I was exhibiting so little regret for his precious view, but I felt compelled to repeat what I'd said a moment ago: I hadn't expected to see anything. Suddenly, as if remembering something momentous, Chen held up the string bag and handed it over. Sensing that this meant Chen wanted to leave, I immediately reached out to shake hands with them: Let's say good-bye here, you go home. But Qi wouldn't take my hand: Don't worry, he said, both hands thrust inside his jacket at the second button, there was still time to see me onto the boat. There's no need, I said, you go now. We've already waited two hours, or longer, Chen said, what's another few minutes? Really, there's no need, I said, off you go. You get on now, Chen said, and we'll go. No, I said, I'll board when I've finished this cigarette, but don't bother waiting. Chen continued to resist: You were telling us to go the minute we got here, he said, but we've been here a whole two hours now. What's a few more minutes when it's already dark? So I said the only thing I had left to say: All along I've been telling you to go—haven't I? But no, you wouldn't. You've wasted a full two hours of your lives, and whose fault is that? Not mine. I never asked you to come and see me off, you came by your own free will. What're you talking about? Chen said. You know time is the one thing I'm not short of, two hours is neither here nor there for me, truly, I don't mind. But I mind! I shouted at him, finally. Understand?

I decided to board. I threw my cigarette butt away, turned, and moved off, without a word to either of them. Also in silence, Qi and Chen ambled along behind me, at an irritatingly sluggish drag. A gangway about a yard wide led up the side of the *Orient*, at the bottom of which, standing to left and right, were two ticket checkers. Most of the other passengers had already boarded, and a foghorn was urging those still on land to board as quickly as possible. As I'd feared, the woman in the black jacket was still standing to one side of the gangway, waiting to walk up. Seeing me approach, she smiled at me, then, as if acting on some prearranged signal, picked up her bag and boarded. A tall, thin girl, a brand-new basket strapped to her back, followed her on. As she boarded, she looked around at me, several times. I hung back, uncertainly. Chen suddenly popped up from behind, his bald head perched on my shoulder like an inquisitive parrot. Who's she? Got a feeling I've seen her someplace before. How d'you know her? Who? I said to Chen. Her, the one with the gold tooth. He meant the woman in the black jacket; it was amazing, sometimes, what his nearsightedness caught. I refused to slake his curiosity. Well, he said, deeply disappointed, this way at least you'll have company, someone to talk to, you won't be lonely. What are you waiting for, on you go. That's what he said to me: You won't be lonely. Qi stepped forward to join us: he knew what that woman was up to, he said. Another bright, this time knowing smile. When Chen instantly began interrogating him, Qi deliberately stalled him. The two of them, fully absorbed by their exchange, forgot all about me, left standing on one side. It was as if they were discussing a question that had nothing to do with me. What further reason remained to moor me to this place called Cape Steadfast? So I boarded the boat. When I got up onto the deck, I heard Qi shouting Hey! behind me. I turned, unwillingly. The same bright smile: Come again, soon. Swearing quietly to myself, I headed off in the direction of the cabins.

★

The *Orient* was crawling slowly upriver, against the current. When the lights of Cape Steadfast finally faded into oblivion, I heaved a sigh of relief. But I still had the feeling the place wasn't done with me yet. After I'd stowed my luggage, I set off in search of a toilet. I'd bought a ticket for a third-class berth, four people to one small room. The other three had already made themselves thoroughly at home: shoes off, they were lying on their beds, all staring at me strangely. Why they should be looking at me like this, I could think of no good reason. The room reeked of their feet and the lower bunk they'd left me was almost impossibly filthy. But now was not the moment to consider these niceties; I needed a toilet, and fast. Despite its prevalent dampness, the corridor through the boat was crowded, on both sides, with people camped out on the floor. Their hair was disheveled, their mood despondent, as if they'd been on the road for days on end. One group, all sharing the same, local accent, was playing cards, while another group with another accent was arguing noisily about something. Back and forth I weaved around them, as if I was doomed to some eternal transit loop around this damned boat. Making as if I knew exactly where I was going, I headed to the back of the steamer, thinking the toilet would be there, but was instead greeted by the thunderous rumble of the engine room. Forced into retreat, I went up a floor and asked for directions from a young man in uniform, after which I finally found what I was looking for, though not the one nearest my cabin. Maybe I'm just stupid, but whenever I'm somewhere new, I always have problems finding the toilet, as if fate is forever throwing obstacles between the two of us. Please once, just once let me find it easily, and I can die happy. On returning to the cabin, I noticed that the man in the bottom bunk opposite me was eating an orange, the juice running down his chin, staring at me all the while, letting it trickle, as if trying to make me feel this very act of consumption was a kind of challenge. I glanced at my string bag: it looked as if it had been opened; or then again as if it hadn't. I took a couple of long, hard looks at the half of orange still in his hand, carefully noting its golden-yellow peel, its elliptical shape. My suspicions were building that it was, indeed, one of mine. He nodded at me, apparently meaningfully. But meaning what? As I considered this question, a piece of orange peel dropped down from the bunk above me, landing just by my feet. I leaned forward to look up: a man in a leather jacket in the bunk above me was applying himself to another orange, chewing on it like he was gnawing on a bone. When I glanced over at the top bunk opposite, I was greeted, with depressing predictability, by the sight of the man the other two called the ghoul, working on yet another orange with a knife on a key ring. All three of them were eating oranges, all three the same kind. Feeling outmaneuvered, isolated, I found myself involuntarily reaching for an orange. Did I genuinely want one at that exact moment? Not in the slightest.

Turning my mattress over, I discovered its underside was even filthier than its topside, leaving me no choice but to lay it out as before. When you're on the road, you take your chances, said the ghoul on the top bunk opposite. I turned to discover my three cabinmates all looking at me. Was he talking to me? Ignoring them, I continued to make up my bed. But I could feel their eyes on me, still. I shifted my travel bag and string bag from one end of the bed to the other, my movements becoming less and less coordinated. The finished product, its sheets twisted and crumpled, was pretty lamentable. If they were still watching me, how should I segue now? I flopped, fully dressed, onto the bed and shut my eyes. Maybe I should have asked them why they were staring at me—I couldn't let things go on this way. Steadying my nerve, I opened my eyes. And discovered, to my surprise, that the two men on the bunks opposite were also lying down, with their backs to me. Leaning forward, I found the man on the bunk above me in an identical position, the only difference being that he had wrapped himself in a grass-green blanket. I got up and took a few nervous paces around the low-ceilinged cabin, deliberately generating a bit of noise, but the three of them continued to lie there, as if in silent collusion, a regular snore droning out of the ghoul. My paths of inquiry exhausted, I lay back down on my bed and closed my eyes. Starting to feel a little hungry, I noted musical noise coming from a loudspeaker outside, and took it as a sign the canteen was about to open. But after spewing out what seemed, at the time, an interminable slew of popular music, the loudspeaker fell silent, without any further announcement. How come the canteen's not opening? I finally said. Although my voice was loud enough, it had an echoey quality to it, as if I knew I was talking to myself. Nonetheless, I still hoped beyond hope one of the men would listen, and say something in response. But no one said a thing. Raising the volume a notch, I repeated my question, the words ricocheting off the walls: How come the canteen's not opening? Still no reply, as if they'd all three of them died in their sleep. I really was hungry; seriously hungry, you might say. So, alone, I walked out of my third-class cabin.

Out in the corridor, I barred the way of a passenger keeping his eyes diligently averted heavenward. How come the canteen's not opening? I asked. As he was holding a cup of boiling tea full to spilling point, he squatted slightly, afraid I was going to jog his shoulder. Hot water's that way, he said. He then walked around me and continued gingerly on his way, as if nervous the ground might collapse beneath him at any moment. Not far ahead, a gloomy young man dressed in denim jacket and jeans was leaning against a wall, smoking. He'd already noticed me and seemed to be bracing himself to receive my question. So I walked over. Excuse me, how come the canteen's not opening? A dense cloud of smoke issued forth. Is it dinner you're after? he said. It finished ages ago. His revelation complete, he fixed a pair of intensely mournful eyes on me. I got the feeling he wanted to prolong this whole exchange, that he was waiting for some kind of response. I continued to stand there in front of him. So he started to tell me things: I'm up from Hainan, on a special trip home, they say my father's seriously ill, I think he might be dead already. This out, he paused and fixed me with a stare of even greater despondency. Before he started up again, he wanted to assess my reaction. This time I felt I had to act fast, before the situation deteriorated further for me. I'm starving, I really am, I informed him, without missing a beat, then walked off. Was dinner truly over? Half in mind, for a moment, to ask someone else for confirmation, I told myself to forget it, to take his word for it. After a period of long, hard thought, leaning against the counter of the boat's kiosk, I finally decided to buy two packets of instant noodles and a bottle of mineral water. Unable to change the bill I had, the shop assistant urged me to buy something else as well. I chose a pack of cigarettes. It's still too big, she said. She had nothing else I wanted, I told her, nothing I needed. After a brief stand-off with me, she set down the hot water bottle in her hands, very grudgingly, fished around in her own pockets, then counted out the right amount of change. I then escorted my two packets of instant noodles, bottle of mineral water, and pack of cigarettes along the left side of the ship back to cabin 11 in the third-class section. Before I went in the door, I glanced, guiltily, up and down the corridor; as I thought he would be, the young man in denim was still leaning against the wall, smoking. He saw me too: what would he be thinking? I hesitated a moment in the doorway. Tucking the mineral water under my left arm, I pulled open the door to the room with my free hand.

My three cabinmates were now sitting on the lower bunks. All three of them were eating oranges. The same sort of orange. With the same intense concentration. I froze in the doorway; stood there, staring. The ghoul was the first to raise his head from his orange and take a hard look at me: Instant noodles, he said. His monotone implied neither desire for dialogue nor admiration for my choice; he was just saying it, trying the words out: Instant noodles. Forcing myself to move, to do something, I bent down to lay the things I'd just bought on my berth. The man in the bunk above me was sitting on my bed; without glancing up at me, he edged his buttocks over to one side, too focused on his orange to do anything else. I had a long, careful look at my string bag: this time it looked to contain several fewer oranges again, but I still couldn't be sure. I was regretting not having left some kind of marker on the string bag before I went out, or counted how many oranges I had. Now, I thought, I could have lost six oranges, without even knowing for sure. I sat down on my bed and sized up the luggage belonging to my cabinmates, hoping to myself they'd been eating their own and not my oranges. They only had one big hemp sack among the three of them, resting on the floor between the two bunks, taking up almost half the space available, tightly sealed with a length of rope. I had, in fact, vaguely registered the existence of this sack when I'd first entered cabin 11, but hadn't thought any more about it. It was only now that I noted how big it was; big enough to make you curious. Could there be oranges inside? Seeing the ghoul had finished his, I plucked up the courage to make some inquiries. What've you got in there? I asked. To maximize my chances of getting an answer, I was careful to make my question as precise as possible, its tone assured and target unmistakeable—I wanted to be sure the ghoul had no reasonable grounds for ignoring it. The moment the words had left my mouth, I regretted them, because if the ghoul took no notice, I'd be in a humiliating quandary. First he smiled. Then replied. It's a dead body, of course—what did you think it was? We've cut it up into pieces so it's easier to carry around with us. I thought he was joking.

But no smiles from the other two. They threw the ghoul these warning looks, as if silently criticizing him for divulging some dark secret. I thought if I didn't run with this revelation, ask something else, right away, the ghoul would think I was scared. Why don't you throw it in the river while it's dark? The ghoul pulled up a corner of the sheet to wipe his hands. Now that would be a terrible waste, he said. We're not done with it yet. You taking it home to make ham? I asked. The ghoul must have smelled mockery in my tone, because a shadow fell over his face. You don't believe me? he said. You really don't believe me, do you? Well, let me open it for you, so you can see for yourself. Be my guest. He started to loosen the rope. The other two immediately panicked and shot forward to stop him. The three of them started swearing at one another in an unfamiliar dialect; I couldn't understand a word. After which the ghoul spread his hands at me helplessly, signaling they were tied, figuratively speaking. A silence. Then the man sitting on my bed suddenly turned to me. Please, he said in a low and serious voice, don't talk to anyone about this.

I started chewing on dry instant noodles, washing them down with swigs of mineral water, my gnawing crunch the only sound in the entire room; mouthful upon mouthful of earache. Outside, a few thumps and crashes suggested the boat was approaching some kind of mooring. I didn't know what precise point in the middle of nowhere we had reached; all I knew was that tomorrow we were due to arrive somewhere called Wan County. I kept doggedly chewing my way through the noodles. Though I was still hungry, very hungry, there was no way I could face doing the same with the second packet. This was unusual for me; generally, I'm the sort of person who can always put on some show of appetite, always get things down me somehow. It's one of my talents. Just something I was born with. Before I was done with the first packet, the other three returned to their own bunks and lay down. That is a fucking awful noise, the ghoul remarked, meaning the sound of me eating. When he was forced to listen to something like that, he said, he knew things were bad beyond hope. His comments reduced my desire for the second packet of noodles to less than zero. I shoved all the random objects I'd scattered over the bed up against the wall, then lay down fully dressed. As the hemp sack slipped directly into my line of vision, I began to feel like the ghoul: that things were bad beyond hope. With a light jolting, the steamer started moving again, steadily up the river. The atmosphere in the cabin was fetid, unbelievably foul; I felt sick, not sick so I could actually vomit anything up, but just a bit, the kind of sickness you can't shake off, that stops you thinking properly.

Come in, come on in. A voice—barely human—inside the cabin broke the stunned doze I had fallen into. Turning over, I pressed my face up against the wall, trying to do my best impression of sleeping like the dead. Come in, come in, come in. It was the ghoul, I now recognized, speaking with a new, louche lilt. When I rolled back over to see what was going on, I immediately shot straight up in my bed. It was the shock of it. The three of them were sitting in a row on the bottom bunk opposite, all eating oranges with this show of exaggerated enjoyment. Nervously, I glanced back at my string bag: squashed flat, it now looked completely different from before. Had they moved it, or was it me who'd flattened it in my sleep? My head was buzzing with questions; this time, I felt, I had to clear things up, once and for all. But the three of them were ignoring me, and staring instead with intense interest at something behind me. Swiveling around, I saw that the door to the cabin had been pushed open a crack, and a woman's head had squeezed its way in. So this is where you got to, she said, smiling at me. Back in a minute. The gold tooth flashed, then disappeared. Back in a minute? What did that mean? My sense of unease was growing. What's that woman to you, the ghoul asked me, she's been hanging around outside the cabin for ages. What could I tell him? She's an acquaintance of mine, I said. The ghoul flashed me a crafty, secretive smile: D'you want us to clear out, give you a bit of privacy? The other two leered their concurrence at me. All right, I said, leave us alone. But it's pitch-dark out there, the man sleeping on the bunk above me pointed out, where's there to go? Just as he was saying this, the woman in the black jacket pushed the door open and came in, slinging her bag on the small empty shelf between my bunk and the door, as if it were the most natural thing in the world. This, she said, now this is what I call traveling in comfort. She then called out to the tall, skinny girl behind to follow her in. The girl went bright red, feeling the room's collective gaze shift onto her, fixed her eyes to the ground, slowly set down the basket on her back, then just stood there, her hands twisted together. There was something gangling and unharmonious about her proportions, as if she'd been stretched out in a distorting mirror. The woman gave her a yank, forcing her to sit down on my bunk, then pointed at me: Say hello—hello, uncle. The three men opposite all started sniggering. I immediately intervened: What the hell are you talking about? I'm not her uncle! Don't say it! But the woman kept nagging at her, more severely insistent each time. After a long, long hesitation, the girl eventually decided to refuse. At last I could relax. The woman pointed at the half bottle of mineral water: That yours? she asked. I said yes. Grabbing it, she unscrewed the bottle top and took a huge gulp. She was dying of thirst, she gasped out afterward.

★

The woman in the black jacket was about thirty, or maybe a bit older, I couldn't say exactly. If you'd asked her directly, you'd have gotten even less precision. On her lower half she had on a less than dignified pair of pinkish slacks. She'd told me her name was Li Yan, a false name I reckoned, but one that I had no thought of challenging. But she knew my name, my real name, which made me feel like I was at a disadvantage. Where are you headed? Li Yan asked me. Wan County, I said. Again, I was telling the truth, but not because I wanted to—I just hadn't had time to invent a lie. Didn't you say the soonest you were going to leave Cape Steadfast would be early next month? That's right, I said, but I'm only going to Wan County to see a friend, I'll be back in a couple of days. Glad to hear that; and will you still be at the Imperial? she asked. That's right, I said, I haven't canceled my room, my luggage's still there. The Imperial was next to a primary school in Cape Steadfast: twenty-odd beds at fifteen *yuan* a night, no bathroom, no television, no phone; air conditioning, but only a cold setting—no central heating in winter. Interesting things happened at the Imperial.

But even if you weren't at the Imperial, I could still track you down, she said. Of course, Cape Steadfast's about as big as the palm of my hand. Once I'd said this, Li Yan seemed to relax, slowing the rapid, staccato tempo of her sentences. She flung herself back, face up on the bed, as if she'd finally come home, exhausted by a long, difficult journey. But this was only a temporary berth—and it belonged to me. Li Yan's sudden recline threw the tall, skinny girl directly into my line of vision: there she sat, withdrawn into herself, separated from me by two substantial pink thighs. I hoped she'd look up at me, so I could get a good look at her, but she didn't. And of course, there was my audience: the three men opposite me, silently goggling, struggling to fathom the situation, to find my Achilles heel in it all. What's your name? I asked, trying to sound a little more relaxed. What? she asked in a heavy local accent, her entire face stained red the moment her mouth opened. Li Yan sat bolt up, tilting her face to glare at me: You trying to pull one over on me? She'd raised her voice, as if afraid the three men opposite wouldn't catch what she said. What're you talking about? I asked. What's to pull over you? How come this time, Li Yan said, it feels like you're leaving forever, like you're never coming back. You're absolutely right, the ghoul said, he's never coming back. Don't let him get away! I glared uselessly at the ghoul, as all three spectators guffawed merrily at his intervention. So what? I said to Li Yan. I can come and go as I like—no one's business but my own. If I want to leave, who's to stop me? I'll go when I want, all right? I was starting to speak faster, I was losing control of myself. That wasn't what I meant, she quickly replied. Of course, you leave whenever you want. But what about the child? the ghoul interrupted, his compadres doubling up with delighted hoots of mirth. What child? I asked the ghoul, without a trace of laughter in my voice. You'd better explain what you mean. Don't take everything to heart, the ghoul said, waving his hands about dismissively, it was just something to say. This, to me, was the last straw. Fuck you! I told him. After a brief, stunned pause, the three men opposite glanced around at one another, a savage glimmer flickering lazily in their eyes. Measuredly, very measuredly the man sleeping in the bunk above me took his leather jacket off, revealing a spare, wiry frame. His nose was so sharp it looked to have been pared down by a knife. What was that you just said? he asked. I wonder if you'd repeat it for the benefit of the room. Like the sound of it, did you? I shot back, without a whimper of hesitation, without any idea where I was getting my nerve from. Happy to oblige: fuck you! Just in time, the ghoul extended a hand to restrain the skinny man, who was clearly about to fly at me. Take no notice, he said, there's time, plenty of time to take care of him. This remark, I think, was half directed at me, designed to terrify me into submission, but I decided to take no notice. Fuck, I said to the ghoul, you take care of me, now that I'd like to see. The ghoul started laughing. I'll give you something to look at, he said, stood up, walked over to the sack, and, squatting down, began to loosen the string around its neck. As before, the other two flew into a panic and rushed over, shoving the ghoul to the ground. The three of them began arguing in their dialect again, violently, and not just shouting, pushing one another around too, until the ghoul was finally beaten down. Shaking his head, he climbed back up to sit on the top bunk opposite me. The three of them had, it seemed, entirely forgotten about the confrontation we'd just had. Ignoring me completely, one of them dug a deck of poker cards out of a pocket and the three of them sat squeezed together on the top bunk opposite, laying out their stakes. What the hell were they playing at? I couldn't work it out. After a substantial silence, the ghoul finally turned around: It's your lucky day today, young man, he told me, you just pulled a fucking long straw. Make sure you enjoy it.

What did that mean? For a moment, for several moments, I could think of nothing to say. So I'd pulled a long straw—I'd actually had some luck. Are these your oranges? Li Yan asked, pointing at my string bag, her lips white with fear, reminding me of the presence of these two equally mysterious women. But at this instant, I felt I could almost believe in them, have the measure of them; at least more than I could the three men opposite. Li Yan seemed terrified I was about to say something that would cause everything to degenerate back into open warfare. Yes, I said, they're mine. Helping herself to one, she prised open the peel with her thumbnail, then bent forward to eat the flesh. The instant I heard her fingernail squeak into the orange, my head cleared. Her hand dripping with juice, she suddenly fished three more out of the bag, took a quick glance at me, then, without waiting to gauge my response, swiftly delivered them over to the top bunk opposite. Have an orange, she said to the three of them, people like us, on the road, away from home, we've got to look out for each other. That's what she said: People like us, we've got to look out for each other. They none of them said thank you. Squatting on the bunk, the ghoul picked one up. Good things, oranges, he said. Then he set it down by his foot and went back to the game. I didn't like what Li Yan had done, didn't like it at all, but neither could I usefully do or say much about it. Why didn't you give her one too? was all I could choke out, meaning the petrified girl sitting next to her. Her? Li Yan said. She won't want one, she's surrounded by orange trees at home, her parents grow them. How d'you know she won't? I said. Give her one! Unable to refuse me, she stuffed one into the girl's hands. Look, she said, she doesn't want it, she obviously doesn't want it. So she wedged the orange between her own legs, planning, from the looks of it, to move on to this second one once she'd finished the orange still in progress. She doesn't want one, Li Yan said, like I told you. Her name's Li Xiaolan, she's my cousin's daughter. Her parents asked me to fix her up, find her something in town; I couldn't say no. Where're you going? I asked Li Yan. You getting off at Fengjie? No, she replied, I told you, we're going to Yunyang. Why're you going there? I asked, just for something to say. She threw me a surprised look. I already told you, I grew up in Yunyang, I'm going home. What're you going home for? What's there to do at home? My questions were starting to irritate Li Yan, who lay back again on my bed. Li Xiaoyan's eyes, I now saw, were shuttered by semitranslucent single lids. How old are you? I asked her. Seventeen, the prostrate Li Yan answered. D'you have brothers and sisters? What? Li Xiaolan said to me. Li Yan sat up again, planting herself between the two of us. Look, she said, lowering her voice, let's just all get off the boat together at Yunyang, okay, you can head off again after a couple of days, I can put you up at home. Okay?

What's there to do in Yunyang? I asked. You tell me what you like, she said. Nothing, I told her, nothing at all.

★

A young man wearing grayed overalls pushed open the door of the cabin, a small notebook in his left hand, a ballpoint refill in his right. Any refreshments for the night, boss? he asked, nodding his head around the room as he spoke. We've a wide range of cooked food, all freshly delivered to your cabin. Whether or not the other three were bosses of anything or anybody I didn't know, but I suppose Li Yan and I were—we belonged to that class of people who're their own bosses. We were very similar, in our different ways. The young man reeked sickeningly of lampblack. There'd been no proper dinner earlier, I was thinking, but now they were pushing food at us late into the night. My empty stomach was violently protesting at the treatment I'd meted out to it. D'you have any rice? I asked him. No, he said, but they did have *baijiu*, Chinese vodka. They'd thought we'd want some alcohol, to warm us up in the cold weather. Li Yan fixed me with a look of almost naked yearning; I knew she wanted me to order something. Not because she was hungry, still less because she was cold; she just wanted to consume. I shook my head at the young man: I didn't want to drink, and certainly not with Li Yan. I just wanted a proper meal, if there was one available. But the three men opposite got very interested—What's the point in refusing drink when it's there? said the ghoul—and ordered several dishes, along with two bottles of *baijiu*. From the piles of money scattered over the bed, they whipped out a large bill as if it were little more than a piece of waste paper, obliging the young man to give them change. In truth, the three of them were betting trivial amounts, no more than a few *yuan*, but each had stacked in from of him a huge, thick pile of hundred-*yuan* notes. At Cape Steadfast, I'd known a few gamblers, but in time they stopped borrowing from me, because my money seemed to be haunted by bad luck. Money that had touched my hands always ended up lost on the gambling table. Compared to the Cape Steadfast crew, the gambling performance being acted out here was little more than amateur dramatics; what I'm saying, I suppose, is their banknotes were only there for show. But Li Yan was immediately drawn to them, her gaze fixed magnetically on the money across the way; I rejoiced at the prospect of some respite.

What's really in that sack? Li Yan, hanging on my shoulder, muttered into my ear, her voice betraying her anxiety. I edged back, pretending not to have heard. But drawing level again, she perched herself, once more, by my ear. You'll be whispering when I'm done with you! the ghoul said without looking up, as he threw his cards violently down on the bed. Li Yan, who'd been about to open her mouth again, shut it, and glanced opposite. When she'd checked that no one seemed to be taking any notice of her, she reran her question: What's really in that sack? Ask them yourself, I told her, impatiently. My voice bounced off the walls of the cabin, eliciting surprised glances in my direction from the three men opposite. I repeated my suggestion for their benefit: She'd like to ask you what's in the sack. Go on, tell her. The ghoul reacted to my request with a show of curiously amicable embarrassment. You'd like to know? he asked Li Yan. Oh no, no, she waved her hands in denial, I didn't ask any such thing. It's fine, the ghoul smiled, friendly as can be, d'you really want to know? His two companions, their faces grim, urged the ghoul to shut up and get back to the game. What's really in there? Is it a python? the words forced their way out of her mouth. No, best if you don't find out, young lady. With an air of finality, the ghoul returned to the card game. The moment the ghoul called her a young lady, Li Yan opened up like a corpulent flower. She twisted forward at her thick waist, as if she was trying to pivot on her buttocks. Go on, she pressed, tell me, what's really in there? After a good long hesitation, the ghoul finally answered: It's a dead body. Li Yan choked up a merry laugh. You don't believe me? the ghoul said. Go over and feel it, go on. Feel free. All right, she said, striding over, I'm not scared. The other two men opposite stopped their card game and squinted across at her, swearing something under their breath. Her hand—an outsized, mannish signet ring threaded onto one of its fingers—froze the instant it came into contact with the sack. She turned back to look around the cabin, a strange expression on her face. She then groped up and down the sack with her other hand, before standing back up and silently returning to her original place next to me. Clearly uncomfortable, she made several valiant, ghastly attempts to produce some kind of smile, but the grin wouldn't come. Was it a man or a woman? The body? Could you tell just from the feel of it? the ghoul asked. The three men opposite burst into hysterical laughter. Unable to peel the strange look off her face, Li Yan stretched out her heavily corrugated left hand, as if to grasp hold of something. After seizing nothing more solid than air, she finally shelved her hand on my right leg until, after a while, it crept back away.

My head aches, I said to her, I want to lie down. It was no less than the truth: my head was splitting from side to side. All right, she said, lie down then, don't mind me, just lie down. I took off my shoes, slowly reclined on the wall side of the bed, and stretched out as best I could. The ghoul threw his cards violently onto the bed: You'll be lying down when I'm done with you! he spat out. You'll be on your back! Li Xiaolan stood up with a start, flushing even redder than usual. Li Yan pulled her back down: It's all right, she said. Li Xiaolan gingerly sat back down, perched only on the very edge of the bed, a long way from my leg. With Li Yan shielding me from the fluorescent lamp, my eyes began to feel a little better. I saw Li Xiaolan look up ever so slightly and glance across at the sack on the floor. I thumped the bed with my heel and she instantly retracted her gaze, lowering her eyes back down to the ground. Li Yan shifted herself over next to Li Xiaolan, stretched her right hand out behind her, and an instant later insinuated it between my legs. In no time at all, her hand had found my trouser fly and I could hear the faint buzz of a zipper being tugged open, bit by bit. I grabbed hold of the hand and threw it to one side. But it returned immediately, this time gently stroking the base of my thigh. I sat up. I've got a headache! I told her. She made as if she hadn't heard. I remade my point: My head aches! This time she turned around. Well, she said, you'd best lie down then. She tried to help me back into a reclining position; I pushed her away. Next, an obsequious smile. D'you want me to massage your temples?

I turned over, without replying, and faced the wall. Could you massage *my* temples? I heard one of the men opposite ask. I couldn't quite gauge his tone. All right, Li Yan said, but it'll cost you. How much? asked the ghoul. A hundred *yuan*, she said. Five minutes, a hundred *yuan*. All right, there you go, the man who'd claimed the bunk above me immediately agreed, without a quibble. One hundred *yuan*. She stood up and went straight over. A few moments later, one of the men started murmuring to himself: Nice, oh, that's nice. Rolling over, I saw Li Yan standing behind him, massaging his temples, smiling at me. Hey, keep time for me, will you, she asked me, it's got to be five minutes exactly, a minute over and I'll be wanting another twenty *yuan*. That's what she said: Keep time for me, will you. The three men opposite went on with their cards, all smiling and murmuring to themselves: Nice, oh, that's nice. I felt a tremor run through my bed—truly I could—and a moment's concentration discerned the cause: a trembling Li Xiaolan, still staring hard into her lap. She was wearing clothes made of some shiny, sky-blue material, a touch too short for her. A red hair clip scraped a few sallowed ends of hair back from her forehead.

★

Anyone else for a massage? Anyone else? Li Yan sat back down on my bed, clearly overexcited. A hundred *yuan*'s too much, objected the ghoul, give us a discount. All right, she said, fifty *yuan*. The ghoul felt fifty *yuan* was still too much; ten *yuan*, it eventually turned out, was the most he'd pay, and he wanted Li Xiaolan, not Li Yan. Give us the ten *yuan* first, Li Yan said, as she tugged on Li Xiaolan's sleeve: Go on, she said, go on, what're you afraid of? Her face blazing red, Li Xiaolan wouldn't move an inch, but I thought she'd give in if Li Yan kept on at her a bit longer. At this juncture, someone outside gave the door a hefty kick: Open up! they shouted. After a brief hesitation, Li Yan leaned up against the glass door panel to look out. It was the young man—the same one who stank all over of lampblack—with the drinks and food. Drink, drink, the three men opposite bayed joyfully. Anyone for a massage? Anyone? Li Yan kept asking, desperately trying to maintain the thread of the previous conversation. But they took no notice, busy clearing the bed and spreading out a brightly printed tabloid; a few moments later, the smell of food and alcohol wafted over to my side of the room. My empty, aching stomach began to torture me even more intensely. Li Yan stood there, asking them all sorts of questions in this affectedly guileless way: how much did this dish cost, how much did that one, this one was highway robbery, that one was far too much. But once her questions were done, there was nothing left for her to do. Whether they were being deliberately or unthinkingly tactless, they didn't ask Li Yan over to have a drink with them; even I started to feel bad for her. She plunked herself back down on my bed and, with the self-assurance of someone who feels they have an absolute moral right to do so, fished an orange out of my string bag. She then took another one and stuffed it into Li Xiaolan's hands: Go on, have one. No, said Li Xiaolan, I don't want it. Li Yan clasped the second orange between her legs and began to eat the first. While this work was in progress, Li Yan suddenly turned to Li Xiaolan: Didn't you just say you wanted the toilet? Li Xiaolan shook her head, slightly taken aback. No, no, Li Yan kept on, you said so, you told me you wanted to go, off you go, go on. No, Li Xiaolan insisted, I didn't. Li Yan's voice grew in stridency: Off you go. Submitting, the sallow, slight presence that was Li Xiaolan got up, carefully opened the door, and went out. She wanted the toilet, Li Yan turned to say to me, she wanted to go, I'm not making it up.

The ghoul and his two comrades, exactly as I'd thought they would, had started to play raucous drinking games. If I'd gone over and asked them to keep the noise down, to have a bit of heart for a sick man, I knew they'd have roared with laughter, and then upped the volume. No clairvoyant skill was required to see this, either, so I kept quiet and refused to feel sorry for myself. Despite everything, though, I still couldn't help nurture a slim, slim hope that Li Yan would keep quiet, would desist from saying anything else to me. But all this time she was keeping a careful watch, preparing, at the earliest possible moment, to supply further conversation; I could sense it. So I turned over to face the wall, closed my eyes, clamped my right ear down hard on the unutterably filthy white pillow, and covered my left ear with my left hand. Although there was less obvious need for it, I kept my mouth jammed shut, only regretting that I had to maintain, via my nostrils, two respiratory links with my fetid immediate surroundings. And somehow, my treacherous nasal cavity seemed to channel all manner of sounds and images up through to my brain, foiling my attempted escape from the cabin's interior. Things being as they were, I began to feel there was little point in trying to deploy my left hand as a seal against the world, and so released it from its rigid guard. Li Yan's voice was the first to take up residence in this re-exposed orifice: Are you really not going back? she nagged, shaking petulantly at my shoulder. What're you talking about? I said. Back where? Back to Cape Steadfast, she replied, where else? I had long since lost the patience to turn back around. Why the hell would I want to go back to Cape Steadfast? Go on—give me one good reason. Have I got some kind of moral obligation? I knew it, she sighed, I knew you weren't going back. It's true: she really did sigh. Go on, go on, goaded the ghoul, banging his chopsticks on the side of a plate. Li Yan shook my shoulder again: There's something I want to talk to you about, she said. Just shut up, I began to shout, will you? I sat up in bed, noticing for the first time that she had taken off her shoes and was lying down. She had, in other words, been lying side by side with me on a narrow bed, even sharing my pillow. I want to talk to you about something, she repeated. While the three men opposite were bellowing out their drinking games—an intriguing tableau, wouldn't you say? Why did I have no idea how long she'd been there? Lying back down was now out of the question for me, so I asked her to move out the way and let me get up. But she just stuck her legs high in the air, as if she was doing floor exercises on a mat, while her upper body remained flatly, immovably where it was. Go on then, she said. Good flexibility! someone over the way shouted, good flexibility! I got up and put my shoes on. The ghoul's face was now red as a baboon's bottom, his gaze wandering. He swayed the bottle in my direction: Hey, how about a drink? You can drink my fucking ass,

I told him. Come on, the ghoul said, there's still a few drops left. Fuck you, I said.

For a while, I stood still where I was. When the ghoul failed to respond in any way, I pushed open the door to walk out. I'll tell you one more time, young man, the ghoul shouted, you drew another long straw, make sure you treasure it more than you did the last one. What on earth did that mean? If I'd been walking along and someone suddenly came up and told me I'd drawn a long straw, I'd have no idea what he was talking about, I really wouldn't know how to take it. Is that right? I said to him. Yup, the ghoul said, another long straw. Your luck always this good? I swiveled back around to face him: And if I don't want this straw? You don't want it? the ghoul asked me. Then you'll end up like him in the sack. I hesitated a moment, my head pounding, then went over to the sack: I had to see for myself. The other two men opposite immediately threw down their chopsticks and leaped up to bar my way, a knife suddenly flickering up out of the fist of the sharp-nosed man sleeping in the bunk above mine. The ghoul was still squatting on the bed, hugging his knees with both arms, his body swaying from side to side in great, exaggerated rocks. Let him look! Let him look! he began shouting, shouting himself hoarse. But they wouldn't let me by, the man from the bunk above me keeping his knife pressed just below my ribs while he turned to swear violently at the ghoul, who refused to keep quiet: Let him look! Let him look! I had no idea what was going on between them: in the end, my two guards left me to cool off by a wall while they went and yanked the ghoul off the bed, knocking two plates of food to the floor in the process. Hobbling unsteadily, the ghoul fell after one push, then was dragged up again for another round. Li Yan chose this moment to join the fray, to try to mediate, we were all on our own here, away from home, she said, let's just talk it through. I took a step back toward the door, to avoid becoming collateral damage. The four of them locked into a kind of diabolic melee, spinning around and around before me like a magic lantern, acquiring greater speed and violence at every turn. I stood there, isolated, without a thought in my head, as if staring down a line of rats in a sewer, hypnotized. I tried, hard, to elucidate a cause, a rationale for the scene playing itself out before me, to find an explanation that could be forced to stand its ground. But it was beyond me. I pushed open the door and walked out.

★

I stood in the corridor, staring blankly around me. I took two steps to the right, then took them back. Because the gloomy young man in denim was still standing there, smoking, leaning against the wall. I turned and followed the corridor around to the right-hand side of the ship. From a window in the roofed part of the steamer, someone hurled a bag of garbage into the river; my heart echoed its thump as it hit the water. I hoped for a little quiet, at least for the time being. Just as I was thinking this, the steam whistle sounded again: long, drawn out, unending. My face, for no apparent reason, was suddenly wet with tears; I could no longer hope to understand even myself. I didn't know how far the boat, now passing along a narrow stretch of river, hemmed in on both sides by sharply rising mountains, had traveled. The air was still, untouched by any river breeze or nocturnal chill, the view surrounding me clearly visible through the pitch-dark, as if the boat was moving through a world existing beyond the usual realities of light and temperature.

Someone tugged on my sleeve. Expecting it to be Li Yan, I shook my arm roughly, without looking around. A few seconds later, another couple of tugs. Turning, mouth open and ready to shout at her, I found not Li Yan but a short, middle-aged man, his neck shrunk back into his shoulders, a tuft of hair drooping over his forehead, an unlit cigarette in his hand. He made a cigarette-lighting motion at me. I drew my lighter out of my trouser pocket and passed it to him, then turned back out toward the river. Was the water rolling eastward? Another tug. I turned impatiently: it was the middle-aged man again, silently returning the lighter. He took a deep drag, and without a word of thanks headed off toward the front of the boat. I lost control. Hey, you! I shouted at him. You want something, why the fuck can't you open your mouth and ask for it? After throwing me a brief, nervous glance, he turned, still without a word, and prepared to continue on his way. I raised my voice, as he retreated: Didn't you hear what I just said? Fuck you! At this, finally, the man spun around and began screaming at me. But not a single intelligible word emerged out of his forest of bright white teeth, only the most basic, bestial roar of rage, squeezed out of the deepest folds of his larynx. His eyes flashed in the dark, like a wolf's, the corners of his mouth coated in white foam, screaming and screaming, so hard his eyes watered. I'm sorry, I said to him, sorry, I didn't know you couldn't talk, I really didn't know you were a mute, I'm sorry. But this only seemed to enrage him further, making me realize I had no choice but to lean against the rail listening, guiltily watching, waiting for him to calm down. Which he finally did when he paused to take an urgent drag, and discovered the half-burned cigarette in his hand had gone out. I immediately got my lighter out again. He tossed the half cigarette into the river, then, drawing his neck in, listed off toward the front of the boat.

I could feel the sweat on me, coming in great waves. Just as I was hesitating over whether to return to the cabin and take a few of the tablets I had in my bag, Li Yan came back to haunt me. So that's where you've got to! Another wave of sweat washed over me. I turned, gripping the rail for support. Li Yan walked in front, Li Xiaolan following behind, head bowed, halting at a discreet distance while her keeper strode confidently up to me. I said I had something to discuss with you, why'd you run away like that? She then called over to Li Xiaolan to come a bit closer, but the girl wouldn't move. I immediately put up a hand to indicate she'd best keep quiet for the time being. What's wrong? Li Yan said, not feeling well? She put on this act of being all concerned, bending in to feel my forehead. I edged away. I want to talk to you about something, she said, something you'll like. Her eyes took on this new, vaguely salacious gleam. Just leave me alone, I said, give me a break, okay? She stood to one side of me, her jacket wrapped tightly around her. Before long, she started up again: Look, it's very simple, a few sentences and I'll be done, all right? No, I replied, it's not all right. Li Yan shut up then, both arms propped on the rail, shifting her weight back and forth between her feet, her heels dully tapping out a monotonous rhythm against the steel floor. If I didn't allow her to say her piece, was she going to just stand there? This was not a good thought, so after much consideration I made a momentous decision: All right, say what you've got to say, quickly, then leave me alone. Li Yan glanced back at Li Xiaolan, then edged a step closer to me and lowered her voice. What d'you think? Of what? I asked. Li Yan motioned behind me with her chin. Sensing that we were talking about her, Li Xiaolan sank her lower jaw even farther into her chest. What d'you mean, what do I think of her? I didn't know what she was driving at. I'm getting off at Yunyang, Li Yan explained. How about you take her on with you? What? I said. This time, she had truly lost me.

★

But what the hell would I do with her? I asked Li Yan. She shook her head: That's none of my business, up to you, just give me four thousand and we'll be square. Four thousand *yuan*? I said. Why on earth would I want to give you four thousand *yuan*? This got her angry. She'd be all yours—she's cheap at the price. Any case, I don't want a cent of that money, it's all going to her parents. I'm just handling the transaction, nothing more, I'm just the one who sorts it out. Somehow, after this, I couldn't quite get a handle on myself and the situation. I merely stood there, unable to speak. Li Yan gestured at Li Xiaolan to come over, propelling her forward by the shoulders. Off you go with your new boss, he'll take you someplace good, you just listen to what he says, do what he tells you to do. That's when the panic took hold of me. I want nothing to do with this, I told Li Yan very clearly, yanking her to one side. You've come to the wrong person. Well, how about you think of it as a personal favor, to me? she suggested, without any audible irony in her voice. You know, take her away with you, make my life simpler. Now why would I want to do you a favor? I asked Li Yan. D'you think I owe you, or something? She then changed tack, after muttering something to herself. It's not just about me, I'm thinking of you too, look, you take Xiaolan with you, you'll have company on your journey, you won't be lonely. Don't worry yourself about me, I told her, I'm not at all lonely. And I want nothing to do with this, go and find someone else. She still refused to leave. How about three thousand? She wouldn't give up. You couldn't give her away to me, I told her. Find someone else. At this moment, the sound of Li Xiaolan's sobbing whined out, a high-pitched, unearthly weeping. You should be ashamed of yourself, look at what you've done, Li Yan immediately rebuked me, you've made Xiaolan cry. That's what she said: You should be ashamed of yourself, you've made Xiaolan cry. By now, my brain had given up any pretense of functioning normally: I began to feel Li Yan's reproach was entirely deserved, that I had in fact committed a shameful, conscienceless act, that I was indisputably in the wrong. Li Yan set about comforting Li Xiaolan, in between hurling mouthfuls of invective in my direction. I just let it all wash over me, all the way back to the cabin, refusing to put up one single word in my own defense; I hadn't behaved well, that I was willing to accept. Far off in the distance, ahead and to the left of the ship, a smattering of lights glimmered into view; the *Orient*, I surmised, was about to dock; where, I didn't know. I suddenly began to sense something was wrong: what was going on here? Why was I allowing this random person to scream at me like this? What right did she have? I had no idea.

I was shivering all over; I had to go back inside. But just as I'd braced myself for it, just as I'd reached the mouth of the stairwell, I looked up and saw a sign by the main door to the second-class cabins on the floor above: ENTRY RESTRICTED. It gave me the reassuring sense that things would be better, quieter up there. A large enamel jar clutched in both hands, a girl wearing the official Wuhan port uniform clicked along the corridor, pushed the door open, and went through, the door crashing shut behind her. Yes, I had a strong sense that things would be quieter there. After a moment's hesitation, I climbed the stairs, pausing after every step.

I don't feel well. The girl didn't even look, despite me attempting my best, most guileless impression of abject misery. Clinic's on the next floor. I don't want the clinic, I want to ask you something. I suddenly got this feeling she was going to say fuck off, what right have you got to ask me anything? I really was worried she might, because she'd have had a point. But she didn't: she even looked up. Though she didn't seem about to swear blood sisterhood with me, she didn't look entirely unsympathetic. After I'd explained things, she agreed that if I paid the difference between a second- and third-class ticket, I could move into one of the cabins on her beat. The gratitude must have been oozing out of my pores, because the look on her face told me my expressions of unctuous thanks were surplus to requirements. But I couldn't stop myself. I handed my identity card over to her, thereby clearing the formalities necessary to move into a second-class cabin. I let out a long, long sigh of relief. By this point it must have been around eleven—a long way till morning still. Holding my identity card in her left hand, she began dashing off a form. Suddenly, she looked up at me in surprise. I couldn't stop the panic surging through me again: had she spotted some problem with the card? For years I'd worried about this: had it finally happened? Were you born on December 6, 1967? she asked me. Yes, I said. She smiled. What a coincidence: we were born on the same day of the same month of the same year. So that's what it was. I immediately got carried away by relief, asking her name, where she was from, whether she liked her job, asked about her family, her husband and children, what she felt about life after marriage. You're quite right, of course: I asked her too many things, too many questions she had no reason to answer. She was probably perplexed by my overenthusiasm. The thing was, a coincidence like this struck me as a good omen, as a sign that perhaps my journey was going to take a turn for the better from this point on. She herself said very little, she was far more guarded: unlike me, she seemed to have some awareness that the distance of adulthood lay between us. The only thing she told me was that her name was Feng Meiyan. I said I'd remember that; she said she'd already memorized mine.

Back in the third-class cabins, the interior of number 11 was wreathed in smoke and alcohol fumes. A cigarette hanging from her mouth, Li Yan was squeezed in amid the ghoul and his compadres, holding in her left hand a pair of very short chopsticks broken out of one regular chopstick. The thin-faced man next to her had a similar pair in his right hand, while his left rested on Li Yan's thigh. Li Xiaolan was sitting alone on my bed, squinting through the smoke, a chicken leg in her right hand. After I pushed the door open, this chicken leg seemed to cause her no small embarrassment. Though she wouldn't let go of it, she failed, even after several attempts, to strike any kind of appropriately casual pose with it; it became a part of, an adjunct to her own angular awkwardness. Li Yan turned around: Come over here, she beckoned me, let me introduce you, these three gentlemen are in the medical supplies trade. I bent down, without replying, and got my luggage together. Li Xiaolan immediately stood up to let me by, holding on all the while to her chicken leg. Come and have a drink with us, the ghoul said to me. My bag slung over my right shoulder, the severely depleted bag of oranges in my left hand, I kicked open the door with one foot and left. Just as I was about to go up the stairs to my new cabin, I felt a yank on the string bag in my left hand. It was, of course, Li Yan, her right hand entangled in the bag, her left still clutching that ridiculous, shortened pair of chopsticks. So you're going? Li Yan asked me. What business is it of yours? I said. Li Yan still wouldn't let go the string bag, tugging it back and forth. Look, she said, if you go now, we might not meet again, ever, at least not in this lifetime. I mean it, not ever. Shouldn't you, you know, mark it in some way? She spoke as if this was an irrefutably reasonable request, but by now my head had cleared, and I knew better. I peeled her hand off my property. I'll never forget you, she said, but shouldn't you leave me with something to remember you by? That's what she said: Shouldn't you leave me with something to remember you by? I peeled her hand away a second time. Come on, she said. Cold! Cold! two passengers in white underpants shouted, as they shuffled by us quickly on slippered feet. Please let go, I asked, as icily as I could. Li Yan fixed her eyes on me, saying nothing. After a brief struggle, I relaxed my left hand: Okay, then. I'll leave you these oranges. As I turned to climb the stairs, up toward the main door to the second-class cabins, I heard her stamp her foot, hard, behind me: Screw you!

she screamed. Once I'd passed through the door to the second-class cabins, I began to feel a disinterested kind of respect for Li Yan's style of farewell.

2

First, Feng Meiyan led me to cabin 9, but a regular, deafening snore boomed out at us the moment the door opened. Could you find me another room, I asked, ideally an empty one? Feng Meiyan seemed less than inclined to comply: There are no empty rooms, she said. The passenger in number 9's going to Yunyang, he'll be getting off soon. I stuck to my guns; maybe I was a bit too insistent, leaving her no choice but to take me on to number 13. Heels clicking against the floor, she continued along the corridor, ignoring my copious expressions of thanks. By now, Feng Meiyan was probably no longer enjoying the coincidence of our birth dates; she was perhaps regretting mentioning it to me in the first place. Perfectly quiet and clean, number 13 was occupied by a bulky, benevolent-looking middle-aged man sitting on the bed, a newspaper in his hands. He nodded at me in a friendly fashion. Feng Meiyan glanced at me: What d'you think? she asked. The middle-aged man hauled himself up, took his luggage off the bed opposite, smoothed over the bedsheets, and beamed me another guilelessly genuine smile. His movements were clumsy, anaesthetized, like those of a sick elephant. Are there really no empty rooms? I asked one more time. Why the hell would I lie to you? she snapped. I sensed that her mood had dramatically deteriorated since our first encounter, and that if I kept bothering her, things would end badly between us. So I said, Fine, I won't trouble you anymore; I'll take this one, it's great. That's what I said: I'll take this one, it's great.

Has the boat just docked? Where are we? How come I didn't notice? my cabinmate suddenly asked, apparently perturbed by the unexpectedness of it all. He had on a pair of gold-rimmed presbyopic glasses with very thin lenses, his eyes bulging out of their vitreous surfaces, like a bull's. No, I said, I got on the boat ages ago. I started off in third class, but I couldn't stand the noise, so I upgraded. Oh, I see. He fell shyly silent for a time. I hate noise too, he eventually supplemented, I really hate it, more than anything else. I stowed my bag securely and got the bed ready, planning to lie down right away. The sheets and quilt cover were of a pure, brilliant white; was it an illusion of the fluorescent light? I wondered. I leaned in close for a careful look: still white. The happiness this brought me, the happiness. After setting everything in order, I took another look around my new territory and discovered the only noisy, disruptive force within its four walls to be myself. Though I thought I could hear high-heeled shoes pacing up and down the corridor outside, I couldn't be sure, as my head was throbbing with a painful, percussive beat. I turned to contemplate my middle-aged cabinmate, piled up massively on the bed. He too seemed to be lost in thought, listening for something. Can you hear anything? I asked him, quietly. They must have gone, he said. I didn't press him on who this "they" referred to. To my ears, at least, the noise had gone. I smiled at him, to signal it was no longer bothering me. I took off my trousers and shoes and lay down on the bed, too impatient to wait any longer, but somehow, a tiny grain of disquiet remained, wedged between me and perfect détente. I put my shoes back on. The toilet's on your left as you go out, he said, just turn and it's right there. I flashed him several friendly smiles, then carefully opened the door and walked out. Before leaving, I noted the bolt on the door: as long as it was locked on the inside, there was no way of opening it from the outside. Locks, especially locks like that one, are wonderful things.

Dressed in my red woolen long johns, I stood in the corridor looking right and left; not a soul in sight. The floor of the corridor in the second-class cabin area seemed, at first glance, to be made of wood. But precisely because it was painted the color of wooden floorboards, I suspected it wasn't genuine. Instead of going to the toilet, I turned right and followed the corridor, all the way up to the doorway to the second-class cabins. Although there didn't seem to be any suspicious noises coming from outside, I wanted to move closer, to put my eye to the crack between door and frame and peek out, but held back, suddenly feeling this was a step too far, or as if I was afraid of seeing something. But what was I afraid of? Nothing at all. The door to the staff room suddenly opened and Feng Meiyan stood in the doorway, both arms crossed over her chest, a puzzled expression on her face that froze over as she looked me up and down. I couldn't quite decide how to react: I tried flashing her a quick smile, but only succeeded in making her more wary. What the hell are you doing here? she asked me coldly. Oh, nothing, I said, nothing, it's fantastic in here, so quiet, so much more comfortable. I'm going to sleep so well tonight, and it's all thanks to you, oh yes it is, so I just came to say thank you again. Feng Meiyan frowned. Without being aware of what I was doing, I came a step closer: I'm so grateful, I repeated, you know, it must be fate that brought us together. Are you not quite right? she asked me. In the head? That's what she said to me: Are you not quite right? This I was not expecting. Why'd you think there's anything not right with me? You joking or something? I'm in no mood for jokes, Feng Meiyan spat out, yanking the staff room door shut with a crash. To be perfectly truthful, her accusation had wounded me to the core. What I later concluded was that I'd already thanked her quite enough for the small service she'd done me, and that coming to thank her again dressed only in my red long johns could, indeed, be construed as puzzling behavior. As I say, though, this dart of enlightenment only came to me long after the fact; in the immediate aftermath of our encounter, I couldn't make any sense of it. People saying I'm not quite right in the head: this is something I dread above all else. Was it because I really wasn't quite right? I now asked myself. Because I was afraid of the truth? I didn't know. Disheartened, I went back to cabin 13, took off my shoes and jacket, and crawled under the quilt. The toilet's to the left, my cabinmate reminded me, I told you, the toilet's on the left. I know, I replied impatiently, I've been. Did you go in the river? he continued to inquire solicitously. Without responding, I turned over and faced the wall. It suddenly occurred to me the door wasn't locked, so I got up and pulled the bolt across from inside, then went back to my bed and lay down again. Throughout this whole process, I didn't so much as glance at the bed opposite, intentionally depriving its occupant of an opportunity to speak. Within about half an hour, as I drifted between consciousness and sleep, my mood slowly began to improve. I was on a river, I said to myself, as if I'd made some great, breakthrough discovery. I was irrefutably, undeniably on my way out of Cape Steadfast, the course of my life plotted, for the time being, by a steam whistle meandering along the Yangtze. Nothing else mattered.

★

As soon as I woke, I groped my watch out from under the pillow. 3:15 a.m., a soft voice informed me. I shivered with fear. Opening my eyes, I blearily turned around and saw that the bulky middle-aged man was lying, semirecumbent, on his bed with the pillow under his back, a beatific smile wrapped across his fleshy face. Challenged by the harsh fluorescent light, I had to reclose my eyes. Are we at Yunyang yet? I asked. We passed it ages ago, he replied, about an hour back. Excellent, I said. Though I wanted to get more sleep, my sense of fatigue had temporarily abandoned me, leaving me victim to devastating hunger pangs. I sat up, intending to turn the remaining packet of instant noodles out of my travel bag. As I did so, I looked up and saw that the huge, dark-complexioned man in the bed opposite was scrutinizing me, a smile still plastered over his face, a box of business cards in his right hand, a single card in his left. When my gaze met his, he deftly nodded at me and passed a business card over. I had this sense he'd been waiting there a long time, holding his card at the ready, waiting while I slept for his opportunity to come. I stretched forward, as far as I could, but still fell a brief distance short. Finally, the middle-aged bloat hauled himself off his bed and, holding it in both hands, personally delivered the card over to me. His name was Lin Yicheng, a salesman for a privately owned battery company. His business card somehow seemed excessively small and delicate to identify an individual of his dimensions. He stood there, at the head of my bed, panting and nodding his head up and down, forcing me to give him renewed consideration: he was like a great, dislodged boulder, swept down the river. I know what you're thinking, he said, smiling at me, a life on the road, it's not a life for someone like me. The reason they made me a traveling salesman in the first place was so that the work would tire me out, slim me down, but after a few years of it, I was still putting weight on, so the year before last I tried stopping for six months, staying at home, but the moment I stopped, the weight piled on even faster. Every night, my wife said, it was like she was being shoved off her side of the bed by a huge, hot hand. So I went back to it. Sure, it made me fat, but not as fast as when I stayed at home—lesser of two evils, I thought. Might I have one of your business cards? he asked. I don't have one, I said. I've never had one. He hovered, indecisively, above me for a while before trying his next gambit: Might I have the honor of knowing your surname then? I have, I replied, parroting his absurd excess of courtesy, the dishonor of being surnamed Li. Might I ask your given name? Qiang, I said, *qiang* as in *qiangzhuang*, strong, or *jianqiang*, determined. Somehow he failed to hear me the first time, and asked me again, which *qiang*? *Qiang* as in *qiangjian*, rape, I explained. This time he heard me. So where are you from then? Wuhan. Where in Wuhan? Wuhan city. Satisfied, Lin Yicheng returned to his bed and sat down, rubbing his hands. I relaxed again: it's unsettling, having a vast stranger looming over the head of the bed asking you endless questions. Fortunately, as my brain was functioning normally again, I could spin a systematic web of lies in response to his questions. In chance encounters, a bit of caution did no one any harm. And I liked fabricating identities: it made me feel good, safe.

Lin Yicheng searched every pocket in his down jacket, then pulled up his pillow and rolled-up quilt, shifting himself around, looking for something in his pants pockets. Given the energy he was expending on his search, anyone watching would be moved to try to help out. I asked him what he was looking for, but he wouldn't say, making me wait where I was. Out of breath, he got down from his bed and moved his possessions off item by item, muttering blast, blast it, to himself. Are you looking for cigarettes? There's some here. No, no, he said, not turning around, I wanted to offer you one of mine, they were here a second ago, what's happened to them? I meant your cigarettes, I said, they're here. I had a perfect view of his cigarette pack, on the table under the newspaper. After finally uncovering them, Lin Yicheng stamped his foot, as if he was furious with them, and clumsily plucked out two using his middle fingers. I accepted the cigarette he offered. I had, in fact, no desire to smoke at this precise moment, but after such a tortuous search, it would have seemed churlish to refuse. The emptiness of my stomach together with the poor quality of the cigarette left me light-headed after a couple of draws. As the cabin slowly jolted up and down before my eyes, Lin Yicheng began to tell me about his work, which he seemed to enjoy. Every year, he went up and down the river he didn't know how many times. To him, these boats were a floating home, carrying him to his target customers in the mountainous areas along the river that didn't yet have electricity, or not much of it, where there might be a need for his Universal Batteries. Universal Batteries were the sun in the darkness of their pre-electric night. It was only thanks to Universal Batteries that they could watch television, and it was only through watching television that they got to see the outside world. He stood up to tell me all this. So, you must sell a lot of batteries then? I did my best impression of looking interested; because I was smoking his cigarette, I didn't have a choice. But the instant the question was out of my mouth, a look of dejection washed over Lin Yicheng's broad face. Tell the truth, he confessed, the last two years I've hardly sold a single battery, the people in the mountains are used to not having electricity in the evenings, and anyway, they're suspicious of batteries, it takes a long time to persuade them. Right now, he told me frankly, the factory's main customers were other factories and mines, and the domestic market was still fairly small. So why does the factory director send you running all over the place? Isn't he wasting his money paying for your tours up and down the Yangtze? Apparently shocked by my question, Lin looked down at his feet and muttered something inaudible, as if I'd forced him to face up to this obvious conundrum for the first time. Unable to find an answer, despite the thought he was giving it, he looked up and smiled awkwardly at me. And there he stood, unsettlingly deadlocked, as if under some moral obligation to give me an answer. I'd just said it for something to say: I didn't care about the reply, there was no need for him to stand there, frozen in contemplation. I tried to help him out. Is it part of a long-term plan to convert the mountain villages to Universal Batteries? Yes, yes, he nodded away at my prompt, that's it, they're thinking long-term, long-term future stuff. I stubbed my cigarette on the side of the table, yawned, and turned over to face the wall, trying to make it look like I wanted to go back to sleep. Because once Lin Yicheng had finished talking about himself, it would be his turn to ask me, What do you do? What on earth do you do? I didn't want to give him the chance.

I could hear someone pacing back and forth behind me. I kept lying stiffly on my bed, wondering whether to turn over, worrying whether the other man would read this as a tacit consent to further dialogue. So I lay there, frozen. When I heard him heave a distressed sigh, I reinforced my efforts to remain still. But, I also thought, surely there was nothing to be afraid of, from talking to someone as honest and straightforward as Lin Yicheng; I stretched out more comfortably, though still facing the wall, and allowed all the muscles in my body to relax. Mr. Li, Mr. Li! someone called out in a soft, almost timid voice. I knew he meant me, that Mr. Li was me, but Mr. Li could hear nothing, Mr. Li was fast asleep. Lin Yicheng coughed twice. Mr. Li, Mr. Li, he called out even more softly, even more timidly. After a moment's hesitation, I turned over. He looked overjoyed to see my face again, rubbing his hands together with delight. Were you asleep just now? You seemed to be, or half-asleep at least. Sorry to wake you, sorry, I hadn't thought you'd drop off so fast, if I'd known you were already asleep, I wouldn't have called out to you. Doesn't matter, I said, I wasn't asleep. Curious as to where this sudden attack of patience had come from, I propped myself up. What did you want to say? I asked. Oh, nothing much, really, nothing important. Lin Yicheng was still rubbing his hands together, still pacing up and down in front of me. His bulk, his sluggishness made his every movement resemble slow motion. I sat there, paralyzed, waiting, but when I saw he wasn't planning to say anything else, I released my elbows from beneath me and lay down again.

I just wanted to say, to say, that you, please don't think this strange, I'm the kind of person who speaks his mind, but as soon as I saw you I felt this bond with you, I felt I'd seen you someplace before. I, for my part, was thinking I'd never met anyone quite as outsized as Lin Yicheng, I swear I never had. And if you had ever seen someone that big, you wouldn't have forgotten them in a hurry. What time is it now? I asked him, very deliberately. He immediately embarked on another flustered search for his watch. Groping for my own under the pillow, I said to myself with this air of exaggerated surprise, almost four o'clock! Best try and have another sleep, I haven't had a good night's sleep in ages. Have another cigarette, he offered. I can never get to sleep. The only time I can sleep is when I've nothing to do. That's what he said: The only time I can sleep is when I've nothing to do. No, really, I said, I can hardly keep my eyes open. I fished my pack of cigarettes out from under the pillow and tossed it onto the table: You smoke, but I really need to get some more sleep.

★

I closed my eyes and lay there for about half an hour, until I finally concluded that there was no way I was going to get any more sleep that night. Because my stomach had begun to ache: the low, indistinct ache of intense hunger. When I focused my thoughts, I became conscious that I was lying on a boat, floating up and down on the water, until this sensation mingled indistinctly with my hunger pangs, holding me suspended in a light-headed, waterborne haze. I rolled myself up into a sitting position, shaking my head. Lin Yicheng was studying a newspaper through his narrow glasses, his posture that of an abnormally fat child pretending to be diligently practicing his reading. He was delighted that I'd woken up, that he, the lonely fat kid, finally had a friend to talk to. I got out of bed, pulled the second packet of instant noodles out of my bag, then went straight back to my bed and half lay down. I had to prepare myself psychologically before swallowing this packet of raw instant noodles, I had to steel myself. I'm not exaggerating. Hungry? Lin asked me. I nodded. You can't possibly eat that. You young people, you just don't look after yourselves, you're signing your own death warrants. That's right, that's what he said to me: You're signing your own death warrants. Clambering down off the bed with some difficulty, he squatted and pulled out of the luggage under his bed a tin of sweet, fruity rice porridge. This is what you ought to be eating, he said, brandishing the tin at me. He walked over to his face bowl, poured in a Thermos of hot water, placed the tin in to warm, then returned to the bed opposite me, rubbing his hands, and sat down, looking extremely pleased with himself. Wait five minutes, five minutes. In truth, I didn't consider his beloved tin of porridge a better proposition than instant noodles: I've never liked sweet things, ever since I was a child. And in any case, the porridge was his, the instant noodles were mine, all nice and clear. No, I said to him, you keep the porridge for yourself, I'll have my noodles. I then started to rip at the packet, but encountered unexpected resistance from the flimsy plastic. While I fumbled, Lin Yicheng staggered off his bed and lumbered over to snatch the packet away. You listen to me, keep eating that stuff and you'll do your stomach in. You wait for my porridge. I'm an experienced traveler, I know what's good for your stomach, you should listen to me. I'm right, you know, Mr. Li. I had major issues with the way he was looking out for me. I really don't like sweet things, I informed him irritably, they make me want to vomit, much better for everyone if you give me back my instant noodles. Please. But the traveling salesman for Universal Batteries ignored me. Sweet or savory, it doesn't matter, he waved his hands dismissively, but when you're traveling you have to eat your food hot, my friend. Anyone knows that. You have to eat hot food. What could I say? Checkmated by such imperiously good intentions, I had, it would seem, no choice but to accept. Grim-faced, I sat on the bed waiting, oblivious to his endless jabbering. There weren't, it suddenly occurred to me, many people around as good-hearted as Lin Yicheng, and there weren't many people like me, either, who had no idea what was good for them.

After five minutes, the porridge was finally served up. Eating sweet things, for me, was like swallowing medicine; I couldn't taste any difference between the two. How is it? How's it taste? Lin Yicheng asked me impatiently. Not so good, I told him, entirely straight-faced. That's what I said: Not so good. After a momentary stunned silence, he roared with laughter: You're a funny one, you're a card. But to tell the truth, I was beginning to feel the warmth of the porridge, the feeling of well-being it spread as it made its way slowly to my stomach and morphed into a faint wisp of gratitude. I smiled at Lin. Beside himself with happiness, my middle-aged cabinmate rubbed his hands together with glee, sat back down on his bed, and lit himself a cigarette, observing me all the while with great interest, his eyes tailing the up-and-down movement of my plastic spoon. A glow of satisfaction, a glow I'd seen before, flickered over his face. Of course, I had no illusions in my own mind about what was happening: a price would have to be paid for allowing this porridge to be foisted upon me. From now until seven o'clock this morning, all hope of getting any more sleep was gone; I was at Lin Yicheng's disposal. As I pondered this, the sense of tepid well-being that had been coerced into the porridge evaporated into nothingness in my stomach.

Are you married? Children? he asked me. Just as I was about to respond, my interlocutor rushed in to reply for me: No, I can see you aren't, you don't look like someone with a family. What're you traveling for? he then asked. I deliberately paused over my answer, and, predictably enough, my interlocutor again chipped in on my behalf: Business? Of course it's business, what else would it be. What line of business are you in, Mr. Li? I knew this would be the next question. I sat there waiting, hoping someone would answer for me. Lin's bulging, bull's eyes goggled at me: this time, it seemed, he wasn't planning to help me out. So I had to answer myself: Anything, whatever comes my way. Even if it's illegal? he asked, very earnestly. Not in the normal run of things, I said to him. But I have a yardstick: even if the end turns out to be illegal, as long as the means don't look to be, I'll do it. This seemed to worry him no end. Look, you're still young, he told me, shaking his head back and forth. Whatever else you can say about me, I'm a few years older than you and you could do worse than listen to me. And I'm telling you now: you mustn't do anything illegal, you want to leave well enough alone, otherwise one of these days you'll get into trouble. You know what I'm saying? The second you break the law, it's like you're making yourself an enemy of society: you're an egg, society's the stone. Think about it: who's going to crack first? Listen to me, you mustn't do it. A tense silence fell after his homily, both of us sitting there, saying nothing, our faces serious. I felt like a criminal awaiting sentencing, as Lin Yicheng contemplated me with the pitying compassion of an older, wiser judge. Yes, I felt like a criminal. After a long pause, he burst into nervously loud cackles of laughter. His sudden mirth intensified my own wariness. An ill-concealed flush of contentment suffused his cheeks. The boat perceptibly lurched upward on the surface of the river, as two different frequencies of steam whistle exchanged screeches. The *Orient*, I deduced, must be passing a big passenger boat coming in the opposite direction.

★

I put the remaining half tin of porridge on the table. I thought that if we had to talk, if we had to keep talking, I needed to maintain some right to take initiative over the conversation, to avoid being led by the nose, being lectured and hectored. I wanted to get my interlocutor talking a bit more, because I didn't want to say anything else about myself. Lin Yicheng came over and picked up the tin, weighing it in his hand: Are you finished? Yes, I said, I don't want any more. There's a bit left, go on, finish it off. No, I really don't want it. Bypassing the spoon, he set about eating it himself, lifting the tin and pouring its contents slowly into his mouth. Where are you getting off? I asked. He was holding his mouth open, waiting for the viscous porridge to dribble down into it. While the porridge clung determinedly to the inside of the tin, Lin answered, with brusque shortness: At the terminus! This said, he reopened his mouth and resumed his expectant position underneath the tin. I shouldn't, it would seem, ask him anything else before this mouthful of porridge was his. And yet still it refused to descend, infecting me with the tension of this ponderous wait. How old's your child? I asked.

Twelve, a girl! Does your wife not mind you always being on the road like this? He slowly lowered his head back down and fixed his bulging eyes on me. What was that? What did you say about my wife? Nothing, I said, I just thought I'd ask, what does your wife think about your job? Oh, that, he said, seeming relieved, she doesn't mind. I immediately thought of something else to ask, but gravity intervened. Fast as he could, he stationed himself back below the tin with mouth wide open; any slower and a mouthful of porridge would have draped itself across his face, like a thick red trail of bird shit. He immediately tilted his head back forward, walked over to the door, and wiped his face with a towel. There was nothing comic about any of this, but for some reason I still laughed. His face suddenly a shadowy gray, he hurled the tin at the bin by the door. He missed, even from such a short distance, and had to heave himself, panting, back over there again, bend painfully down, pick up the tin, and place it in the bin. When he sat back down in front of me, he seemed to have become a different person: dejected, listless, muttering indistinctly to himself. One mention of the wife, fuck, that's all it took, and things started to go wrong.

Eyes downcast, Lin Yicheng silently drew a cigarette out of his pack. I immediately pulled out my own cigarettes, threw one over to him, and put one in my own mouth. There was something a little moldy and definitely unpleasant about his cigarettes. But I must have reacted a little overquickly, as he widened his eyes back at me. Are you saying my cigarettes are second-rate, they're not premium quality like yours? There was something belligerent, aggressive to his voice. I don't care what grade they are, I told him, but they're moldy, I can't smoke them. You sure? Lin sniffed at his cigarettes a few times. They're not moldy, he said, they're just a bit wet, it's the humidity, everything's damp around here. No, I said, they're moldy, they really are. Smoking one moldy cigarette is as bad for you as one hundred normal cigarettes, you know? He smelled his cigarette again, then threw it to one side: All right, he said, I'll smoke yours. After taking several long draws, one right after another, he inhaled very deeply. Your cigarettes are a bit better than mine, he admitted. What d'you mean a bit, I said, they're much better. He started chuckling, repeating back to me what I'd just said: Much better, much better.

Mr. Li, I need to talk to you. The shadow had fallen back over Lin Yicheng's face. I did my best to lighten things up: Weren't we talking just now? We've been talking for hours. I want to have a serious talk with you—would you hear me out? He was still looking very solemn. This got me worried: Well, what d'you want to talk about? I'll be getting off soon, very soon, in fact. There's time still, he said. What're you worried about? I want to talk to you about something personal. I gestured frantically at him to stop: No, please no, I'm sorry, but really, I just can't listen to people talk about personal stuff. I'm sorry. He became even more intently beseeching. What's the problem? Just talking about stuff isn't going to involve you in anything, is it? But I've just got to talk to you about this. That's what he said to me: I've just got to talk to you about this. The more he went on, the less I dared say anything in response. My head was full of regret that I'd eaten half—more than half of his tin of porridge. What else would have given him the right to talk to me like this? So I decided it was time to sort things out. I took five *yuan* out of my pocket and placed it on the table next to him. Of course, I tried to do this in the most natural, relaxed way I could manage, smiling as if it was something I'd suddenly remembered: I almost forgot, I owe you for the porridge. I'll just leave it here, in case I forget when I'm getting everything ready to get off. Lin Yicheng dully eyed the money on the table, saying nothing. Now, I thought, now he had no right to ask me for anything else. He shook his head: Is this just to avoid listening to me? he asked. Am I really that bad? It's not just that, I said, debts need to be paid. And I don't think you're that bad at all, it's just that I find it really difficult having serious conversations with people, they make me nervous, more nervous than anything else. Lin Yicheng wiped his eyes with his sleeve and pasted a smile over his features: All right then, he said, let's not have a serious conversation, that's fine by me. I'll say what I want to say, and if you don't want to know, you can pretend you're not listening, okay? This seemed to leave me with no further grounds for refusing. But just as he was about to return the five *yuan* to me, I stopped him: If you don't keep it, you can forget about having our little chat. All right, he finally agreed, a pained expression on his face, I'll keep it, but the tin cost four *yuan*, so I owe you one *yuan*. He searched out a one-*yuan* coin from inside his pockets and threw it onto my bed. I kept it, of course. The tin, he repeatedly explained, he'd bought on the boat, that's why it cost four *yuan*, if it had been bought on land, it would have been no more than three and a half, things on the boat are always a bit more expensive, you realize? On and on he swore to me he'd bought it on the boat, that if I didn't believe him I could go and check with the woman in the kiosk. Irritated and bored by this unending deposition, I began to feel uneasy, even apologetic about the whole business. I didn't know what was wrong with me. So I tossed him another cigarette. But he threw it back and groped one out of his own pack, saying he was used to moldy cigarettes by now.

The words began pouring out of him in a chaotic torrent; when he got worked up he slipped, without realizing, into a dialect I couldn't understand. What he was saying seemed to revolve around the boss of his battery factory, his wife, and his daughter. But there my understanding ended, far short of unraveling each tortuous strand of the complex, intertwining relations that bound them together. To abide by the terms of our agreement, I noted that Lin Yicheng was keeping his tone scrupulously relaxed, peeling his mouth open at regular intervals into a smile, set incongruously within the grim mask into which his other features had frozen. Several times during his narration, he had to stop altogether, readjust, then continue in a self-consciously light-hearted voice. I found myself so nonplussed by the bad fit between the tone and the content of what he was saying that I eventually stopped listening, and fell instead to counting in my head, or taking my pulse by my wristwatch. In, I suppose, the inevitable way of these things, though, every now and again his voice would modulate up or flatten out, as if he'd reached the nub of some impenetrable mystery or some crux in the narrative, obliging me to tune back in. He used to work in a factory making wireless electrical elements, he said, he'd liked it there, but then it'd closed and even the director had had to look for another job. These few phrases I caught fairly clearly, but because what came after was incomprehensible to me, I immediately lost patience again and went back to counting. Before long, however, his tone would modulate again, subtly, forcing me to listen carefully to a few more sentences. On and on it went like this, as if I'd lost all personal right to speech. When it finally got too much, I stood up and began pacing up and down. But this had no impact on his epic narration: on he talked, gripped by his own rhetoric, continuing with the same rhythms of speech and tone, happy when he was happy, still acting happy when he was sad. But despite his efforts, despondency seemed to billow around us in great, gloomy clouds, forcing me—seated back down on my bed, straight-backed, opposite him—to respond by setting my own face with appropriate solemnity. After a violent fit of coughing, Lin threw his remaining half cigarette onto the floor and stubbed it out with his foot. He then looked up and fixed me with an expectant stare: So what d'you say I should do? What d'you think? It was only then that I realized he had completed his soliloquy, that now it was my turn to produce a few soothingly conciliatory, irrelevant words, but as I'd long since lost the drift of what he'd been telling me, how could I respond? My brain began spinning, trying to fit together the few segments I'd heard, hoping to fudge the main sequence of events. Impossible. He was still staring at me; but still I had nothing to say. It was at this precise instant that Lin Yicheng, traveling salesman for Universal Batteries, burst into noisy tears. Somehow, magically, and just in time, his sobs provided a perfect memory jolt, marshalling into line the mess of plot links washing around my head; I finally understood. The whole thing was, in fact, very straightforward; it was only his inefficiently meandering narrative that had made it seem complicated.

Two years ago, Lin Yicheng's boss in the battery factory, the director, started having an affair with his wife. Everyone in the factory knew, even Lin Yicheng, but there was nothing he could do; the boss paid his wages, simple as that. The director, according to Lin, was younger than him—and it was bad enough a middle-aged man begging his pay off someone his junior; that he should have to share his wife as well made it all much worse. Although, by staying on the road all year round, Lin Yicheng never managed to make much money, he could at least make things less difficult for his wife and his boss. So, out of a kind of appreciation for Lin's cooperation, his boss decided not to make a clean break, not to sack him; and of course, he wouldn't help Lin Yicheng find a new job. Both sides gave a little of themselves. Lin Yicheng didn't seem entirely critical of his wife's way of going about things: a family had to get by somehow, it wasn't easy putting a daughter through school. But the minute he set off on his travels, he couldn't stop thinking about his wife and his boss together. It upset him. So much that he couldn't hold his middle-aged tears back in front of a young stranger. I might not have gotten every detail straight, but this, more or less, was what Lin Yicheng had wanted to tell me. What could I advise him? I didn't feel the slightest bit of sympathy. Luckily, he didn't want me to tell him what to do; it was enough just to have said it. What I could do was, inch by inch and limb by limb, lay his vast form out on the bed, then cover him up with the quilt and turn off the bedside lamp. Lin Yicheng's tears were beginning to dry: Thank you, my friend, he kept saying, thank you, my young friend. Returning to my own bed, I lay down and looked at my watch: 5:15 a.m. The boat seemed to have stopped, the low, rumbling roar of the engine stilled. The *Orient*, I supposed, had reached the mouth of Wan County gorge, and here we had to wait for dawn. Though we'd almost arrived, I was suddenly hungry for delays, for protractions in the journey: I didn't want to reach my destination so quickly. Because we were still in limbo, only temporarily moored, I hadn't yet decided where I should head first after docking, I hadn't even thought about it; not that thinking about it would have been much use, of course. The miraculous sound of a low, but increasingly resonant snore reached me from the other side of the room. But my initial gratification at Lin's loss of consciousness quickly wore off when the snoring took on a painful monotony, as startlingly monumental as his physical bulk. Several times I thought of waking him, but couldn't quite find the heart. Suddenly, having gotten Lin Yicheng to sleep no longer seemed such a personal triumph. But I'd made my bed.

I'd reached a point of paralysis in my mental processes, unsure of whether I'd fallen asleep or not. When a heavy knocking sounded at the door, I jumped up in fear, standing by my bed in bare feet. Where was I? Who was the man opposite me snoring so thunderously? I could feel the ground shaking under my feet: why, what was it? Someone on the outside had stuck a key into the lock and was struggling to turn it: what was going on? Finally realizing that I'd been asleep, very deeply asleep, I shook myself and walked over to open the door. Feng Meiyan stood in the doorway, a black folder in her hands, looking extremely displeased. What did you think you were doing, she barked at me, bolting the door like that? I didn't, I didn't, I immediately explained, I locked it by mistake. Rubbing my eyes, I focused an affably apologetic gaze on my birthsake. She looked back at me, blankly, holding her file. Neither of us spoke. I felt we'd managed to understand each other. No one expects these precious glimmers of entente so soon after waking, while the dust of sleep is still in your eyes. I kept gazing at her, as if I'd slipped into a near-trancelike state. Feng Meiyan's eyes widened into a glare: What the hell are you standing and staring like that for? You've got to get off. Lin Yicheng sat up in bed, startled: Who's got to get off? he asked in a panic, groping wildly around his pillow. Don't worry, I said to him, it's my stop, you've a while yet. I found my bedding token and gave it to Feng Meiyan, who handed me my boat ticket back in return. Just as I was hesitating over whether to take this opportunity to say a couple of words of farewell to her, she put her folder on a leatherette sofa by the door, then strode past me over to my bed and swiftly remade it. Before I'd put my shoes back on, my bed had recovered its original, standard-issue appearance, as if no one had ever slept in it; it was no longer my bed. She picked up her folder again, then went off to other rooms. Just as she was about to leave, she told me to get a move on, the boat was going to dock very soon. I was still hesitating, wondering whether I should find an opportunity to say something, whether I ought to thank her. But I sensed that the way she didn't so much as glance at me as she left was a pretty clear sign that being in my presence brought her little personal gratification. Lin Yicheng climbed out of bed and laboriously got dressed: Hold on, he told me, hold on, wait a minute, I'll come and see you off. His air of frenzied haste perplexed me: What did you say? I asked him. See me off? Yes, he said, I must see you off the boat. There's really no need, I quickly said, why'd you want to do that? The boat'll go straight off again once it's docked. He leaned against his bed, strenuously hitching up his trousers: No, I'll definitely come up, the boat stops half an hour at Wan County, I've checked, I'm sure, and I'll get to stretch my legs a bit on the quay, wait a minute, hold on.

★

Another indistinctly misty morning. Standing on one side of the deck, I inhaled mouthfuls of cold air, damp but invigorating, choking with my greed for fresh oxygen. Slowly, measuredly, Lin Yicheng thumped me on the back with his fleshy right hand, its fingers splayed, fanlike. I had more coughing inside me, but suppressed it. I was quite tall, but he was a whole head taller than me, and of course many times wider; in the true light of dawn, he seemed to have swollen an extra layer of flesh. Standing next to him amid the overcast mass of passengers waiting to get back onto dry land, I became a good deal more conspicuous. I wished, uselessly, for more distance between us. He, again uselessly, tried to help me carry my bag off the boat. After I got on shore, I immediately concentrated on getting away from the crowds, on fleeing, on climbing the steps up from the packed quayside, all thirty—at least—of them, my spirits rising with every step. I was in a new place, somewhere I'd never been before. Someone was shouting behind me: Lin Yicheng, of course. It broke your heart to watch him climb those steps. I paused and stood where I was, preparing my good-byes to the traveling salesman for Universal Batteries. Once he'd reached me, he bent over and spat through bleached lips. I then stepped forward, extending a hand: Well, then, thanks, good-bye. My original plan had been to shake his hand and go, but he hung on to my right hand, heaving great gasps of breath. I knew I had no chance of going on my way before he'd recovered enough to choke out the handful of weighty valedictory phrases preying on his mind.

Fate, my friend, brought us together. Meeting you has made me so happy. His right hand grasped mine even tighter, jerking it up and down. Yes, I nodded, same here. I tried to withdraw my hand, but sensed this still wasn't quite the moment. He then straightened up, his face solemn: Li Qiang, I hope we'll meet again. You've got my address and telephone number on my business card: if you pass by my neck of the woods, please let me know, we must have a drink, several drinks together. Okay, I said, okay. Saying this, I successfully retracted my hand with a sudden exertion of force. Good-bye, I said, good-bye, then hurried off in some, any direction. He pursued me a couple of steps: Your friends aren't here to meet you, he shouted, d'you know where you're going? I've been here hundreds of times, can I help you with anything? No need, I said, my friend lives near here, I'm headed there right now. After walking a certain distance, I turned to discover he was still standing there and waved back, but he took this as an unexpected cue to rush at me again. Wait! he shouted, wait! He fished out of his pocket a brown telephone book and a pen. This is where I write names down—I almost forgot! Leave me your address! He seemed very embarrassed at his near oversight. Lin Yicheng, I now felt, was probably, it was fair to say, an unusually good person; there was no harm in him. I hesitated a moment: I might not, I thought, ever meet this person again, but he still doesn't know my real name, which doesn't seem quite right, or necessary. So I wrote my real name and contact address. Lin Yicheng took back his book: Thank you, he said, over and over, thank you.

But I thought your name was Li Qiang? he frowned. The hand holding the telephone book was, I noticed, trembling slightly. He was looking straight at me, his eyes filled with tears. I felt ashamed, I couldn't help myself. I tried to explain things to him, even dug out my identity card to show him, explaining over and over that at least now I was leaving him with my real name. But isn't your name Li Qiang? he repeated. I realized, regretfully, that he hadn't listened to a word I'd said. So I stopped explaining; I'd done enough, I felt, I'd tried to make amends. I stood there next to him. Why did you lie to me? There was no need to lie! He began crying, crying in these great heartbroken sobs. Let me tell you, it's an unsettling thing, having a blunderbuss of a man standing opposite you, eyes and nose streaming. I looked anxiously around me, at the morning just begun, at the long line of breakfast stalls stretching to the left and right, at the great hordes of people coming and going, beginning a new day. There I stood, head empty of thoughts. Before long, we had an audience, eyeballing me with idle curiosity as they stuffed hunks of breakfast into their mouths. It was too much for me, truly, it was too much. What the fuck are you crying about? I asked Lin Yicheng. But he just cried even harder, his teardrops three times bigger than normal people's, and tinted an unnerving yellow. Why does everyone always lie to me? That's what he said: Why does everyone always lie to me? This was now a great deal more than too much for me. What do you mean, everyone? I asked him. Fuck you, fuck you, fuck you! I was surprised at myself, at my anger, at the stars of spittle it was generating. My swearing done, I wanted to break out of our crowd of spectators, walk away, but no one would give way; they seemed to be entreating me to stay where I was, to entertain them a bit longer. Lin Yicheng suddenly stopped weeping, slowly lowered his clammy hands from his face, and looked straight at me, his head shaking from left to right. Before I knew what was happening, I was on the ground, lying face up, carried backward by an overwhelming blow to the chin, the crowd gathered behind rapidly fanning out into a broad mass. Although the course of my fall was obstructed, at various points, by other bodies, I'd taken on an unbreakable momentum, staggering seven or eight paces back before collapsing flat down on the ground, the world spinning in glorious Technicolor around me. He hurled himself at me again, directing a string of violent kicks at my lower abdomen, growling to himself, You lying, lying bastard, you lying bastard. Incapable of putting up any resistance, I suddenly tasted this strange, raw sweetness—a mouthful of blood—then a rank, rotten rush of aftertaste. But my mind was clear. I hauled myself up with some difficulty: I felt fine—surprised, but fine. A pale Lin Yicheng stood there, his entire body convulsing. I offered him a crooked smile; I couldn't help myself. You trying to piss me off? he roared back at me. You trying to piss me off? He charged again. Kicks to my chest, the soft part of my ribs and my back, this much I know, but whatever followed remains a fog.

When I became aware of myself again, I found myself sitting on a chair, Lin Yicheng beside me, solemn, straight-backed, a different man from the one I'd known on the boat. Three policemen were seated opposite us, two of them huddled around a stove, the third sprawled over a table, one leg swinging from left to right. Both sides of the window were shut, a mass of human faces compressed behind them. My bag had been thrown into the right-hand corner of the room, a corner smeared with sticky mud. The room was warm; no one was speaking. One of the policemen around the stove was picking away at a small piece of skin peeling off his hand, which he eventually threw into the fire, where it disappeared with a faint burning hiss. Without turning around to face us fully, the policeman sitting on the table gestured in our direction: Go on, he said, tell us what happened. Lin Yicheng cleared his throat: Do you want to tell them or shall I? You do it, I said. So he told it from the beginning. After each installment, he'd turn to me: Isn't that how it was? Isn't that how it was? He meandered into endless trivial details, with the three impatient policemen continually having to remind him to pick out the important bits. I had nothing to add, because everything he said was the truth. The policeman sitting on the table shook his head and thumped the table: Anything inside that fat skull of yours? he asked, pointing at Lin Yicheng. A guy tells you one lie and you do this to him? Did you hit him back? the policeman asked, turning to me. No, I replied. Good, he said, then this has nothing to do with you. You go and wash your face in the water trough, then get checked out at the hospital, get whatever you need, just ask for a receipt. You're going to let him go? Lin Yicheng cried out, springing up in his agitation. Why did he lie to me, why? You saying I'm in the wrong? The policeman sitting on the table thumped the table again: Sit down! Sit the fuck down! Or do I have to make you? Screwing up my morning. He doesn't know you, why should he care what he says to you?

How old are you? Forty-eight, Lin Yicheng said. Eight or forty-eight?
Forty-eight. The other two policemen by the stove began sniggering.
The policeman on the table thumped it again: People like you, you
piss me off, you know, every day of your life you must have eaten
shit, every one of your forty-eight years. Shit! Because you have shit
for brains. His swearing began to hold my attention: it was clearly
giving him satisfaction. After a brief preliminary wail, Lin Yicheng
burst into tears again, crying in this desperate, broken-hearted way,
as if he'd suffered some terrible wrong. Well pleased with himself,
the policeman hopped off the table, picked up a cup, and headed to
one side of the room to get himself some water. Suddenly, without
warning, Lin Yicheng hurled himself across and deadlocked his arms
around the policeman's scrawny neck. The cramped room immediately disintegrated into chaos. The two policemen guarding the fire
sprang up, grabbed rubber police truncheons off hooks on the wall,
and began beating Lin Yicheng. But he seemed to feel nothing. Despite his clumsiness, his sluggishness, within five minutes all three
policemen were on the ground, mumbling in pain. And one of the
truncheons was in Lin Yicheng's hand, his face bathed in blood, as
he stood grim, solemn guard in the center of the room. He turned
to me, still panting hard, his eyes bloodshot. He drew a step closer,
oppressively closer: You're coming with me, he said. I remained on
my chair. Where to? I asked. Don't worry about that. But you're coming with me. By now he was shouting, hysterically, brandishing the
truncheon as the blood spattered off it. I didn't feel I had a choice.
All right, I replied. I pointed over to the corner. But I want to take
my things with me. Saying nothing, Lin Yicheng stepped slowly over
a policeman's body, threw down the truncheon, and bent to pick up
my bag. I noticed him almost topple forward with the effort onto one
of the policemen—who would surely have been finished by the impact—then, just in time, steady himself against the table. Lin Yicheng
yanked out the telephone cord lying across the table, scrunched it
into a rough kind of ball, and stuffed it into his pocket. I threw him a
surprised, quizzical glance. He wiped the blood off his face with one

sleeve. They'll take us otherwise—dead not alive, he informed me, his voice low, his tone mysterious. That's what he said to me: They'll take us otherwise—dead not alive. Us? I said. He nodded, portentously. He drew up alongside me. Let's go, he said.

★

I got up. By the time I'd reached the door, both legs felt so weak they'd almost given up. The pain in my left rib was boring right through me. Lin Yicheng slipped his right hand under my left armpit, forcibly keeping me upright. You all right? he asked. So-so, I said. I stretched my hand out to open the door of the People's Police staff room and a couple of men lying against it almost fell forward into the room. The area outside was crowded with our earlier audience, through whom our reemergence generated a wave of intense excitement. We strode out the main door, single file, the crowd voluntarily parting to let us through. As he left, Lin Yicheng shut the door of the staff room behind him. Though every step I took was agony, somehow I couldn't suppress the laughter bubbling up in me. But then laughing made everything hurt more, so I stopped. Otherwise, I would have roared till the tears came. Our audience followed on our heels at a sedate, steady pace, keeping their distance. Lin Yicheng stopped in the middle of the road and hailed a taxi. We got in. I looked back as it drove off. Our crowd of spectators were mounting their bikes, or simply jogging along after us, struggling to keep up.

After only a couple of hundred yards, Lin Yicheng asked the driver to stop. Once Lin had helped me out, the taxi revved off in a cloud of exhaust fumes, without even claiming its fare. It was only when I heard the blast of a steam whistle from over by the river that I realized we were back at the quayside. In the distance, I could see the *Orient* still waiting where it had docked, its loudspeakers urging passengers to make their way quickly on board: The *Orient* will set sail in five minutes. Lin Yicheng swung my bag up onto his back: Quick, he told me. But I stood where I was, not moving. I turned and saw our dense mass of spectators hurrying toward us, perhaps shouting something as they ran. Quick, he called to me again. I shook my head, wiping a frothy dribble of blood from the side of my mouth. Wait, I said, where am I following you to? I have to know that first. He reinserted his unnervingly forceful right hand under my armpit: I'll tell you everything after we get on the boat, okay? I'll take responsibility, I'll make sure you're all right. But you have to come with me now. That's what he said to me: you have to come with me now. His eyes were bloodshot with desperation, the blood pulsing impatiently through his forehead. I hesitated a moment. All right, I said, let's get on. Thank you, thank you, he said, apparently moved by my acquiescence; he'd pay my fare, he promised. And after we were on the boat? I couldn't begin to imagine what he had in mind after that. Of course, it wasn't my place to talk back, it was my job to agree. But at the same time, it did in fact occur to me that maybe getting back on the boat would be no worse than staying in a place like Wan County, a place where I didn't know anybody or anything.

WHEELS

IT MUST HAPPEN all the time: you're on your bike, your concentration slips, you bump into someone, you find yourself in a whole load of trouble. It's a bit like catching a cold: almost everyone gets one at some point and doesn't give it a second thought when they do. Practically ever since they emerged from the primordial swamp, humans have had four choices in how to get from A to B: first, walk or climb; second, swim, the precondition for which is knowing how to swim; third, fly, for which you need to grab hold of an ample bird to whom you have clearly explained your desired destination. The final option—rolling—has proved the most popular across the centuries and millennia. Now, this last mode of travel comes in motorized and nonmotorized forms, the former dividing into further subcategories according to size and power of engine. Nonmotorized modes of wheeled transport come in two varieties, animal- and human-powered, easily distinguished by a respective tendency, or lack thereof, to defecate in public. But all types of rolling have one point in common: every single one effects spatial motion through the agency of wheels. The crucial historical shift, the force driving humanity ever forward, ever faster toward meltdown, is the move from two legs to the wheel. At this advanced hour in history, even I, a mere boiler serviceman in an electrical factory, can sense that we're freewheeling helplessly, inexorably toward some kind of doomsday.

One day, as I set about my work, safety-helmeted and wielding my wrench like a young girl off to pick mushrooms in a steel forest, I struggled to imagine how my naked ancestors Adam and Eve passed their time in the Garden of Eden before the Fall, knowing nothing, doing nothing. And then an idea suddenly came to me: it should have been a big, shiny golden wheel hanging on that fateful tree, not an apple. But as every edition of the Bible seems pretty adamant on this point, that it was an apple and not a wheel, I've never had much truck with Christianity. I've always had more of a soft spot for Buddhism, with all its wheels of reincarnation. I'm not that bothered about what its doctrines actually say or mean: as long as there's a wheel in there somewhere, they can't be too far wrong. Centuries ago in the West, one of those medieval Europeans devised a whole Wheel of Fortune theory, which had some winged guy up in heaven with a hotline to God cranking the needle of time around the seven stars of government, bringing good or bad luck to the poor helpless bastards down below. But this theory strikes me as a bit simplistic, a bit like ancient Chinese divination—different technique, same idea. Wheels are everywhere, sometimes working invisibly, moving in beautiful but mysterious ways. They're the very devil. . . .

Because wheels move faster than legs and are harder to control, humans sometimes have to face up to the unexpected consequences of wheeled movement, viz. traffic accidents. Some claim that the Asian economic crisis and the Gulf War were caused by traffic accidents. Or that the Second World War was just one particularly long, drawn-out, and harrowing traffic accident. I like explanations like this: there has to be something in them, because they bring vehicles and wheels into the equation. Nostradamus predicted that in July 1999 a cataclysmic traffic accident would engulf the world. I won't comment for the time being, as it's already 1998 and history will soon speak for itself.

And while I'm on the subject, I might as well point out that wheels are implicated—heavily—in AIDS, the most terrifying viral threat of the last twenty years of the millennium, too. It's thanks to wheels that people can now get around like they do. Wheels carry people over enormous distances to have sex, spreading AIDS as they go.

But let's get back to everyday sorts of traffic accidents, thereby enriching our understanding of larger-scale traffic accidents. In my experience, rollers don't get along too well with walkers, who tend to cast themselves as victims. It isn't surprising that walkers hate rollers: the wheel-less are always going to hate the wheeled, just like poor people hate the rich. There are also splits within the rolling ranks: nonmotors hate motors, two-wheelers hate four-wheelers. Even four-wheeled motors are a fractious bunch: Fiats hate Volkswagens, Volkswagens hate Audis, Audis hate Porsches, and so on. Basically, wheels mean trouble.

In this big unhappy family of rollers, I'm a fully paid-up member of the nonmotorized two-wheeler class. I'd now like to give you a full and frank introduction to the bicycle that has been my faithful companion for eleven years: it's a black Phoenix 28, minus bell, minus mudguards, minus kickstand, minus rear brake (though the front brake functions gloriously). In short, it's the kind of crappy old bike you could leave unlocked in front of the railway station and still no one would steal. But: it does have a spanking new lock, which didn't come cheap. My colleagues laughed at me when I got it fitted: it was the lock, not the bike I should be worried about people stealing, they said. But I've always stuck up for my faithful companion, who, like all of us, was young once, and beautiful too. She's carried me safely around for ten years now, and put up with all sorts of crap along the way.

I've heard that because so many mailmen suffer from the occupational hazard of swollen testicles and inflamed prostate, the government's trying to recruit women—or at least women without testicles or prostate—to deliver the mail. I don't see any reason to blame these injuries on bicycles: as long as you're careful how you sit, you won't suffer any ill effects. Look at me: I've been cycling for eleven years now and my bike's almost completely done for, but there's nothing wrong with me. And on the few occasions I don't have my bike and have to walk, my knees always act up, limping creakily between heavy and light steps. In China, where the bike rules supreme, where nobody listens and everybody shouts at each other, we'll never be half decent at a running game like soccer. But this, we should remember, is a sign of necessary evolution, of progress. If we follow this train of thought through to its Darwinian conclusion, human legs will eventually wither away into two neat little Catherine wheels in order to facilitate wheeled motion.

While I'm on the subject, researchers in the West have shown that in all mammals (humans included), the male sexual organ is progressively shrinking due to changes in lifestyle, triggering a sharp decline in reproductive capacity that many find deeply disquieting. Personally, though, I see this as another necessary and inevitable part of evolution. If, like me, you belong to the oppressed majority that is the nonmotorized two-wheeler class, you're bound to see what I mean: cycling would get very awkward if your thing were any bigger. The wheels of daily existence turn those of evolution. If the world doesn't end in a massive traffic accident in July 1999, the science textbooks of the future will surely hypothesize that the male human sexual organ will shrink further and further to accommodate the wheel, until it retracts inside the abdominal cavity, just as giraffes' necks have grown longer and longer to reach leaves higher up. Humans will finally, at evolutionary snail's pace, succeed in ridding themselves of their second tail.

My room was a couple of bus stops away from the factory, a perfect biking distance. The route took in a steep slope, about the distance between the two stops, of around one in twenty-five, I'd guess. My journey to work took me down the hill, my journey home took me up. Descending the hill was, of course, hugely enjoyable, but because I was always hurrying in late to work, I was never in the mood to appreciate the delights of gliding downward, while having to climb back up the hill after a mind-numbing day at work made me feel even worse than I already did. My most cherished dream during that period in my life was for my room and the factory to swap places. Given the chance, in fact, I'd have swapped a whole lot of things in my life. When my spirits and energy were at a low ebb, I'd have to dismount halfway up and push my two wheels the rest of the way on legs that had turned to cotton. At times like that, the hill felt like the back of a huge whale adrift in the unbounded darkness of the ocean: after one arbitrary roll, I'd be left buried at the bottom of the sea. As you can see, once people get off their wheels and stand on their own two feet, they're only a trip and a limp away from self-pity. The stop at the top of the hill was called Xinzhuang, the stop at the bottom Xiejiadian, and the locals called it Big Xie Hill.

My unexpected encounter on Big Xie Hill was so ordinary it can be explained in a few sentences. No one knocked me over, nor I them; all that happened was I brushed against some old man's arm as I rode down the hill. But this old man and his bloodsucking relatives sank their fangs into me and insisted on a hospital checkup. Not just a regular checkup, a full checkup, in which it was discovered the old man had a tumor in his stomach the size of a broad bean. Not long afterward, the old man, who'd lived perfectly happily up to that point, kicked the bucket.

All this happened in 1992, six years ago, but I sometimes think back to that fateful cycle ride down the hill and still can't feel sure I really did bump into that old man. Every rush hour, morning and evening, the hill would be a black, swarming mass of bikes, with a sprinkling of pedestrians blurred into the torrent, emerging into view only after most of the swarm had departed, like a scattering of solitary stalks of wheat fortunate enough to be left standing after a plague of locusts. Collisions were always happening, but nothing too serious. That evening, as I toiled up the hill on my way home, a skinny guy wearing biker glasses and wielding a chain lock blocked my path upward. Get off! he shouted. My heart quailed when I heard his strong local accent: this was obviously going to be sticky. The factory where I worked was in an industrial area—segregated from Nanjing proper by the river—which had started out as a small town renowned only for being the most murderously violent hole in the entire Jiangbei region. More recently, the government had purposely developed it into a satellite zone, where almost all Nanjing's industry was now concentrated. It must, of course, also have entered into the government's calculations that a satellite can get hideously polluted without having much effect on the mother planet. A satellite, as it spins merrily around, will trace one massive wheel in space, and wherever there's a wheel, there'll be trouble. In addition to the usual difficulties faced all over any developing country, Nanjing's industrial zone suffered from certain specific social problems, namely that the local residents were not the kind of people you'd want to have to dinner every, or any, night. The whole area was rife with triads, always fighting one epic gangland war or another. I stopped but didn't actually dismount, resting one foot on the ground. What do you want? I asked, affecting total nonchalance. The skinny guy took off his glasses, stuck one earpiece into his buttonhole, and pointed to the side of the road: Over here, he said. He then turned and walked there without a backward glance at me. Not so long ago, some local criminal had stopped a university graduate newly arrived to work in the steel factory around Xiejiadian and asked him for a pack of cigarettes. As the ex-student only gave him one, not a whole pack, he and a whole gang of his associates dragged the graduate kicking and screaming to a public toilet nearby, where they buggered him one by one. If I'd found myself in a similar situation, I reckon I'd have given him two packs, no questions asked. So I warily followed the skinny guy over to a noodle restaurant at the side of the road. In the mornings, this noodle place did pretty good rice balls, and as the portions were on the generous side as well, sometimes I'd stop and buy a couple on my way to work. Still without looking in my direction, the skinny guy frowned and said, Leave your bike over there. He had this look of total disgust on his face, as if I'd already pushed him to the edge and beyond. Hurry up and say what you've got to say, I said. My bike doesn't have a kickstand, I can't just leave it anywhere. He glanced at my bike, still without looking at me. Slowly, deliberately, he proposed, in a tone that suggested he was exercising remarkable self-restraint, Can't you lean it against the wall? There was something in what he said, I thought, so I wheeled the bike over to rest against the wall of the noodle place. Meandering over behind me, the skinny guy locked my bike with the chain he was carrying, all in the most casual way imaginable, as if he were locking up his own bike, pulled out the key, slipped it into his trouser pocket, then walked over to a stool in the doorway of the shop and calmly sat down. I snapped out of my stupor and went after him: What the hell're you doing locking my bike up? I asked. Acting as if he hadn't heard me, the skinny guy bent his head over to light a cigarette.

Thought you could run away, did you, you little fucker? Try running after I break both your legs! a voice like a wheezy gong boomed out somewhere behind me. Turning to look, I discovered it belonged to a white-haired but burly old man, seated on a square stool, his back resting against a table, a blue cotton jacket, filthy with grease, over his shoulders. His body listed slightly to the left, with his right hand supporting his left shoulder. His head was the size of a bucket, his face a dark purple expanse of pure fury, in which browless eyes darted about like a pair of jumping beans, the corners of his mouth furred with snowy spittle. His hair was completely white, but it was still thick and stood straight up, half an inch all over, like a toilet brush, although, weirdly enough, the straggly, uneven moustache on his upper lip was still black. All he was wearing under the jacket was a yellowish-brown sweater over a filthy, open-necked white shirt. None the wiser, I looked at the old man, then back at the skinny guy. So the old man kept on barking at me, stringing every word together with emphatic urgency—his entire body shaking with the effort. While riding down the hill that morning, he made abundantly clear to me, I'd bumped into his left arm, which was now completely paralyzed. And as if this wasn't bad enough, he'd yelled after me for all he was worth, but I'd just pedaled off. I had absolutely no memory of this: Sure you haven't got me mixed up with someone else? I asked him. The old man glared at me, his eyes bulging like fish balls: I might forget your face, but I'd recognize that bike of yours again anywhere. I had to admit my bike was rather more memorable than I was, and forced myself to go contritely back in my head over the events of that morning, but I still had no idea what he was going on about. The old man got up, his right hand still supporting his left shoulder, and shrugged his shoulders without dislodging his jacket. Follow me, he said, jutting his chin out. We crossed over to the opposite side of the street, him in front, me behind, then climbed a few steps up the hill. The old man stopped, looked both ways: Yep, he said, it was here all right.

I squinted back over at the other side of the street, where the skinny guy was still sitting at a table by the entrance to the shop, smoking in between gulps of noodles. The old man reenacted the scene over and over, spattering my face with gobs of spittle as he got increasingly excited. Frankly, he was boring the pants off me. So I said to him, perfectly politely, Look, you old . . . gentleman, I heard you the first time, and I really don't know what you're talking about. But, as you're so sure, and we're not talking about anything really serious here, I'll take your word for it. So how do you want to settle things? The old man calmed down a fair bit and took a sidelong squint at me: What factory are you? was what he wanted to know next. Electrical, I said. Soon as I'd said this I regretted it, because although none of the big factories was in clover, electrical was at least doing a bit better than some, so the locals all thought the people who worked there were millionaires. So I wasn't that surprised when the old man made a few quick calculations in his head, then named his price: Five hundred *yuan*! The moment the words were out of his mouth, he involuntarily retreated a step, blown backward by the outrageous size of the sum he'd demanded. While I computed, just as fast, that his mouth was big enough to stuff 500 in small change into. I dug out all the money I had in my pockets, even the cents, which in total came to only a few dozen *yuan*. See for yourself, I said to him, straight up, I'm stone broke, I have to borrow money at the end of each month just to get by.

We kept arguing all the way back to the noodle restaurant. Or, I said, how about we all go to a hospital and I pay for your treatment, however much it costs, even if the doctor says he's got to saw your arm off and swap it for a leg, I'll pay, all right? The old man didn't like this idea one bit; it was the money he wanted. He'd gotten this far in life without ever setting foot in a hospital, he said, he hated them. The skinny guy didn't look too keen on getting involved, just stayed on his stool, studiedly picking his teeth. But I noted the expression on his face: embarrassment at the exorbitant sum—*500 yuan*—the old man was demanding. As it was getting dark and I really didn't want to get in much deeper than I already was, I ended up saying to the old man, okay, you win, how about I give you my bike and we call it quits. I then walked off. After a couple of steps, I paused, twisted the bike lock key off my key ring, and chucked it at him. Neither of them came after me. Although they'd said they wanted 500 *yuan*, I figured they knew in their heart of hearts they were doing well just to get a bike out of it. By the time I got to the building where I lived, I'd started to miss that crappy old bike of mine. Lots of times I'd thought of giving it away and getting a new one, but I'd never managed to offload it onto anyone. And it would've been a waste just to put it away somewhere to collect dust, so I'd had no choice but to keep riding it. But now everything had turned out for the best in the best of all possible worlds: I'd finally gotten rid of her and could get on with enjoying missing her.

I thought the whole Big Xie Hill incident was over and done with—little did I know it was only just beginning. The next day, I hitched a ride to work on my roommate Hao Qiang's moped. Hao Qiang was a local, a ladies' man, liked his women almost as much as his moped. Dozens of them he'd ridden, without committing himself to a single one. The question is, could someone that promiscuous with his vehicles be counted a member of the motorized two-wheeler class? His favorite vehicle, according to acquaintances, was the moped, followed closely by young women, then by girls. He was always most popular on the journey home from work, when two-wheeling, nonmotorized colleagues fought among themselves to grab hold of one of his shoulders to give them a boost up the hill. That morning I sat behind him, hanging on to his waist, both of us with no more than half a buttock each on the moped seat. Cold air rushed down my neck once the moped got going, but I still felt all warm inside, because tucked in my jacket were all the savings I'd scraped together during my frugal bachelor existence and that I was planning to splurge on a three-gear mountain bike in the market west of the factory. I was like a man who'd just kicked out his wrinkly old wife and was running, tail wagging, into the open arms of a sweet young thing. When we were about to ride down the hill, Hao Qiang turned around: Don't stick that thing of yours in my back, all right? he warned me. Or we'll have an accident on our hands. After we'd gone just a little way down, I spotted over Hao Qiang's shoulder a few people standing to one side of the road. Two of them I'd met the day before, the old man and the skinny guy wearing biker glasses; to the other side of the old man stood an even skinnier guy, quite tall, and dressed from head to foot in tight denim, so new I could almost hear it squeak. He was short on top, and more than half of what hair he did have had gone gray. There was one other man with them—tall, dark-skinned, dressed in a suit, hair slicked back, piercing eyes—talking into a flip-open mobile phone. He stood slightly back from the others, maintaining a certain distance from the three of them. They all stared straight ahead, their lines of vision projecting forward like perfectly spaced teeth on a comb, raking over the sea of bikes rolling before them. I shrank back: Bad news, I said to Hao Qiang, the guys who robbed me yesterday are standing over there. Hao Qiang reacted instantly, taking his foot off the accelerator and merging his moped into the mass of bikes immediately in front, then edging sedately toward the middle of the road. But Hao Qiang's moped was still too conspicuous: the skinny guy with the motorbike glasses spotted me and yelled, Get off that moped! Take no notice, I whispered into Hao Qiang's ear, keep going. We're in the middle of the road, they're at the side; they'll never catch us through all these bikes.

So you can imagine my amazement when Hao Qiang's moped did a funny little U-turn and stopped right in front of the four of them. Quick as he could, Hao Qiang plastered a smile all over his face and started sucking up to the guy in the suit: Aha-ha, Mr. Black, good to see you again, aha-ha-ha. Slimy little creep. So I didn't have much choice but to effect an awkward dismount from his slimy creep of a moped. My crappy old bike I spotted leaning against a slim birch nearby, its weight bending the tree over backward. The man he called Mr. Black nodded slightly, flipped shut the mouthpiece on his phone, and pointed at me with the finger that had been wrapped around it: You know him? he barked. Hao Qiang glanced back at me, then replied, with touching reluctance, He's, ah, a friend of mine, we, uh, room together. After staring at his big toe and muttering to himself for a while, Mr. Black looked up: Get lost, he told Hao Qiang, this is nothing to do with you, it's your friend I've business with. Hao Qiang hesitated, casting anxious looks first at me, then at Mr. Black. I told you once, Mr. Black started to lose patience, Get lost, nothing'll happen to him he hasn't got coming, relax—and get lost. For some reason this reassured my roommate, who turned his moped work-ward: I'll tell them you're not coming in, he offered, with his back to me. Then he turned and made an odd, twisted face in my direction. His fine, pale face was even paler than usual, his lips two thin white lines across his jaw. It was only later that I learned, courtesy of Hao Qiang's explanation, that this face was a warning to me not at any cost to rub Mr. Black the wrong way. Now although this was the first time I'd met Mr. Black in person, the name was already familiar to me. He ran a small restaurant near the 45000 Agricultural Market specializing in soy-braised meat, called Mr. Black's Pot-Roast Goose. The goose meat served there was delicious: tender on the inside, crispy on the outside. But rumor had it that Mr. Black's pot roasts were made from goose carrion. Every day the local livestock wholesaler ended up with a load of dead geese and ducks, which Mr. Black bought at a knockdown price, then pot-roasted. His restaurant was pretty small, but around here he was Mr. Big. If he walked up to a peasant trader, hands folded behind his back, and told him, that's dead, that goose of yours, the peasant would have to sell it to Mr. Black for the price of a dead goose. If he had the balls to say to Mr. Black it looked perfectly alive to him, he could kiss any more business good-bye. But at Mr. Black's pot-roast goose restaurant, any customer who complained he'd been given dead meat wasn't too far from becoming it himself. Basically, what Mr. Black said, went around here: if he said a goose was dead, it was dead, and vice versa, and soon enough it occurred to him that life would be much simpler if he exercised the same powers of attorney over humans as well. Anyway, once Hao Qiang had disappeared in a cloud of exhaust smoke, Mr. Black took a step forward: You've brought the money, haven't you? he said right in my face. Let's see it. Soon as he said this, I just stood there, overcome by a paralyzing heartache. The skinny guy walked over, mouth full of smoke, and started searching me; within a few seconds he produced from the pocket of my cotton jacket the envelope that contained the sum total of my worldly wealth. He took the money out and counted it in front of everyone: 800 *yuan*. The old man went mad when he saw all that cash: You little shit! he roared at me, telling us you don't have any money—where's all this come from? Rob a bank, did you? This is money to buy a bike, I said. I can't get to and from work every day without a bike, can I? Mr. Black looked sunk in deep thought, not angry in the slightest: That's your bike over there, he told me, pointing behind him, we brought it along to return to you. So let's not waste any more time: are you ready to be reasonable? 'Course I'm going to be reasonable, I said. Good, he said. My granddad's shoulder here, it's still hurting, been hurting all night. Now what d'you say we do about it? The old man quickly clutched at his left shoulder with his right hand and glared daggers at me. Like I said yesterday, I replied, let's go get him checked out at a hospital, I'll pay all the medical costs. Mr. Black immediately nodded: Fine, he said, let's go. He took the envelope from the skinny guy and waved it under my nose: How about I look after this for now, he said, and we'll settle up when we leave the hospital, whatever it costs, okay? Remember, there's exactly 800 here, we won't take a cent more than you owe us.

This was not an offer I could refuse.

Bahuajian Hospital was at the top of the hill, a mere hop and a skip from where we were, but Mr. Black insisted on going to Nanhua Hospital, a good four bus stops away. They told the old man to sit on the back of my bike, told me to walk in front pushing him. Mr. Black, the skinny guy, and the even skinnier guy followed behind, swinging their arms as they walked. That old bastard on the back weighed at least half as much as an iron pylon, I reckoned, a dead weight he was, and forever shrugging his shoulders to stop his crappy cotton jacket from falling off. As I pushed it along, the bike took on a life of its own, winding forward in an S-shape, almost tipping over on every bend. I could feel every single particle of air being squeezed out of the back tire as the wheel frame scraped painfully along the ground. Just at that moment, I felt worse possibly even than my bike did, so bad I wanted to kick the thing right over. But, my bike said to me, what'd be the point in kicking me? You're the one who's dragged me into your own fine mess, I shouldn't be having to suffer like this, not at my age. How can you say that? I said to her. Are you enjoying seeing me get skinned like a dead goose? Way you're walking now, she answered back, you're an insult to dead geese. After I'd staggered along for a while, smarting from the hurtfulness of this last remark, Mr. Black nipped forward and poked me in the chest with his index finger: I've been pretty easy on you so far, but you're not exactly meeting me halfway. You better start putting your back into this pushing, because if the old man takes another fall thanks to you, there'll be no more Mr. Nice Guy, got that? This thing's no picnic to push, I said to him. Let's take a bus, I'll pay. Show us your money then, he said with a smirk. I haven't got any money, I was forced to admit. Then cut the crap and get pushing! he replied. He might have had a suit and leather shoes on, but I could still smell the roast goose on him. Although he was all smiles on the outside, he was, I realized, hard as nails on the inside. I don't like your attitude, I said. I've spent good money at your restaurant in the past and I might do so again. So I have really serious issues with your attitude. Mr. Black looked momentarily taken aback and I thought for a second my speech had really gotten to him—until he grounded me with a hefty kick around the back of the knee. The three of us—me, my bike, and the old man—collapsed in a heap.

The skinny guy and the even skinnier guy hurried over to pull up the old man, who was face down in the dust. Picking up the blue cotton jacket, they gave it a few pats and helped the old man put it back on. The old guy's great moon face was swollen red, like it was pumped full of pig's blood, like his head had grown a whole size bigger. After brushing the dirt off his rear, he brooded silently for a remarkably long time, glaring venomously at Mr. Black, who stood there, paused, head slightly tilted to one side. The old man spat noisily on the tarmac road: I'll remember this, he finally said to Mr. Black. What're you talking about? said Mr. Black irritably, with a dismissive wave of his hands. Look, Granddad, I didn't do that on purpose. What d'you mean, not on purpose? the old man said. Ask your brothers, did he do it on purpose? The old man turned to the skinny guy and the even skinnier guy, but the pair of them were too busy looking blank and cross-eyed to say anything. Just then Mr. Black's mobile phone rang; he looked at the number, then flipped it open to answer it. Meanwhile, back on the pavement, my right hand was stuck between two spokes of a wheel and my poor traumatized bike was still hanging on to the rest of me for dear life. After slowly extracting my hand, I placed both palms flat down on the ground, preparing to lever myself up. Looking for someone to vent his anger against the world on, the old man charged over like a mad bull and kicked me in the ribs. I collapsed back down again without a sound, clutching my stomach. A few passersby got off their bikes and gathered around to watch the fun. Mr. Black faced the street, talking on the phone and waving his hands at onlookers like a traffic policeman to shoo them away. Although clearly unwilling to abandon such an entertaining spectacle, one after another our audience got a handle on their curiosity and remounted their bikes. Soon as Mr. Black shut his mobile phone, he poked the old man in the chest with the antenna: Any more funny business and you're on your own. I won't lift a finger even if you get your head sliced off. See if I care, said the old man, standing his ground. I'm your granddad, where's your respect? Just give us the money and go. The skinny guy and the even skinnier guy broke the two of them up, telling them to quit arguing and gesturing at the body they'd left lying on the ground. Mr. Black turned, walked over, and lifted my chin with his square-toed shoe. Get up, he said, like he didn't want to hang around much longer.

In the end it was Mr. Black who pulled me up by the armpits, straightened my jacket for me, even gave the zipper a bit of a tug. I've been beaten up more times than I can remember, he told me, brushing the dust off my chest, had the shit kicked out of me, I'm not kidding you, really kicked out of me, till I genuinely couldn't get up. Like my whole body'd been cut into bits and I couldn't move any of them. My point being: I know what it's like when you really can't get up. So don't try telling me you can't now. You know, I really don't want to have to hit you. Sincerity seeped out of the open pores that pitted his swarthy face. I began to feel the last few seconds had contained some valuable lessons for me. More crucially for my well-being in the immediate short term, my bike-pushing skills now dramatically improved. Once I'd gotten the hang of pushing the thing, the old man no longer weighed so heavily on the back seat. Peak rush hour had passed and the crowds on the street were slowly thinning out. As I silently pushed along in front, I began to feel like an old hand at the whole bike-wheeling game, able to derive satisfaction from a job well done. Wait up, Mr. Black shouted out from behind. I brought the bike to a halt. Got any cigarettes? he asked. I pointed at the left pocket of my jacket, rather embarrassed: They're not very good, I told him. He groped out the yellow pack of Red Peach cigarettes. They'll do, he said. He passed the pack to the skinny guy, who rubbed his hands, picked one out, licked one side of it with his tongue, and stuck it in his mouth. Mr. Black then passed the pack to the even skinnier guy, who waved his hands in refusal. Ignoring the way the old man sitting on the back of the bike followed the pack's every move, Mr. Black then drew a cigarette out with his teeth. The skinny guy chose this moment to extend a hand, pull another one out, and pass it to the old man. Mr. Black, the skinny guy, and the old man each took out a lighter and each lit his own cigarette. Mr. Black stuffed the cigarette pack back in my pocket: Bit tricky smoking while pushing a bike, he said, so guess you won't be wanting one? No, I said, I never smoke and walk at the same time.

A train track from the iron and steel works intersected the road around Xiejiadian. The front wheel of my bike got so stuck on the track I couldn't budge it, however hard I tried. I turned around to look at the old man, but as he was focusing all his physical and mental energies on sucking the life out of his cigarette butt, he was taking no interest in my difficulties. I tried lunging forward, giving it a mighty push, but still it wouldn't move. My left leg—the one that Mr. Black's foot had introduced itself to—felt completely paralyzed, as if the tendons had been ripped to pieces. Hey Granddad, Mr. Black, who was bringing up the rear, called out, can't you get off a second? What the hell would I want to get off for? the old man grunted. Tell him to push harder! When I tried to lift the handlebars, the bike suddenly reared up like a frightened horse, and we all watched helplessly as the old man slid off the back onto the ground like a piece of rubbish. After a good long pause, the skinny guy and the even skinnier guy finally remembered to haul the old man up, then helped me push the bike over the tracks. Once we were over, the old man started muttering to himself. He'd never wanted to go to the hospital, he said. Look, Mr. Black said, we're going, we've already talked this through; anyway, you're not going to get a needle stuck in you, so what're you scared of? Come on, the skinny guy and the even skinnier guy said, no harm in getting a checkup. Waste of money, said the old man, I've lived this long without paying a penny to any hospital. It's not your money anyhow, said the skinny guy, so what's your beef? How's about, said the old man, you take me home and take your mom to the hospital instead. Why the hell would we want to do that? Mr. Black asked. Your mom's got lots wrong with her, the old man said, but she can't afford to see a doctor. She's the one who needs to go to the hospital, not me. It's not a question of who needs to go most, Granddad, Mr. Black said. Can't you get it into your thick skull? You're the one who got run down, not Mom. Your mom was run over last year too, remember? the old man said. Her back's still not right. Didn't you say it got better, the skinny guy, or maybe the even skinnier guy, interjected, after she got that heat suction thing done? Fine sons you are, the old man said, you haven't even noticed your mom's still bent left! I always thought she bent right, Mr. Black said. What d'you mean, right? the old man said. It's left! It's left, he's right, the skinny guy agreed. Personally I thought it was right, the even skinnier guy countered. Look, you fuckheads, the old man cut in. . . . And so it went on, with the old man still not wanting to go to the hospital, his last and final excuse being he couldn't bear the smell of hospitals, it made his head ache. Doesn't matter, Mr. Black said, long as your shoulder stops hurting, I don't give a fuck about your head. They remained utterly oblivious to my presence throughout this entire conference, as if I was some ox or mule pulling a cart. Thinking about it, that's how I often saw myself, too, either as an animal pulling or as an animal being pulled on a cart.

As I passed the main gate of the electrical factory, I started walking faster, afraid of bumping into one of my colleagues. Is the dance hall in your factory's social club still open to people from outside? the skinny guy asked. Yup, I said. Is it still five *yuan* to get in? he asked. Dunno, I said, never been. Well, what do you do in the evenings then? the skinny guy asked. I didn't know what to say to that. The old man made a big thing of twisting his head around to look at the new factory gate: Fuck, he said, they must be rolling in it, pissing money everywhere like that. At that moment, a bicycle stopped dead in front of me and rang its bell. When I looked to see who it was, I froze: it was Xiao Qi, the only woman on our team, just over thirty, recently divorced, with a seven-year-old son and a face like a sour pumpkin—well preserved, but a sour pumpkin all the same. Where're you going? she asked, taking off her face mask. She must have been arriving for work, she was always late. Everyone in our workshop, from the team leader to the director, wanted to screw her, so she could arrive as late as she liked. She never even looked at men who wanted to screw her; she was only interested in leading on men who didn't want to screw her, right up until the man *did* want to screw her, at which point she wouldn't look at him anymore. But I should add that, as little as I knew of her, she was a pretty decent sort of person. I stammered out some kind of response, that I was taking this old gentleman to the hospital. What? she said, unflatteringly astonished, out of the goodness of your own heart? She then put on this great show of rolling her eyes heavenward. That's right, Mr. Black quickly interrupted, absolutely. My granddad fainted, and he just happened to be passing by. I just stood there with nothing to say for myself, concentrating on looking appropriately bashful, like some idiot Samaritan doing a good turn he didn't want other people to know about. Well, blow me down, she said, that's beautiful—I'll tell the boss where you are. She then put her mask back on, straddled the crossbar of her bike again, and rode off with a very straight back. I sighed with relief and moved on. Nice skin, the skinny guy sighed admiringly. What good's nice skin, Mr. Black said, when she's ugly as that! Face might be ugly, the skinny guy begged to differ, but her cunt won't be. Bet she's gone rusty down there by now, said Mr. Black. I couldn't keep walking along, listening to them all slandering my colleague like this. I turned around: Look here, I said rather hesitantly, I don't like what you're saying. The skinny guy poked me in the chin: What don't you like? he said, trying to goad me. Screwed her yourself, have you? I didn't have anything to say to that, just shook my head and turned back the other way. Just then, Mr. Black called out to a taxi cruising by on the other side of the road to stop. I've got some business to sort out, he said to the skinny guys, I'll meet you at the hospital entrance. Before getting into the car, he patted me meaningfully on the shoulder, a warning not to pull any funny business, I knew. The car turned in front of us and revved off in a cloud of dust. The old man gave a disgruntled kind of snort. When I got to the big Shicun roundabout, I thought back to what Xiao Qi had said: yes, I suddenly thought, damn right, I *was* doing a pretty damn good turn out of the goodness of my own bleeding heart. As I was starting to overheat quite seriously by this point, this new insight into the morning's traumas washed soothingly over me, making me feel slightly better about the way things were turning out. Faster and faster I pushed, leaving the skinny guy and the even skinnier guy far behind. Slow down, the old man sitting on the back seat spat at my neck, what the hell're you going so fast for? This isn't an appointment with death, y'know.

When I reached the entrance to Nanhua Hospital, I scanned all around but couldn't see Mr. Black anywhere. The skinny guy and the even skinnier guy looked even more exhausted than me. The even skinnier guy was in particularly bad shape, panting heavily and clutching at his spleen, with his jean jacket unbuttoned and sweaters rolled up. Four thick sweaters he was wearing—he must have been skin and bones underneath them all. The old man slipped off the back seat, slapping some life back into a leg that had gone numb from the ride. But even before he'd gotten his balance back, he was barking at the skinny guy: Well, where is he then? Eh? He's inside looking for someone, the skinny guy said. Hold on a bit, he'll be here. Soon enough, Mr. Black emerged together with a middle-aged doctor dressed in a long white coat. This latest addition to the party had a white hat scrunched up in his hand, wore glasses, and was pretty bald, apart from a few long hairs on the left combed flat over the vast, desolate firmament of his head like shooting stars. If you stared straight at his scalp, you found yourself unconsciously tilting leftward. I've got to go now, Mr. Black said to the old man, but just follow Dr. Wu and you'll be all right, don't worry about anything else. The old man was less than overjoyed: Off again! What're you in such a hurry about? I'm a busy man, Granddad, Mr. Black said, not like you. He then called the skinny guy over to one side, where they turned their backs on us as he fished out from inside his jacket the envelope printed with the name of my factory. After taking a look inside the envelope, the skinny guy seemed to start arguing with him about something. His ears pricking up, the old man hustled over to see what was going on. But before he'd gotten anywhere near, the argument was over and the two of them spun back around again. Mr. Black waved a quick thanks and good-bye at the bald doctor. I thought he was going to turn and say something else to me, but he didn't. He left without a single look back. The old man yanked on the skinny guy's arm: How much he give you? he whispered. Maybe because I was there, the skinny guy turned away, refusing to respond. This enraged the old man, who wouldn't let go of the skinny guy's arm: Let me see! he kept pestering. Dr. Wu clapped his hands: Let's not waste any more time, he said. Come on, the skinny guy said, taking this opportunity to prise the old man's fingers off his arm. Just to make everything more fun, the old man started muttering to himself again that he wouldn't set foot in that hospital dead or alive. Nothing the skinny guy or the even skinnier guy said made any difference. I actually started to find it funny, the way the old man was dragging his ass like a sulky kid. The more they yanked at him and his clothes—exposing his back like a blotchy red side of bacon—the more stubbornly terrified he got. In the end, it took some bedside manner from Dr. Wu to calm the old bastard down again. The old man seemed to find him even more reassuring when he covered up his bald spot with his grubby white hat.

It was the skinny guy who accompanied the old man in to his
checkup, telling me and the even skinnier guy to wait at the main entrance. I was quite happy to comply, as I had no great love of hospitals
myself. If the smell of hospitals gave the old man a headache, then it
made me sneeze everywhere. Undignified and exhausting, I know, but
I couldn't help myself, and once it started, it'd go on for two weeks.
Clearly less than ecstatic to be spending this quality time with me,
the even skinnier guy ambled across to the other side of the entrance
and squatted down on the ground. I wheeled my bike over to lean
against the back of the phone booth by the entrance, then sat down
on a short pillar on the pavement. I took off my right shoe, pulled off
the sock, and examined the sole of my foot. As I'm flat-footed, the
long walk I'd just been on had left me with two big blisters. A bicycle-
bound specimen such as myself lives and evolves by the wheel—set
me back on my own two feet and I'm done for. As there was a nip
in the air, I couldn't spend too long mourning the state of my sole.
But while I was putting my sock and shoe back on, a disconcerting
image suddenly flashed through my head: when that old man pulled
at the skinny guy's shoulder a minute ago, he'd used his left hand.
And given it a good old yank—there wasn't anything wrong with his
left arm. I'd suspected this all along, but I still felt outraged to have it
confirmed. I replaced my shoe, stood up, and hurried straight over to
the even skinnier guy. He was staring off into space, so by the time
he noticed me, I was already parked in front of him. Struggling to
lever himself up, he almost fell over backward in his eagerness to reestablish some distance between the two of us. Squatting back down
again, he propped his hands on the ground and finally got himself upright by bouncing up and down a few times like a long-legged locust.
What the fuck you playing at? he warbled, a little nervously. I tried
facing him down for thirty seconds, until the absurdity of the whole
situation overcame me. I gulped down a mouthful of saliva (I've
tasted better) and groped for something random to ask him: Why're
they taking so long? The even skinnier guy relaxed: They'll be ages
yet, he said. He looked like a malnourished, overworked old peasant, nothing like a big city mafioso type. Is the old gentleman your

grandfather? I asked. He nodded. Are you three brothers? I then asked. He nodded again, but slightly reluctantly, as if he wasn't keen on answering any more of my questions. But still I plowed on: Is Mr. Black the eldest? I wanted to know. The even skinnier guy didn't nod. What's it to you? he said after a pause. Nothing, I said, just making conversation. The even skinnier guy eyed me suspiciously, then mumbled, like he had a steamed bun in his mouth, I'm the eldest. He then ambled back to the other side of the entrance and sat down on the concrete pillar (the purpose of whose existence remained unclear) that I'd just been parked on.

Finally, at around eleven a.m., the skinny guy reemerged from the hospital with the other two. I was about to faint with hunger, as I hadn't had breakfast that morning—I would have gotten a bowl of noodles or something at a snack stall nearby while I was waiting, but I didn't have a cent on me. The skinny guy handed two big plastic bags containing all sorts of medicines to the even skinnier guy to hold, then walked over to me, clutching a great handful of receipts. Suddenly he stopped and swiveled back again, beckoning at me to follow him. He walked over to a fruit stall, borrowed a calculator from the one-legged stall holder, and passed it to me: Add it up for yourself, he said. Then he ceremoniously presented the receipts one by one to me: X-ray, CT scan, liver function, blood type. . . . What the fuck, I couldn't stop myself saying, your granddad applying to be an astronaut or something? Taking no notice, the skinny guy then set about declaiming his list of drugs: Precious Kidney, Yellow Bile Essence, ginseng, Golden Brain. . . . I forced out a laugh: My mistake—it's immortality, not space travel your granddad's into. I handed the calculator back to the skinny guy, declining to do any more calculations. Any case, he told me, comes to the same whether you count it or not. I've added it all up, 781 *yuan* and 56 cents. We'll keep the change, as we've got to come back for the result of the checkup tomorrow and we'll need it for the bus fare. Go on, add it all up, why not? No thanks, I said to him, but you'll let me go now, right? The skinny guy grinned at me: Hey, don't put it like that, makes it sound like we forced you into this. Cheer up, this is for you. He stuffed the receipts in my face, pretending to look all sympathetic. I pushed his hand away: What the hell're you giving me these for? I said. They're receipts, the skinny guy said. This is where I really lost it. I screwed up my courage and yelled (with heroic defiance, I thought): Fuck your receipts! at him. Once I'd gotten this out of my system, I headed straight for my bike. After standing there stunned for a moment or two, the skinny guy started after me. Let it go, the even skinnier guy pulled him back. Come on, it's getting late.

Tell the truth, inside I was still pretty afraid my outburst would bring me new trouble. I pushed my bike out from behind the telephone booth, but it was only when I saw the three of them walking over to the opposite side of the road that I relaxed. Thank fuck, the whole thing was at an end. Just then, though, I heard the fruit stall holder shout at the three of them as they walked off. He'd gotten so worked up about something that he was trying to lever himself wobbily out of the wheelchair using his walking stick. Turning around to look, the skinny guy remembered he was still holding the stall holder's calculator, so he went back to return it to him. The stall holder must have said something back to him, because the two of them started arguing. I couldn't catch what they were actually arguing about, but after a few exchanges, the skinny guy grabbed a huge Tangshan pear from the stall and hurled it at the ground. The stall holder sat up straight in his wheelchair and suddenly jabbed his walking stick out from beneath the stall in a well-concealed maneuver that got the skinny guy right between the legs. He collapsed forward, grabbing at his crotch. Not sure what had happened, the even skinnier guy ran over there with the plastic bags, yelping, What's going on? Speech was still beyond the skinny guy. So the even skinnier guy transferred both plastic bags to his left hand and gripped the stall holder by the scruff of his neck with his right. What's going on? he demanded. Without further warning, a blade suddenly flicked up out of the stall holder's fist. Next thing I saw was him somehow manage to leap unsupported out of his chair and take a slice at the neck of the even skinnier guy, who didn't quite dodge back in time, and swipe at his ear. Now badly overstretched, the stall holder toppled right over, bringing the stall down with him, apples, pears, melons, kiwis, all rolling around together on the ground. Seeing the way things were going, the old man shrugged his jacket off, charged over, picked up the stall holder's crutch, and smashed it down onto his left shoulder, knocking the knife out of his left hand. The one-legged stall holder screamed, rolled onto the road, and started crawling desperately away like a stung lizard, all hope of climbing back into his wheelchair way beyond him. Now the skinny guy was back up on his feet, the three of them had the stall holder surrounded and launched into a frenzy of kicks that soon had their victim howling in agony. The even skinnier guy concentrated his efforts on the stall holder's face, transforming it, in no time at all, into a fleshy, bloody blur. On and on the even skinnier guy went, while his own lacerated left ear—holding together only at the very base of the lobe—flapped backward and forward with every one of his movements, spouting blood all over his neck and left shoulder. Despite the massive kicking he was getting, the stall holder managed initially to keep shouting abuse back at his aggressors, but soon all he could do was beg for mercy. The old man and the skinny guy were the first to leave off, but the even skinnier guy wouldn't stop, ignoring the stall holder's yelps and wails. In the end, the skinny guy had to pull his elder brother, now completely out of control, away. Kneel three times to our granddad here, the skinny guy offered the stall holder, and we'll let you live—today. The stall holder covered his head with both hands, muttering something to himself. Y'hear? the skinny guy stepped forward to direct another kick at the stall holder's belly. Nervously relaxing his arms from around his head, the stall holder edged himself up to a sitting position with his back against a fruit box, looked at the three men standing opposite him, shifted his one decent leg over, tilted his body forward, propped both hands on the ground, and knelt three times to them. Fucking useless, the skinny guy snapped, keep your back straight! Once the stall holder released his hands off the ground, his body slid over to one side. You're fucking useless, the skinny guy repeated, do it again! Some old woman keeping a surreptitious eye on proceedings picked up a big apple and popped it into a wide-necked Thermos, followed, in a short while, by a kiwi and, another little while later, by a handful of lychees, before she finally stepped forward and tugged at the skinny guy's clothes: Give him a break, she said, how can he kneel, with one leg? But the skinny guy took no notice. The stall holder tried once more, and fell over once more. Still clutching his ear, the even skinnier guy darted forward again and delivered another savage volley of kicks: Stop playing dead, you fucking cripple! he screamed. Kneel! Kneel! Kneel!

I'd seen more than enough, so pushed my bike unsteadily over the road, got on, and pedaled desperately away, not stopping until I was back in my room. That was the quickest I'd ever made it up Big Xie Hill in my entire life, quicker even than I'd ever ridden down it. Once back in my room, I curled up into a ball and crammed packet after packet of instant noodles into my mouth until, by evening, I'd finally calmed down. Hao Qiang came back around eleven o'clock, with a girl in tow who, despite the heavy lipstick slapped onto her baby face, I guessed wasn't yet out of high school. This would usually be my cue to make myself scarce, to give him some personal space, but that day I just sat there, refusing to move. Hao Qiang had no choice but to take the girl elsewhere. He was back within the half hour, looking as if he'd managed to solve his little difficulty somehow, and now he was no longer waiting for anything, he was much more tractable. His hands'd been tied this morning, he said, no one around here wanted to pick a fight with Mr. Black and his family, not because they were afraid, but because it just wasn't worth it; who in their right mind messed with cinder scavengers? This term, "cinder scavengers," I'd heard plenty of times but had never bothered inquiring into, so I asked him what it meant. Hao Qiang said that quite a lot of the people from around here had moved from nearby Subei before the Communists took over in '49, scavenging coal cinders along the railway tracks. After a while, they reckoned they could scrape by here, so they stayed. Now, of course, there were no coal cinders to be scavenged, but they had other ways and means of picking up bits of money—everyone has to get by somehow, right? Long as you give them money they won't give you any grief, they didn't treat you like that fruit seller cripple, stabbing them for no good reason like that, you're all right, aren't you? They didn't touch a hair on your head. Now I'm from Subei myself, so listening to what Hao Qiang had to say didn't make me feel too great, but I kept my feelings to myself. When I told him about the business with the fruit stall holder, shivers still ran down my spine. Forget about it, Hao Qiang told me, ten to one the stall holder was a cinder scavenger himself, only cinder scavengers pick fights with other cinder scavengers, you can't stop a dog-eats-dog fight, don't think about it, go to sleep. But I tossed and turned, unable to sleep: those 800 *yuan* still stuck in my throat. I was up and down all night, either for a drink of water or for a piss, annoying the hell out of my roommate: You still thinking about that 800 *yuan*? he eventually asked from out of the darkness. Who me? No way, I immediately replied, furious that he'd asked me something like that. And, that he'd hit the nail on the head. I thought back over my own path in life, how I'd left Subei behind, chugging along the railway line to study in Nanjing, not all that different from cinder scavengers. Fuck, I was a cinder scavenger myself.

However much Hao Qiang insisted this unfortunate incident was all behind me, I had a premonition there was more to come. Just to be on the safe side, I avoided Big Xie Hill over the next few days, and took a detour around by the district Party Committee building. I also used a side gate into the electrical factory, instead of the main entrance. As a result of all these detours, the proprietor of Mr. Black's Pot-Roast Goose made a personal visit to my room one evening a week later. As soon as Hao Qiang opened the door, he made this panicked yelping sound and just stood there, petrified. I was sitting on my bed reading at the time, wrapped in my quilt, and assumed it was some big cheese from the factory. In fact, Mr. Black looked and acted more convincingly like the factory management than the genuine article did, what with the document folder tucked under his arm and the circuit he paced around the room as soon as he came in. Out you go, he told Hao Qiang. Hao Qiang, who'd been frozen to the spot all this while, finally came to, scooped up his jacket, and slipped out the door quick as he could. Wait a second, Mr. Black called him back. That thing I gave you, you still got it here? Yes, it's here, Hao Qiang whispered back, afraid I'd hear. Mr. Black muttered something to himself, then said, Let's see it. Deeply embarrassed, Hao Qiang walked over to his bed, lay down on his front, and hauled a cardboard box out from under the bed. He then took out a battered old pair of rust-speckled scissors used for cutting goose guts and waved them in Mr. Black's direction. Mr. Black nodded his head: Off you go then, he said. I was observing all this with quizzical surprise, but Hao Qiang headed out the door, eyes down and without a single look in my direction, carefully shutting the door behind him. Inside the quilt, my legs had started trembling uncontrollably. It occurred to me that huddling on the bed was too passive a stance, and I started making movements to throw open the quilt. Mr. Black gestured at me to stop, walked over, covered me up again, then sat down on the side of the bed. He tapped his knees with his document folder: Got any cigarettes? he asked. Just smoked my last one, I said. After rummaging around for ages in the inner pocket of his suit, he produced a cigarette and lit it. I got the feeling Mr. Black didn't want me to know what brand of cigarette he smoked; from the first puff he exhaled I could smell it was the most inferior kind of blended tobacco. Mr. Black cleared his throat: So then, my granddad's got the results of his checkup back, there's a black spot about so big in his stomach, near the bowel. The doctor's afraid it's a tumor, he'll need to do another examination before he can say for sure, but Granddad won't agree, says there's no way he's going back into the hospital; you know what he's like. Is his shoulder all right? I interrupted nervously. Mr. Black closed his eyes, took two deep draws on his cigarette, and ignored me. He opened his folder and spread it out in front of me: Have a look at the diagnosis for yourself, expect you'll make more sense of it than me. I flipped through, then looked up: How come there's no X-ray of his shoulder? Why d'you keep going on about his shoulder? Mr. Black asked, glaring at me. We're talking about a tumor here. In the stomach. You'd best get your granddad checked out, I said to him, let's hope it's not malignant. Mr. Black bowed his head and looked tragic. After a pause, he shook his head and sighed: We don't need a doctor to tell us the score. Last few days, my granddad's wasted away to nothing, like his face's been ironed flat, he can't keep anything down. Well, what're you waiting for then? I said. Get him into the hospital right away. Mr. Black nodded his head: That's all very well, he said, but where's the money going to come from? There's no state health care, we've no medical insurance, granddad doesn't have a cent to his name, how're we going to pay for a doctor? At this point, Mr. Black gave me a good, hard, direct look. Of course I understood what he meant. I had a think, leaned back, and pointed around at the room. Look, I began, this is everything I own—Cut the crap! Mr. Black interrupted, don't try getting out of this, now it's gotten this serious. If you hadn't run into Granddad, he would never've gone to the hospital; if he hadn't gone to the hospital, he wouldn't be in this mess now. These are my terms: give us 3,000 *yuan* and the whole thing's out of your hands, whether Granddad lives or dies. Soon as I heard the words "3,000 *yuan*," I knew a brief moment of madness. Now *you* be reasonable! I screamed, banging my head against the wall like a lunatic. Did *I* ask *you* to be reasonable today? he said. I don't think so. So stop changing the subject.

As he was starting out the door, Mr. Black restated his terms to me: I'll give you a week, all right, get 3,000 *yuan* to my restaurant, not a cent less, or I'll personally pot-roast you. Soon as he was gone, Hao Qiang tiptoed back in. After giving me a quick once-over, he opened the quilt, felt my legs, and stuck his hand in my crotch: That's funny, he said to himself, all present and correct. He was trying to get a laugh out of me, but I told him to fuck off and leave me alone. What's your problem? he shouted back at me, feeling rather aggrieved by his frosty reception. Bet you didn't tell *him* to fuck off, did you? We'd never fallen out, not in years of sharing a room, but right then I must admit I felt an overpowering urge to rip his head off. How come Mr. Black knows where I live? I wanted to know. Hao Qiang shook his head at me and refused to give an answer, apart from a click of the tongue. After a while, he walked over to his own bed, bent down, took out that pair of scissors from the cardboard box, and threw it onto the concrete floor in front of me. See for yourself, he said. I took another look, but they still looked like a pretty unexceptional pair of battered old scissors. But once Hao Qiang had told me the history behind them, I started to see them in a rather different light. The year before, Hao Qiang (who was, remember, quite a ladies' man) had gotten very heavily involved with a married woman called Chen Xiaoyun. They were always off dancing together, and even went on vacation to Yellow Mountain. He actually introduced us and asked what I thought of her: Great, I said, though her ass is a bit flat. Time and again their trysts drove me out of house and home, had me wandering through the streets like a destitute. Since Chen Xiaoyun's husband couldn't control Chen Xiaoyun himself, he had no choice but to pay Mr. Black to scare Hao Qiang. First of all, Mr. Black beat him up pretty seriously; then he delivered this pair of scissors with the message, Any more funny business with Chen Xiaoyun and you'd best cut your dick off yourself; leave the job to me and I'll have your balls too. I can bear witness to the fact that Hao Qiang made a totally clean break with Chen Xiaoyun; it was as if they'd been snipped apart by those scissors. I couldn't understand it at the time: Where's that Xiaoyun, the one with the flat ass, gone? I think is how I delicately put it to my roommate. Hao Qiang angrily kicked the scissors over into a corner. And the worst of it, he said, is I don't even dare throw the scissors away, because Mr. Black warned me, I have to keep a close eye on them, and if I don't produce them whenever we meet, he'll personally pot-roast me. I smiled at Hao Qiang: People destined for pot-roast should look out for each other, I said. To my surprise, Hao Qiang turned deeply serious: What're you smirking about? Everyone around here's terrified of Mr. Black! He's not joking, you know. Why d'you think his pot roasts taste so good? It's no accident!

I started to feel a little unwell, because that very evening I'd had half a pot-roasted goose for my dinner. After asking me for details, Hao Qiang reckoned the old man's tumor was probably made up, just another money-making scam. But he still urged me to pay, even if I destroyed myself financially in the process; it was, after all, only 3,000 *yuan*. I leaped up and told him straight: I'd given boiler servicing some of the best years of my life and never even got near having so much money. He frowned: What does money matter, he argued, long as you live to fight another day? That time last year, before Mr. Black actually did anything to me, he told me, I'll accept money, you know: I mean, sure, he said, you're going to get a beating today, but I'll give you the choice, d'you want to be dead or alive at the end of it? Alive, of course, I said. Well then, Mr. Black said, cough up 2,000. I only had a few hundred on me, but I whipped off my necklace and watch and gave them to him as well. You saw the results for yourself: a few surface wounds, sure, but I was fine once I'd slapped on a bit of mercurochrome. Your family's loaded, I said to Hao Qiang, 2,000 *yuan*'s nothing to them. I don't have that kind of money. You've got the wrong attitude, he said, it's not about money. You're too fucking stubborn, that's your problem, you need to get a bit of perspective. Take me, for example: sure, I was 2,000 *yuan* down by the end of it, but I must have screwed Chen Xiaoyun at least 200 times, which works out on average only 10 *yuan* a time. Cheap at the price, I figure. So get a grip. What do you mean, get a grip? I said to him. I haven't screwed that old bastard with the tumor. He stamped his foot in irritation: You're so fucking unimaginative! All right, he suggested, how about we call it your 3,000-*yuan* donation to Help the Aged?

However hard Hao Qiang tried to persuade me, I just couldn't cross this 3,000-*yuan* threshold. I was already in agonies after the tragic loss of 800—another 3,000 would break my heart. The next few days passed as follows: during each sleepless night spent bathed in cold sweat, things would start to look a bit clearer. An egg has no good reason to run into a stone, a head has no business being split open like a watermelon. Money is just an external, let it go. So every tormented night I'd decide to go and borrow the money the next day, deliver it to Mr. Black, and get myself half a pot-roasted goose while I was at it. But every morning as the sun rose, I'd get some fire in my belly, from God knows where: fucking hell (I'd think), he was just a pot roaster, right? What's so scary about that? Screw the lot of them, a life lived in fear, et cetera, et cetera. Then, as the day dragged by, my brain would go into shock mode, able only to perform a few mechanical tasks (but as my work had never made anything but mechanical demands on me, the daily routine could continue entirely as normal). On the evening of the sixth day, Hao Qiang told me he was going back home to toast his baby nephew's hundredth day tomorrow, that he wouldn't be back that night. He took out 1,000 *yuan* from inside his leather jacket and threw it down on the table. This is a loan, from me to you, he said. I don't care whether you repay me, but you'll have to find the rest yourself. I found this all deeply moving: I'd always thought I only had a 500-*yuan* friendship with Hao Qiang; now it turned out I was worth a thousand to him. But I stuffed the money back in his pocket and told him I'd decided not to pay up. You mad? he asked. Don't you give a fuck about yourself—aren't you worth 3,000 *yuan*? That's another question altogether, I said. But I can't keep taking shit like this, it's bad for my sense of masculinity. It's a self-respect thing. Bollocks to masculinity, he said, I'm still leaving the money. Let's see how your self-respect's doing once your face's been ripped to shreds. I deliberately kept him arguing a good long time, to nail my own resolve. After finishing work on the seventh day, I had dinner in the cafeteria, had a wash in the factory baths, then cycled back home. Problems, I decided, were like pigeon shit: if they've decided to fall on your head, they'll fall on your head anyway, it's no good trying to dodge them, best get them over and done with as soon as possible. I stashed the 1,000 *yuan* Hao Qiang had left in a shoe I found under his bed, then opened the window and put both shoes out on the windowsill. In order to prevent the wind blowing them off, I weighed them down with a dumbbell. The iciness of the dumbbell against my hand woke me up, suddenly made me think: might Mr. Black put the other dumbbell to use on my skull? Considering this less than ideal, I took the other dumbbell, placed it on the windowsill, then shut the window tight and closed the curtains, which normally only got drawn when activities of a sexual nature were ongoing.

Eleven o'clock that evening: still no sign of Mr. Black. I was tensing up at every movement along the corridor; it was like being in love for the first time all over again—the physical, mental exhaustion of anticipation. But Mr. Black stood me up. The funny thing is, I had no problems falling asleep that night, I slept like a log, maybe because I was so tired. Early the next morning, Hao Qiang rushed back over, expecting to go shroud shopping, but ended up just waking me for work. When I opened my eyes, the first thing I saw was Hao Qiang, eyes blood-shot, hair like a bird's nest. You'd have thought he was the one in the shit, not me. Anyway, a whole week went by, but still Mr. Black didn't show—it looked like I was in the clear. Hold the celebrations, Hao Qiang said, let's wait another week. Another week passed, and still no Mr. Black. As I gradually got used to all this waiting, the whole pro-cess became far more relaxed. What the hell's going on? Hao Qiang wondered. Maybe Mr. Black's got a sense of humor, after all. It's not a question of humor, I told him, it's a question of right standing up to wrong. If you don't play ball with him, nothing he can do.

A few days after this, a Wednesday it was, I remember, I was ped-aling asthmatically up Big Xie Hill as usual on my way home from work. My work unit happened to have distributed toilet paper that day, forty rolls per employee, as if we ate the stuff three times a day. Twenty of them I stuffed into my tool locker, the other twenty I or-ganized into two bundles of ten each, stuck one on the back seat, the other on my handlebars, and set off back home with them. I took in the view as I cycled along, analogizing away: Big Xie Hill was a river of two-wheeled vehicles flowing upstream, crowned by a foaming crest of Pure Refinement Toilet Paper (the brand favored by my fac-tory), with a few eccentrically shaped pebbles washed up on one side of the bank. And that's where I choked on my analogy. The skinny guy, the even skinnier guy, and Mr. Black were all lined up by the noodle restaurant, dressed unusually somberly, with black mourning bands tied around their right arms. The even skinnier guy stood in the middle, the tallest, with white gauze wrapped around his head, like a soul-summoning prayer flag mounted on a pole. Though they were all facing the road, they didn't seem to be focused on anything except introspection. None of the pedestrians who passed by them failed to be affected by their air of solemnity. Seized by a sudden desire to put this whole business behind me, I hurriedly dismounted, catch-ing my leg on the toilet paper and almost toppling right over with the bike as I did so. Without any real consciousness of what I was doing, I pushed the bike over to where they were and stopped. None of them said anything, as if they hadn't noticed my presence. After a good long pause, a red-eyed Mr. Black sniffed and bowed his head, still without a word. I sensed the even skinnier guy finally looking at me, the distracted expression in his eyes slowly gaining focus, like two blunt nails being sharpened. Eventually, I lost my nerve and broke eye contact. Your days are numbered, he pronounced. Once our mourning period's over, you're pot roast. Don't forget: seven times seven, forty-nine days you've got, we've done four already, another forty-five to go. Enjoy. The three of them then headed down the hill. After a few steps, the skinny guy turned back and heaved ten toilet paper rolls off my bike: You won't be needing all these, he said.

Five nights I didn't sleep, just stared up at the ceiling contemplating the nightmare I'd woken up into. Hao Qiang didn't mince his words: I told you way back, but you wouldn't listen! Now what're you going to do? You're just too fucking stubborn, that's your problem. Hao Qiang, who normally never had any trouble dropping off, joined me in my sleeplessness, tormented by sharing a room with the living dead. His own terror alleviated my own a bit, as the need to comfort him gave me something to do: Don't panic, I said, maybe things aren't as bad as all that. When we were relatively compos mentis, we'd discuss ways of dealing with the situation. Plan A: go public, ask our work unit or the police for help. Hao Qiang was immediately down on this idea; the authorities were never much use around here, he said, they might be able to help you once, but they couldn't help you your whole life. Anyway, it would just make everything worse, because Mr. Black hated the Public Security Bureau. Plan B: fight fire with fire, get a triad boss on our side. Although Mr. Black was pretty powerful around here, he still wasn't quite the hardest tiger in the concrete jungle. Get someone even harder than him to mediate, like Princess from Yangzhuang, or Old Pimple from the phosphate factory. This plan, of course, required money. But it was a double-edged sword: anyone who'd had dealings with the triads would never be able to shake them off. Plan C: submit completely. Give Mr. Black the money quick as you can and grovel like there's no tomorrow. Plan D, go into hiding for a while or leave the area for good. But you can't go, Hao Qiang grabbed my hand, if you go I'll be stuck. When I reassured him I wasn't going anywhere, Hao Qiang produced the 1,000 *yuan* I'd returned to him a few weeks ago. Totally done for by this point, I followed his suggestion to the letter. Swallowing my pride and scribbling IOUs as I went, I borrowed money from six of my less objectionable colleagues, cobbling together a round 2,000. Then, in accordance with local custom, I wrapped the 3,000 in red paper, bought a set of quilt covers as a funeral gift, and together with Hao Qiang, went looking for Mr. Black. But halfway there, I started to have second thoughts: I might as well keep the money and die, because if I handed it over, it meant I wasn't worth 3,000 fucking *yuan* anyway. After a violent argument, Hao Qiang ended up having to grab the money and quilt covers off me and go on alone. About nine o'clock that evening he despondently came home, threw the red packet on the table, then sat numbly down on the bed, weeping with his head in his hands. I'm not in tears yet, I shouted at him, so what business have you got crying? Mr. Black took the covers, Hao Qiang said, but he threw the money onto the road, said it's not about the money anymore, said he'd made a vow to his granddad's spirit tablet. . . .

When I decided to adopt Plan E, I still had a whole month to go before the day of my death: 30 days—720 hours. Plan E was, in short, to wait for death. Though I'd made this decision, I was in no great hurry to return the 3,000 *yuan*, as I still had vague hopes of using the money to get me out of trouble. Hao Qiang insisted I use it to approach Princess from Yangzhuang. Princess was, in fact, a man: fine-featured, quite feminine in appearance, and not particularly tall, but utterly ruthless. People said he'd made his pile peddling flour; now he threw his money all over the place—Yangzhuang's biggest, most impressive building, Haitian Hotel, belonged to him. Someone from outside Yangzhuang bringing him a piffling 3,000, he might not even bother to meet. Anyway, my heart wasn't in it. So we started arguing and ended up having a falling out. I'm staying out of this now, Hao Qiang said. If you're in the shit, learn to swim. I just gave the 1,000 *yuan* back to him without another word. A few days later, Hao Qiang moved back in with his parents, while I headed off to work every day and kept up an outward show of normality. Except for my new habit of heading to the bathhouse after work and soaking for several hours. The plan was to soothe my nerves, but all I ended up with was a droopy scrotum. Even if I lived to 100, I thought, things would go on just the same. Going to work, coming home from work, retiring when I can't work anymore—the sooner this kind of a life finishes, the better. One afternoon, when Xiao Qi and I were left alone together in the staff room, she suddenly asked, What's on your mind? I glanced at her: Nothing, I said. What d'you mean, nothing, I've been watching you for days now, you look like you've been dragged out of the morgue. Come on, what's up? Nothing, I repeated. Once Xiao Qi's curiosity about something was up, she was unstoppable. As Hao Qiang sometimes observed, no wonder she got divorced. There was no escape for me now, so I tried fobbing her off: Nothing—nothing— I'm just in love, that's all. All this did was stir her up even more. Who is it? She was completely out of control now. Go on, tell me, who is it? She kept on shaking my arm, would have stuck her hand down my gullet to dig it out of me if she hadn't been holding a wrench. I masterfully controlled my intense irritation: Why you, of course, I told her. Staring, dumbstruck, at me, she took her hand off my arm: Think you're funny, don't you? she said, turning furiously away. It's no joke, I said to her, it's true. By this point, I'd amazed even myself. She gave me another long, hard stare: No way, absolutely no way. She shook her head. I'm much older than you, and divorced, and I've got a kid, while you, you've got a degree, a— None of that matters, I interrupted her, as if possessed by the devil himself. Sitting down numbly on the chair opposite me, she bent over and bit her nails. A dead quiet fell over the staff room. After a while, she lifted her head and looked straight at me, her eyes moistening as soon as she began to speak. If you're joking, she said, you deserve to rot in hell. This brought me back to my senses almost immediately, but by then I'd maneuverd myself into a corner. I did the only thing I could: nod.

Things between me and Xiao Qi developed at breakneck speed, too fast for anyone to slow them down. The news bubbled away all

over the factory. Xiao Qi was totally transformed, radiant and ener-
gized, that sour pumpkin face of hers no longer so sour. And because
of her, my relations with colleagues, especially with colleagues of
around forty, underwent a subtle change. Once Xiao Qi, her son, and
I took to strolling around the old Confucian temple of a Sunday, I
realized I really had no idea how to finish the thing. Feeling I had to
do something, I remembered I hadn't used this year's vacation allow-
ance up yet and immediately arranged for home leave. Xiao Qi sensed
something was up, but didn't do anything to stop me. When are you
leaving? she asked me. First thing tomorrow, I said. D'you want me
to see you off? she offered. Don't worry, I said, you've got a kid to
look after, your life's difficult enough already. After a brief pause, she
asked, D'you want me to buy anything to take back for your parents?
No, no, I quickly said, thanks, but no. She fell silent, as if a cloud had
settled over her, as if something had been spelled out loud and clear.
I returned the 2,000 *yuan* I'd borrowed, ripped up the IOUs, and left
work. But instead of going to the bus station, I headed for the whole-
sale market, where I bought an entire box of instant noodles, then
went into hiding in my room. I only got one home leave a year, so
these brief periods when I wasn't obliged to labor up the hill to work
every day were very precious to me—I never wasted them. As I was
due 21 days' leave, it struck me as rather a shame I only had 13 days
to live. I chewed on my instant noodles as slowly as possible, keeping
absolutely still, leaving the light off until evening, waiting for my colleagues to go to work before venturing out to the washroom or going
downstairs for a Thermos of hot water. Most of the time I spent lying
on my bed; I used my foot basin to piss in. I wasn't drinking much
water, but I pissed a lot. At the beginning, I found time every day to
go empty it, but that stopped after a while. The room must reek, I
thought, but as I was inside all the time, I couldn't smell anything.
One night, at three or four in the morning I woke up, turned on the
newspaper-covered lamp by my bed, and sat up, gazing at that basin
full of urine, at its mirrorlike surface, gleaming under the radiant orange glow of the lamp like a river at sunset. Time, I felt, had stood
still. I suddenly wondered whether I ought to go back home for a few

days to see my parents. The idea flashed across my mind only briefly, but long enough to fill my eyes with burning tears.

Soon only three days remained. I had long lost the ability to distinguish between the taste of instant noodles and the smell of piss; all I knew was that a combination of the two flavored the air I breathed every day. At noon, I went downstairs and had a big feed at a little restaurant near the dormitory compound, then went for a long bike ride. After so many days spent inside, my skin prickled to feel the sun's rays on it again. When I passed by a building site, I stopped, found a piece of steel pipe half a yard long, and wedged it under the back seat of my bike. I cycled straight through the 45000 Agricultural Market toward Mr. Black's Pot-Roast Goose. There was no one there except a fat old woman wrapped in an apron, standing in front of the chopping board peeling something; three or four customers hovered in the doorway. I threw my bike down on the ground, grabbed the steel pipe with both hands, rushed in, and began wildly smashing around with both eyes shut. All I heard was a succession of crashes and terrified screams. When I opened my eyes, I found nothing much left to destroy: the floor was covered in shards of broken glass and cold stewed meat, and the fat old woman had disappeared somewhere. Blood was pouring down the steel pipe from a deep cut between my right thumb and index finger. I sighed deeply, kicked in the glass in the door, then sat down. A growing crowd of spectators was gathering, the ones at the back trying to jostle forward, the ones at the front pushing backward, unwilling to get too close to me. I looked down at my trembling hands to avoid making eye contact with any of them. I kept the pipe to hand, ready to knock senseless anyone who made a false move at me, waiting to get knocked out myself.

AH, XIAO XIE

THE POWER PLANT our factory was building was originally projected to cost a billion *yuan*, but at the point my story begins, 1.5 billion had already been invested, and no one seemed to think there'd be much change out of at least another several hundred million before the whole thing was done. One reason for the runaway budget was that the basic setup for the plant had been bought from Russia before 1991; only about half the goods had found their way over the border into China when the Soviet Union collapsed. The problem now, though, was too much, not too little money: as the whole thing was a national showcase engineering project, cash was always coming in from somewhere. Because it was so easy to get investment, the more money the government hurled at it, the more creative the management got at asking for more. Once the plant started working, their reasoning went, any debts would be cleared by the profits from the electricity generated.

The only task left to us, the workers and future masters of this power plant, was to complete our technical training. Our factory manager told us 3 million had been set aside for this in the original budget, but 5 had already been spent, and probably another 3 or 4 were still needed. Peanuts, admittedly, compared to the 1.5 billion thrown into the plant itself, but it was a lot of money for a glorified boiler serviceman and his colleagues to think about. By this point, we'd already been training for 4 years at various thermal power plants—it was like graduating from college, then being told, Hey, have another 4 years to piss away. The only problem was, having nothing to do was finally starting to get boring. A colleague of mine, a computer programmer, decided he'd had enough and resigned. Xie Weigang was his name: we graduated the same year, from the same university, just from different departments. Now you may find this surprising, but computers are different from boilers. Every day, in computers, someone, somewhere does something new; they're never static, they're always twitching and responding, like some kind of deranged, hypersensitized nerve system. So I suppose that if you work with computers, it helps to be a deranged neurotic yourself; by that logic, Xie Weigang was a born code monkey. Designing computer software is a young man's game; having stagnated for 4 years after graduating, Xie could see his prime hurtling past him—he wanted out before the factory used him all up.

But for some reason, the factory bosses took his resignation as a personal insult and refused point-blank to accept it. The head of the personnel department had something wrong with his spine that meant when he stood up, he was always leaning to one side. He looked fairly normal sitting down, but the moment he got up and started walking, you noticed it—he listed along like an exhausted glider. But somehow, the minute he saw Xie approach from any direction, at any distance, he managed to take off. Xie's only remaining hope was to get advice from the Municipal Human Resources Exchange Center. But they told him they couldn't do a thing, because it was government policy to protect national showcase projects, to prevent the outflow of human resources. Xie tried to get around them all by pulling a huge, extended sickie. Luckily for him, he had a pretext in that he really did have something wrong with his liver, something to do with his trans-animase index being abnormally high—or so he said. Although the factory was apparently disastrous for his liver, it seemed to thrive in the Taiwanese computer company where Xie started working on the side. The factory very soon got wind of his new job and ordered Xie Weigang back to the factory hospital for some more examinations. I felt quite sorry for him, having to have all those blood tests. The few times I saw him, he was always at the food stall by the factory gate, face down in a bowl of noodles and an enormous oily plate of sliced pig's head—someone had told him intensive lard consumption was a surefire way to wreck your liver performance. I was worried about him—things must have been tough: endless grease, lies and blood tests at the factory, then long hours working at the new job. He was not what you'd call an impressive physical specimen in the first place: stick-thin, mouth full of skewed fangs, Adam's apple sticking out a mile, glasses that had one earpiece stuck on with first-aid tape, cunning glint to his eyes, filthy fingernails—pretty much your standard computer-genius-on-the-brink look.

Everyone around the factory called him Xiao Xie, *xiao* being a Chinese diminutive, meaning little or young, that you tucked in front of a surname, in an affectionate kind of way. I don't know how it started, but somehow we all reached a spontaneous consensus that this was the name for him. It slipped beautifully easily out of the mouth: the *x* like a sh with extra hiss, *iao* like yow, *ie* like yeh—ssh-yow ssh-yeh—you just let the jaw hang and the job was done. Say it and enjoy it: Xiao-xie, Xiao-xie, ssh-yow ssh-yeh, ssh-yow ssh-yeh. And somehow the sibilant wispiness of these sounds meshed peculiarly perfectly with Xie Weigang's physical appearance and personality. Some people are just born to be called Xiao Xie. His real name, Xie Weigang—Xie the mighty and indomitable—was nothing like him at all; it was too big, too pompous. To the best of my knowledge, Xie Weigang also answered to three other names: Weigang, Liver, and Se-ba-C-ba. The first two, being his given name and his problematic organ, are fairly self-explanatory. The third probably needs a quick glossing, being the phonetic Chinese transliteration of the Russian word for thank you, *spasibo*, which in turn was the Russian translation of *xie* ("thank you" in Chinese). Though it was a bit harder to say, being foreign, it enjoyed a brief currency, together with the other two. But in the end, Xiao Xie beat them all in the popularity stakes.

I had another colleague, called Wang Yalin, who, now I think about it, also graduated from the same university as me, though he'd taken his degree at evening classes. I had nothing much against him and his big white moon face, only that he tended to keep you talking just a bit longer than was interesting. He'd gotten his job here through personal connections: whenever one of the factory management saw him, they'd bow, ever so slightly. I never worked out what the nature of these precious connections was, but they must have been fucking amazing. Not long after they began excavating Xiao Xie's liver, Wang suddenly left to start another job: no warning, he just said he was going and off he went. Almost everyone I knew wanted out: because we were still being trained, because our nonexistent power plant wasn't generating any profits, and because our salaries had been squashed as low as was humanly possible—most of us were getting several hundred *yuan* less per month than our contemporaries who'd graduated at exactly the same time but who had jobs elsewhere. For those trying to scrape together the money to get married, our salaries were a serious problem. It was a clash of calculating cultures: the municipal government thought in hundred millions, the factory manager in millions, while we ordinary workers measured our profits and losses in paltry hundreds. Soon enough, the entire factory workforce was a seething mass of discontent. And another thing: if building work had kept to the original schedule, the power plant would have become the nation's very first supercritical unit, an accolade that might have kept the alpha males among us quiet, but what with everything getting so behind, we'd been beaten by plants in Shanghai and Hebei, both fitted out with heavy industrial products made by top Japanese and Swiss manufacturers. When we went to visit them, we all thought we'd died and gone to thermal energy heaven. Our shaky self-esteem just about held together after the first trip: okay, our plant was behind schedule, okay, it was slow and heavy and brutish, but it had a certain safe, nostalgic appeal as a Soviet period piece. But on the way back from the second visit, group morale started to collapse: we felt like we were caught in an industrial time warp, back where the West had been in the early 1950s, left behind in the dust years before we'd even generated a single spark of electricity. What was the point? Why go on? The whole venture had obviously been one big mistake from the very beginning, and now we were all stuck. When Xiao Xie heard about Wang Yalin leaving, he rushed back to the factory from wherever he'd been, to have another try at persuading the factory bosses to accept his resignation. A lot of people encouraged him to really go for it, giving him all the gossip there was about the factory manager, in case, presumably, it came to blackmail. One rumor, for example, had it that the manager was a repressed homosexual, that he'd promote anyone who buggered him. This, I suppose you could say, was one possible route through, or up, the back door. I admit the manager did have a bit of a, you know, look about him, but I still couldn't quite believe he was that way inclined. Xiao Xie, however, made careful mental note, as though it were gospel truth, and formulated his plan of attack accordingly. The route to the manager was through the director of office staff, but the moment he saw Xie Weigang approach, quick as a flash he'd say the manager was away on business. So Xiao Xie implemented Plan B: for three whole days he draped himself over the men's toilets across the corridor from the manager's office, until the manager, and an opportunity, finally presented themselves. The moment he got his belt undone, Xiao Xie lunged with such precipitation, it was reported, that the manager screamed out in terror. The whole thing did Xiao Xie no good at all; in fact, that very day, the factory canceled his sick leave, told him to come back and report for work, and issued a serious disciplining order. Things being now as they were, we all reckoned Xiao Xie should just go AWOL and force the factory to fire him. Instead, bizarrely, Xiao Xie obeyed and docilely went back to training with the rest of us, albeit with a martyred look on his face. Xiao Xie, we all agreed, had made his own bed.

After work, I spent most of my time in my room, pottering about or sleeping. Like most things our factory tried to build, the unmarried accommodations hadn't been finished, so for people like me the management had rented some extra rooms in the dormitory block belonging to a chemical engineering company. We were supposed to be two to a room, but because I came out of the ballot as a single lot, I ended up being put with a guy who worked as a designer in the chemical engineering company, stuck on the fourth floor while all my co-workers were on the third. My roommate's name was Hao

Qiang: delicate almond-shaped eyes, high-bridged nose, tall, slim, fond of the ladies, always out dancing (at which, incidentally, he was very averagely talented). Basically, he was one of those people who discovers the joys of dancing quite late in life but becomes unstoppable once he has. All this meant he spent very little time at home, in the room. I couldn't believe my luck, having a roommate like him: girls often came looking for him when he wasn't there, and if I was in a good mood, I'd let them in, just to give them the once-in-a-lifetime opportunity to discover how much more charismatic I was than my roommate. This used to save me no end of time, and made me appreciate the virtues of staying in even more than I had in the first place. Of course, sometimes Hao Qiang would bring a girl back with him, which meant I had to go kick around the streets for a while. But it didn't happen that often, so he must have had other places besides our room he could use. After a while, I started to feel a little uneasy about the type of women who came knocking on our door—all of them young, married, and in heat. Sooner or later, I worried, Hao Qiang's taste in women was going to get him into trouble.

Xiao Xie was prickly as hell after the toilet debacle, and seemed to be continually falling out with people around him. His roommate, Xia Yuqing, who was from Wuhan but graduated from Xi'an Communications College in the northwest, in the same subject as me, was always sniping at Xiao Xie about chickening out of the whole resignation thing: no self-respecting dog, he said, goes back to its own vomit. Another favorite pastime of his was joking about Xiao Xie's name. Now, Chinese has a great many ideograms but not that many sounds, so one phonetic combination can be written in several different ways and mean several different things; aural understanding depends on context. The sound *xie*, apart from the rich comic possibilities offered by the pun on "thank you," had almost 40 other, alternative meanings, the most negative and derogatory of which Xia Yuqing delighted in seizing upon. Your surname, Xie, he'd ask, now would that be the *xie* meaning shriveled and limp, or the *xie* meaning premature ejaculation? Either way, guess it explains why you're such a loser. Pretty soon, Xiao Xie was ready to put Xia Yuqing to a slow, painful death, if only he'd dared: his roommate—who lifted weights—was approximately 99 percent muscle. To avoid any fatalities, I instead offered to swap rooms with him, a suggestion Xiao Xie gratefully accepted. The evening of the day after the move, Xiao Xie had fetched himself a Thermos of hot water for a bowl of instant noodles and a foot bath and was about to settle down with an English-language computer magazine when suddenly two men entered the room. Is that your shirt on the ground outside the building? they asked. Xiao Xie stepped into his slippers and went over to the window to look. Where'd you say it was? he asked, squinting out into the dusk. Without any further elaboration, the two of them lifted Xiao Xie up and threw him deftly out of the window.

I could never persuade myself to feel much affection for Xia Yuqing. From the moment we first met, I knew there was something not quite right about him, that he was the kind of person I'd never take to. But after I'd roomed with him for a while, we did manage to get along, and eventually, I suppose, we got more or less to be friends. Though I hadn't been at college with Xia Yuqing, I could tell what he'd been like around campus, what his family background was. The only exceptional thing about him was, I hazarded, that he'd been a Communist Party member as a student, but when I asked him about it, he denied it, eyes flashing. I did get accepted, he went on, a note of regret in his voice, in my fourth year, but the formal admission got held up because of the student protests, so all my application materials and references got transferred to the factory. 'Course, in the normal run of things, I would've been let in a year or two after starting here, but what with building the new plant, nothing's gotten done, so it's still in the pipeline. Because lately Xia Yuqing had lost interest in weight lifting, the quality of his physique was in visible decline, and his (once gloriously) bulging pectorals began to look more like plump, slack silicone implants than muscles. Unfortunately for me and other casual observers, however, he was still very attached to an old white vest of his, one with a low, baggy neck that left practically nothing of his chest area to the imagination. I must say, seeing him sashay about the room in that state of undress was very detrimental to my psychic tranquility. Please, I had to beg him, very seriously, please wear something else. Xia Yuqing glanced down at himself, smiled, and squeezed his two breasts together to produce a deep, still ravine of cleavage. That night, I couldn't sleep. When, finally, after tossing and turning for hours, I dropped off at dawn, I started having these bizarre dreams. I dreamed I was buggering Xia Yuqing really hard, when I suddenly realized it wasn't Xia Yuqing, it was someone else. Get up, I said, slapping the mystery man's ass a couple of times, get up and show me who the fuck you are. The man turned his face toward me and gave me the most melting smile. But I still couldn't think who he was. After wiping from his forehead the beads of sweat neatly lined up like snake spawn, he groped for a pair of glasses lying by his side. It was only then that I recognized our revered manager. After he'd gotten dressed, when he was about to leave, he left his name card on the table. Anything you need, anything at all, he said, just call me. I felt sick for several days afterward.

Any young man who wants to get ahead in a new factory has to have something about him, or he'll never find an opening. Xia Yuqing's chosen route to promotion was gambling and booze. Thanks to his love of mahjong and *baijiu*—the 55 percent liquor beloved of those who have no further use for their livers—Xia Yuqing quickly set about networking his way out of our peer group, all of us university graduates with similar qualifications and experience. There were a few differences between Wuhan and Nanjing mahjong, but this didn't hold him up for long. Anyone with a weakness for mahjong loved Xia Yuqing, because apparently he was a fantastic player. Actually, someone else told me he was useless, but that was quite possible, too—sometimes, the longer you'd been playing, the sloppier you got. *Baijiu* was another great way to make friends and influence people: get two cups sloshing around someone's stomach, and in no time at all they'll practically be offering to donate you their kidneys. Xia Yuqing drank his way through just about everyone of any importance in the factory. The day he invited them for a drink, Xia Yuqing would always buy a pack of quality cigarettes, and carefully tear a perfectly square, regular hole in the silver paper underneath the lid. He would then lay the pack on the drinking table with one cigarette poking out of the opening, offer it to whichever figure in authority had become his latest drinking victim, then in a single, deft movement sweep up the lighter, tightly cradle the flame with his cupped hand, and solicitously light the cigarette for his esteemed drinking partner as if they were standing in a force-ten gale. *Baijiu*, before it does other, less sociable things to your insides, tends to open people up conversationally, and Xia Yuqing's powerful guests all opened up wide: on and on, endlessly promising him a promotion. Unfortunately, it was all so much alcoholic hot air; in our factory, the only word that counted for anything was our manager's. And he was a pretty strange sort. This is how the factory management career ladder seemed to work. One, appoint your manager when he's close to retirement, to guarantee he goes intensely and thoroughly power-mad during the few years of absolute rule left to him. Two, he starts sacking and reappointing the entire middle-level management to annihilate the *ancien regime* and ensure absolute personal loyalty to him. Next, he turns into this industrial man of mystery: no one knows where to find him, or the most basic personal details about him, such as where he lives, whether he likes spicy food, whether he has a wife and children, even whether he likes karaoke. But as soon as someone from a senior administrative department comes on an inspection or there's some ceremony to mark the completion of a building, or an anniversary of the founding of the Communist Party, or National Day, up he pops, out of nowhere, surrounded by his retinue, shaking hands like he wants to dislocate everyone's wrists, mouthing platitudes like they're God's own truth. The people who worked in the factory's TV station must have been the best in the business, because their industrial propaganda flicks somehow managed to make the manager look more like the chairman of the Communist Party than the head of a small provincial factory employing no more than a few hundred people. So mahjong and *baijiu* with the management small fry were never going to get you anywhere; it was the manager's ear you wanted. Xia Yuqing told himself to be patient, that Rome wasn't built in a day. But in his more introspective moments, he began to think that after four years Rome was no nearer to getting built than our electricity generator, and he couldn't keep this up much longer. He started to grumble. He got bitter.

One day, I returned to our room to discover that the mess of objects usually piled up on our table had been cleared away to make room for a few plates of food and a bottle of *baijiu*, and Xia Yuqing was lying on his bed, staring up at the ceiling, exhaling smoke rings. My bile instantly began to rise: nothing irritated me more than when he brought his dinner parties back to our room. Astonishingly, however, today the wine and food on the table were for me, the single, honored guest. I really didn't want to seem ungracious, but two little details niggled their way into my consciousness, impeding my enjoyment of this convivial gesture: the first was that the bottle of Yang River liquor was only a little more than half full, obviously left over from his previous banquet; the second was that although the seal on the pack of cigarettes on the table had been meticulously ripped back, just as usual, it was not the premium brand Xia Yuqing bought for his more esteemed guests. He divided the just-over-half bottle of *baijiu* equally between two tooth mugs, and passed one to me. Well, then, he said to me, like the relaxed, generous representative of the upper-level management that he wasn't, isn't this nice? Must be months since we . . . in fact, have we ever sat down and had a drink together? This time he wasn't wearing that low-necked white vest, thank God, the one that gave me nightmares. Instead, he had on a tight black vest that I found equally traumatizing. Look here, I said, I'm happy to sit down and have a drink with you, but I insist you put something else on. Xia Yuqing wasn't exactly overjoyed, but he capitulated in the end and yanked a shirt over his head. Problem was, the shirt neck was still wide open, so the black vest underneath started to look like a bra, giving his breasts even more definition and uplift. Sorry, I had to tell him, you've got to button it up properly. To the neck. Xia Yuqing slammed his glass down on the table, his eyes narrowing into angry triangles. Just when it looked like he was going to get really angry, he shook his head. Fuck, what's wrong with you? he complained. It's roasting today! Well, if you really think there's something wrong with me, I could have answered, you ought to humor a sick man.

Furious at being made to button his shirt, Xia Yuqing sat there for ages refusing even to look at me, until finally he went off to cool down in the toilets. I don't know what he did there, but when he came back he was clearly feeling much better. He raised his mug and clinked mine, took a swig, picked up a fried goose leg from one of the plates, and started to chew on it. I'd just gotten the mug to my mouth when I suddenly got this massive whiff of some sickeningly sweet, Chinese brand of toothpaste. I wrinkled my nose and set the cup down. This, for Xia Yuqing, was the last straw. He pounded the table and stuck his finger about a quarter inch from my nose: This time you've gone too fucking far! he started yelling. There's me, trying to be nice, offering you a drink, licking your ass, and that's the fucking thanks I get! Did I say you could lick my ass? I countered mildly. D'you think a cup of minty *baijiu* is all it takes? Only momentarily wrongfooted, Xia Yuqing shoved the table between us to one side, then clenched his fists, ready to fight. Though his eyes were flashing like Christmas lights, I kept my cool. None of this was surprising to me: I'd always expected we'd end up having a fight—to some interpersonal problems, violence is the only answer. Bring it on, I thought. I don't like fighting, but once I've started I fight dirty. In the end, though, Xia Yuqing chickened out, pulled the table back into place, then sat down and drank, hard. Not because he was afraid of me; he was just worried that if it got around, a fight with a colleague would make him look bad in front of the management and sabotage his chances of promotion. I've got proof, too, because I saw him fight someone else later on, and that time there was no holding back: one punch and three of his opponent's incisors were off with the tooth fairy. (Hao Qiang, my old pretty-boy roommate, was the man suddenly in urgent need of a dentist.) But back to the evening in question: Xia Yuqing ripped open all the buttons on his shirt and settled down to a private domestic bender. Preferring to leave him to it, I went off wandering the streets until about midnight, by which time I figured that Xia Yuqing would either be out playing mahjong or playing by himself under his blanket. But there he was still, sitting all quiet and peaceful by the table, as if waiting for me. What the hell was he doing there? This time he really had me worried, worried that he was waiting for me to fall asleep before murdering me in my bed. Xia Yuqing languidly lifted a pair of misty, drunken eyes in my direction, then picked up the pack of cigarettes and tried to pluck one out. After the last of several badly coordinated attempts finally succeeded, he promptly dropped his prize on the floor. He bent over, with signs of enormous effort, picked the cigarette up, then suddenly passed it to me. I don't remember too well what we talked about that night, and I'd guess he doesn't either; he was slurring his words so much he had to repeat every sentence two or three times. He had himself draped over my shoulder like a dead camel, going on about how neither of us were locals, we were far from our families, our homes, how hard life was for us, how we had to look out for each other, help each other out. I immediately took my cue to help him as fast as I could onto his bed, an act of charity that strained my back and left me walking at a 30-degree tilt for the next week. The lesson being: helping other people seriously damaged my health, and I wasn't cut out for it.

After getting Xia Yuqing settled, I staggered off to the washroom to brush my teeth. This was not a particularly joyful event, because my tooth mug still reeked of booze. Smells matter; they need to harmonize. That principle holds for human relationships too: if someone doesn't smell compatible, I say stay well away. Rice and dung I could smell together without flinching, but booze and toothpaste was just one of those combinations I couldn't handle. When I went back to the room, I was just about to lie down when Xia Yuqing suddenly shot up in bed like a sleepwalker, grinning like an idiot. He said he wanted to ask me something. His voice had this confidential tone to it, as if he was about to tell me about some treasure map and he was worried the walls had ears. To cut a potentially agonizingly long story short, I immediately told him the map was old news, everyone in the factory had a copy, and we should get some sleep. But no: he had decided now was the moment to talk about our factory manager's ass, about whether therein really lay the passage to promotion. D'you think it's true? Xia Yuqing asked me, with deadly seriousness. Of course it is, I replied, my patience wearing thin. After chewing this over for a while, Xia Yuqing felt an inner compulsion to ask me something else. Wouldn't—wouldn't it be a bit unhygienic? What? I said. Xia Yuqing looked a bit embarrassed. Wouldn't there be, you know, shit? I don't know, I said, but a bit of shit wouldn't put anyone off who was really desperate for a promotion. Xia Yuqing was still giving the whole matter serious thought. Another thing, right, he asked, adding an illuminating gesture, how d'you, like, jam the thing in? Just can't see how it could be done. By this point, I'd had enough of the whole exchange. Look, I said, I'm sure so many people have been down that passage by now, there's probably room for two in there. Just do it, Xia Yuqing, I said. Make things easy on yourself, get your promotion and be happy. I immediately regretted these incautious words of advice: he'd have to be really drunk not to realize how offensive I was being and beat the shit out of me. But he clearly was exactly that: eyes half shut, he sank into deep, peaceable contemplation. What the hell, I'd really gotten him thinking. After a good long pause, Xia Yuqing shook his head: Nah, wouldn't work, he said to himself. What d'you mean, wouldn't work? I asked. Xia Yuqing's face went blank, then broke into a grin. Without another word, he lay back down. The moment his head hit the pillow, he was snoring like a train whistle.

His fall only briefly interrupted by a clothes rack suspended from a second-floor window, Xie Weigang slipped through its slats onto the bags of garbage left outside the dormitory building and fainted. (I suspect he'd already fainted from fright by the time he reached the ground. A minor point.) As this unconventional descent occurred on a weekend, hardly anyone in the unmarried block was around, and no one who was in his room noticed this botched murder attempt. There Xie Weigang lay, under the watchful guardianship of thousands of rats, before he woke up sometime in the middle of the night. Consciousness, and the slightest movement, he soon discovered, were pure agony, so, abandoning any pretense at quiet dignity, he bawled his head off. After he was taken to the hospital, the results of the checkup reported little short of a miracle: apart from a bit of soft tissue damage, he was right as rain. The factory authorities took a very serious view of the whole affair and gave the local police station every assistance in their inquiries. But the verdict of the investigation was extremely bad news for Xie Weigang. Because there was no trace of any struggle in the room and the door had been locked, everyone put two and two together—that Xie Weigang had been under severe psychological pressure, and that he was a bit flaky at the best of times—and concluded it was attempted suicide, not murder. To avoid putting any further strain on Xie Weigang's nerves—which had already been proved fragile—the management spread the word that the subject was not to be discussed around the factory. The head of office staff was deputed to visit Xie Weigang at the hospital and to communicate the manager's latest views on the question of his resignation: viz., that this path called life is very long, its tapestry is very rich, et cetera, so if you're still determined to go, how about you revise and resubmit your resignation? Xiao Xie, hypersensitive and paranoid at the best of times, immediately sensed what was being implied, went into an enormous huff, and refused to leave the hospital. Feeling a bit responsible because of the room swap, I decided to ask Hao Qiang a few questions of my own; I was convinced he had to know something. But Hao Qiang told me to get lost, he didn't know a fucking thing. A couple of days later, he was seeing things differently. Point of fact, he wasn't seeing very much at all, as his head had been smashed in with a steel angle joint. Only when Hao Qiang, his head a bloody mess, went into the hospital would Xiao Xie agree to come out. Soon as he was out, he handed in another letter of resignation to the factory bosses. By then, he was telling everyone he met that he was on the verge of collapse, that there was no way he could stay on, and that he didn't know what he might do if he was forced to. Most of the management, apart from the manager himself, were on Xiao Xie's side, and after a special meeting called to discuss the matter, they finally gave him a straight answer. They'd let him go, but only after he'd reimbursed them for the costs of training him all these years; the accounting department would do the math. For the rest of us workers, the idea that we were all one big, bad debt was very damaging to our sense of self-esteem: we suddenly realized that, in the eyes of our state employers, we were little better than indentured laborers, or prostitutes. When we left, we had to buy back our freedom, like slaves. Xiao Xie argued back that the factory should compensate him for the loss of his youth. Figuring that Xiao Xie, released into the free-market world, was never going to make it big and reflect glory back onto his old employers, the manager stuck to his original ruling. A personnel crisis resulted.

A group of four computer programmers resigned in protest against the leadership and just walked, without waiting for a response. In the end, they were all officially fired by the factory for going AWOL beyond the accepted time limit. As all four of them were code monkeys, they didn't need to worry about finding another job. Our factory had only had eight computer programmers to begin with; now it'd lost half of them, and with Xie Weigang also determined to go, the department as good as collapsed. Well and truly outmaneuvered, the factory bosses frantically started firing off requests to the head office for new staff, while desperately trying to woo back the absentees. Of course, they still didn't give a rat's ass about anyone else, because they knew they didn't have to. Take me, for example: what's a graduate in thermal energy to do except waste his life in a doomed, sub-Soviet electricity plant? Even if I wanted to leave, where would I go? The factory soon became obsessed with what the four escapees went on to do. Almost no one wished them well: what everyone most wanted was to see the four of them run into brick walls, hard, then crawl back like concussed dogs. But things never work out the way you want them to, and as soon as it became clear they were all doing very nicely, everyone lost interest. This is about the sum total of what I know. The ringleader, Jin Zhiyang, got a job at a big Hong Kong computer firm. He was quickly promoted, put in charge of about 100 people, began earning more than 10,000 a year, and acquired a Hong Kong accent. Li Minghao started up a computer company with a few friends on Zhujiang Road, but after some management difficulties he left to work for a credit company run by the provincial government, where things went so well for him he got a contract to set up an Internet system for a negotiable securities firm. He got rich, bought a house and a car. Apparently, his connections in the provincial government were so good our deputy manager used to go begging him for help. Yu Jiang, the one I knew best out of the four, soon abandoned computing altogether and began messing around in stocks and shares, buying and selling all sorts of stuff—VCDs, stove parts, rice, plastic bags—and running a restaurant. Everyone said he'd done the best out of them all, but how well, no one really knew. I passed him on the street earlier this year, but he stared straight ahead, over my shoulder; we didn't say hello. The last, Hu Jinbiao, went back to his hometown in Jiangxi and got a job in a petrochemicals company: another iron rice bowl, just someplace else.

But Xie Weigang still insisted on resigning formally, however pointless his computing confreres had made that look. He was like someone who was always saying good-bye but never actually left; it got plain irritating. Fortunately, because he'd been going on about it for so long, it was now possible pretty much to ignore him, let him get on with digging his own hole. Exhausted by the whole performance, the management just wanted Xie Weigang to hand over the cash and be gone. In their finest creative hour, the accounting department calculated the sum total of the repayment to be 50,000 *yuan*, minus the statutory 10,000 *yuan* legally owed to employees as severance pay. So anyone who wanted to ransom their freedom had to scrape up 40,000 *yuan* from nowhere. When Xiao Xie was told, he almost fainted dead away from fright. After a certain amount of bargaining, the factory offered to halve the ransom; that, they said, was as far as they were prepared to go. But even 20,000 was still out of the question. How was he going to make that kind of money, and fast? Everybody gathered around to offer suggestions, which Xiao Xie carefully recorded, one by one, in a special notebook, pressing for further details as he made his notes.

1. Solicit contributions. Set up a fund-raising center in the unmarried accommodations block.
2. Go northeast to trade. Although Chinese-Russian border trade was slowing down after a busy couple of years, it was still worth a try. Head northeast, sell a truckload of down coats to the Russkis, get a truckload

of steel in return, and who knows, maybe that's your 20,000 *yuan* made. Because of our factory's import links to the former Soviet Union, we'd all had language training in Russian. This way, Xiao Xie would get some use out of it. But where was the initial capital going to come from?

3. Sell stuff. Anything he could get cash for. Blood? Probably not healthy enough, faulty liver and all that. Flesh? Illegal, and no one was sure he'd find a buyer. The manager might pay up; problem was, no one knew whether he wanted to be buggered or do the buggering himself. Further clarification required.

4. Steal. There were plenty of valuable objects around the factory, technical instruments, electric cables, and the like. The thermal department used electrical contacts made of platinum. It was just a question of picking the right moment. The factory's screwed you, the advice-givers reasoned, time for some payback. Or: break into the old workers' toolboxes, where most of them were hiding their bonuses from their wives. They deserved it, the mean old bastards.

5. Advertise for a husband. Describe yourself as a young female of outstanding natural beauty, indicate clearly that any interested parties should accompany their letter of response with an administrative fee of 50 *yuan*. This sounded too much like fraud, Xiao Xie objected, and anyway, personal ads never normally ask for money. But you've got to ask for the money at some point, his advisors rejoined, it's just a question of when. And what contact address to give? puzzled Xiao Xie.

6. Get married. A little while back, at the steel and iron factory across the way, after a worker was killed in an accident, his widow had received tens of thousands of *yuan* as compensation. Find someone to act as a go-between; problem solved.

7. Win the lottery. Spend a whole month's salary on lottery tickets—fortune favors the brave.

8. Amputate your left hand, and leave it on the manager's desk. He'll never ask you for anything again.

While Xie Weigang was wavering among these various schemes, the factory took another surprising step backward. Xiao Xie could resign, effective immediately, and leave the 20,000 *yuan* outstanding.

When he'd repaid it, he'd get his personal work files back. Someone in management, who felt sorry for Xiao Xie, even hinted there was no need to worry about owing money to the state, it wasn't like a private debt. If he left it long enough, everyone would probably forget all about it. I rejoiced for Xiao Xie: he didn't need to waste his time here anymore, he could leave and get a decent job. Okay, so he was never going to be China's Bill Gates, but he might do all right for himself as a software designer somewhere else.

But Xiao Xie refused to either exit along this olive branch or give any kind of explanation for his schizophrenic behavior. Everyone felt snubbed. The manager immediately dropped the conciliatory act: This isn't a hotel, he told Xiao Xie. You wanted to leave and now we're letting you leave, so leave! In the blink of an eye, the deadlock had done a 180-degree turn, with Xiao Xie insisting on staying and the manager insisting on kicking him out. After this latest bizarre twist in the saga, Xiao Xie struck an even more pathetic figure around the factory. Because there were so few computer programmers, they'd all been put under the direction of the electrical department. Following instructions from the factory manager, the head of department stopped allocating work to Xie Weigang, and even gave his desk away to someone else. The personnel department cut off his salary, and even his monthly toilet paper/soap/shampoo/et cetera ration. Xie Weigang responded by showing up for and leaving work perfectly on time, spending the intervening hours sitting in a corner of the office, like a rather unusually shaped cactus. Unable just to stand by and watch this happen, colleagues walked over to offer yet more advice about what he should do next; soon, Xie Weigang had a whole sheet of suggestions. He tried submitting a personal pledge of good faith to the factory manager, a blown-up copy of which he stuck on the ground floor of the office building, acclaiming the manager as "our brilliant, great, kind leader." When I read it, I almost vomited. Surprisingly enough, the manager didn't like it either, and ordered Xie Weigang to tear the poster down immediately. This is a public office area, he said. You can't stick posters and pictures up wherever you like. Xie Weigang and his pledge then disappeared altogether from public view. But he was still there, collapsed in his room after suffering a complete physical breakdown. Soon afterward, the parents of our wayward computer genius hurried in from out of town: both plain, simple country people, perfectly normal on every count, tearfully begging anyone they thought looked vaguely powerful for help with Xiao Xie's case. Finally, the manager managed to generate a bit of human sympathy and agreed to let Xiao Xie stay. Even after he was allowed back, though, most of the time Xiao Xie seemed barely there at all.

If Xiao Xie were obviously mentally ill, his abnormal behavior would have been very easy to explain. But the truth of the matter was, a lot of the time he didn't seem all that different from the rest of us. So why did he suddenly refuse to leave? There were, in summary, three different general opinions on the matter. First, the majority view of the factory workers was that after seeing his fellow computer programmers go, Xie Weigang figured if he stayed, he could get to be the head of the computer section, then if the computer section later became a department in its own right, he'd get to be the head of the department. Promotion jackpot. Second, as Hao Qiang later remembered, it was at about this time that Xie Weigang first set eyes, in their room, on Yin Hongxia. Plump, fair, generally radiant, Yin Hongxia was indisputably the most attractive thing ever to come out of the phosphate fertilizer factory—a subsidiary of the chemical engineering company—where she worked as an operator. When Xiao Xie saw her, he practically started drooling on the spot. Although Yin Hongxia ignored him almost completely, Hao Qiang agreed to try to set Xiao Xie up with her. In other words, Xiao Xie decided to stay for love, an interpretation that has a heart-warming kind of appeal to it. The third explanation came from Xie Weigang himself, told to me in confidence, long after the events in question. He said that just as he was getting his bag ready to go, he discovered blood in his shit. It broke his nerve. Assuming it was a delayed-reaction consequence of his three-story fall, Xiao Xie started to see his life flash before his eyes. The bleeding went on for another ten or so days, increasing in volume with his anxiety. Though too scared to tell anyone, much less go for a checkup, he instinctively felt that quite soon he might need a state health insurance program very badly indeed. Even now, Xiao Xie often shits blood for a few days in every month, though he doesn't lose sleep over it anymore. But the first time, Xiao Xie explained to me, he went out of his mind, like a girl getting her first period. I nodded silently, keeping my doubts to myself.

It was round about this time Xia Yuqing developed a new, psychosexual-linguistic theory about what was wrong with Xiao Xie: Xie Weigang, he surmised, had been destroyed by his surname and its homonyms (premature ejaculation, shriveled, limp, etc.), by hearing it fifty times a day, day in, day out. It must have undermined him, on a deep psychological level—it would have worn down better, stronger, truer men. Everybody thought Xia Yuqing had a certain point, and for a while "Xiao Xie" became a multipurpose colloquialism around the factory. Sometimes it meant premature ejaculation, sometimes it meant impotence, sometimes it meant neither, just the routine goings-on of married life. For example, if a married colleague showed up for work one morning with a sour look on his face, someone would ask him, Have a Xiao Xie last night with the wife, did you? Sometimes it was used in its original sense, sometimes it was used as a metaphor, extended by various degrees. After a while, it came to mean practically anything you wanted it to, until it got focused back in on a sense of unfinished, aborted, failed, the most typical and obvious example being: if things go on like this, the electricity generator's going to turn into one big Xiao Xie. Here's the phrase at work in a sample conversation:

Did you watch the game last night?

Only the first half. Fuck, the Chinese are completely Xiao Xie at soccer.

I don't know, they're all right.

They're crap, all of 'em, every one's a Xiao Xie. They're a fucking disgrace.

Come on now, the last match, okay, it was Xiao Xie in the end, but they almost won.

What do you mean, almost? So near and yet so fucking far. As I say, pure Xiao Xie.

Okay, sometimes they're Xiao Xie, but sometimes they're not bad.

D'you want to bet on the next one? A hundred *yuan*?

Nah.

Xiao Xie-ing on me, hey?

Usually, it was impossible to grasp the precise implications of a "Xiao Xie" outside its immediate oral context. Occasionally, however, it was the other way around: the deeper you got into a context, the less you understood what "Xiao Xie" really meant. Once, on night shift, a colleague standing next to me stared up at the stars and sighed, "Ah, Xiao Xie." Maybe, I thought, he meant something along the lines of "Ah, life." Or maybe I'll never know.

After about a month, the expression began to fall out of use, as if everyone were responding to a secret signal to drop it. The phrase "Xiao Xie" dissolved away into nothing, like a grain of salt on the tongue. If it happened to flicker back through your head, it was like the memory of a faint, saline aftertaste returning long after the original particle had been washed away.

In order to stabilize plummeting staff morale, the factory decided to put us to work immediately on the power plant building site itself. The whole project had been contracted out to two electricity companies, one local and one from the northeast. These two companies then subcontracted the work out to a series of smaller outfits, who had very little idea what on earth they were doing on such a big job. At the same time, a work team from the Provincial Institute of Electrical Experimentation was beginning some preliminary testing, picking its way around a vast, ever-present cohort of dust- and earth-covered peasant labor, settled over the work site like a black cloud. So we were part of a pretty miscellaneous bunch on site. Our task was to familiarize ourselves with the facilities, identify any faults, check on deliveries for the next stage of work, and prepare for the plant's first dry run, together with a dozen or so engineering experts from the Ukraine, who had come over to assist us. They were very serious about their work, running around the site all day, constantly grumbling about the quality of installation work carried out by the Chinese electricity companies. But the Chinese either ignored their complaints, like they were so much wind past the ears, or openly laughed at them. I suppose when a nation's slipped down the hierarchy of world powers, when politically and economically it's on the skids, it gets easy to start treating all its citizens, however well qualified they are, like disenfranchised refugees. Although the Ukrainians got the regulation, foreign expert red carpet treatment, earning great shovelfuls of dollars, they lived very thriftily, only buying the cheapest goods that no one else would buy at the market, so even the local stall holders treated them like cheapskate crap.

We were divided into four teams, working three-shift rotations with the electricity companies. Even when there was nothing to do, we had to stay on the work site, because we were supposed to put in regular work hours and our attendance was being monitored. Having finally achieved his life's goal—being made a team leader—Xia Yuqing became obsessed with sacrificing his own comfort to the collective, especially on the long night shifts. He'd man the staff room on his own and tell the rest of us to go and find somewhere to sleep. When the weather was warm, you just lay down on any bit of flat ground, but from November onward, sleeping options were much more limited. There was a bed in the electricity company's staff room, but unfortunately there was always someone in it. So the rest of us had no choice but to gather in our own staff room and nap on the tables. Someone brought in a semiconductor so we could pick up radio broadcasts, and a local call-in program called "Bridge at Midnight to Your Hearts" became the soundtrack to our long night shifts. Pretty soon, I hated it with all my body and soul. Only two types ever seemed to phone in to expose their gnarled psyches to the presenter: people experiencing marital problems and people suffering from impotence. In the latter case, the caller's opening gambit was always: "I have a friend. . . ." There was a phone in the staff room, and when we were bored and had nothing to do (in other words, almost all the time) we'd take turns calling the radio station, pretending to be impotent, to enjoy a bit of sympathy from the presenter and his audience. So that we didn't make the caller laugh, we left whoever was doing the phoning on his own in the staff room, while the rest of us went outside and huddled around the semiconductor to listen. In the end, after an exhaustive process of comparing and contrasting, everyone agreed that Xia Yuqing was the champion impotent impersonator, that he'd gotten the jerky, quick-slow, coy-desperate delivery that marked the genuine article. He was so good that some of us began to suspect he might secretly have problems in that department himself. Soon we were demanding a show from our star performer on every long night shift; if he refused, we'd go on strike. Finally, something snapped in him: we were all listening to him talking away when suddenly, out of nowhere, he screamed Fuck you! at the presenter. Though we were pretty shaken, the presenter kept his cool perfectly. Don't adjust your sets, he said, we're just experiencing a technical difficulty, we've reconnected, next caller. . . . Hello, caller. . . .

About four or five o'clock that morning, I went out for a piss. Afterward, I wandered around in the cold, trying to shake off my persistent fatigue. When you were on a three-shift rotation, the second long night shift was usually the hardest. Passing by the electricity company's staff room, I peered through the window in the door and saw, to my amazement, that the bed was empty, and the room completely deserted. Without a moment's hesitation, I opened the door and lay down fully dressed. The quilt was thin and the bed rock-hard, but at that moment, I felt like I was in paradise. After snuggling down, I discovered, to my slight unease, the quilt was perceptibly warm. A few instants later, the door was kicked open and a young man with curly hair rushed in, swearing about the cold. He'd gotten as far as the bed when he spotted me. Who the fuck are you? he shouted. Bloody hell, I go out for a shit and somebody's taken the bed! He spoke in a very strong northeastern accent and had a big mole on his chin; I knew him by sight from around the work site. Embarrassed, but too tired to explain, I climbed out of the bed and surrendered it back to him. Don't worry, the young man said, rubbing his knees, move over, there's room for two. After a moment's hesitation, I agreed and edged over to one side. He then lifted up the quilt at the other end and lay down. After a bit of shifting and fidgeting, both of us found fairly comfortable positions, and lay still. S'not bad, I heard him say, just now it was a bit cold in here, much warmer like this. I tucked the quilt tightly around my shoulders, trying to hermetically seal his smelly feet inside. In a short while, he went to sleep, his heart beating steadily into the soles of my feet pressed along his spine. I didn't sleep a wink myself, but I was happy enough just being able to lie down. I stayed there more or less until breakfast time, when I quietly climbed out and went back to my own staff room. Looking around at my team's faces, waxy with exhaustion, I felt I'd not done too badly for myself.

After two long night shifts we had a day off, then a short night shift. I quite liked short night shifts, because I never knew what to do with myself anyway between four o'clock in the afternoon and midnight; having to work at least kept me out of trouble. As an added bonus, at six o'clock the factory canteen sent over some dinner and at eleven o'clock they sent over a bedtime snack. Though the food was pretty poor, if you were an unmarried man like me, it was better than having to fend for yourself. That evening, I'd just gotten back to the staff room and was about to take off my safety helmet when I heard that the day before yesterday someone from one of the electricity companies had been killed after falling off the temporary elevator on the work site. Although the door opened, the elevator itself had failed to come up, and the poor guy had stepped into nothingness. I immediately thought of my bed partner, the one with curly hair, but said nothing, much less made any further inquiries, afraid of having my fears confirmed. Everyone else was spreading this around like it was a piece of good news. If you don't spill a bit of blood on a big build, if you don't have a few people die, the old workers used to say, it doesn't get finished. So this meant there was still hope for the plant and everyone working on it. While we were waiting for dinner to arrive, everyone was comparing this accident with Xiao Xie's: both had fallen from about the same height, so how come one of them was dead before they got to the hospital, while the other could take himself there and walk out again? Of course, by the end of this seemingly endless discussion, everyone had agreed there was only one possible, plausible explanation for the complex medical mystery: fate.

After dinner the head of the electricity generating department came and announced that two representatives would be sent to attend the memorial service and cremation tomorrow morning, and that he was looking for volunteers. Whoever went could go home early tonight, and have a half day off tomorrow. Everyone, naturally, wanted to go, because a cremation had to be better than watching their own time go up in smoke at work. The department head put Xia Yuqing in charge of selecting a volunteer, then told him to contact the engineering department, because they were also sending someone and he needed to discuss with them things like whether to go halves on a big wreath or to buy a smaller wreath himself, et cetera. As soon as he had gone, everyone crowded around Xia Yuqing, begging for the remaining place. Reveling in his new power and popularity, Xia Yuqing dragged his decision out like a master playing with his slaves. Finally, he pointed at his empty food box on the table: I'll take whoever washes that up, he said. Though some balked at this precondition, others stampeded over to the table. As I happened to be sitting just next to it, I snatched it up and took it out to the sink. Like everyone else, I wanted the half day off. After I'd washed the box, I went back home to my room, as I'd been told I could. Xia Yuqing came back much later, at eleven o'clock, lugging a huge wreath with him, which took up most of the available space in the room. This would make things a bit simpler tomorrow morning, he said, when the engineering department car arrived for us. Hanging on either side of the wreath were two blank strips of paper, where the elegiac couplet to the deceased—as yet unwritten because no one knew what the dead man had been called—was supposed to go. Xia Yuqing said I had to remind him the next morning to find out the name as soon as we got to the ceremony, so he could scribble it in. He'd just lain down in bed when he heard the sound of mahjong being played on the other side of the wall. He put his trousers back on and rushed out again in a state of obvious excitement.

I slept incredibly badly that night. The wind was whistling in through a gap in the window frame, making the paper strips on the wreath flutter and rustle in the draft. I sat up in bed, turned on the lamp, and opened, then reclosed the window. Finally, at two, or maybe three o'clock, I got to sleep. But it seemed I'd hardly been asleep two minutes when I felt someone pushing at my shoulder. It was Xia Yuqing, presumably just back in from his game. The fluorescent lamp overhead was so bright that I could barely open my eyes. What? I said. Who filled the couplet in? he asked in a low voice. I leaped out of bed, all desire to sleep gone. I walked over to the wreath, pulled the paper toward me, and there, in pompously large, regular script, were the words: We'll never forget you, Comrade Xie Weigang! All this time, Xia Yuqing was hovering behind me, sending shivers up my spine. Fucking stand in front of me, I told him. Xia Yuqing unwillingly inched forward and ran his finger over the ink marks. Just been written, he said, examining his finger. After I went out, did anyone come in? No, I said, after a quick think, the door was locked, who could get in? The more we thought about it, the more confused and uneasy we felt. Xia Yuqing lit a cigarette. You don't think, he started saying, Xiao Xie would have. . . . I told him I thought we should go upstairs to look for him. Xia Yuqing ripped the strips of paper off, scrunched them into a ball, and chucked them into a corner of the room. Nah, he said, forget it. Let's go to sleep, we've got to be up early tomorrow.

But I wouldn't let it go, and forced Xia Yuqing to follow me upstairs. We went all the way along the corridor to the room at the very end, then knocked lightly a couple of times. No answer. I then knocked twice again, this time more heavily, but still no one answered. Xia Yuqing called out Xiao Xie's name a couple of times, then Hao Qiang's a couple of times, but there was no response. I then remembered that I still had a key to this room, but it was downstairs. I told Xia Yuqing to wait at the door while I went to get it. By the time I'd gotten it and gone back up, I discovered the door was already open a crack, and a sleepy-eyed Hao Qiang had poked his head and naked torso out. What the fuck? he asked, yawning away. It's the middle of the night, what the hell is it? I'm really sorry, I said, but is Xiao Xie in? Hao Qiang was nonplussed. Xiao Xie? he said. Who's she? You know, I said, Xiao Xie! Xie Weigang. Your roommate. He's not here, Hao Qiang said, haven't seen him for days. Why didn't you tell us? Xia Yuqing barked at him.

What's it got to do with me? Hao Qiang replied impatiently. I do my job, you do yours, how should I know what's going on with him? You share a room with him, 'course you should know! Xia Yuqing shot back. For God's sake, Hao Qiang said, you used to share a room with him, did you give a shit? Stop arguing, I interrupted, look, is Xiao Xie there or not? No, Hao Qiang said, shaking his head. Why would I lie to you? We want to go in and have a look, Xia Yuqing said. You can't, said Hao Qiang, who seemed rather alarmed by this idea. While we were talking, Hao Qiang had taken care to wedge himself firmly in the doorway, to block our further progress into the room. With one hand, Xia Yuqing shoved the door open, almost knocking Hao Qiang over backward. I groped for the light pull and gave it such a violent tug the cord broke. The fluorescent lamp flickered a few times, then came on. See for yourselves! Hao Qiang shouted furiously, pointing around the room. Where is he? Where is he then? He was right: no Xiao Xie. His bed was empty, piled with a quilt and a chaotic mess of clothes and books. A plump, fair woman sat up in Hao Qiang's bed, covering her chest with a blanket.

Feeling guilty, I put my hand on Hao Qiang's shoulder and tried to apologize. Hao Qiang pushed it away. We'll leave as soon as we've had a quick look to see whether Xiao Xie's left anything, I said, just a couple of minutes. Xia Yuqing and I started whipping through Xiao Xie's bed, desk, and cupboard, with no idea what we were looking for. After a while, the woman in the bed interrupted our search. I think I can see a piece of paper under his pillow, she said. We pulled out a note written on printing paper, the kind that has holes down the side. A few random sentences, a kind of last will and testament, I suppose, were scrawled on it: I wanted to resign from my job. Now I resign from life. Screw you all. As Xia Yuqing and I read it, we started to feel very bad indeed. I passed the paper over to Hao Qiang. By this point, Hao Qiang had cooled down enough to comfort us. Don't worry, he said, Xiao Xie's never stuck to a decision in his life, he's probably just fine. Just as we were trooping out the door, I thought I ought to apologize also to the woman in the bed. But when I took another look at her over Hao Qiang's shoulder, I couldn't believe my eyes: it was the ravishing Yin Hongxia. I yanked Hao Qiang over to one side: Didn't you agree to set Xiao Xie up with Yin Hongxia? I muttered. Yup, replied Hao Qiang, completely unconcerned. What the fuck d'you mean, yup? I asked with growing agitation. You're sleeping with the person you were supposed to set Xiao Xie up with! Look, Hao Qiang said, here's the situation. Way before I made that agreement with Xiao Xie, I'd already slept with her. I don't care about that, I said, you shouldn't be sleeping with her now! After a quick glance back at Yin Hongxia, Hao Qiang pulled me outside the room and put the door on the latch. Just leave it, all right, he said. Whether you sleep with a woman once or a thousand times, it's still the same thing! I've already slept with her once, so what's the harm in sleeping with her again? No! Xia Yuqing added his own, unusually animated view. Sleeping with her now is completely different! Hao Qiang unceremoniously elbowed Xia Yuqing out of the way: Mind your own business! I scowled and said nothing. No one said anything for a while. The cold air of the corridor started to make Hao Qiang, who was still wearing nothing on his top half, keener to make peace and get back into the warm. Okay, he conceded in a gentler voice, it's not ideal, I admit, but ever since my head got smashed in, I've had to be very careful about who I sleep with. All those married women out of bounds. So Yin Hongxia was . . . Look, I had to sleep with someone. Forces beyond my control. There: that's my last word on the matter. He then made as if to return to his room. My own anger was vaporizing. We had no good reason, I felt, to blame everything on Hao Qiang and his libido. Xia Yuqing, however, saw things differently. You fucking bastard! he screamed. We don't know whether Xiao Xie's dead or alive, and you want to go and screw his girlfriend! You're too fucking much! By the end of this little announcement, Hao Qiang was lying face up on the floor of the room. After scraping himself up, he turned his head left, right, then bent forward and spat out three front teeth into the palm of his hand. Somehow, without front teeth, Hao Qiang looked like he was laughing, laughing as he gurgled blood.

Early on the morning of the following day, we carried the wreath downstairs to wait for our transportation. I was wearing the dark blue factory uniform that I hated so much, as this was the most formal item of clothing I had. The crowds of people rushing in to work stared at us like we were flower-bearing aliens. Xiao Xie was among them, running downstairs with his bag under his arm. Where are you off to, then? he asked. Before I'd thought how to reply, he'd swung his leg over his bicycle and pedaled away at top speed.

The engineering department said the car would come at eight o'clock, so of course it didn't come till quarter past; a bad start, as the service and cremation were due to begin at nine and we were miles from the funeral home. From the moment the car arrived, our troubles multiplied. The engineering department had sent a hatchback car that was far too small to cram the wreath into. But they said yesterday they were going to send a van, Xia Yuqing complained. No one told me anything about it, said the guy sitting in the front seat, shrugging. Xia Yuqing started to get wound up. What do you mean they didn't tell you? he said. I okayed it with your boss. Nah, no one told me anything, the guy still insisted. We hated the engineering department more than any other department in the entire factory, partly because they had this massive superiority complex: they thought that they were the only ones doing any work, that everyone else was a bunch of useless no-hopers. But their major failing, the fatal flaw that guaranteed universal revulsion for the factory's engineers, was the fact that their bonuses were always much higher than any other department's. After a long and fraught negotiation, the car drove off, leaving us to fend for ourselves. Spitting obscenities, Xia Yuqing told me to wait where I was while he went off and made a phone call. Don't worry, he said confidently, I'll get head office to send another car. Ten minutes later, Xia Yuqing came chugging back in a wheezy old minicab. Unfortunately, he said, all his very good friends in head office were in a very important meeting. As time was running out, we squeezed into the back, each of us holding onto one of the wooden props, completely smothered by the wreath. As soon as the minicab cranked up and crawled off, we knew we were never going to get there on time. Xia Yuqing was still whining about the useless bastards in the engineering department, probably thinking he'd lost face.

Personally, I couldn't have cared less, particularly as, now that we had all but disappeared under the wreath, neither of us actually had any face to speak of. When the taxi began limping uphill, he suddenly turned to me and said, Of course, I could have phoned the manager, but I was a bit embarrassed, you know, to bother him over such a small thing. In case I didn't believe him, Xia Yuqing gripped the wreath support between his knees, groped around in his pocket, and produced a business card, which he passed over to me. I glanced at it: it was the manager's card, all right, a rash of personal titles printed above the name. For some reason, it looked vaguely familiar. By 9:30, when we'd gotten about halfway there, I suggested we give it up. Forget it, I said to Xia Yuqing, by the time we get there, he'll be toast. Let's just find a place to chuck the wreath, then go home. Xia Yuqing hesitated, uneasy about how he'd explain this back at the factory. But I won in the end. We got out; Xia Yuqing paid the fare and asked for a receipt. Forget it, the driver said, I don't do receipts. Meanwhile, I was looking, unsuccessfully, for an inconspicuous place to ditch the flowers. It's amazing how hard it is to dump an outsized funeral wreath when you actually try. Everyone stared at us, as Xia Yuqing, the wreath, and I staggered off through the streets, searching all the while for somewhere to abandon it.

POUNDS, OUNCES, MEAT

ONE BURNING HOT afternoon last June, I had to go to the telecom tower to pay an overdue phone bill. Because before this, I'd paid, overdue again, an electricity bill and overdue fines for the past half year, for a while I'd not had the money for my phone bill. The telecom office issued me two warnings, then cut my line off. Now, after finally scraping together the money to pay the phone, I was hoping against hope this month's electricity bill would have a heart and come a bit later than usual. Electricity and telephone bills are, I suppose, what you might call a contradiction of everyday life. On the bridge by the old Drum Tower I was stopped by a shabby individual, clearly someone who'd wandered in from out of town, with a black bag tucked under his arm and an unnerving gleam in his eyes. He told me my physiognomy was most unusual; he simply had to tell my fortune, he wouldn't charge a cent. The plastic on top of the bridge had melted tackily in the sun: crossing felt like walking over spat-out chewing gum, or smoker's phlegm, or snot, or semen, or fresh dog shit. I include these comparisons purely to illuminate, not disgust, you understand. If I were to suggest you imagine it was raw meat underfoot, now that, I admit, would be nauseating. Fuck off, I told him as impatiently as I could manage. Briefly, all too briefly, the man was transfixed by shock, too transfixed to manage any kind of response, till I'd reached the end of the bridge's elevation and was about to set off down the steps on the other side. Good luck's coming your way this year! he screeched vengefully at me across the asphalt. About fucking time, I muttered to myself as I descended. When I was halfway down, I happened to look up and see a girl with a healthily tanned face coming toward me up the steps, carrying a black parasol and a copy of *I Love Dollars*. My heart began to pound. I wasn't sure, at that moment, whether this counted as my good luck or not. In subsequent weeks and months, I often thought back over this scene, about this girl and that book, about how she kept the latter pressed beguilingly up against her chest, blinding me to its obvious flatness.

One evening two months later, after a blazing argument, my new, healthily tanned girlfriend and I went to the market to buy something to eat. As we turned to leave for home, now the proud purchasers of a premium piece of pork fillet, we discovered that a great lump of bone had magicked its way into our meat, and went back to have it out with the stall holder and his cleaver. Never one to be pushed around, my girlfriend got right in, using her voice box exactly as God intended. Easy there, lady, said the unfazed butcher. He took back the plastic bag in which the meat was encased, pulled the bone out from the middle, and threw it onto his table: So, according to you, how much should this weigh? he asked. Four hundred grams, I said, we bought 400 grams of fillet. Fine, he said, and put the meat on the electronic scales. You want to know how much it weighs? he said. See for yourselves. My girlfriend and I crowded around. The funny thing was, it *did* come to 400 grams, even a bit over. The stall holder smiled beatifically at us: That's cleared that up, I think. I threw in the bone for free, it makes a lovely soup stock. Weighing the bone in his hand, he was about to throw it back in the bag when he suddenly raised his eyebrows at us: I'll ask you first this time, so you don't get the wrong idea. D'you want the bone? No, we replied emphatically, ever-mindful of our dignity. Without another word, my girlfriend picked up the bag and headed for the reweighing stall at the front of the market. I followed close on her heels. The old man in charge of reweighing looked up at us from his knitting: Where'd you buy this? Fourth stall on the right, we said. No need to check, then, he said serenely, pushing the plastic basket containing his wool farther up his arm. He won't have shortchanged you. That's Cao Hong, he's been the best stall holder around here for years now, won prizes for it, you don't need to worry. Still skeptical, we put the meat on the scales; perplexingly, still 405 grams. By now, my girlfriend had the light of battle in her eyes and the bit between her teeth: He's bound to be in cahoots with the stall holders, she muttered to me. Just look at him, how can you trust a man who knits? Come on, let's go and check elsewhere. If I'd expressed any opposition, she'd have turned on me. So I immediately murmured my agreement. But the problem was, where could we find a dependable set of scales? There was a set of old-fashioned suspension scales at a fast-food stall not far off, but they were no good: everyone knows scales like those can be tampered with. A little farther down, there was a set of greasy electronic scales at a state-owned osmanthus duck stall. We had no problem with osmanthus duck, naturally, but were the scales beneath it to be trusted? My girlfriend was beginning to regret not having brought her pocket-sized spring balance out with her. But even if she had, it wouldn't have been much use: the springs were so old they sometimes turned 500 grams of chestnuts into a kilo. You didn't know when you'd been lucky or when you'd been had. I think we should go by feel, I said, after thinking it over. All we need is an expert to do it for us.

Just then, an old lady with thinning gray hair hanging down over her shoulders happened to be walking by, away from the market, carrying a basket full of food. Smiling as ingratiatingly as I could, I approached and made my request. Without another word, she set down her basket and began slowly unlocking her shoulders, backward and forward. I held out toward her the plastic bag containing the meat. But she didn't take it. Wait a second, she said, I've just been carrying a heavy basket, I need to readjust or I won't be able to guess right. There was something in what she said, I thought, so I stood by and waited patiently. Once she'd loosened her shoulder joints, the old lady sighed, then started shaking out her wrists, one flick after another, first quick, then slow. Just as I thought she was about to stop, she restarted the entire process. My girlfriend threw her head back like a warhorse and snorted several times up to the heavens. She was getting impatient, I could tell. Unmoved, the old lady next threw herself into massaging, then pressing down on her right hand with her left, listening for a crisp crack from every joint.

All right then. Hand it over.

What?

The meat!

Oh. Suddenly remembering, I quickly passed her the bag. I watched as the old lady curved her index finger like a hook, hung the plastic bag on it, and slowly focused on the task at hand, lowering her eyelids as she did so. After a very, very long pause she reopened her eyes and looked briefly, but intently at me.

Should I count the bag in?

What?

The weight of the bag, should I count it in?

Eh? Oh, don't mind, up to you.

I need an answer!

All right, count it in.

The old lady nodded, then reclosed her eyes. My girlfriend tapped her heels restlessly on the cement road, darting furious glances at me. My throat was dry with the tension. The old lady was still refusing to open her eyes. Excuse me, I eventually croaked out, deeply embarrassed, we really need to get going, any chance you could hurry up?

A little under a pound.

What? What d'you mean, a pound?

About fifteen ounces.

Ounces? No, no, no, we need to know what it is in grams.

You young people don't know how much a pound is?

No, we don't.

All right, then: one pound is 0.454 kilograms. You do the math.

My new girlfriend and I stood there like idiots. The old lady returned the plastic bag to us, swung her basket back over her shoulder, and prepared to set off again. I quickly reached out to stop her escaping. She frowned. I'm warning you, young man, let me pass, I've a dozen people at home waiting for me to cook them dinner.

Don't leave us in suspense like this, I begged her, just tell us what it is in metric. The old lady looked me up and down. Don't you know how to convert? she asked. Why should I lie about something like that? I said. Please don't keep us in the dark. This was not what the old lady wanted to hear. Work, work, work, dawn till dusk, that's all I do, all day, every day. Where d'you think I'm going to get the time to waste keeping you in the dark? Just figure it out. Saying this, she slipped under my armpit without even needing to duck her head. In a few decisive strides, I was once more barring her way. Please, I said, tell me what this weighs in grams, I'm begging you now. The old lady twitched her chin. Stop whining. If you really want to know, I can tell you, but first admit you can't work it out yourself. All right, I said impatiently, I admit it. The old lady shifted the basket over to her left hand: You youth of today! She pointed her liberated right hand up at my nose. You can't cook, you can't convert pounds into metric, you can't do anything! You don't study, you can't tell rice from beans, you treat your family like dirt. You're all useless. Look at you! You've hands and feet of your own, why d'you need an old woman to cook your meals? Working her fingers to the bone. You should be ashamed of yourselves. And I know I shouldn't say this, but I'm going to anyway: what if I keel over one day, what'll you do then? Go begging? Even if I'd wanted to, I couldn't have gotten a word in edgewise, so I just let the old lady get it all out of her system. The beginnings of a tear shone in the corner of one eye: Best not to start, only gets me angry. I've had it, slaving my guts out for you! Is this your idea of fun? Because it's not mine. She flung her basket violently to the ground, sending tomatoes and potatoes rolling everywhere. No, I said, feeling a response was finally required, it's not, actually. But by now the old lady was bent over, scrabbling to retrieve her purchases, racing after errant tomatoes and potatoes on their bid for freedom.

A trailer-bicycle piled high with vegetables pushed along by a clean-shaven, middle-aged man ambled toward us, crushing to a pulp the tomato at the head of the pack. Whipping back her outstretched right hand, the old lady crouched, face down on the ground, her eyes closed in heartbreak. After replacing some of the potatoes and tomatoes in her basket, I tried to help her up. Pushing me away, she clambered a couple of paces forward and solemnly peeled off the ground, using both hands, the flat, muddy pancake that had once been her tomato. Levering herself up on a crooked elbow into a kneeling position, she shakily straightened out one leg, then the other. Almost breathless from the effort, she then turned and ran a few steps to catch up with the trailer, which hadn't gone far. Holding his handlebars steady, the middle-aged man was asking a peddler how much his round chopping boards cost. Five *yuan*, the peddler said. Three, countered the man, before finally agreeing on four. After digging four one-*yuan* coins out of his trouser pocket, he was placing them, one by one, in front of the peddler when the old lady poked the small of his back with the tip of the steeple her hands had made over the tomato. Tickled, the man flinched back and chortled, almost dropping his bicycle. Turning, he leaned over to one side and pulled in his neck, as if to guard against any more involuntary gibbering.

Who—who are you?

What d'you mean, who am I? As if you care.

What the hell is this? Hey, don't stand in my face.

A fine mess you made!

And so the old lady and the middle-aged man joined battle, the former accusing, the latter refusing to admit anything. You won't get away with this, the old lady said. Take it from me, this tomato was squashed thirty seconds ago by that front wheel of yours. Go and look for yourself if you don't believe me, the wheel's bound to be wet still. Standing and watching, I began to feel a little worried for the old lady: she was trying to be just a bit too clever, I thought. What if the wheel was dry? Tomatoes these days are all grown under plastic covers: the flesh is dense, but there's hardly any juice. Exactly as I'd feared, the middle-aged man walked forward, lifted his handlebars and the front wheel off the ground with one hand, and spun the spokes with the other. So where is it then? The old lady moved in close: not a trace of juice. She moved in even closer. The man began whirring the wheel with extra, exaggerated effort, almost scraping the tip of her nose. The old lady darted back.

Okay, there's nothing there, but that doesn't mean you're innocent!

I don't have time for this. Hey, I already told you once, don't stand in my face.

Her patience long exhausted, my girlfriend yanked the plastic bag containing the meat out of my hand. Come on, let's get out of here, they're all mentals. But just then, the old lady started waving desperately over at me. I glanced, in consultation, at my girlfriend, who veered, glowering, off to one edge of the fracas. Obviously, if I heeded the old lady's appeal, I'd get in trouble with my girlfriend. To my left I had a wizened old lady, to the right my young, attractive girlfriend; an easy choice to make, you would think. Making for the old lady, I bent down to her level and waited obediently for instructions.

Hey, young man, you tell him what happened!

What?

Who squashed my tomato?

I pointed, with due circumspection, at the middle-aged man: It was him.

You hear that? Now which wheel was it?

I pointed at the front wheel: That one.

You sure?

What?

Are you sure?

I'm sure.

Anything else to say for yourself? the old lady, now overbearing in triumph, asked her defendant, hurling the squashed tomato down at his feet. After thinking it over, he shook his head. All right, he said, so it's not my lucky day. But what do we do now? The old lady said she'd bought 6 tomatoes, costing 2.5 *yuan* altogether, making each tomato 0.41666 *yuan* on average. Rounding it up, he owed her 0.42 *yuan*. After a brief, stunned pause, the man demanded to see the other 5. The old lady brought over the basket from the ground and, one by one, rummaged out the tomatoes from in among the potatoes, cauliflower, asparagus, lettuce, ginger, onions, long chilies, and pickled garlic. I disagree, the man pronounced after thorough investigation, these 5 are all quite big, but the one I squashed was obviously much smaller.

The old lady glared upon her adversary, suddenly realizing he was not yet a spent force. Well, what do you say we do? The man pulled out from his bicycle trailer a carrot and laid it in front of the old lady: Look, I bought 4 carrots, 625 grams altogether. At 2.4 *yuan* a kilo, they cost me 1.5 *yuan*, which makes each carrot 0.375 *yuan* on average, but because this one is the thickest and the longest, it's bound to be worth more than 0.42 *yuan*. Take this and we're even. The old lady closed her eyes a while, out of habit, then grabbed the hostage carrot and tucked it into her own basket. But take it from me, she added as an afterword, though the current official price for carrots is 2.4 *yuan*, you can sometimes get them down to 2.3. As I'm running late and I've got to get home to cook for my children, I'll leave it here for today. The man stared, dazedly, at his elderly opponent: They broke the mold when they made you, he mumbled to himself, and no mistake. Swinging his leg unsteadily over his crossbar, he moved off. The old lady pulled the carrot back out and repositioned it in a more appropriate gap in the basket. Then she looked up at me.

Hey, young man, what time is it?

What?

I said, is it 5:30 yet?

Er, 5:40.

Heavens, they'll be starving. But then that's a good thing. Let them.

Without any kind of farewell, she swung the basket over her shoulder and rushed off. Though I still felt I had some kind of unfinished business here, I couldn't for the time being remember what it was, and stood there, staring after her as she moved farther and farther away. I then turned to look for my girlfriend, who, just as I expected, had long since disappeared. Normally, whenever this happened, I could never find her again, however hard, however thoroughly I looked. The harder I looked, the harder she was to find. So I just stood where she'd been a minute ago, lit a cigarette, and slowly smoked it down. And, as anticipated, half a cigarette later, a flat-chested but otherwise healthy-looking girl with a plastic bag walked up to me, hyperventilating with rage. I threw down my cigarette and walked after her.

Slow down a bit. Did you find some scales?

Yes!

Nice one. So how heavy was it?

405 grams!

Fuck!

Fuck what?

Fucking 405 fucking grams!

Go fuck yourself.

In an effort to catch up with her, I broke into a brief trot. Spotting what I was up to, she responded by walking even faster. Normally, whenever this happened, walking faster only left me farther behind. So I just slowed down. Now who, at this precise moment, should approach and block our forward progress, both arms outstretched in joy at seeing us, but my old middle-aged, clean-shaven, now-minus-one-carrot friend. My girlfriend, without another word, swept him aside with a single arm movement, and continued on her inexorable way. Once he'd recovered his balance, he grabbed me tightly by the waist.

You can't leave me like this!

What?

Here's what had happened. The middle-aged man had paid four *yuan* to the plastics peddler for a round white plastic chopping board, but in his hurry to get away had walked off without taking it with him. When he came back, the peddler refused to honor the purchase. After wrapping both his arms around my torso and immobilizing me with his gelatinous bulk, the man dragged me, willing or otherwise, over to the peddler's stall and demanded I testify that he really had paid that four fucking *yuan*. I twisted my head around, watching anxiously as my girlfriend weaved her way through the crowd. As well as plastics, the peddler also sold a small selection of stainless steel kitchen implements—fish slicers, slotted spoons, knives, and the like. However loudly and persistently his dissatisfied customer complained, the peddler took no notice, busying himself with the endless, engrossing permutations of rearranging his knife display.

My head was all over the place: I truly couldn't recall whether my captor had in fact paid for that board. And if I'd barely noticed what was going on in the first place, how could I bear reliable witness now? I quietly communicated my feelings to him. Nooo! he began shouting in a sudden transport of passion. You must remember! I was so obvious about it, I took out four coins and put them down in front of him one by one, like this! Like this! I just stood and stared. To refresh my memory further, he then picked up his bike, which he had previously propped up out of the way, and pushed it over in front of the stall. His right hand on the handlebars, his left dived symbolically into his trouser pocket, groped around, then mimed, again and again and again, the action of throwing coins down. With a disdainful smile, the peddler mimicked the middle-aged man's actions back in my direction. Any onlookers would inevitably imagine the middle-aged man was throwing some mysterious, invisible object to the peddler that the peddler was then throwing at me. Both pairs of eyes finally fell on me, the logical conclusion to this triangular transaction. But all I could do was shake my head and wonder where my girlfriend and our 405 grams of pork fillet had gotten to.

Do you remember now?

What?

After a brief paroxysm of anxiety (expressed through stamping his feet), the middle-aged man got a grip back on himself and refocused his energies on his throwing mime, only this time reducing its speed and frequency. I'm very sorry, I said to him, but I have to go. My mind's a blank. With a roar, he swiveled his entire bicycle so it sprawled across my path. You won't get away with this, he muttered furiously. None of this would've happened if you hadn't spoken up for that old bat. You either help me get my four *yuan* back or pay it back to me yourself, it's up to you. I turned and looked off into the distance, standing on tiptoe: my girlfriend was now nearing the end of the street, her entire person and the 405 grams of fillet an ever-shrinking dot on the horizon. I had to make a choice. Raising my right foot, I jammed it against the seat post, bringing the bicycle and the unlucky individual leaned against it crashing to the ground. I then stepped calmly over his head and strode off in pursuit of my girlfriend. But by the time my lung capacity had abandoned me, my girlfriend was still no bigger than a two-cent coin. As my ultimate ambitions lay in enlarging her into a five-cent piece, I broke into a trot and, after a good deal of pain and effort, finally fulfilled my dream. But the instant I relaxed my efforts even a little, she shrank back to two cents and then, before long, to one. Dispirited, I stopped. This pursuit, it seemed, was not going to be the piece of cake the first one had been. So I hailed a taxi. When it was five meters behind my girlfriend, I got out and quietly followed along behind. My girlfriend and I were yet another contradiction of everyday life. It was the same with the next one too. How the hell had I ended up with this psychotic girlfriend? And then I was struck, stirred, even more powerfully than usual, by the sway of her perfect, rounded buttocks. I hung back behind, making silent plans to unite our contradictions before dinner.

After we were done, we lay together on the bed, neither of us wanting to get up and cook. Normally, when this happened, I'd take on the job. Because I'm tall and well-built, I need my food more urgently than others, because I'm never hard on myself, because I love myself more than any girlfriend. Heaving a long sigh, I rolled out of bed and started to get dressed. Languidly curling her well-muscled legs underneath her, my girlfriend suddenly remembered something. Pass me the dictionary on the table, would you? she said. What? I asked, puzzled. Apparently too tired to repeat her question, she merely pointed lethargically. Walking over, I weighed the bricklike dictionary in my hand, then spun around, lifted it over my head and made as if to smash it down on hers as hard as I could. Screaming, my terrified girlfriend cradled her head in her arms. I was only joking, of course. Slowly lowering the dictionary from its raised position, I placed it lightly by her pillow. Still frightened out of her wits, poor thing, she kept going, "I hate you, I hate you," over and over, calming down only after she'd kicked my right kneecap several times and almost broken the bone in the process. I limped around to the other side of the bed and continued dressing, while my girlfriend leafed through the dictionary, half-sitting up in bed. What're you looking up? I asked her. Don't you know how to spell "fuck"? 'Course I do, she replied, it's "bastard" I'm not sure about. Flipping through to the last few pages of the dictionary, she tilted her head to one side, as if calculating something.

Hey, how heavy did that old woman say it was?

What?

The meat!

What meat?

For God's sake.

Oh. Just under a pound, about fifteen ounces.

Amazing. Almost exactly right.

My top half still bare, I went and crouched down over the dictionary, wanting to see for myself. There was a conversion table for measuring units in the appendix at the back, but the letters were too small and the room too dark to see properly. My girlfriend rubbed her shoulder against me: Put the light on, would you? Do it yourself, I told her, stop telling other people what to do all the time. Normally, when this happened, she'd come over all wheedling, after which I'd give in—normally. As anticipated, she rolled over and gave me a hug, just a quick one, then released me. So I could immediately get up and do her bidding. I didn't move. Another hug. This time a bit longer. If I failed to move again this time, I expected she'd hug me even longer, even closer. As anticipated, she rolled over again. But this time, I felt only resentment, deep, long-term resentment at the pressure of her flat chest against mine.

Fuck off, do it yourself!

Why're you being like this?

Like what?

Like a schizo! Nice one second, a bastard the next!

I told you, I'm fed up with you telling me what to do!

And how do I do that, then?

Do this! Do that! Come here! Go there! Buy this! Buy that! What d'you call that? In the two months I've known you I haven't gotten a single thing done, and why? I've been running after you every single day—so what d'you call that?

You're crazy! Fucking crazy! And I suppose you've never forced me to do something I didn't want to?

No! Never!

Well, isn't that funny. How about just now, when we came back from the market? I was really tired, I didn't want to do it, but you made me! Did I complain?

What?

What d'you mean, what?

That's different.

Different how?

My girlfriend, entirely out of character, started sobbing violently, her tears slowly cooling my overheated brain back to something approaching a normal temperature. Recognizing something mysterious, something out of the ordinary in this explosion of temper, I apologized, then, unasked, went and turned the room light on. Half an hour later, she accepted my apology and asked me something else: Pass me the pen in the drawer, and a piece of paper, would you? I naturally complied. Then we both lay on our stomachs on the bed, revising our multiplication and division skills. The old lady, it turned out, had been almost exactly right. Sure, it was impressive but, I said, stroking my girlfriend's prominent bicep, not that surprising; I mean, she's been buying food for years. I could be just as good as her, I ventured, turning over to kneel on the bed. Shut up, my girlfriend replied. You'd need to do a lot more food shopping than you've done to get as good as her. It's not like I'd try to stop you. I shook my head: All right then, you've never told me your weight, or made me ask you, have you? I could pick you up now and tell right away. I bent down, gathered my strength, and lifted her up. Seeing as how you're so sure of yourself, she said, I'll give you a 3-pound margin for error either way. No more. I closed my eyes and pondered the weight in my arms. 130 pounds and 5 ounces, I choked out and released her. As my bed was hard-slatted, it wasn't a particularly light fall for her, but she scrambled back up, unbothered, and immediately started doing sums on the paper. After a few calculations, she threw down the pen: Fucking hell! she said.

So, was I right? Like hell, said my girlfriend. If I got it wrong, I said, must be because you broke my scales, 110 pounds is about my limit, normally. A light suddenly entered her eyes: I'll guess how much you weigh! she shouted, rolling me onto the bed. After several attempts, she very naturally had failed to make any headway in lifting me up. So I offered a suggestion. Think of it like this, I said. I'm like a set of suspension scales, so I weigh things by lifting them, but you're a set of flat scales. You know how they work, don't you? I stretched my body evenly out over hers, as a peasant might spread the corn of a bumper harvest over a balance. She seemed to be having difficulty breathing. She closed her eyes. So, how much do I weigh? I asked.

After we were done, we lay side by side on the bed, neither of us wanting to get up to cook. Normally, when this happened, I'd take on the job. Because I'm tall and well-built, I need my food more urgently than others, because I'm never hard on myself, because I love myself more than any girlfriend. So I got up and cooked the entire 405 grams of fillet like I bore it a grudge. Because I refused to take any time or trouble, the meat didn't tenderize or take on any flavor in the cooking. My girlfriend laid down her chopsticks after half a mouthful. But I chewed indomitably on. Though it was like eating wood, though it got stuck in your teeth, it was still meat. Meat. It contained the nourishment I needed. I was starving—weak with it.

He just wanted a decent book to read ...

Not too much to ask, is it? It was in 1935 when Allen Lane, Managing Director of Bodley Head Publishers, stood on a platform at Exeter railway station looking for something good to read on his journey back to London. His choice was limited to popular magazines and poor-quality paperbacks – the same choice faced every day by the vast majority of readers, few of whom could afford hardbacks. Lane's disappointment and subsequent anger at the range of books generally available led him to found a company – and change the world.

'We believed in the existence in this country of a vast reading public for intelligent books at a low price, and staked everything on it'
Sir Allen Lane, 1902–1970, founder of Penguin Books

The quality paperback had arrived – and not just in bookshops. Lane was adamant that his Penguins should appear in chain stores and tobacconists, and should cost no more than a packet of cigarettes.

Reading habits (and cigarette prices) have changed since 1935, but Penguin still believes in publishing the best books for everybody to enjoy. We still believe that good design costs no more than bad design, and we still believe that quality books published passionately and responsibly make the world a better place.

So wherever you see the little bird – whether it's on a piece of prize-winning literary fiction or a celebrity autobiography, political tour de force or historical masterpiece, a serial-killer thriller, reference book, world classic or a piece of pure escapism – you can bet that it represents the very best that the genre has to offer.

Whatever you like to read – trust Penguin.